SARONG
PARTY
GIRLS

SARONG PARTY GIRLS

CHERYL LU-LIEN TAN

WILLIAM MORROW

An Imprint of HarperCollins*Publishers*

SARONG PARTY GIRLS. Copyright © 2016 by Cheryl Lu-Lien Tan. All rights reserved. Printed in the United States of America. No part of this book may be used or reproduced in any manner whatsoever without written permission except in the case of brief quotations embodied in critical articles and reviews. For information address HarperCollins Publishers, 195 Broadway, New York, NY 10007.

HarperCollins books may be purchased for educational, business, or sales promotional use. For information please e-mail the Special Markets Department at SPsales@harpercollins.com.

FIRST EDITION

Designed by Leah Carlson-Stanisic

Library of Congress Cataloging-in-Publication Data has been applied for.

ISBN 978-0-06-244896-5

16 17 18 19 20   OV/RRD   10 9 8 7 6 5 4 3 2 1

FOR MY FATHER,
TAN SOO LIAP

AUTHOR'S NOTE

This book is written in Singlish, which is the patois that most Singaporeans speak to one another. It's a tossed salad of the different languages and Chinese dialects that the country's multiethnic population speaks—English, Malay, Mandarin, Hokkien, Teochew and more. It's packed with attitude and humor and often is deliciously vulgar. Despite its allure, it has been the target of the Singapore government's "Speak Good English" campaigns in the past. Fortunately, Singlish has turned out to be like a weed—it lives on.

SARONG
PARTY
GIRLS

CHAPTER 1

Aiyoh, I tell you. If we do nothing, we are confirm getting into bang balls territory. We have to figure out how to make this happen—and we have to do it now.

After all, we've wasted enough time already. And we don't have any more time to waste! We are not young anymore, you know—Fann just turned twenty-seven, my twenty-seventh birthday is two months away and Imo's is not far behind. If we don't get married, engaged or even nail down a boyfriend soon—my god, we might as well go ahead and book a room at Singapore Casket because our lives would already be over. In many ways, in Singapore, our kind of age is already considered a bit left on the shelf. Ordinarily, I don't heck care about such things. Hallo—Jazzy here knows she's quite power. Usually, unless the guy is blind or stupid or some shit, whatever guy I have my eye on I also can get, even at my age. You ask any bookie out there—my odds are damn good.

But it's true that Singaporean men are a bit fussy—especially when it comes to older girls. But luckily for us, we still have one big hope: ang moh guys. That's what we need to be thinking about. These white guys—they really catch no ball about Asian ages. Us twenty-something-year-old Asian girls, if you wear a tight tight dress or short short skirt, these ang mohs will still steam over you. (Some of them even go for the really old ones—thirty-year-old women also have chance!)

Even so, we cannot waste time. And we must be serious, because once you manage to marry a white guy, then you are only one step away from the number one champion status symbol in Singapore—a half ang moh kid. The Chanel of babies! But, how to get an ang moh husband?

I used to think getting an ang moh husband was quite easy to do. I mean—hello, we girls are always out there, meeting ang mohs, letting them buy drinks for us, dance dance rubba rubba a bit, so surely one day we'll just naturally end up with an ang moh husband, right? At least that was the thinking lah. Recently though, I realized something that started making me nervous about achieving our goal. And it only hit me on that super cock night—the one where we lost Sher.

I tell you, I cannot even talk about that night right now without vomiting blood. Sher is so pretty, so sweet, so thin, has such fair skin. She could have had any guy she wanted!

After that night, I realized that yes, we've been quite focused over the years. If you count up all the guys our group has dated since secondary school, most of them are ang mohs. Not always good quality ones—some of them, I have to admit, are the don't-wear-suits-to-work type—but still, in this small country, to be able to say that most of our boyfriends and flings have come from England or some shit is quite good lah. Most girls here end up with local boyfriends the whole time. What nonsense. I tell you, if an SBS bus runs me over on the street tomorrow, Jazzy here will go up there with no regrets.

Once we lost Sher though, I realized that our ang moh husband strategy was not so good because . . . we had no strategy! You ask Sun Tzu or Lee Kuan Yew, they confirm will say that every important thing also must have strategy. I tell you—if only we had paid closer attention to all that shit during Chinese proverb classes. If we had, maybe Sher would still be with us today.

So, first things first—must call a meeting. After work: Wala Wala bar at Holland Village. Of the four of us, there were only three left—me, Fann and Imo. Time to get serious.

Long time ago when we were in secondary school, the four of us used to be quite shy about coming to Holland Village. This neighborhood is not say super atas—although the hawker center there is damn bloody expensive. One stupid plate of wanton mee can cost you four dollars and fifty cents! If your family is printing money and you have all the cash in the world to pay American prices for Singaporean food then OK lah, please—you just go ahead. Also, you know how things are around here sometimes. If you are not ang moh and don't speak good English or wear a school uniform from one of the expat schools or at least one of the right kinds of schools, people will sometimes look at you a bit funny. Like, why are you hanging out here? Don't you have your own kampong to squat in? That kind of cock attitude.

But once we got a bit older and started going on dates with ang mohs who sometimes brought us to Holland Village, we started to see the bar scene, get to know some of the waiters and bartenders, then OK lah, we started to fit in. Now, at all the tapas bars and happening Irish pubs along there, even if we're not on dates and it's just us girls hanging out, we feel more OK about showing our faces in Holland Village.

Since I was the first to arrive after work, judging from all the texts from Fann and Imo about being late, I decided to slowly slowly walk to Wala Wala. Never fun sitting there for too long before your girls show up, after all. If you sit there for too long with your one drink, just waiting and looking, waiting and looking—aiyoh, even if the bartenders don't think you are pros, I tell you, someone confirm will come and sit down with you and ask "How much?"

Holland V was happening as usual for a Thursday night. Of

course it was still a bit early—since our work shift is more normal we can knock off at five o'clock, so we can come out earlier and start our night. I know sometimes if you work for ang moh companies or those British law or banking firms, even if you are a receptionist or assistant, then still must work late. Sometimes my job at the *New Times* is also like that lah, since I'm assistant to the editor in chief and all. But luckily Albert didn't keep me too long today, because even that early on a Thursday, the narrow street that most of Holland V was on was already quite packed. The tables outside the bars and restaurants jammed on the pavement were already filled with people drinking and smoking. And I could almost taste the smell of grilled meats coming from some of the fashion-fashion yakitori places on the street.

Because it's so crowded—and sometimes filled with families and kids, that kind of crap—Holland V is not usually my favorite place to go. But it's good to check out the scene and be a part of it at least once in a while, show face and all.

When I got to Wala, I ordered their super shiok chicken wings. If the girls are late, it's their problem. More wings for me. But bang balls, man—Fann and Imo showed up just when Ahmad brought the wings to our table. Fann didn't even wait to sit down before grabbing one and stuffing it into her mouth. This one, I tell you, if I didn't know her better I would have said she confirm would end up marrying some lousy Ah Beng squatting by a longkang.

"OK, you all know there was a reason that I called this meeting," I said, making sure when I paused to stare hard at Imo. This one as usual was not paying attention, searching through her bloody handbag for god knows what.

"This is a meeting? I thought we were just drinking tonight," Imo said, finally taking out a gold Chanel compact to powder her nose. Fann signaled to Ahmad to bring a round of our usual drinks over. After coming here for so long, Ahmad knows lah—cheap white wine first, good stuff later, especially if by then we have met ang mohs who want to buy us rounds.

"Yes, yes—but there's something we need to talk about . . ." I started to explain. "This is serious. Listen—I think we need a plan."

Fann and Imo looked worried. I cannot blame them lah. We whole life never talk about serious things at all. Yes, when Fann's dad died and Imo—aiyoh, Imo—when all that drama happened after junior college with her father and his second family, then, yes, we were serious. So they must have thought something really bad happened.

"Eh, you OK or not?" Fann said.

"OK, OK . . . but listen, I've been thinking, we don't have much time. Look at us three—this is a happening Thursday night and the best plans we have are going out with each other. No husband, no two-carat diamond ring, not even a boyfriend. What kind of cock life is this? If we want to marry ang moh guys, we cannot go to SPG bars and just anyhow shoot arrow. No wonder we haven't win yet. We must have a method!"

Imo looked skeptical. "If we just go to Chaplin's or Hard Rock, meet people, dance dance dance, sing sing, hiau hiau a bit," she said, "aren't we just doing it because it's fun?" Fann shrugged and nodded.

"Fun—your head lah!" I said. "Like that maybe for one night or a few nights, of course it will work. But if we want to get married, then we must be more strategy! So, listen—I came up with this idea. Got four parts."

Imo leaned forward—I could tell she was a little curious. Of all of us, she's the one who's most focused on getting married. Her father—aiyoh, my god.

When we were in secondary school, we didn't see Imo's dad

much. Uncle was always traveling for work—each week he would disappear for a few nights, often over the weekend. So every time we were at her house, it was mostly just us hanging out with Auntie. Auntie never seemed to mind though—whenever Uncle came back from his travels, he always brought something nice. Sometimes got duty-free perfume lah; other times if he disappeared for longer trips, he would actually come back with a Prada handbag, that kind of thing. But of course Imo always liked it best when he showed up with those big Toblerones—so big that each piece alone was the size of a McDonald's hamburger! The few times we met him, he seemed nice, not anything special—people's father is just people's father after all. Unless you bump into them in a club or something—my god, later on, after our school years, that actually happened with some of our friends' dads—you don't really think about them that much.

And Uncle was so boring we definitely didn't think about him at all. He was like my dad lah. Or Fann's dad, who we didn't really care about until he suddenly had a heart attack. But then right after we graduated from JC, like just the day after our final exam and we hadn't even had time to go chionging to celebrate and all, Uncle and Auntie sat Imo down after dinner and said, "We have something to tell you."

Imo said everything happened very quickly—once Uncle started talking, everything also just anyhow come out. Apparently, his job was actually not a traveling type of job. He works in a local insurance office! First, he said, Imogen, you know your Mummy and I love you very much, right? Everything you want, we also give you. (When Imo first heard this, at first she thought he was dying—at that time Fann's dad had recently passed away, so we were all quite scared, wondering which Uncle is the next to go.) So Imo just nodded and kept quiet—when she told us about it, she said she was almost crying.

But then Uncle said, "Now that you're old enough, almost a woman already, your mummy and I thought you should know something: You have two brothers."

At first, Imo was quite confused. She didn't know what he meant. "But how could my mum have two other kids that I don't know about? Cannot be! She had me when she was so young and then I don't remember her being pregnant anymore. Where got two sons?" She was still thinking hard about all this when Uncle continued talking.

"I have another family," he said.

Imo looked across the dinner table at her mum, who was looking a bit blank-faced, except that her eyes were staring down. She said Auntie was blinking and looking hard at her fingers, which were pulling apart at one corner of the carefully ironed white tablecloth that she spent four months last year crocheting. This was the table-cloth that Auntie cared about so much that she even bought a special clear plastic cover for it for Chinese New Year so when people brought curry or whatever over, her tablecloth will still be Number One OK. So Imo knew that if her mum was actually cho cho-ing with this tablecloth—then, confirm: this conversation is really serious.

Uncle continued: "When I met your mum, I already had one son. And then just around the time you were born, I had my second son. They look a bit like you actually . . ."

Imo is usually quite toot lah. So at this point, when she told all of us about it, we thought the situation was pretty clear. But Imo was actually still confused! So she asked her dad, "But . . . you had your mistress before mum?" She still wasn't getting anything or understanding what was going on. When she told me, Sher and Fann all this—my god—we all just wanted to reach over and slap her one time. Where got people so stupid?

That was when Uncle looked a little bit embarrassed. And she said her mum by this time couldn't even look up from the tablecloth.

"Imo, I care about your mum very much. And I care about you very much. The two sons I have are with my wife. They live here—in . . . well, a town center quite far from here so you were definitely never in the same schools of course. But now that you are all grown up, have wings, can fly already, we wanted you to know you have brothers out there. Just keep that in mind whenever you meet new people. You just . . . aiyah, you just never know. And we were thinking now that you are getting older, going out and dating dating all, sekali something weird happens. Better be safe. So we might as well sit you down and tell you everything—just in case. So, um, if you ever have any news about new guys you are meeting, might be getting serious with, you just be sure to keep us informed ah? OK, come, come, let's eat some oranges."

And then after that Imo's mum just got up, peeled two oranges for them, went to her room and turned on the TV to watch her Cantonese serial and they didn't talk about it anymore.

Walao eh! Crazy lah!

When Imo told us, at first we weren't quite sure what to say or think. We all hugged her of course. And then we just looked at each other. Finally, Sher smiled, reached over to squeeze Imo's hand and said: "Eh, Imo—you are lucky you're a sarong party girl. Like that, you confirm won't end up snogging your brother by mistake. Even if your dad's wife is white, her sons will only be half ang moh. As if you'll even think of going home with a loser like that!" Even Imo had to laugh over that one. Sher always knew just the right thing to say.

So ever since then, Imo has been quite determined: Get an ang moh husband or bust, man!

"Come, set. Tell us your strategy," Imo said. The guniang had even closed her mirror and put it away, so now I really knew she was listening.

"OK, number one," I said. "Looks. Obviously we are quite chio, otherwise how come we have so many ang moh guys always chasing us? But girls, think about it. If you look carefully, the types of Singaporean girls that ang moh guys like to pok and the types that they end up marrying is quite different! So we must make ourselves look like those girls they want to marry."

"But who?" Imo asked, already looking a bit lost.

Aiyoh, I tell you. I tried very hard not to roll my eyes though. Instead, I pulled out some of the pictures I looked up on my phone that morning. Best one: Maggie Cheung. "This one ah," I said, "very power. Marry the best type of guy—European! French some more; sexy sexy one. Rich also." Imo and Fann were nodding.

Actually, I was not really joking when I said that since we are so chio, why must we plan so hard? For starters, we were all quite skinny—Imo was the smallest of us, short short cute cute one. Got dimple on one side of her face so at least she looked half like the cute Japanese teenagers in those Kao Biore face soap advertisements. (But without that one big side tooth jutting out—my god. Those dentists in Japan, I also don't know how they spend their time, man. Why are their girls' teeth all so terok?) Imo's skin was also very fair—so fair that she definitely didn't need to buy SK-II whitening cream. Lucky girl. Also, right after school she worked at Robinson's at the Shiseido counter for a while, so that girl really knows how to put makeup on and all. Her eyes are always nicely outlined so they look round round, big big one, like those Japanese anime girls that guys always want to pok. And since she now works at Club 21 boutique, she gets a 40 percent discount on everything they sell, so her clothing and handbags always quite designer, quite fashion one.

Fann, to be honest, is not so cute. Her nose is a bit big, her eyes only have a double eyelid on one side, so no matter how much she tries to put on eye makeup nicely, her face always ends up looking a bit crooked. And some more, even though since secondary school, she's always carried around a packet of powdered blotting paper wherever she goes, her skin is always oily! My god, when it's hot, like June or July type, her face—it's a bloody blooming garden! Everywhere also got pimples opening flower. But still, she's a very nice girl lah. And her job is quite serious—she opened a pet store with her uncle and all—so guys usually know she's not after them for money or something funny. I think she gets extra points for that. Also, her backside is quite round and sexy, so confirm guys will always try to rubba her in clubs. And I guess she must be quite good in bed since usually, even when they wake up the next morning, the guys always take her out for breakfast, still ask for her phone number so they can text her again type.

Me, I think I'm OK lah. Can still make it. Not as sweet as Imo but luckily, not as bad as Fann. The ang moh guys I've met are always talking about how glossy and black my long hair is and how soft and smooth my skin is—so I guess I at least have two things going for me. Of us all though, Sher was the best looking—skin very fair like a Japanese princess, eyes not as big as Imo's but beautiful almond-shape type. And she really knows how to put on eyeliner so the sides of her eyes look pulled out a bit, like those exotic Asian girls in ang moh movies. Also, she was the tallest of us all. But she wasn't the skinny giraffe type—her breasts were small but quite nice (at least got cleavage, unlike Fann or Imo), and with her small small waist and legs long long and so shapely, my god, when she wears a miniskirt she almost looks like a Barbie doll. When she walks along Orchard Road, guys always steam. Even the atas guys also not shy—they stare until crazy.

Which is why, really, the way things turned out for Sher, it was damn bang balls to think about how everything was just so bloody wasted.

"You see ah," I continued, before the girls could get distracted, "Maggie Cheung actually, her features are not so pretty. Her teeth are so big, got gap some more, her eyes are so small, cheeks a bit fat. But still, ang moh guys love her! Because, you know why? She's quite mysterious. Joan Chen also same thing—her face flat flat also ang moh guys still steam. So we must learn—better to be mysterious a bit. When we meet a new possibility, cannot same night everything also whack."

Fann waved at Ahmad for another round of drinks and took another chicken wing—typical, never pay attention. Imo on the other hand, had taken out a little notebook and was writing things down. Good. The way her fishnet mind works, I know if she doesn't have anything written down she confirm won't remember.

"Number two—is behavior. You see ah, ang mohs in Asia, step one for them is to look for girls to pok. This one is not hard lah. SPG bars, office . . . everywhere in this country is easy for them to find girls. But once they are used to this, it's quite difficult to get them to think differently. So the best thing is to grab them FOB—if you snatch the ones who just moved here one or two weeks ago, then confirm is a win. But if you don't manage to do that, when you meet them, you must act quite differently from those girls who just want to give them one–two nights good time type. Eh, Fann, I tell you ah, if you want to get married you better stop stuffing your face and write this down." I pointed to her handbag and she fasterly opened it to pull out a pen and paper.

"OK, until now, we have been quite good at the laugh laugh drink drink wink wink type of thing. But if we want to be more serious, we must know what kind of things ang moh guys like—football, rugby, maybe things like rowing or tennis are also quite good. We don't know much also must learn—so every day, we'd better read the *Straits Times*. English league, Italian league, German players, World Cup—everything also must know. If we know more, then we have more chance to talk more cock. If we talk more cock, then it becomes more like a relationship! Not just one night garabing garabung then everything is over already. If they think that we like what they like, then an actual relationship more likely is can."

Even Fann was very seriously writing things down now. Imo, however, asked, "What about them learning about the things that we like?" Fann nodded. I tell you—sometimes Imo's tootness is just really number one. "Hello," I said. "If you are waiting for a guy who wants to hold your hand and have long conversations about the new Shiseido eye shadow then you'd better take off your shoes and sit down comfortably—because you are going to wait forever!" Fann started giggling; Imo just blinked at her.

"Next, we must understand the enemy. Cannot be like Jackie Chan in those kung fu movies—in the beginning he's always the goondu, everything also don't know, don't understand then alamak, suddenly his balls get whacked! No, if we want to win, then we must know who we are fighting: number one: China girls. This one is the worst one. Since they come from China and are desperate not to go back, they anything will also do. No standards at all! Old old, ugly ugly, smelly smelly also they don't care. But because they are so willing and so pretend-sweet, ang mohs like them! Some more they have no guilty conscience—if a guy has a wife, a girlfriend, is engaged, has kids, they don't care. All, they will also whack. China girls, aiyoh. This one is the number one to watch.

"Number two: Filipinas—this one is quite dangerous because they are quite ang moh already, so it's very easy for them to talk to ang moh guys. They have a lot in common. Some more they sing so well—if we see them in a karaoke lounge, I think we better just siam. No chance there. Better don't fight.

"Number three: other SPGs—this one is quite easy to spot in a bar lah. But girls, we are all on the same side, all looking for the same thing, so if we see them, just show respect. No need to fight unless they try to potong your catch—if they potong, then we hantam them one time.

"Number four: ang moh girls. This one is actually not so dangerous because they're all so fat and white chicken-skin type. Some more their hands and legs are usually damn hairy! If ang moh guys want that kind of thing, aiyoh, they know that if they go home there are better ones there lah. Down here in Singapore, these ang moh women know that Asian girls are better. But still, sometimes, the ang moh girls also can win. So it's just better to keep an eye on them."

At this point I was a bit hungry but Fann and Imo were so quiet I thought I'd better carry on. I was starting to feel like I was giving one of those opposition rally speeches you see on the Internet. My voice was getting louder and louder, Fann and Imo were both sitting up, leaning forward, listening carefully to each word. If I waved a flag, I tell you, they confirm will shout "Merdeka!" (At least, this is what I was thinking in my head lah.)

"Last one: This one is not hard," I said. "We should just know the places to go. We already know the bars—Hard Rock, Studemeyer's, Chaplin's, these are all good places to spot ang mohs. But we also must try and see them in normal situations—for example, ang mohs like brunch! And hello, I'm not talking about going eat roti prata or prawn noodles type of brunch. Pancakes lah, eggs lah—that kind of thing. Even if we don't really like to eat that crap, we must also whack brunch. Cannot just whack the bars and clubs. Sunday lunchtime—must try.

"OK? Now, we must be serious a bit. If this is what we want, then we must really understand all of this. Cannot anyhow anyhow anymore."

The two of them were very quiet and looked at each other blankly. "Jazzy," Fann finally said. "I think this plan—we cannot be like that lah. Love and relationships must be natural, not so calculative. We cannot plan plan plan until like this. Otherwise, what does it all mean? We might as well be like our parents."

My god, when she said this—this really got me upset. The whole point of my plan, of us trying so hard on all this, is exactly so we won't end up like our parents. Fann of all people should know— when her father dropped dead her mother was actually happy! No one to kau beh and fight with her for the TV when she wants to watch her Cantonese serials anymore. No one to sit on her sofa, smoking and peeling dried skin off his toes for hours each evening. Finally—after all those lousy years, peace inside her own house!

"Fann," I said, blinking hard at her. "You wake up your own head! If we don't follow this plan, we will end up like your parents, my parents or even worse—Imo's parents!" Even though I was angry, I felt bad about saying that last part lah—hello, this guniang here isn't heartless after all. But when I looked over at Imo and said, "Eh, sorry," she just shrugged.

"It's true," Imo said very softly. "We can't end up like them."

All this, I know, was a lot for Fann and Imo to think about. But you look at us—now, we are still chio, still happening. But twenty-six and twenty-seven is not young already, you know. Fann has always been a bit cannot make it lah, and Sher is a gone case already, but Imo and I still have a chance! Even then, I can already see, sometimes when I look at our old photos, that last year and the year before that, we were even more chio. So if we carry on like this, that means next year we will be even less chio! This matter of getting an ang moh husband—if we are smart—it's best to try and fasterly settle.

"In fact," I added, "I think we actually must hurry up a bit. If you are serious about this, then, come, we set deadline. Today is Feb first—by end of month, must try and confirm something."

"Like what?" Fann asked. "You want us to be married in a month? Be engaged?" Imo joined in. "Crazy, lah!" she said. "That's only a month! I'm very busy at work, you know. Our big Club 21 sale is happening this month!"

Aiyoh, my god. These people! Hadn't they been listening to anything I said?

"Look," I said, "no one is asking you to hold a wedding banquet in thirty days. All I'm saying is, by the end of the month, we should at least have an ang moh boyfriend—a serious one. If we really focus and put our minds to it—and follow the strategy—this one, I tell you, is probably can. So how? Set?"

Imo looked at Fann, who looked back at her for a moment. "OK," Imo said, raising her glass and waving her hand at Fann to follow. Together, we clinked our glasses and said, "Set!"

CHAPTER 2

I still remember the night when everything went to shit.

Of course I didn't want to go to the wedding banquet. Sher, if she could actually bring herself to give a flying shit about our donkey's years of friendship, should have known that. After everything that happened, after everything we discussed over the years and everything we planned and tried for, and then everything just going to hell at the end because of some cock decision she suddenly made—just the fact that she was asking me to come to her wedding was damn bloody daring.

But then she texted me one day, and then that night, and then the next day asking—no, actually, begging—for one small favor. "I need you there, Jazzy. Sit at the reception desk, Jazzy. You don't have to do anything, Jazzy. Just smile and greet people and be there for me, Jazzy. How long have we been good friends, Jazzy? You know you are practically my own sister."

That last bit was the part that made me feel bad lah. I don't have that many people I still know—or care about enough to actually text and see—who have been my kaki since primary school days. Or people who were there with me at Zambo until 3 A.M. in the morning on so many nights, holding my hair back as I'm throwing up into a longkang by the side of the road after a really good night out. At the end of the day, I have to honestly say I have never had a better friend than Sher. Friends like her are really A-plus-plus, man. Long long then will come one time. This, I always knew—and I always assumed we would be best friends until we were old fat aunties sitting in our rocking chairs looking out at our colorful English gardens, sipping tea or whatever it is they drink over there.

So, I felt a bit bad. After all, even though Sher changed her mind and abandoned the three of us in the end, I couldn't ignore the fact that we used to be good friends.

I remember when we first started really hitting the SPG bars— Studemeyer's was one of the first places everyone used to go. Right when the club first opened awhile ago it had all these good-looking ang moh guys hanging out there on weekends. But then very quickly all these Ah Bengs in their old-fashioned pleated baggy black pants, shiny silk shirts and overgelled blow-dried hair starting rushing in and taking over the club on weekends. Aiyoh—when I see those guys I just want to throw up. I know these Ah Bengs are Chinese-Singaporean guys who probably feel like they need to action a bit more to stand out—but I don't understand how people can actually want to look so low-class! Even so, Sher wanted to see Studemeyer's and we'd all never been. So somehow we ended up there on a Friday night—Louis had started reserving a table there on weekends the moment it opened, so we had a VIP spot. I didn't mind going for that. Otherwise, I confirm won't go.

When Louis saw me at Studemeyer's, he was nice as usual, holding up the bottle of Chivas after we double-kissed. "Better faster get high," he said, starting to pour even before I could find a place to put my handbag. "Where have you been? We've all been here since eleven drinking already. You'd better catch up. No fun being sober when we're all so high." After that, he just kept pouring. Every time my glass was even half-empty he would bring the Chivas over. I can't remember whether he was also pouring so much for Sher, Fann and Imo. He must have—I think—but then in the end, it was only me, about one hour and six double-shot whiskey sodas later, who was suddenly feeling like not dancing anymore.

"Ehhh," a voice came, so close to my ear I could feel a sticky hot-ness. I didn't need to turn around to know who it was. I could feel him already, the front of his bulky jeans rubbing against my bum. Sher and Imo were convinced that Kelvin stuffed his crotch with socks—no way someone so short could be so big. "Aiyoh, please lah," I said, turning my head around to shout so he could hear me. "Guniang here mabuk almost to the point of throwing up already and you still want to be like that." But he just kept rubba-ing and didn't go away. By the time I fully turned around so I could actually push him back, I could see from his saggy lids and big smile that he was quite gone. Kelvin just blinked and stumbled off to try his luck with some fresh girls near the next table.

"Jazz, you OK?" Sher had finally come back from wherever she'd gone. Neither of us had seen Imo—or Louis, for that matter—in a while.

"You look a bit . . . too high," she said, cupping my face.

"No lah, I'm OK. Don't worry. I just need some air."

I turned back around again, leaning against the cool stainless steel railing that kept us from falling over onto the sprawling dance floor beneath. I could feel Sher rubbing my back. It felt good. Her face leaned in next to mine. We both looked over at the floor be-neath us, filled with bodies jammed next to each other. I couldn't remember the last time we went to a club and didn't have a VIP table—we were all getting older already lah. Going clubbing on the main levels is for the youngsters—us old birds have no energy any-more to push and squeeze and get noticed in such a crowd. Sher was pointing at something below, a group of Ah Bengs in a small circle with one of them in the middle. Each one stood firmly in a spot, holding on to his pleated pants waistband with his right hand, as if trying to steady himself while he rocked violently from the waist upward. The other hand was raised up high waving above his head. Even though we were one floor up, we could hear them shouting, "Yo ah yo! Yo ah yo!"

Aiyoh—this phrase so old already still want to say! Back in the eighties everyone was lousy at dancing lah, so the main way was just to yo back and forth to the music and shout "Yo ah yo!" Nowadays, everyone knows much more about dancing, but these Ah Bengs somehow are still out there doing this nonsense.

"Oi!" Sher suddenly shouted, leaning over slightly as she waved and pointed at the group. "Yah—you, Ah Beng! This one not 1985 anymore, you know. You still Yo ah yo? Lau pok lah!" The Ah Bengs stared up, looking confused. When they saw Sher waving her third finger at them, they started to whisper to each other, holding their hands up to cover their mouths as they talked. Typical brainless type—we are so far up, how to hear anything?

My god. It was too much. I started laughing, at first just a little bit, but then when Sher started laughing also, we held on to each other and just started laughing louder and harder. I even slapped my hand on my thigh so hard I could feel it getting hot from how painful it was. But then suddenly I started to feel something else—it began in my chest. A burp, I thought? Next thing I knew I was leaning over the railing, shooting crap out of my mouth like one of those big fire engine hoses—I could taste Chivas, and some green tea mixed with bits of the noodles my mum made me eat before coming out.

I remember two things happening as it started—Sher's left hand catching my shoulder as I bent over, and her right hand quickly grabbing and holding back my hair. She waited one minute for all of it to really finish before saying, "Eh, we'd better faster siam." When

I opened my eyes, I saw the Ah Bengs all staring up at us, pointing and shouting. A few of them were touching the tops of their heads and then pointing even more. I could hear myself start to laugh again as I wiped the corner of my mouth, making them point even harder. Then one of them pointed toward the staircase and they all started to move. Sher grabbed my hand, swiped my handbag from the booth and we both started running for the secret back VIP exit, not even stopping to see where Louis was so we could give him his two air kisses goodbye. We didn't stop laughing until we reached the roti prata stall ten minutes away.

"Aiyoh, Jazzy," Sher said as she clinked her mug of hot ginger tea to mine when we had laughed until there was no more sound coming out and we actually had to buy a twenty-cent packet of tissues to wipe our tears dry. "You tonight ah," she said, "were really number one."

So, when it came down to it, when Sher begged me to come to her wedding, after all the nights we'd been through over the years, how could I not give her face?

Outside the wedding banquet hall, Imo, Fann and I were standing around, looking chio and dressed in gold just like Sher texted us to, and saying hallo to her relatives all. "Auntie, congrats ah?" I said when I saw Sher's mum.

Auntie looked like she'd lost some weight, maybe to fit into the turquoise and gold cheongsam she was wearing. She looked at me a little bit sad, like she wanted to say something. I felt bad lah. I had seen her almost every week since primary school, though I had been avoiding their place for months. But we both knew that now wasn't the right time. So she just smiled sweetly and squeezed my hand. "I think Sher wants us all to line up right on the inside by the door," she said, leading me through the large double doors to the ice-cold banquet hall and pointing to the area just to the right.

The music started the moment I took my spot. I almost started to cry—I only needed to hear five beats to know what it was: Richard Marx's "Right Here Waiting." Sher and I used to sing it all the time in secondary school. And then also after that lah—but by then the song was not so happening anymore, so we secretly sang it, like, only when we were in the house type. (Outside the house, if we hear people singing it, we'll just blink and stare at them as if they are bloody kampong idiots. Which is true lah.)

After I didn't do so well in my A levels and I applied to uni in Australia, Sher would always say, "Just think of Richard Marx and this song. We will always be best friends even if you go. Don't cry, don't cry." In the end, something lucky happened—I failed the entrance test, so I kena stuck in Singapore anyway.

But why would Sher purposely play this song at this moment?

The lights dimmed and a small, sharp spotlight came on, swirling around the room in big loops before stopping at the doorway. The circle of light got larger and larger until suddenly two figures stepped into it. Everyone in the room started clapping.

Sher was glowing in the dress she had eyed for five years now, the one that was slim and silky, designed to look exactly like Carolyn Bessette Kennedy's negligee-style wedding dress. "Marry an ang moh prince must have ang moh–style princess dress!" she had said when she showed the magazine photo to us a few years ago and we all told her the dress looked too plain.

In the end, Sher was right about the dress, of course—when I saw her stepping through the door to her wedding banquet, she looked just like a princess. Her hair was done exactly like the photos of Carolyn that she had cut out and stuck on her mirror—tied in a loose bun in the back with some of her fringe draping across the side of her face.

I saw her looking around the room to the sides of the door, looking for someone. Looking for me. But just before she caught my eye, I turned away.

Ang moh princess, my foot. I couldn't see her husband yet but I knew who he was. Mr. Lim Beng Huat. Black spiky hair, oval wire-rim glasses when he wasn't wearing contacts, bumpy button nose. Rolex watch, one gold tooth. Typical Chinese guy.

I couldn't even look at Sher. I just kept thinking over and over, *There goes her Chanel baby.*

CHAPTER 3

Of all the bosses in the world, Albert is not the worst.

He's quite funny lah. But definitely not the worst. Sure, there was the time when he almost got in trouble for rubba-ing the neck of a new NUS grad when she was on deadline one day. It wasn't even anything special—everybody knows he does that to everyone, after all. But this guniang happened to be one of those modern women types—you know, those girls you are hearing about more nowadays, those who cannot take a joke. When she got angry and said she wanted to file an official complaint, he just laughed and explained to her that aiyoh, that's just the way he is—just being the fatherly uncle type, wanting to help people feel less stressed when they are on deadline so he just goes around the newsroom giving them neck massages. To make sure she wouldn't really go and file a complaint, after that, for a while, Albert had to go around rubba-ing various people around deadline, just to prove that he's not lying. Older women, ugly ones, even guys—everyone got his special neck rubba. My god, for a while we were all a bit uncomfortable, but really—we had no choice. In the end, the girl had no case lah. And Albert took us all out to Front Page for big drinks when she finally quit and it was all over.

That wasn't even one of the funniest things he did. I still remember when I first started six years ago, he was a bit more daring then. One day, he was walking around the newsroom—slow news day, nothing happening, so he was feeling bored lah. He sent out an email calling for a meeting in the middle of the newsroom. Since he rarely does that, of course we all took it damn seriously. I even wondered whether he was going to announce his promotion! Everyone had been waiting for years for him to become the publisher of the company. But that day, when the meeting started, Albert just started naming people. If you got arrowed, then you had to come to the middle of the news hub. Of course we started to realize something was going on when we noticed that he was only calling girls' names—moreover, he was calling up all the girls who were wearing a skirt that day. Once there were about ten girls up in the front he asked them all to turn around and said, "Eh, look at this. We have some of the most chio girls in the country working for us. We must show some appreciation—come, let's vote. Tell me who you think has the most happening legs!" OK, even I have to admit it was just a little a bit weird, but Albert is such a good-natured guy that we all knew he meant no harm. It's all good fun after all. So, the girls were all good sports, and in the end the whole thing was quite fun. (I don't remember who won but we all had a good laugh about it at happy hour that night. That Albert really knows how to get everyone in a happy mood lah.) But these days, with more and more girls showing up like that NUS grad, even Albert knows he has to watch it a bit. So, life in the newsroom is not so much fun anymore.

Usually at the start of the day though, Albert is in a very good mood. After spending the night and early morning with his wife and their daughter doing all those boring-as-fuck family things, Albert always cannot wait to come into the office and bother all of us. Sometimes he'll even take the lift to the skywalk and cross over to the next building to flirt with the bimbo girls in circulation. He has such a big title at the *New Times* that even though he's not good-looking (mouse eyes, flat backside, a bit too skinny and walks a bit funny) the circulation girls always laugh at all his jokes and flirt back lah. I think one or two of them are a bit like his spare girlfriends, even though no one dares to talk about it too much. (No matter how good-natured he is, Albert is the boss after all. We should never forget that.) Girls in the newsroom—Albert knows they probably are a bit too smart for him to mess with. If you start going out with them, confirm will have trouble. When things don't work out (and hallo, you know that is usually what happens), you still have to see the guniang's face in your department every day. Like that, where's the fun?

Plus, especially now, when we all have to go to sexual harassment seminars and all, trying to pok girls in the newsroom really is a lousy idea. But the circulation girls—they're not as smart or bossy so you can count on them to not want or expect very much. (And I guess since they are technically not directly his staff members, it's a bit more OK.) And his wife also doesn't really seem to notice or care. He makes big bucks after all—and has the atas title along with it. So when he tells his wife he has to work really late, she also knows she doesn't have anything to say. That's why from Monday to Friday—those are Albert's days for being really happening.

Even though I was his assistant, he had so much to catch up on—he always has to do a lot of hello hellos to the guniangs all over the building lah—that he didn't even notice me that much until after tea. "Wah, Jazzy, tonight hot date is it?" he said, suddenly appearing next to my chair. He must have meant it because his rubba-ing then was not just my neck—I could feel his hand going down the back of my red silk blouse. "No lah," I said. "Hot date? As if!"

"Good," Albert said, continuing his rubba-ing. "By the way, on Monday, wear something nice like this. That night, I have to entertain some people at Front Page—you come along too. Don't worry, this will be early. I just need some pretty girls there for them to look at. Just drink, smile, listen, don't interrupt—you know how to do it lah. Just be yourself, Jazzy."

Even though Albert would never say so, I know that part of the reason he's kept me on for so long is that I actually bother to show up at work looking nice. Before me, his assistants were all young young cute cute ones—they'll join him at twenty-two years old; by the time they hit twenty-four, Albert will have already moved them on to some bumfuck job somewhere else at the *New Times*. No one seems to know where they go because nobody ever sees them again. It's not as if they mattered before, when they were Albert's assistants, but after he shoved them off somewhere else, they really didn't matter to anyone anymore. The point is, Albert was done with them. And they were now out of the way.

Everyone knows that Albert likes his assistants young—partly because he likes to bring them to all these industry things he has to go to, or when he's entertaining visiting media types, having a chio little girl to smile and laugh at all these bosses' stupid jokes, is a confirm win situation. But this guniang here actually likes this job—and I know how to dress. And no matter how expensive those SK-II creams are, I always buy them—it's an investment, after all. If I actually start getting wrinkles anywhere on my face, aiyoh, I know my job will be gone already. Also, whatever Albert asks me to do, I'll always do it. No questions asked. I make sure that no matter what happens, he always knows that I have value.

Of course, it also helps that I am actually good at being his assis- Guniang may not be smart enough to be a lawyer but I am very ized. And Albert always has so many appointments, so many to think about, he knows that if he doesn't have me around him keep track of everyone, his life will be one big problem.

"This week, you have a lot of things on, Albert," I started to tell him.

"OK come come come, let's talk inside," he said, finally stopping the rubba-ing so he could quickly walk into his office and wave for me to follow. He's very impatient, so whenever he moves I know I'd better fasterly move behind him. So I quickly grabbed my pen, notebook and his printed schedule and ran behind him.

"Close the door," he said after sitting down in his black fake leather big boss chair and leaning back a bit to get comfortable.

Oh. It's that kind of meeting.

I closed Albert's heavy door and went over to the wide bookshelf by the sofa. It's quite funny that Albert has such a big bookshelf with so many serious books because everyone who works with him knows that he hates to read. "That's why I went into newspapers," he always tells us at Front Page after he's had a few. "The stories are all short!" In fact, since he took over as editor of the *New Times* ten years ago the stories in the paper have only gotten shorter and shorter. (Except for the sensational ones—anything involving politicians, rich men and sex, he'll let reporters write as much as they can and he'll put the stories all over the top of the front page.) But his strategy clearly works lah—circulation has only gone up and up since he was in charge. I can only imagine that his salary is also the same story.

I guess even though Albert doesn't like books, he is the editor of the *New Times* after all, so his office must look respectable a bit. That's why he has this gigantic bookshelf in his office with all the important books—Margaret Thatcher's collected speeches, *Quotations from Chairman Mao Zedong,* and of course right in the middle, displayed facing outward, is Lee Kuan Yew's *The Singapore Story.* One time, someone tried to give him that book that Hillary Clinton wrote about helping children or some shit but he just laughed and said to them, "Please. She's a wife." People should really know better lah: hallo, the editor of our country's newspaper cannot look like he's too open-minded. Display this kind of ladies' book on his office shelf? He might as well start wearing panties.

I think I am the only one in this whole building who knows that of all these books he actually has only read one: *How to Win at EVERYTHING*, which he squeezes into one of the dark corners of the bookshelf. (Ever since the Hong Kong tycoon who wrote that book got jailed last year for embezzling, it's now quite not fashion to read this book anymore.) But sometimes when I pop into his office to tidy up before going home, this is the one book that will be on his desk. I always know to quickly hide it away so no one sees it.

The most valuable thing in Albert's tall bookshelf is actually the cupboard he has at the bottom. Once you slide the heavy wooden door open—there's a full bar inside! Chivas, Grey Goose, Hendrick's— and if you want Japanese whiskey, he's got all the expensive kinds.

"Jazzy, it's raining a bit so let's try something mellow," he said. "Maybe some Yamazaki—the twelve-year-old one, not the eighteen. Today's not anything special."

After I filled half a crystal glass with Yamazaki and brought it ver to Albert, I moved the two chairs in front of his desk to one side d went to sit on the sofa. When I first started, it took a few weeks ore I figured this out—if I'm wearing heels and a tight or short , then he wants me to sit on the sofa, not the chair. The sofa is . Albert always likes a good view.

n though my skirt that day was not that short, it was bunching r my backside because his sofa was so low. I'm sure Albert e my red panties! But aiyah, I didn't care. I just leaned back ed my legs just a very little bit—not so much that it's slutty, mind you. Just enough for a sneak preview. Let the boss look lah. Job security is always good, right? Besides, no matter what, I know Albert will never try anything funny with me. After having to deal with all the scandals from people pok-ing each other in his newsroom over the years, he is the first one to tell everyone: "Please, don't shit where you eat."

Even though Albert is damn lecherous with most girls, when it comes to me, I know that he just likes to window-shop. He might be quite old—although you can't really tell since he dyes his hair boot-polish black all the time—he's a guy lah, so if there are panties and legs for him to see, of course he's damn happy. If you have to be stuck in an office doing some crap job, might as well try to have something nice to look at while you are doing it, after all. Some people hang nice art on their walls; others look at legs. Who can't understand that? But at the end of the day, I know he actually feels protective of me, like he's my uncle or something. Last year when some editor over at the *Business Post* kept bugging me to go out with him, the moment I mentioned it to Albert he went over to their newsroom upstairs, popped his head in and shouted across the whole office, "Hello, Cedric—please control yourself. Leave my girls alone!" Wah, the guy was so embarrassed he doesn't even dare to say "Hallo" to me now even if we are both queuing up for kopi in the cafeteria at the same time.

From the squeaking of his chair, I could tell Albert was trying to lean back and relax a bit more. Since my desk had no window—or wasn't even remotely near a window so I can sort of peek out—I didn't even know it had started raining until I was in his office. Through the large wraparound windows of his spacious corner room, I could see that it was really coming down. All the sparkling glass condominium towers around were just blurry gray smears;

fat ribbons of water were racing down Albert's window. Despite the pounding machine-gun rain, I could hear him sigh a bit. Good. A calm Albert was always better than the hyperactive manic one that the newsroom usually saw. He seemed to be in a solid mood.

"Eh, boss—focus!" I said. "Next week, you're very busy. Monday is your mum's death anniversary but don't worry I already called the temple and donated eighty-eight dollars for you. They said they would send their best sweeper to help your wife clean up her grave since you cannot make it. Just remember to mention it to Mrs. Lim later tonight so she knows you remembered. Wednesday is Mrs. Lim's birthday—I already bought a pair of pearl earrings for you to give her and one of those romantic cards she likes. Do you also want me to buy some of those handmade chocolates she likes from the Four Seasons?"

"No need, no need!" he said. I could see his face suddenly turning black. In his mind, he's probably kau-behing over how he must now spend Wednesday evening with his wife just because it's her birthday. Poor guy.

"I tell you," he said, really frowning now. "I don't know what kind of food she's spending her money on these days but that woman is really putting on weight. And not in the right places."

I figured I'd better quickly move on to the next topic. "OK, then on Thursday you have that lunch with the new minister for the environment and water resources," I continued. "I booked a table for you at Iggy's . . ."

"Iggy's? No, no, no—no need to take him somewhere so nice! He's only in charge of the environment—not say, information and communications. Who cares?" Albert said. "Just book a table at the Shang and be done with it. Not the nice steak restaurant. Just do the Chinese one below it."

I could see that Albert was getting a bit impatient because all of this was stressing him out and not letting him enjoy his whiskey. So I very quickly went over the rest of his schedule, being very careful to not mention any other appointments that might really stress him out, and closed my notebook. When I got up to leave, he wiggled his second finger at me, asking me to come to his desk. As I got closer he waved his hand to get me to come around to his side.

It felt weird to just stand there so I leaned back on his desk, which I guess was the right thing because he smiled and started to really look at my legs. So I decided to get even closer and half-sit on his desk. His smile got even bigger.

Albert took a slow sip of his whiskey and set down the glass, sighing again. He put his right hand on my thigh for a moment, thought for a minute, then removed it and took my hand instead.

"Jazzy, how old are you now? Twenty-four?" he asked.

I wasn't sure where this was going but it didn't feel good. Twenty-four is that age when he turns his assistants into pumpkins! Luckily I had two kopis that morning so I could still think quite quickly. No matter how bad twenty-four is, twenty-six is worse! So I just nodded and smiled as sweetly as I could. At that moment I really wished I had one of those Japanese-girl dimples. Everyone knows that Albert likes his girls fair, with big eyes and a cute smile—Japanese-y lah.

"What do you want in life?" Albert asked. He was still looking at my legs; I could feel his thumb stroking my fingers.

I started to feel a bit weird at this point. Sure, after too many drinks at Front Page, Albert sometimes got touchy-feely with the girls—at those times of the night, even I would sometimes get some of that, regardless of his big policy about not shitting where you eat. But whenever that happened, Albert was usually just very huggy, sometimes maybe kissing you on the cheek—you know, playful shit. But this time, he wasn't drunk and he was looking quite se-rious. My god—would I actually have to consider whether I would have to say yes to my boss or not?

"Well, I like working for you . . ." I said.

"But Jazzy, you are a smart girl, you know—you must have bigger goals, right?" he asked.

This, I wasn't sure how to handle. Of course I have a goal—but obviously I can't tell him I am hoping to meet some expat Prince Charming and live a better life, right? Not that many Singaporean guys are so understanding about life ambitions like that. They think it's some big insult to them that we don't want to marry an Asian guy, like they're not good enough or whatever fuck. (OK, that may be true. But even so, they really shouldn't be so petty and take it personally. Life is just like that.)

So I just said, "Eh, boss, I'm very happy where I am—you don't need to worry about me. OK?"

Albert sighed again. "You are not getting younger anymore, Jazzy—you have so much potential," he said, squeezing my hand and patting my thigh. I guess the conversation was over.

"I just want you to carefully consider what I've asked you," he added, leaning back now. "It's time to grow up. If you really don't have any other options—have you thought about working in circu-lation?"

CHAPTER 4

First, we figure out the Chinese bitches.

At least that was the plan. (Part one of it anyway.) If girls from Mainland China were coming over here to try and steal our men, we need to figure out how they're doing it! I had texted Fann and Imo first thing Friday morning before going to work that day—I'd just laid out my strategy to them the night before after all, so it was still on my mind. Besides, I was trying to find a way to distract myself from my mum, who I suspected would try to drag me out to the wet market before work that morning. My god, that woman really had never met a chicken backside she didn't like—whenever I go marketing with her, each chicken backside also must stop and look ten times before walking on. "Meet outside Lunar—11 p.m.," I said to the girls in my text. "Last one buys first round."

Then, just when I was lying there, thinking of our strategy, what to do tonight at the Lunar, a club that we'd heard was just filled with China girls, my mum of course decided to bang on my door and nag at me. Hello, people here have a serious mission, you know— after giving the girls that big lecture last night with all those Excel spreadsheet-type points, we need to follow through tonight!

"Huay ah! Sleeping still?" my mum was shouting. I could tell from how her voice was getting louder that she was starting to open my door and pop her head in. Aiyoh, I don't know why, after so many years already she's still calling me by my Chinese name. My god, Ah Huay is so cheena! I told her how many times already that my name is now Jazeline, but she still catch no ball. Before I started working, I changed my name already—not in my passport lah. That would be too much work. But starting from secondary school I already told everyone—from now on, just call me Jazeline. This name is quite power, you know—I know I made it up lah but it's a name that nobody else has! Jazeline is not Jasmine or Celine or any boring name like that—it's damn special. In the whole of Singapore, only I have this name. When people hear it, they confirm know they'd better pay attention to me. All these things, I told my mum so many times already. If she wants me to succeed outside of her small world, how can I do it without an ang moh name? Why she cannot understand?

"So lazy!" my mum said, shouting even louder when she saw I was still in bed. Aiyoh. "I need your help to buy things from the market—you better hurry up otherwise I got nothing to make for your pa's dinner tonight!" She didn't even wait for me to say anything before slamming the door. I knew that if I didn't just jump up to follow her, she confirm would come back in two minutes so—no choice is no choice.

By the time I quickly put on some clean shorts and T-shirt and brushed my teeth, my mum was already sitting by the door holding her wallet, wearing her slippers, looking damn grumpy. When she saw me come out, she just jumped up and started walking out the door. I swear, this woman moves faster than anybody I know.

When we walked to the wet market, I realized how late it was—no wonder she was in such a bad mood. If you want to go to the wet market, you must 6:30 A.M. wake up and fasterly go. Eight A.M. then go marketing? At that hour on a weekday, a lot of market uncles got air also they won't bother selling to you. They're tired already—time to close shop and balik kampong.

So by the time we started walking around, her favorite fish uncle was holding a fat red rubber hose, washing his stall and splashing pink water everywhere. Even though my mum tried to smile at him a bit, he had nothing to sell her. "Sorry lah—even my reserve fish all no more already," he said, actually looking apologetic. "Hallo, now what time already! You now then come?" Luckily her second-choice fish uncle still had a few pieces and the pork uncle also hadn't packed up his stall otherwise my mum will confirm spend the whole weekend saying I made her to go to NTUC and buy not-so-fresh fish and pork.

I was feeling quite sotong at this moment. Damn tired, first of all—didn't sleep enough, of course, since I ended up having more drinks with the girls last night to celebrate our plan. On top of that, my mum was walking so fast through the wet market, trying to get to her vegetable boy and the flower auntie before they closed shop. Since some uncles had already started cleaning up, the floor was damn slippery; running water sloshed around our toes. But my mum was not affected, of course—she just glided through the market as if she were going down a slide. Guniang over here was just desperately trying to keep up—and not splash any pink water on my legs.

Whenever my mum stopped, she would try and give me some lesson. "Huay ah, when you buy chicken or duck ah, if the uncle doesn't kill it in front of you, you must remember to always press the skin a bit—got bounce back then it's good. Never bounce back then don't buy. Too old already." Or, "Make sure you see the color of the fish eyes before you buy—cloudy one means not fresh."

All these things—I don't know why she's wasting her saliva to tell me. I've heard it all how many times already! Finally, I got a bit fed up. "Ma, you damn long-winded lah," I said when she kept trying to push a winter melon into my hands to make me feel it. "If you use less saliva, maybe you can finish your shopping faster."

Wah—that's when she got angry.

"You think I'm just being naggy for the sake of nagging you, is it? Ah Huay ah, you how old already? You won't always have your mum here to buy food for you, cook for you every day, you know? One day when you get married, who is going to go shopping for you? You'd better learn now otherwise nobody will marry you! Or worse, you get married and your husband so unhappy he divorce you. Then your life will really be over. With men—you must always know how to feed and pamper them otherwise their stomachs will lead them outside."

I almost wanted to laugh. Me? Go shopping in a wet market? As if! When Jazzy gets married, a Filipino maid is going to do all her marketing. Some more, the kind of shopping my family will do is confirm not shopping at a wet market—it's the "drive your car and go to Cold Storage on Sunday with the kids" type of shopping. More expensive also no problem. You think Jazzy's husband is going to want food bought in a low-class wet market with bloody water and chicken shit all over the floor?

I know this is all my mum always expected from her lousy life—in fact, all things considered, it's much better than the life that her mother had. Her ma grew up on one of those old pig farms! But please—my mum should know that their lives will not be my life.

"Ma, please lah—this kind of lesson, I don't need to learn," I told her.

My mum stopped walking. Right in the middle of the wet market corridor some more. When I saw her eyes, my god, I knew that now I'm really going to get scolded.

"You ah—I tell you, just dream dream dream only," she said

loudly. "You think I don't know what you think you can get? Some ang moh prince to come and bring you home with them, far far away from me and your pa? You better wake up your head, Ah Huay! Once we are gone, you'll have no one to take care of you if these are the kinds of guys you want. These ang mohs—they only want one thing. When they take already, they don't need you anymore. You think I don't have eyes, is it? Cannot see what is going on with you? See you how late then come home all the time? You think I don't know what you do when you are outside, is it? See how you dress, put lipstick and perfume all? You think the neighbors don't ask me why you always have strange ang moh guys sending you home so late? I tell you—seeing your daughter do all these kinds of thing, break your pa's heart only. He want to talk to you also don't have words to say."

I, on the other hand, had many things I wanted to say, but my mum had talked for so long and was clearly so angry that I was scared she was going to cry. In fact, people walking by us were staring a bit by then. If she cried, then habis. The whole neighborhood will start gossiping about how Jazzy made her mum cry in the wet market.

"Ma, please don't be upset," I quickly said. "Sorry, sorry. I promise I will listen."

My mum looked like she didn't really believe me, but she also didn't know what else she could say.

"One more thing," she said, "you'd better watch your language, Ah Huay. I heard you say the word *damn* just now—do you know how chor lor that is? That word is a men's word, you know—women are not supposed to use it! Please—don't shame your pa and me by saying bad words like that."

I guess it's a good thing she never spies on my texts with me and my friends. My god—with all the kani nah here and cock there, Ma confirm will vomit blood.

Like that, I guess my mum's lecture was finished. So she turned around and started walking again.

We were both damn quiet on the walk home—guniang made sure to walk a few steps behind the old lady so we had no eye contact. I didn't want anything to somehow get her started up again.

Her words, even though I don't agree, actually upset me a bit, I have to say. Clearly she and Pa think I'm no better than one of those KTV lounge girls. And obviously, I know they worry about me. Pa spent his whole life working in some cock factory as some lousy low-level manager and never earned that much lah. And Ma—I'm not sure if being a hairdresser in one of those super old slightly sleazy hairdressing parlors really counts as a job since she basically earned peanuts. And once they're gone, I'm really on my own since I'm the only child. But this one is also their fault. Who asked them to take the government's population control campaign so seriously? All the government posters clearly said "Two is enough" but they wanted to be super patriotic so they just stopped at one. So now, if I end up alone, whose fault is that?

Also, hello, she should know that our guy friends and the ang mohs we meet and fool around with don't pay us for anything. We are free modern women! (Drinks are just drinks lah—even at three hundred dollars a bottle, it doesn't count. Everyone is just having a good time.) And please, it's not like we were like those China girls who were coming to Singapore in herds to marry rich guys. In fact, it's girls like that who were pushing us to go out that night. Our goal: to find out how Mainland girls hook our men.

When I sat down to think about getting to the bottom of how these China girls operate—it seemed very straightforward. If you want to understand the mind of the enemy, then you must bravely go into their territory! If they want to come over to our country and steal our men, then we must invade their turf and learn what their strategy is. And with these girls, everyone knows there are many places where they like to do their business. But for the more decent ones—or rather the ones who try to attract guys in decent areas that me and the girls would actually show our faces in—there's only one place that we can go to see the most daring (and successful) cases: Lunar, in crazy Clarke Quay.

Of course, everybody knows about Lunar. The location of this club, I tell you, is super primo. It's right in the middle of Clarke Quay, where—confirm—all the most happening bars and clubs are right now in Singapore. And on Friday or Saturday night when you want to meet your friends outside a club first before going in together—you know, so when you walk in the door, people automatically know you're with a group instead of being some fucker who has no friends—usually you will choose a meeting place in the middle of everything. So people always just say, "Come, we meet outside Lunar."

So that Friday night, after guniang here got ready steady nice and sexy, I quickly hopped in a taxi. Looking out the smudgy window, I wondered how everything got so boring. After all these years in Singapore, honestly, I'm quite tired of the scenery lah. All the buildings look the same—every year even if new ones get added to the skyline also at the end of the day, nothing looks different. If I knew this early on, aiyoh, Jazzy here confirm would have become an architect, man—get paid big bucks to design new buildings that look exactly like everyone else's? This one really is win. Half-sleeping at work also can become millionaire. But then sometimes at night, like now, looking out of a taxi as it's zooming through traffic, past the Singapore river, past the stupid tourists and expat drunks on Boat Quay, past the flashing lights of the towering bank buildings, OK lah, this is when I think, maybe this island is not so bad. I guess once I meet my ang moh and move to London or Melbourne, maybe—maybe—I will miss this longkang.

Things were damn happening by the time I got to Clarke Quay. The moment I opened my taxi door, people were rushing over to try and snatch the cab before it got to the taxi queue. I never understand these people. Now only eleven o'clock—hallo, most of the clubs are only just starting to fill up with people besides Ah Bengs and their smelly girlfriends. Why would anyone be so toot as to leave right now?

Although, we should all be glad that some losers were actually leaving and clearing some space. Even though it was still quite early, the wide open-air concourse slicing through the heart of Clarke Quay was jammed with the usual sea of warm bodies—each one feeling all the more sticky as I pushed through because of all the sleeveless tops and too-short skirts that everyone was wearing. This was the part that I hated the most. Technically it should only take about three minutes to walk from the taxi queue to Lunar—and hallo, guniang here is talking about doing this in my four-inch heels, OK! But because of all these babis and wannabes, the walk always takes damn fucking long. Like tonight lah—I purposely planned my outfit so I could look super chio in front of all these China girls at Lunar, but the crowd at Clarke Quay was unbelievable! By the time I got to Lunar, not only were my arms coated with this thin film of Ah Beng sweat, but I also almost fell down from trying to avoid some lumpar flicking around his cigarette as he pushed through.

Sher, Fann, Imo and I—of course we'd been to Clarke Quay many many times. We never want to admit it lah, but we'd been to so many of these clubs so often that we usually don't need to pay cover charge to get in. Once the bouncer sees us, he just knows to let us in. Unlike those people who come in, order one drink and sit in one corner, watching other people dance and go crazy all night because they themselves are too shy or too low-class to participate, these bouncers know that not only will we buy drinks ourselves but also we usually dress nicely enough that other guys confirm will buy us more drinks. Of all the clubs though, the one place we had never been was Lunar. If you are a guy, and you specifically want to meet a China girl—like, not one from one of those red-light shophouses in Geylang or a sleazy KTV lounge, then Lunar is the place to go.

So, why would we ever have reason to go there? Those guys who want China girls usually are not the type to chase us. Singaporean girls to them are too bossy, too opinionated, not quiet enough. But, as I told the girls, if we want to understand the competition, then Lunar is confirm must.

Louis had been to Lunar a few times before—China girls actually prefer rich Singaporean guys to ang mohs. I also don't know why. Sometimes I think maybe they're scared of big cocks or something. Or maybe they're not used to so much hair? Sometimes it's true lah—ang moh guys, if you rubba them too long, it's like fucking sandpaper. Anyway, when Louis goes to Lunar—he confirm can always score. For these China girls, the other thing also is that Singaporean guys are easier to control. Ang moh guys often want to be independent and all that shit. When they meet you, even if they really like you, they usually want to date a few people at a time type. After months and months where you end up having to hang out with their boring friends for all these nights playing darts and pretending that you like drinking Guinness, then maybe they suddenly will wake up one morning and think, okay lah, this girl not so bad—can go steady.

But Singaporean guys, aiyoh, if you hook them properly and fasterly, they will pamper you for a long time. So when I told Louis we wanted to go, he texted his guy at Lunar to book a VIP table. Since it was our first time there, Louis agreed to come out earlier to meet us. This wasn't easy. His wife, Mary, usually doesn't start her mah-jongg game until 11 P.M. so Louis cannot leave until then. But tonight was a special case—we were not meeting at the usual club and in this Lunar world, we quite toot, China girls are quite fierce. So, Mary—once she heard where we were meeting, even she was OK with Louis coming out early just this time. After all, she probably thinks, if us girls slowly one by one get married, maybe Louis will see his friends settling down and he'll start staying at home more. Even though Louis never talks about it, we all know that it's getting to be time for him to pop out a son. And Mary, of course she wants that too—once that happens, she's really set for life! Dowager status—earned.

"Eh, Jazzy, tonight is really happening ah?" Louis said when Imo, Fann and I finally got there and made it through, past the VIP bouncer. I tell you, this was the first time he was so on time. Must be he's a bit worried for us. Louis of course was nice as usual, holding up the bottle of Chivas after we double-kissed. We used to just hug when we saw each other, but then last year he and Mary went to Paris for a holiday. When he came back, he started doing that Frenchy double kiss that you see those atas people do. So now, like that lah.

"Jazzy, you're looking good," he said, running his right hand through his nicely styled fringe and smiling. He was not bad-looking for a Singaporean guy, actually. Married lah, but I still might have considered. His family is so rich—who wouldn't want? Except that we all knew Imo had her eye on him. She never told us if anything happened, but sometimes we could see her drinking very little and then waiting for Louis to offer to send her home. Sometimes she had to wait for hours, watching him drink Chivas after Chivas, pulling random girls from his office or sometimes me, Fann or Sher close to him if we happened to be nearby during one of his favorite songs. Whoever it was, he would wrap his arms around the girl as he sang each word, his mouth so close it sometimes felt as if he was eating our ears. Imo never got upset—pointless, after all. Dancing is just dancing. And she knew she didn't have any real right to be upset. Not that we knew whether anything was going on, or wanted to ask. These kinds of things, better not to know too much. It made it easier on those few nights when Mary actually agreed to set aside her mah-jongg game and come out with us. If none of us actually officially knows anything about Imo and Louis, when his wife is out with us, we all can still smile, say hi hi and everything is OK one.

"Of course lah," I said to Louis, pulling back my new sexy black tank top and puffing up my small boobs. "People went shopping all—just for you!" Louis rolled his eyes, stuck out his third finger and then held up his other finger to ask me whether I wanted one shot or two. "Aiyah, two lah, two lah," he said, shaking his head and starting to pour. I could see him looking around to mentally count how many drinks he had to pour, and he had a slightly confused look for a moment when he saw that Sher wasn't there. "Married," I said. I could see him sighing and blinking his eyes; he shook his head and started pouring.

After handing out glasses to the three of us, he rubba-ed my neck a bit and whispered in my ear, "China girls! They are havoc, man. You sure you want to be in their territory? You can still change your mind, you know. Terence is holding my table at Studemeyer's until one A.M. if we want it."

"Crazy! You think I'm scared?" I said, holding up my hands and hitting my left palm into my right fist. "Lumpar lah!"

Louis thought for a moment, then just raised his eyebrows and nodded, smiling. He raised his right hand and gave me a big thumbs-up. He should know better. He's known me for how long already—and he still dares to ask me this kind of rubbish question? China girls are nothing compared to us!

Actually, to be honest, we were a bit scared when we walked in. When we walked in, the first thing we heard was this damn loud Hokkien singing. Yes, I know some Hokkien but walao, this song was so cheena that even I couldn't understand what the guy was singing about. Something about girls and love and other cock stuff, I'm sure. The waitresses were all wearing these bright red glittery cheongsam-style bodysuits that were super tight and super short. From the looks of them—hair dark dark and straight straight, fair skin, flat nose, crooked teeth, concave chest—I could tell that they were all really from China.

When we first started seeing China girls popping up in the 1980s—at first in Geylang around the brothels but then after a while, everywhere—we at first thought these girls were so plain-looking, what harm could they be? With faces like that, how can they win? Especially back then, those SK-II type face creams were all still quite expensive so not everybody had fair skin—some were still a little dark-looking, like those coolies in padi fields type. But I tell you ah—these girls are quite cunning. They only look simple—if you see their eyes close-up . . . scary! Each and every one of them, they all have that hungry look. Even if a guy has a wife, girlfriend, kids, grandkids, they also heck care one. All they care about is what they can take—Singapore citizenship is number one. Coach handbag, condo, car and cash even better—nice, but not so necessary. If they win the man then everything set already—no need to go home to their longkangs in China.

At Lunar, the whole place was filled with these girls—the cheong-sam sluts were fawning over the guys, some even daring to sit in their laps out in the open. Walao eh, we couldn't believe it—this place is a decent club in Clarke Quay, you know. It's not say super atas like the Orchard Road bars—but it's also not sleazy like Geylang at 3 A.M. Kani nah—so daring! And in all the little white shiny banquettes on the side there were groups of China girls just sitting around, looking pretty—as pretty as they can try and look lah—and trying to catch guys' eyes. Fann and Imo were quiet, looking around quite shocked. We were dressed up rather nicely—that day, Imo came from stylo work drinks so she was wearing a little black dress (new one—Marc Jacobs, don't play play!) and Fann, well, Fann was looking as nice as she can. And I was feeling quite chio in my new Seven jeans. If any guy is not staring at my backside tonight, I tell you, he is confirm agua.

When we came out, we knew we were looking damn steam. But these cheongsam sluts—walao. The competition really was a bit unfair. I stared at Louis and he shook his head, leaning over to my ear. "Woman," he said, "don't forget—it was your idea to come here."

Aiyoh. Well, since we were here, we might as well stay, I thought. Better don't waste a Friday night. Louis poured another round of double shots to make us feel better. It worked. After a few sips, we could actually relax a bit. Soon after, when a few of Louis's guy friends showed up, we were already a bit high. So high in fact that we actually forgot why we went there. Until the Ah Beng emcee in the sparkly purple suit and the Elvis Presley hairstyle got in the middle of the stage and started shouting some nonsense in Hokkien that we couldn't really understand. But from the way he was pointing at the crowd and shaking his mike around, we could tell that something was about to start.

In our VIP section, Fann, Imo and I all stood up so we could see better. We were all squinting squinting at the stage, trying to see what was going on but eh? Nothing was happening. At this point the lights had gone down and the place was quite dark except for these two bright red circles of spotlight that were chasing each other around the room. This kind of light show—fucking toot, man. I was just about to whisper to Fann, "My god, this is damn boring," when Louis tapped me on the shoulder. "Guniang, look over there," he said, pointing toward the center of the room. When we first walked in, I had noticed this big divider in the middle of the room—there were two long lines crisscrossing in the middle, separating the room into four parts. Quite strange. Usually these clubs like to have a large, more open space so people can have more dancing dancing and all. But then I thought, well, Lunar is owned by some old man from the Mainland, after all. These kinds of modern stylo design features, how is he supposed appreciate?

The lights suddenly all came on at once and the Ah Beng emcee started singing this old Hokkien song—I could understand the first part, since sometimes people sing it at weddings. Some love song about two people sharing an umbrella—a bit toot, yes, but when someone explained the lyrics to me recently I was actually quite touched. So I thought, OK, this is not bad. But only the first few lines were sweet and slow—after that, this Lady Gaga–type disco beat suddenly started and then the umbrella song become half romantic, half Rihanna's "Umbrella." And the red spotlights started moving around like crazy again and everyone started cheering and clapping because these long rows of China girls started coming out from the four corners of the room, dancing down the aisles between the tables and then climbing onto the crisscrossed divider in the middle.

Each girl was wearing shiny black shoes with a small button strap across them, like those shoes you see schoolgirls in England wearing except these had very high heels. Some more they were wearing knee-high white socks and tight white buttoned shirts that were so see-through you could see that underneath them, each girl was wearing a sparkling red bra—their tetek were all so big the bra is confirm push-up one. They all had hair tied up in two ponytails, eyes painted big big, super long eyelashes—fake one lah. But the thing that all the old Ah Peks and Ah Bengs were really staring at was their skirts—aiyoh! These China girls—kani nah! Not shy! Each of their little black skirts was so short it couldn't even cover their whole backside—whenever they moved you could see their white frilly panties underneath. And then the way they purposely danced, they kept pushing up their backsides for everyone to see.

Walao! By this point, Louis and his friends were all out of control, shouting and clapping like crazy. One of them even started loudly saying over and over "Teng kor! Teng kor! Teng kor!" (As if those girls would actually take off their panties—mad! I almost told Kelvin, "Hello, you buy them a Coach bag first then maybe can negotiate. If buy Louis Vuitton, then they confirm will suck your pretend big cock.") Fann, Imo and I just looked at each other—we had nothing to say.

Like this—how can we win?

Just the other day, my mum was lecturing me about life again. These days ah, in my house, people cannot just quietly drink kopi and eat toast. Now, every day, breakfast is my mum's big lecture time. The topic never changes: my future.

That day, mum had clipped out this Singapore Airlines advertisement from the newspaper. They were doing their annual recruitment, looking for new Singapore girls and stewards. Every year when this advertisement comes out, every year my mum confirm will cut it out. "Huay ah—you see?" she said, pushing the paper to me.

"Aiyoh, please lah. Guniang here so old already—as if they want me!" I said. She should know this better than me—Singapore Airlines, they usually want those twenty-one-, twenty-two-year-old girls. "Old birds like me? Please lah. If I apply, they sure laugh until fall down."

"You cannot think like that, Ah Huay," mum said, trying to push the advertisement in front of my face again. "The cutoff now is a bit older. Not like my time, when only young girls can apply. You got chance, why you don't want? Flying can really change your life you know, Ah Girl—SQ will teach you how to dress, how to put on nice makeup, how to eat properly at those nice restaurants, look pretty, meet the right kind of men. You not young anymore, you know—please lah, why you don't want to find a good husband? Your ah pa and I won't be around forever to take care of you, you know."

This argument ah, she every week also say. I don't know why she still tries. She knows I listen until tired already. Cannot listen anymore.

Yes, of course I know she always wished she could have joined SQ. Then maybe she could have done something more with her life than be a hairdresser in a sleazy Excelsior Plaza salon where only cheapskate housewives go for those 1980s tight spiro perms. My ah pa is an OK guy lah, but he's not rich, definitely not handsome, boring job, whole day watch football or go downstairs to the kopitiam to drink Tiger beer and smoke cigarettes type. Of course when you add all those things together, my mum was not happy. This kind of life, my god, if you dare to offer to me I confirm will tell you, "Eh, thank you ah—but balls, lah!"

But my life is actually not bad—I don't know what my mum complaining about. Be an executive assistant to newspaper editor, you think it's an easy job? Boss is always grumpy, I sometimes end up staying late because there's always some news breaking somewhere. And now with texting, I'm somehow always on call—late at night also sometimes get text from the boss to ask me to book a table or buy a present or make an appointment or something. This one is not an anyhow kind of job you know—it's a real career! Got future! My boss is a big guy, which means I am actually quite important. If my boss someday becomes publisher, then I'll be the publisher's assistant. Serious one! Don't play play.

Yes, I know some of my school friends, all the smart girls, they managed to grow up to be lawyers, accountants and banking types. Even one of them actually became a surgeon—I also don't know how. When we found out about it, we were all damn stunned. I mean, I didn't go to the most terrible school in Singapore but even I also know that judging from the kinds of girls who went to my government school, for any of them to become a surgeon is almost as difficult as winning the Toto big prize. (Although if you saw this surgeon girl and the kind of backside face she has, you can tell that she's quite smart.)

But me, I may not know much but at least I know what I can do—and I know what is just crazy to consider. I know I'm smart enough to be a secretary or executive assistant. But to become a doctor, lawyer or banker? I'm smart enough to know not to dream about it.

Don't talk about becoming a doctor, I can't even imagine marrying a doctor. Usually they are not the types of guys that you meet at the clubs and bar. At least not the ones we usually go to. But then again the doctors who come here from America or Australia are usually older, married already, stay-at-home type. I guess it's a bit weird if you see them at Clarke Quay at 1 A.M., chionging in the SPG clubs. And the doctors who are Singaporean—my god, please, those are the most boring. Sure, if you marry one then your life will be good money-wise, but I tell you, those guys are the ones with the bossiest mothers, who will live with you and interfere with every single thing you try to do with your husband and kids. Give me that kind of life—hallo, I'd rather stay at home with my parents until I drop dead.

This Singapore Airlines issue though, I've explained it over and over to my mum until I'm fucking tired. It's just wasting my saliva to even try telling her again.

But seeing the China girls at Lunar tonight, I started thinking that maybe my mum actually has a point. Maybe joining SQ or some shit like that is better than us trying to run around Singapore and anyhow hit balls. So many girls out there, so many different things to fight. I suddenly felt quite tired. And I also suddenly wished Sher was there at Lunar with us.

If Sher was here, confirm she would find something funny to say. (Also, usually when Sher is around, more guys talk to us, even if there are other chio girls around for them to look at.) I was trying to think where she was tonight. The wedding was a few nights ago— where did she say she was going for her honeymoon? Langkawi? Or Batam? Typical Ah Beng honeymoon. Marrying an ang moh means you get a honeymoon that's not a cheapo Malaysia or Indonesia trip. Our friend Dolly last year went to Paris for her honeymoon when she married that American guy, OK! He's not even that rich but he said Paris was very romantic, so honeymoon must go there. By the time Dolly came back, she was pregnant already! Talk about number one win. But if you marry an Ah Beng, aiyoh—they just want to bring you somewhere nearby so you don't need to fly for so long and there's cheap local food so they don't have to pay big money for Western crap. All they want is to garabing garabung—fast fast one so then they can smoke a cigarette, text their friends and play Candy Crush.

What time is it now? One something in the morning? I'm guessing that Sher's Ah Huat confirm must be snoring away already. If he had anything to drink then he's probably been sleeping for hours and hours. Whatever lah. Her life; she chose it. As long as Fann, Imo and I don't end up like that, I heck care what happens to Sher.

Just thinking about Sher made my blood boil all over again. No—no matter how fucked up Lunar and its China girls were, my mother was not right. Sher was not right. There was a better future for me, Fann and Imo out there—there had to be. We just had to push out there and get it. Cannot be scared.

"Eh, girls," I said, tapping on Fann and Imo's shoulders and pointing at the Lunar VIP section exit. "Come, let's siam." We tried to air-kiss Louis goodbye but he was still staring so hard at the dance show that even Imo couldn't get his attention. So we just left. Nobody looked even once at us—not even at my chio Seven jeans backside—as we squeezed our way through all the guys to get to the door.

Outside, I was so angry I just started walking. Fann and Imo quietly followed—I didn't know if they were drunk or just being blur. As long as I could hear their click clack heels behind me I didn't quite care. Before we went to Lunar, I was thinking OK lah, we go, we try to understand their game, then we can try and figure out how to beat them. But those bloody cheongsam and schoolgirl China girls—they have no standards! Even the ones who were not performing, those just there to flirt and hook husbands and boy-friends, they're all the same! Unless we are willing to just do any-thing to hook a guy, we have no chance against them.

"Oi—Jazzy! Don't walk so fast lah!" I heard Fann shouting behind me. "People's feet pain, you know. Where you going?"

I actually didn't know. It was only 1 A.M.—too early for supper and definitely too soon to go home. I was feeling quite sad and had no mood for partying anymore. But then Imo pointed at the queue in front of us. "Eh," she said, "the bouncer at Attica tonight is Louis's old friend." Win Toto lah! This means we wouldn't need to pay the thirty-dollar cover charge.

"OK," I said. "Let's go in and see how."

The music was damn loud the moment we walked in. At that time in the morning, Attica was just starting to get happening—they have a license to close at six, after all. So 1 A.M. is when people really start showing up. The front part of the club is nice—newer-looking, less grungy, got nice shiny podiums for people to dance and all. But this part is where they play hip-hop lah—so unless you want to meet black guys or those wannabe black guys, you'd better fasterly walk through and go to the second building in the back. I tell you, Singaporean guys who want to act black are the worst—all attitude and they think they're so cool, but when you get to know them better you find out that they are just as no-balls as all the other Singaporean guys. Some more the ones who are really into trying to be black are usually short short small small one. You just need to see them one time and you know—if you go home with them, their cocks confirm will also be short short small small. Waste time only.

So Fann, Imo and I quickly walked through to the building in the back, where a different crowd hangs. This second building—my god, the first time I went there, I remember I was quite scared. Sher practically had to hold my hand the whole time and push my backside up the carpeted stairs—the stairwell was so dark I couldn't see where I was going and it was so narrow that there were people pushing and shoving, trying to come down right when we were walking up. Kani nah—fucking annoying! The whole thing was so small, tight and scary I felt like I couldn't breathe. I almost wanted to go home, but Sher said she had heard the place was very worth it. So, even if I was scared also better keep walking. In the end, once we got to the second floor and got used to the super loud Euro techno music, it was quite a good evening lah. Those really white really skinny ang moh guys always seem to like Euro techno the best. So this club was quite the primo place to hook them. We were with Louis at that time so we had a VIP table and of course, Chivas bottles. We met some cute Scottish guys and Fann ended up going on a few dates with one of them. So overall, it was worth it—even if Fann had absolutely no idea what cock her guy was saying every time he opened his mouth.

Tonight was different though—we didn't have Sher. And usually she's the one who starts conversations with guys. Or rather, guys try to start talking to her first. Also, we didn't have Louis there, so we didn't have any bottles. So we all knew what had to be done: fasterly find some guys to buy drinks for us. Fortunately, Imo's dress was looking exactly the kind of chio that these Euro Euro guys like—small black dress, a little bit more sophisticated-looking, sexy sexy one. So the moment we got there, some ang moh guy from the VIP area came down to the bar to ask if we wanted to join his friends.

The rest of the night, I was quite blur. I remember doing tequila shots. Then drinking beer from a jug. Then someone ordered champagne. Then I remember Fann getting quite sick. By that time I was already a bit gone. And I was dancing with this guy whose face I couldn't really see—it was so dark! But he was tall, no glasses, quite skinny and his accent ah—super British, man. Like those old butlers in those British movies—sexy!—but as far as I could tell, he wasn't that old.

At that time, Imo started ignoring everyone because she started texting like crazy. Ah, must be 4 A.M. already—Louis was probably looking to leave Lunar. I guess he didn't find any Chinese backside that he liked.

"Jazzy, ah," Imo said, tapping me on the shoulder. "I think I'd better make a move first." I was so high by that point that I just nodded and kept dancing.

"Eh, Jazzy—I'm going to send Fann home with Louis. You leave also lah—we can send you home too." I could tell she was a bit worried about leaving me alone there. Usually we have Louis or one of his friends around to make sure we're OK—to either send us to a taxi stand or make sure that if we're going home with a guy, that the guy is decent. But these people, we'd only just met them a few hours ago. We didn't know anything about them beyond the fact that they were British and they all worked in Jurong on one of those oil refineries. (Which means they confirm are not rich.)

But aiyoh, guniang over here was finally having good time tonight—why must Imo be so naggy? I just waved and said, "Aiyah, no need lah. I how old already—I don't need another mum, thank you very much. I'll be OK." She still looked a bit worried. So I pointed at the guy behind me rubba-ing his crotch into my backside and touching my stomach with his hands as he danced.

"Please," I said, giving her two thumbs up in case she couldn't hear me since the music was so loud. "He'll take care of me—don't worry!" So she just said "OK" and started helping Fann off the couch and toward the door.

After they left, I started to panic. The music was so loud my feet were hurting from the "boom boom boom" I could feel from the floor. Each time there was a "boom" the guy behind me was rubbaing into my backside even more, pushing me forward, until I felt like I was almost going to fall over the railing in front of me. Walao! I wanted to say something to him but then I remembered that I actually don't remember his name.

Some more I couldn't even hear what song was playing because all techno songs sound the same. And the laser lights shooting all over the room were starting to make my eyes a bit pain. I looked at the dance floor in front of us and it was jammed with all these ang moh guys and Singaporean girls, all of them rubba-ing and hugging and pushing and touching. Long black hair was flying around; white hairy arms were holding on to backsides and waists all over the floor. Maybe Imo was right. I should have left with them.

"Hey, sweetie," my ang moh suddenly said in my ear. So I turned around. And the moment I did that he just started kissing me—big, wet slobbery ones. His chubby lips were like suction cups, man. And he kissed me for so long that one of his friends started pointing and cheering, actually spilling beer all over himself because he was jumping up and down. Kani nah—never see people hook up before is it?

The kissing actually wasn't that shiok. His tongue and my tongue were not quite in sync and some more he was quite the aggressive type—move head, move hands, everything also rubba. I started thinking, now it's maybe four something? If I leave now, the cab queue is probably still quite short—no need to wait for so long. Maybe can even buy supper on the way home.

But then I thought about how chio I looked tonight. In my Seven jeans, my backside was super power! And my small black tank top was damn sexy. Even so, all those guys at Lunar didn't even look at me one time once those China girls came out. How can like that? I know Louis had warned me about the situation. But that was total defeat. And Jazzy cannot lose!

No. Even if this guy is a lousy fuck, I must have something to show for tonight.

So I stopped kissing him for a moment. He looked a bit confused, but then I smiled sweetly at him, then looked a bit demure and all, even fluttering my eyelids a little bit. (I tell you, ang mohs—especially drunk ang mohs—really love that geisha shit.)

Then I slowly slowly moved my right hand to the correct position—and squeezed his cock.

CHAPTER 5

"Aiyoh, what is wrong with you?"

Kani nah, people here are just trying to quietly sit and drink kopi on a Saturday morning also cannot. Why does Seng bloody hell have to come and bother me? I even went to the kopitiam quite early that day. Early for me, that is. After all, I came home at 10 A.M.—after showering, I didn't want to listen to my mum complain about me coming home so late (especially after her lecture at the wet market yesterday). And the thought of having my dad join her in hantaming me—my god, I knew I'd better fasterly get out of the house. And on a Saturday morning, the kopitiam is the best place to go and stone for a bit lah. If you go to one of those atas western cafes with the croissants and shit, these smiley waitresses with the high-pitched singsong voices won't leave you alone! "Miss, do you want more of this or that crap?" and all that bullshit. But in a kopitiam, the uncles there will usually leave you alone to sit and stare into your kopi for as long as you want. The only drawback—for me, anyway—was the bang balls possibility of bumping into Seng.

"What's wrong?" Seng asked again, pulling out a plastic stool from under my table and sitting down. "I whole life never see you so quiet before."

I couldn't even really move my head that much. I just lifted my sunglasses and stared at him. "I got ask you to sit down with me, is it?"

"Eh, this one is free country, you know. You don't own all the seats at the table. If got free seat—then anyone can sit lah! Now—what the hell is wrong with you today?"

Of course, Seng was the last guy I could tell. Even though the fucker was getting so comfortable at the table he took out his Marlboro Menthol Lights and nodded at the kopi uncle, giving him the "one" sign. Before uncle—in his long pajama pants and singlet that was so thin you can practically count all the hairs around his nipples—brought his kopi over, Seng had already moved the rusted empty lychee can near his elbow and lit his ciggie. I tried not to watch him slowly scratching his chin with his one long fingernail. I don't understand when Seng suddenly became such an Ah Beng, growing a sharp fingernail on his little finger for digging his ears and nose and all. And why was I so unlucky to be sitting at a smoking table? Never think properly lah. I had wanted to avoid all those Saturday mothers with their noisy fat kids but now here I was, ending up talking to Seng. Really bang balls, man.

"You don't want to tell me I also know lah," Seng said, flicking his ciggie into the lychee can and exhaling through his nostrils. Actually I don't usually mind Seng so much. Last time when we were young, before he became an Ah Beng, we actually hung out at the kopitiam together a fair bit. At that time, we were just seventeen—we still had no money to go clubbing so much, so might as well just sit in the kopitiam and drink Anchor beer. It was quite fun lah—on Saturday nights, you would see all the old neighborhood Ah Cheks and then the two of us sitting there, drinking beer, talking cock. Uncles would try to share their sad life stories, wanting to tell us young people all the mistakes in life to avoid. Crazy! As if we can't see with our own eyes what their pathetic lives are like. Seng and I would always just laugh. Of course we're smart enough not to end up drinking in a kopitiam with these old Ah Cheks when we are forty years old. Seng is not say very good-looking but he knows how to dress up nicely, saving up to buy Prada sneakers sometimes, carrying a Dunhill wallet and all. And he's not big and buff like those ang moh guys we all like but his body is not terrible. (At least he's not fat like some of his chubby friends. One good thing about his smoking, I guess.) And we all know how chio I am lah. So all those Ah Cheks should know better. Unlike them, people like us actually have dreams. As if we need their advice!

At that time I was not yet happening like I am now, where I have these guys at clubs buying me drinks and all. Back then—we were all damn poor, man. Must save up for a week so we can afford even one pitcher of Long Island Iced Tea at a club. To make the most of it, we knew we had to drink the pitcher fasterly so we could get a quick high. If your head immediately feels pain a bit then confirm is success. But if you drink so fast it's not always shiok. Such highs always only last so long. But the good part is, if you are high and act happy a bit, sometimes guys will notice you more and come over to offer to buy you drinks. So in the end the strategy might have some payoff, after all. As tough as those days were, you know what those aunties always say—better to know hardships early in life, otherwise later when you have a good life, you won't appreciate it.

Later on, once Seng finished army, we all had a bit more money, but he and I would still go to the kopitiam sometimes. Drinks at clubs were expensive after all—so if you sit in a kopitiam first, drink four or five Anchors, get mabuk already then that's the time to go clubbing. When you get to the club already high, you don't need to spend so much on drinks there. Seng even hung out with us girls sometimes back then, but we hadn't invited him in a long time. If you want to meet ang moh guys, if you bring a Singaporean guy along—aiyoh—you might as well just give up before going out.

(Louis is different. A rich guy buying bottles for everyone—who doesn't want to hang out with him? Even ang moh guys also like him.)

Seng also taught me to smoke back then—he said it would make me look sexy. The last time I smoked with him, he was trying to teach me how to do this stylo move, pushing smoke out through his nostrils like a dragon. But no matter how many times I tried, until my nose was fucking pain, almost want to nosebleed, I also couldn't do it. This skill—Seng knows he is champion, and he was doing it now. My head that morning was so painful, however, I just sat there and watched him make those long dragon smoke puffs. Everything was quiet. I had nothing to say.

Earlier this morning—my god. I was still trying to not think about it.

"You hungover lah," Seng said, taking one sip of his kopi that was so big that almost half the cup disappeared. I never understood how that guy can drink so fast. Kopi, whiskey, all the same. One sip, two sips—time for a refill already.

I didn't want to respond to his cock comment. Usually better not to encourage him. If I answer one question, I will have to answer ten more. "This kind of obvious thing," I just said, "no need to say lah. Waste saliva only." Seng just put out his ciggie and pointed one more time at the kopi uncle, who immediately stood up, pulled up his pajama pants and shuffled over to make more kopi.

"Guniang, you last night didn't vomit is it?" he said, shaking his head. I didn't move, hoping that if I didn't say anything he would just shut up. "You ownself ask for it," he said, lighting another ciggie. I could see him looking at me—at first I thought maybe he's pitying me or some shit but actually, it was quite funny. The fucker looked like he was concerned. Must be my lucky day.

"You should know this what," he continued, "if you are going to get that mabuk, then must make yourself throw up before sleeping. Otherwise, if you get hungover until like this, what's the point of drinking?"

It's true lah. Right then, I was thinking, what is the point? That morning—aiyoh. That morning. At first, when we left Attica, I planned to just go that guy's place, finish already then make some quick excuse and go home. But then, my god, guniang here was so tired and mabuk I just fell asleep! Not to say that the guy was that good—but luckily he was quick. So even though he was also quite mabuk it was almost literally like, garabing garabung then everything over already. If he didn't shout one time when he came, I probably wouldn't even know that anything happened. When he suddenly said "GOD!" guniang was actually lying there, still slowly adjusting my hair on the pillow and all, wondering whether I should try and turn over so I wouldn't have to see his nose, which, once we got outside of Attica and I could actually see his face, I realized was not only big but also hairy as fuck. Kani nah, next time I go to Strip I'd better ask them whether they wax noses or not. If they don't, next time I'm not even going to consider guys like this. I would have turned over from the start so I didn't have to see that shit lah, but the first time with a guy, sometimes if you turn over they get the wrong idea. Hallo—guniang here don't do backside.

Once the guy was done he went and got us some water—sweet of him lah. That move, I appreciated. But by the time he came back I was already asleep. Then this morning, aiyoh. When I woke up at around nine, I could actually see that his apartment was not very nice. It's not small—one of those older condos, so it was quite spacious because when government first started granting land for building them, they parceled out bigger lots, so all of them were big big one. But even though it was not bad, it was totally empty! There was nothing on the walls—just white and more white. In the living room, there was just one sofa, one coffee table and one giant flat-screen TV and PlayStation. The fridge was empty. And walao eh, clothes were all over the place—half-rolled-up socks, dirty T-shirts, all thrown all over the living room floor. The bedroom (I guess maybe he doesn't spend so much time there) was at least a bit neater.

I was still walking around the living room, thinking of what else I could look at, when he came out of the bedroom and said, "Hey babes. Hungry?" In the daylight he wasn't, say, terrible-looking. The nose, it's true, looked quite bad. (In the morning light I could see even more clearly just how much hair there was.) But his body— which I could see even more now since he was still naked (and also since I wasn't mabuk and feeling a bit cross-eyed anymore by this point)—was quite thin and nice; his smile, quite cute. If I didn't know by now that I'd probably have to end up picking up his rotting underwear from the floor my whole life, then I actually might consider. Also, I couldn't remember his name. Babi, why didn't I think of going into his wallet and find out while he was still sleeping? Now, what should I call him?

So I just smiled and said, "Not really hungry, sweetie." I was about to pick up my handbag and tell him I'd better go. But then the guy came over and hugged me from behind. I didn't know what to do. Usually they're not so sweet. So I just turned around and he suddenly kissed me, the open open type. I was going to push him away since we both hadn't brushed our teeth yet—why would he want to kiss like that now? Damn gross, man. But then I could smell something minty. Wah—fucker brushed his teeth! I was so touched I actually wasn't thinking and just kissed him back. Then I could feel that he was getting a bit hard. And I remembered that he was actually quite nice-sized. Also, last night, since I was so tired, fucker came but guniang here didn't finish. (Actually, don't say didn't finish lah—the fucker was so quick that guniang never even started.) So when I thought about it a bit—OK, might as well not go home just yet.

Overall, it was all OK lah. At least the second time, both sides also got action. But the bad part is, hooking up like that tends to mean that it cannot just be a one-night thing. So when he asked for my number, I felt a bit like I couldn't say no. Also, since the girls and I sometimes go to Attica, I might bump into him again! So better don't give a fake number, I guess. The good part is, at least when we exchanged numbers, guniang here had a number one idea. I pretend-told him I don't know how to spell his name, asked him how to spell it and all. So he slowly spelled out for me: R-O-Y.

So, now—like that lah! I don't even know how, man. With a nose like that and with his lousy apartment and I don't even know what cock job he has, this situation—aiyoh, it's not good, man. Really not good. Confirm will end up wasting time. By the time I got back home, I already got a nice text from him. This one—is really susah.

"Guniang, your kopi so cold already—come, I buy you new one," Seng suddenly said. I had forgotten he was even there. Actually, I even forgot that I was there.

Just the other day, my mum actually said to me: "Please lah—why don't you just go out with a nice boy like Seng? You know, last week he brought me and your dad breakfast—I think he came looking for you, but in the end he just gave it to us and watched us eat. This kind of good heart—I can tell you, a white-skin man definitely don't have."

Seng? My god. Of course in my mum's mind this is the kind of dream husband for me—Goh Kwok Seng, major Ah Beng to the extreme! But my mum mainly loves him because even though outside the house these days, he is one of those kwailan assholes who likes to go to Marina Square and stare at other Ah Bengs and ask them "You staring at what?" before throwing down his cigarette and whacking them one time, at home, Seng is very sweet to his mum. Only son, after all. And after his dad died a few years ago, if Seng doesn't pamper her, who will? Plus his mum and my mum used to be old kakis, so Seng is very "auntie-auntie" around her, always finding all sorts of ways to carry her water.

But expecting Jazzy to marry this kind of guy? Talk cock lah!

I don't even know what Seng's job is—one time he told me he was applying for some fuck job at a shipping company and I zoned out. Please—I know shipping is a big business in Singapore, but people (especially those at Seng's level) who are in it are basically nothing better than the coolies that our grandfathers were, working at the docks. And no matter how many TAG Heuers he buys for himself or Prada shoes he wears, at the end of the day, a coolie is a coolie.

So even though guniang here wouldn't have minded a free kopi from Seng, better not say yes. Don't give him any funny ideas.

"No need lah," I said. "I better go home already. Must help my mum clean the house." This one—I know is lies. Seng also knows is lies. But whatever lah. As if he cares.

After I started walking away toward my block, I looked back and saw him lighting another ciggie and slowly checking his phone. He wasn't even looking up at me. Since that first time that I met him at the bus stop way back in primary school, he always super act-cool one. Fucker doesn't need anybody.

=====

I didn't want to go home though—with my luck my mum would actually be cleaning the flat that day and guniang here will have no choice but to help. Imo didn't live far away from me though—two bus stops—so I started walking to the bus stop. Normally, of course I don't take the bus—come on, no matter how good the air-con or seat cushions are, you are still sharing that nice air-con and seat cushions with all the types of people who have no money to buy a car or take a taxi. But Imo's house, two bus stops? Can endure a bit lah.

Imo had already warned me that she was helping her mum clear the storage room so if I come by, I'd better help out. This one, I don't really mind—of all the aunties out there, I actually liked Imo's mum the best. It's true that now she is damn boring—looks like an auntie, acts like an auntie; whole life long doesn't do much except cook, watch TV serials and crochet at home when Imo is not there. But her life before Imo and Uncle—from some things she says now and then about going to this club or that party, we all imagined that she probably was damn happening!

Before we found out about Imo's dad's first family, we didn't think much of how auntie spent her time. In Singapore, so many men travel for work or get posted overseas but leave their families behind, it's no big deal to see mums and aunties sitting at home with nothing to do except wait. But since we found out about Uncle's first wife, every time I see auntie sitting at home cleaning the already-quite-shiny altar for the fifth time that day or rearranging the framed photos of Imo on the living room wall again, I can't help but feel a bit sad lah. Who wants to always be number two?

The bus doors opened, and I stepped out of the super power air-con into the sticky morning. It wasn't even noon yet but I already felt as if someone had thrown a gummy blanket of steam over my

face. Even though Imo didn't live far from my place, the two neighborhoods could not be more different. Looking out the smudged
windows of the bus, you can always see it. First, in my government-
housing neighborhood, there are the skinny streets jammed tight
with white blocks and blocks of flats; trees, each one a perfectly
rounded blur of green zooming by, interspersed by rows of dusty
old hardware stores, provision shops and kopitiams and then,
one or two gigantic buildings that on their own look quite boring
lah, except that they're wrapped all around with flashing neon
Chinese characters and words like HENNESSY and RÉMY MARTIN.
Then, slowly slowly the roads get a bit wider, the buildings a bit
shorter, the puffs of green get bigger and bigger, the trees fuller
and darker.

By the time the bus doors open outside Waikiki Towers, there's
no neon anywhere around. Even Imo's bus stop is atas—a cube
of shiny metal and clear glass. Every time I get off here I always
think—the government damn toot lah. If you are going to make
something so shiny, atas and clean, why not make it the front
window that bus drivers have to look out of instead of some fucking high-class bus stop that people in this neighborhood never
use anyway because everyone has at least one Mercedes in their
covered car park?

Even though the security guard station to Waikiki Towers is right
next to the bus stop, walking into Imo's building is quite terok, especially this close to noon. The driveway to her building is damn
fucking long for starters. Then, it's also obviously not a space designed for people to actually walk—after all, everyone here has a car.
The pavement got not much space one—some more, got no shade!
But once you get to the lobby, everything is all OK again. Pure white
marble everywhere, everything is always clean, the air-con is always

power. The first time I visited Imo, I remember thinking that this place was a bit strange—if it's called Waikiki Towers, then why is it not beachy like Hawaii? Back then, we were all still in primary school but Imo already knew what she wanted to do in life.

"Aiyoh," she scolded me, "you are the toot one lah. Hallo, Waikiki is not just stupid stuff like palm trees, beaches and bikinis. Those kinds of things—excuse me, even low-class towns in Malaysia also have! It's not special one. No, what's special about Waikiki is all the shopping there—how come you don't know this? Japanese tourists and people from all over the world go there to buy branded names and all. Apparently there's even one shopping center in Honolulu that's so big that the corridors are bigger than Singaporean roads. And in the center of it all there's a four-corner walkway—north, south, east, west, each one has a big store. Louis Vuitton one corner, Gucci, Prada and Chanel on the other three.

"I tell you," Imo said, her voice suddenly turning less fierce, "one day, I will go to the real Waikiki and visit all four corners."

Imo's door was already open by the time I reached the twenty-first floor and I could see that auntie had set out cold packets of barley water on a plastic tray by the foyer for us. Visiting Imo is always quite fun lah, since auntie always takes care of us like this. (When anyone visits our flat, they're lucky to get even a hallo from my ma or pa. Want some water or soft drinks? Please. I will be the idiot fetching it from the kitchen—or even worse, being sent downstairs to NTUC to buy some for my guests because there's nothing in the house. So yah, people know that if they get thirsty in my house, they can go ahead and wait until tomorrow.)

"Hallo!" I heard Imo say from the dining room. "In here."

Old photos were scattered all around the dining room table—I could tell they were quite old because a few of them were square, with that crinkly white border all around the picture. Most of them were faded rectangular ones though—I could see that they were mostly filled with people, not scenery. Before I could look closely at any of them though, Imo waved me over, quickly turning the big photo she was holding facedown on the table.

"I bet you you've never seen this before," she said, smiling. "Ready?"

After waiting a moment for me to come and sit down next to her, Imo turned the photo over. At first, I didn't quite understand what I was looking at. It was some glamour head shot, like those you see in that wall of frames outside KTV lounges or cheap Chinese nightclubs. From the haircut, I could see that the photo was from the 1980s—shoulder length, layered tight curls, a bit like old TV show *Dynasty*. Since it was a head shot, you couldn't see much of the dress except that it was sparkly and red, with silver sequins all around the neckline. And the makeup was equally fierce. Glittery glittery type—and greenish-blue eyeshadow!

"You show me this for what?" I asked.

Imo just laughed, handing me the photo. "Aiyoh," she said, "you blind is it? Look closer."

I held the photo closer to my eyes, squinting a bit so I could see it more carefully. Puffy hair, pencil-thin eyebrows—the old-fashioned kind where the hair is plucked until there's almost nothing there and you can really see the dark pencil lines—and eyelashes so thick, long and dark that even if you looked at this person from two floors up you confirm can tell it's all fake. But the eyes . . . and maybe the nose? There was something a bit familiar about them, even if the dark red glossy lips didn't quite seem to match the face that popped into my mind. I looked at Imo, squinting at her eyes and her nose and then looked back at the photo.

"My god," I said, putting the photo down.

"Yeah," she said. "It's my mum!"

Her mum? I couldn't believe it.

"But . . ." I started to say. I had so many questions I didn't know where to start.

Imo put her finger on her lips, making a very quiet "Shh" sound, pointing to the storage room nearby where we could hear her mum moving some boxes around. Rummaging around all the photos on the table, she finally picked up a small brochure and handed it to me. It was one of those folded pamphlets that you'll see in boxes outside shops or offices trying to get your business. Although it was quite old, a bit yellowing, it was in good condition. I could tell from how sharp some of the corners were that it had obviously been very carefully stored.

The front of it was filled with square photos of what looked like a quite happening nightclub—not the sort that Imo and I go to in Clarke Quay but the kind that businessmen will bring clients visiting from Korea or Japan, that kind of thing. There were a few glamour shots of women who were dressed and made up just like Imo's mum, along with some photos of a big stage outlined with bright lightbulbs. In some shots, the center of the stage was packed with a few girls in short sequined dresses, dancing; in others, there was just one singer, always a woman, in a long shiny gown, holding a microphone. Across the top, in large words: "Golden Lotus Night Club."

Walao eh! Auntie was a nightclub escort? OK, this time, even Jazzy didn't know what to say.

Imo saw how shocked I was and just laughed.

"I tell you," she said, leaning close to me so she could whisper, "I've never seen your face like this!"

Of course, all of a sudden, this explained everything.

The thing about Imo's mum is—yes, she's quite chio and yes, she's very sweet and nice. (And also has become quite a champion crocheter over the years, as you can tell from the cushion covers and blankets that you see all over the apartment.) But something I always wondered is how on earth she managed to get a semi-rich man like Uncle. I mean, Uncle is not super rich—hallo, Imo lives in Waikiki Towers, not in some two-story bungalow with a swimming pool—but still, he's rich enough to give them all this. (And obviously more—but all the best stuff goes to his first family of course.) And Auntie after all is not say super hot or very smart and her personality is about as happening as a piece of paper.

But this photo, this brochure. Now, I see.

"It's how they met!" Imo said, after I finished thinking through all this and looked at her again. "It was a long time ago though. She left the business when she fell pregnant."

She looked like she was going to say something more but then Auntie suddenly came back into the dining room, holding a box. "Imo, talk less, finish faster," she said, setting the box on the table and dusting off her hands.

Watching Imo's mum's round backside slowly leaving the room in her auntie auntie housedress, I guess I could see why she never told us about any of this. I'm sure, even though Imo thinks it's funny—and now I have new respect for Auntie—it's something maybe she's a bit ashamed about. Also, I guess this is why Imo also never really sees her mum's family—in fact, I think she's only met her grandparents a few times, a very long time ago. Her mum told her that her family lives in Penang and we all just believed it. Who knows? They probably live in Singapore also, maybe even nearby! But of course once Imo's mum became an escort they probably wouldn't have wanted to have anything to do with her anymore lah. I guess if you think about it, it's sad to see parents treating their children this way but, what to do? At least, in the end, life sort of worked out for Imo's mum. Come on—Waikiki Towers! Don't play play!

I was about to ask Imo something else but Auntie poked her head in again. "Girls," she said, "stop daydreaming!"

CHAPTER 6

The cool thing about Charlie is how she says the word *know*.

She's Singaporean, yes. But then her life changed—she went to Australia for uni and came back sounding different. Now when she says some words, there's this sexy sexy twang. Like *know*, for example—instead of just "know" like we all say, she says "naeiooe." My god, when ang mohs hear it, they also steam. As if she's Nicole Kidman or some shit.

But the thing that's quite happening about Charlie is that even though she's not in Ozzie anymore, the way her life is, it's almost as if she's still living there. Even after she came back, she still only dated ang moh guys. Plus, they're all serious serious, crazy about her. (Not like all our one-night stands or one-hour rubba rubba in the club and never see them again type.) The guys Charlie sees all want to see her again and again and take her to nice restaurants and all.

Charlie, even though she went to Ozzie to study, at the end of the day, she actually is just like me, Imo and Fann. (But less cute than Sher.) We all look quite the same—quite chio but not so pretty that can say, win Miss Chinatown or something. And it's not like she has a super power job or her family has a lot of money. So if she can have so many ang mohs wanting her in a serious way, maybe we also have chance! When I look at her—wah, I feel very inspiration.

When I called Charlie after leaving Imo's place and asked her for help, she suggested meeting her at her usual bar that night, even calling it her "office" and all. Really vain, this one. Since when is a bar someone's office?

Even so, I knew the evening was going to be productive. In fact, Charlie taught us her first lesson even before she showed up: Always be late. Walao, this woman. Tell us to meet her at Harry's at 9 P.M. then don't show up until almost 10 P.M.? By the time she showed up we had just ordered the third round of vodka Ribenas so we were definitely a bit happy. When Charlie sat down, she just looked at us.

"Aiyoh—mabuk already?" Charlie said, blinking at us one time while she pulled out her cigs from her handbag and threw them on the table. This woman was really damn action! Her eyes are quite big and pretty, so she knows that when she acts drama a bit with them, men confirm will steam when they see it. Some more she always outlines her eyes with thick thick black black pencil, so it makes them look even bigger and darker, a bit like those chio Bollywood actresses. This type of move—yes, is quite obvious drama, but that night, I thought to myself, Jazzy, better take notes. If you can pull this off well, it can be quite useful.

Even though Charlie was talking to us as she was sitting down, her eyes actually were not looking at us. Instead, I could see her scanning the whole room, trying to see who's there. A few times she would smile and wave "Hi hi," blowing kisses at people sitting who knows where. When she saw Imo and Fann trying to turn their heads around to see who she was waving at, she just blinked at them one time and rolled her eyes. "Guniangs," I whispered to them. "Try to act a bit cool, OK?" The two of them just quickly picked up their drinks and hid their faces a bit. I felt quite bad scolding them, but they should know better—if you're going to go to Harry's, must act cool! Of all the SPG bars in Singapore, this one is damn history. Must respect a bit. Before Harry's, I don't know where decent girls went to meet ang mohs. Last time we only had those sleazy Orchard Towers bars where the ang moh sailors and tourists go for cheap hookups or Thai prostitutes.

Now, we avoid Orchard Towers (unless we're craving Thai chicken wings from that stall on the second floor) but that one time years ago when we decided to go just to see whether the place had cute guys or not. The scene—my god—was damn scary man. First of all, all the corridors in the entire mall were filled with the smell of smoke—you know that kind of smell where you step in the building and you know right away that you confirm must wash your dress the next day. Then, everywhere we looked, you could see ang moh guys with these very young-looking girls in super short skirts— schoolgirl schoolgirl type—in very high heels just walking around, arm in arm, the guys sometimes rubba-ing the girls' butts as they walk. All along those narrow corridors there were bars, yes, but also massage parlors, cheap Thai restaurants and also these small provision shops that not only sell all the kinds of cigs you want but also had gigantic displays of condoms. You know me—I very not shy. But when I saw these condom displays—my god, even guniang over here started to feel a bit embarrassed.

We decided to go into one of the bars, even though Imo and Fann didn't want to, saying they were worried about what kind of guys were in there. But Sher and I thought, we've never been here before—at least check one out. What's the harm? Maybe it would at least be a bit entertaining—and from the looks of just the outsides of the bars, I could tell that we could emerge with many stories to tell our friends even after just one drink there! So, why not?

Also, I know it's a bit crazy to think this in Orchard Towers of all places, but you never know where you can find love. Sometimes even nice ang mohs also go to sleazy places—maybe they're there because their friends have brought them or it's some compulsory office party they have to attend or some shit. And we had already been talking about how, if you want to meet guys, sometimes you must adventure a bit. Cannot be so close-minded and judgmental. Anyway, since we were already in Orchard Towers, I said, "Let's go." So we just picked one of the bars that looked more open—not one of those with blacked-out glass windows or bitchy-looking Thai girls standing outside to check your ID and charge you a thirty-dollar cover fee if they think you're a girl that is potential competition. The one we picked seemed decent—it even had a large barrel painted on the side of the door, giving it the same look as some of those touristy English pubs near Boat Quay. But once we walked in, we almost walked out. My god, the place was damn fucking sleazy.

The bar was filled with girls—all wearing high heels and short flared-out skirts. Most of them had long black hair, some tied up in sweet little ponytails. And their faces all had that fresh, clean kind of makeup to make them look even younger. I couldn't tell how old they were, but if I had to guess—maybe seventeen or eighteen? And that's because I'm Asian—I can tell they are actually not as young as they look. If I weren't Asian, I confirm would think they look more like fourteen or fifteen years old. And the whole bar was filled with these girls! Except for one—this woman who looked quite ragged, maybe thirty years old or something. She was wearing simple black pants and one of those patterned auntie blouses and she had one of those big bulky fake Coach handbags on her arm. The moment we walked in she just sat in one corner and stared at us the whole time.

We ordered a drink—we figured since we were there, we'd better order something or mamasan confirm will come over and whack us one time. When the drinks—and bill—came, we instantly regretted it. One simple gin and tonic—fifteen dollars! Some more the drink was damn watered down. "Never mind lah," I said to Imo when I saw her making a face. "Research is never free." Once the drinks came, we didn't know what to do so we decided to just sit there and look-see look-see. Fann got excited when she saw there was a small pool table in the corner. "Hey, maybe we can play a bit!" she said, starting to get up. Luckily, Sher acted quickly and pulled her back down before Fann could make a move.

"Guniang," Sher quietly said to Fann. "Don't be so blur. Look around the table—is anyone actually playing pool?"

It's true—even though there was a game in progress, and there certainly were people walking around carrying sticks, the only action we were seeing was when the girls would come and bend over the pool table, stretching for a really long time, sometimes even propping one of their legs up on the table until can see panties and everything. No one actually seemed to be noticing the game. The girls were just anyhow shooting—striped ball, solid ball, anything also whack. Ball never go in also never mind one—this game was really damn toot. Since when do you have people playing a game and not caring about winning?

If the girls missed a ball, they just covered their mouths and giggled like those teenagers in Japanese toothpaste ads. We watched this carry on for a bit, not quite sure what to do—Imo at some point just gave up and started texting with god knows who—until Sher suddenly elbowed me. She nodded her head very slightly toward the dark corner near the pool table. I had to squint a little bit at first but there was some tall, a bit fat oldish ang moh guy sitting on a bar stool and rubba-ing this girl. At first, it seemed normal—not like anything we hadn't seen in Attica before, except this guy was balding, had super gray hair, at least two chins and such big boobs that no decent Singaporean girl would ever give him chance. Hallo, even though he's an ang moh guy, us SPGs still have some standards, please.

This was all still sort of OK, but then once or twice when the girl started moving away from him, he would grab her wrists and pull her back so she was facing him, her thighs wedged between his legs. This guy wasn't even wearing pants or jeans—he was wearing bermudas! Some more they were not even branded berms— got no logo! As we watched, the guy got more daring—he not only started reaching underneath the girl's skirt to rubba her backside but at some point he turned her around to face his friends on the other side of the pool table. His fat fingers were all over the front of her shirt, rubba-ing her stomach and everything and then moving down to her skirt. Sher looked damn angry. We thought all this was quite bad already, but then the guy lifted up the girl's skirt and started rubba-ing her through her panties, pretending to try to pull them down. His friends just started laughing and cheering. Aiyoh! No shame! We thought the girl would give the fat guy one tight slap but she just giggled a bit and patted his hand, firmly moving it away. Mamasan in the corner was keeping an eye on all this, even though she had this heck care look on her face. What kind of mamasan is this? Where got people give things away for free?

"Should we do something?" Imo asked. When I looked at her, she looked like she was going to cry. It's true lah—the four of us have seen all sorts of public rubba-ing in our lifetime of clubbing (and also participated—a bit—of course) but this, my god, this really made me want to vomit blood. The girl was so young, the guy was so old and ugly—some more from the looks of him, he confirm is not rich. Not even middle-class. Where got point? No amount of money he gives you can be worth that shit.

Then suddenly we saw mamasan raise her right hand and rub her thumb against her fingers. Cash sign. The girl turned around and kissed the guy on the cheek then whispered in his ear. He smiled, nodded; then she took his hand and led him around the pool table, right past us and headed to the darkest corner of the bar. We had seen the door in that corner earlier—some thin wooden one with a slightly frosted glass window. At first I thought it was a karaoke room because through the large window we could see a couch and coffee table. But then there was a sign on the purple wall saying STAFF REST AREA. Quite weird, I thought at the time. Working as a bar girl—is it really that strenuous that you need a rest area? But once the girl brought the ang moh into the room, closed the door and turned off the lights, I realized how toot I was.

Which is why, once Harry's opened—thank god. If you want to meet ang mohs, then you didn't need to be so LC as to go to Orchard Towers. All Harry's bars are confirm not low-class—they have nice tables, waiters treat you like normal girls, and the menu even has atas drinks with happening shots like Lemon Drops.

Of course, if you are truly happening at Harry's, you don't need to look at the drinks menu. In fact, Charlie was so famous here she didn't even need to order her drinks. The moment the bartender saw her walk in, he already started mixing. So by the time she pulled out a ciggie to put in her mouth, the waiter had already brought over a vodka green tea. He even stood to one side, waiting for her to be ready and all so he could pull out his lighter to light her cigarette. Imo, Fann and I all looked at each other—kani nah, this woman was damn impressive.

Charlie looked sexy. In fact, I don't think we had ever seen her not nicely made up, but tonight she looked more chio than usual, wearing a tight short dress. "Is it one of those Harvey Leggy types?" Fann whispered to me. I wasn't sure but with the stretchy bandage-straps crisscrossing her chest, showing off her B-cup tetek, it very well could be. Her hair at that time was quite short, in a very straight bob, fringe long long one, swept to one side so when she leaned over to talk to you, she always had a fan of hair brushing across one side of her face, making her eyes look even bigger. For those guys who like those Sailor Moon kinds of blue movies, Charlie is the shit lah. Since secondary school days, she was always quite cute—but back then, her kind of cute was mostly the sweet sweet type. It wasn't until she came back from Ozzie that she suddenly became so sexy. I don't know what happened to her there, man—or why she never stayed. But when she came back last year and we met at Zambo the first time, we almost didn't recognize her. All the guys we were with that night got super steam the moment they saw her. But because none of them were ang moh, all also knew they had no chance with Charlie.

Midway through her cigarette at Harry's, Charlie was leaning back, crossing her legs, looking quite bored and blinking her eyes a bit as she slowly smoked. Fann and Imo looked at each other, then looked at me, both not sure what to do. Toot is toot. So I just started explaining. "Um, Charlie—you know, we've all known each other how long already . . ."

Charlie just rolled her eyes and sighed, leaning over to put out her ciggie in the ashtray. "Please lah—cut the crap," she said. "I naeioo you how long already—no need to bullshit me. You just want to naeioo my secrets, just admit it."

I could see Fann's face was starting to turn black—I knew she never really liked Charlie. Charlie just blinked again at Fann and looked back at me.

"You want my advice?" Charlie said. "Then listen. Stop being so desperate. Please—you girls keep going to the same places over and over, meeting the same groups of guys over and over. And when you go there you're always in the middle of everything, chitchatting with the same arses each weekend, dancing with them, going home with them—or not going home with them but then seeing them the next weekend anyway. Aren't you bored? If you want people to notice you—really notice you—then you must hang back a bit, be in the shadows, let the guys discover you and want to naeioo you. These ang moh guys, hallo, all they want is the chase. If they want to run after you—let them run! The harder they have to run, the more they want you. Even after you get married, must still make them run! When they stop running is when they run away."

Wah, this was the longest I had ever heard Charlie talk. But it made sense. I was thinking about that guy I just pok'd—what was his name? Obviously, that one was a mistake. Even though in the end he seemed like maybe a decent guy, at this point, guniang here cannot start over with him again. My flower—all give away already. I even stayed over on the first night! The chase hadn't even begun but everything—aiyoh—everything was over already. If the guy didn't have such a hairy nose I might feel a bit sad. But my god, that nose!

"Hallo, Jazzy, are you even listening?" Charlie suddenly said. So I made sure to look back at her again.

"Also," she said, looking around at all of us and scrunching her nose, "language, ladies. You and I know how we always talk. But kopitiam chitchat is different from ang moh chitchat. Guys don't like it. Even if they think it's a bit exotic, they in the end will think that you are just too LC for them. Want them to take you seriously, then you must give them the impression that when they bring you back to Melbourne, Chicago or whatever shit longkang like Manchester they came from, that you also can fit in and be the perfect wife. So yeah, among yourselves, you can talk talk however you want but when you want to hook ang moh guys, you must sound more atas."

This one is true. When we get to the point of hanging out with ang mohs and their friends, whenever we talk, they sometimes catch no ball, asking us to repeat what we said—slowly. Quite embarrassing. Charlie was right. If they cannot see us fitting into their world, then confirm we have no serious chance.

"Plus, this"—Charlie started saying again, pointing her second finger at all of us, making a circle in the air—"I can tell you, is not going to work."

"What do you mean?" Fann said. Her dark face came back again.

"You three are too similar!" Charlie continued. "You think this one is what—army is it? Everyone all the same one. No, your approach must be different—your role model should be girl bands. See, even though they are one group of girls, all around the same age, all chio, you can always tell them apart. Each girl has a distinct personality—got Posh Spice, Sporty Spice, Baby Spice . . . I'm not saying you should dye your hair different colors and wear costumes or some cock shit but maybe each one of you can find something to play up.

"Like you," Charlie said, taking out another ciggie and waving it at Imo, "pretty face, nice clothes—maybe you are the atas one. So maybe talk less, be standoffish a bit. Jazzy, you are more of the spunky type. Many ang moh guys like daring girls."

Charlie gave Fann a hard look—we could see her eyes going from her hair to her face to her body and back up. "You," Charlie said, "you—aiyoh. OK, I'm sure if you really put your mind to it, you can find something interesting."

The bartender had come over with another vodka green tea for Charlie. All of us were sitting right in front of her and none of us had noticed that her glass was almost empty but somehow the guy managed to arrow it with his eyes from the other side of the room and fasterly make a new one for her. After he set it down, he lit her cigarette, waiting for her to take her first puff and smile sweetly at him before he walked away.

Charlie was quiet now. Her advice was good but it was a lot to think about—things to practice. Maybe must even go shopping. But tonight—tonight was still early. I guess maybe we could hang around a bit and have some drinks. It wasn't even 11 P.M. after all—although this was quite late for Harry's. Usually ang mohs like to go there for after-work beers or earlyish drinks and then run home to their wives before it gets too late. If not for Charlie, who knows the whole staff at this Harry's, we wouldn't be here. We didn't like this particular Harry's bar, in Boat Quay, because it was very touristy. And all SPGs know tourists are like sailors—in and out so quickly, confirm will have no results. My whole life I only knew of one guni-ang who managed to hook an American sailor on shore leave who wrote her love letters for six months then came back and asked her to marry him. Wah, that one is damn lottery! Now she lives in some chee bye little town in Virginia lah—boring military wife and all. But still at least she managed to make it out.

Tonight though, the ang moh crowd at Harry's was older; many of them had wives or girlfriends by their sides so it was all a bit pointless. Just when the Filipino band started playing "Wonderful Tonight" and we were wondering whether we should go somewhere a bit more lively, some short Malay guy popped up by our table, wink-ing at Charlie and all. We thought this was quite funny—even Fann started smiling. If Charlie doesn't even want Chinese-Singaporean guys—Malay guys where got chance? But Charlie just laughed and patted the cushion next to her and he sat down.

"Rahiman—girls; girls—Rahiman," Charlie casually said.

Rahiman jumped back up, leaned forward, smiling and shaking all our hands quite hard, asking each one of us what our names were. Even though we were quite stunned, we managed to be polite.

"Babe," Rahiman said to Charlie, "drink?"

Charlie nodded and waved him away. The three of us just stared with our mouths open as Rahiman ran off to the bar.

Imo was the first one to ask. "Charlie, who is he?"

Charlie just shrugged. "Auntie tonight too tired to work hard—this one, always eager, always shiok," she said, bending closer toward us, cupping one hand by her cheek to whisper. "Big tongue."

Three of us didn't care about being polite now and started stretching our necks to get a better look at Rahiman, who was at the bar chatting with the bartender. Every time his mouth opened, all I could think about was what was inside.

"Eh, girls," Charlie said, snapping her fingers to get us to look back at her. We had been staring at Rahiman for so long that he was already picking up the two vodka green teas and heading back to our table.

"Advice session over," Charlie said. "Now bugger off."

CHAPTER 7

I was still thinking about Big Tongue when I woke up the next morning.

After Charlie chased us out, all of us were so depressed we decided to just go home. We didn't even have the heart for supper. Charlie was our hero, you know. And she's secretly screwing a Malay guy? We never would have imagined it. She's so pretty—she has her pick of all these ang moh guys. Good quality ones some more! So wasted. What would her parents think?

But when I woke up, I understood. Needs are needs. As long as Charlie is not so open about it, fooling around with Big Tongue maybe won't affect her chances so much. But if it was me, I really don't know if I could somehow bring myself to do it. Even if no one knows, you yourself will always know. So, somehow you must always maintain standards.

I still remember when we were teenagers and Marina Square was just built—my god, the air-con was so powerful, the cinema was so big, the Isetan there had so many floors and one whole section was filled with all the best makeup counters (Dior, you know—don't play play!). Sher and all of us just started going there every weekend. At first, it was still quite high-class—mostly families (Singaporeans lah, but at the time we were not so focused on ang mohs yet so it didn't matter) and teenagers like us. Sometimes the American schoolkids would pop up also, but at that age, they always stuck to themselves and were not so interested in making friends. In fact, if we even said hallo to them they always looked at us a bit shocked, probably wondering how come we don't understand that we're too LC to be trying to talk to them. Only the Ozzie international schoolkids might be a bit friendly. But that's usually because the boys thought we might be an easy snog or something. (Which Fann more than once proved to be true lah. But that's another story.)

After a while though, all these Ah Bengs started taking over Marina Square! These gangs of guys with their spastic gelled hair and baggy pleated pants and their Ah Lian girlfriends who, even though they're already sixteen or seventeen years old they're somehow still choosing to wear Hello Kitty hairclips, just started showing up everywhere. If you go and see a film there, you confirm will find Ah Bengs in the last row talking loudly in Hokkien throughout the show. Sometimes in the food court there were even fights for tables and all—especially near the famous chicken rice stall. So low-class!

We were already considering not hanging out there anymore, especially since the *New Paper* started doing reports on "Marina Square Kids" after not only Ah Bengs but even their Ah Lian girlfriends started having quarrels and fights all over the place there. When Ah Lians fight, it's not as happening lah—mostly a lot of shouting about wanting to "whack your face" and then pulling each other's spiro-perm hair until the Hello Kitty hair clips fly. But some of the Ah Beng fights were actually quite serious—one time, according to the *New Paper,* one of the guys even pulled out a Swiss Army knife.

But still, habit is habit. So on a Saturday afternoon, if we had nothing to do, then we didn't mind meeting at Marina Square. One Saturday, Sher and I were sitting outside McDonald's waiting for Fann. I think we were maybe seventeen years old at the time? Sher was looking chio as usual; me, not so much—I still had a few pimples back then (must carry paper to blot my skin, type). At the time, none of us had handphones, so when Fann didn't show up after one hour, we panicked a bit. Call her house also got no answer. So we tried calling her pager, which meant that we ended up having to sit next to one of those old orange coin phones to wait for her to call us back. Normally, we didn't really mind waiting like this. Fann was very often late and Sher and I always could find nonsense to talk cock about for hours. But this time because we had to sit next to the coin phone outside McDonald's, we were right in the middle of foot traffic. Not only that, it was Ah Beng foot traffic! Normally when we see them we just try to stay out of their way. But McDonald's is like a giant Ah Beng magnet, man. And if you have two nice-looking girls sitting outside McDonald's—walao, Ah Bengs confirm will suddenly damn steam. After the fourth oily Ah Beng asked Sher, "*Xiao jie, yao bu yao zuo peng you?*" I finally couldn't keep quiet anymore. I know he and his friends and his parents all probably speak Mandarin or Hokkien to each other all the time lah but hallo, doesn't he have eyes to see that Sher and I were more atas than that? Yah, I mean, my parents still speak Hokkien to each other at home when they don't want me to understand what they're saying, but even they know that English is the future. That's why we always try to speak proper English!

"Be your friend?" I said to the Ah Beng, blinking at him and then quickly looking away sideways before looking back, like you see those bitchy girls do in all those Cantonese TV serials. "Who wants to be your friend? You think we what? Desperate, is it?"

Wah, Ah Beng became damn angry. After his face turned color a bit, he turned around and used his finger to signal his friends to come over from their McDonald's booth. And once they all stood up, even without hearing the sudden rumble of many many chairs, I realized they were quite a big group. I was a bit scared but I knew that there is one golden rule—unless it's your own girlfriend, Ah Bengs don't hit girls. (If this guy had an Ah Lian girlfriend there, then I would really be scared. Girls can always whack other girls, even if it's not their fight. That's fair game.) Even though this Ah Beng was angry, I could see that he suddenly remembered that, so he knew he had to back off. Sher stepped in to do what she always does. "Um, sorry ah," she said, smiling very sweetly at the Ah Beng. "My friend today a bit moody lah. You know, the usual girl stuff."

Ah Beng was quiet for a bit—his friends were all surrounding him now like idiots, not knowing what to do because they weren't quite sure what was going on. (I tell you ah, the brainless group mentality of Ah Bengs is always amazing to watch. If I ever meet a professor at Harvard I confirm will tell him to come to Singapore and do a study.) Then Sher extended her right hand and said, "Come, OK, let's be friends." Ah Beng's sour face suddenly disappeared. Now, happy lah—even though it had to come to this, he finally got what he wanted. The fucker smiled and quickly shook Sher's hand, asking, "What's your name ah?" Sher just said, "Oh, we are waiting for our boyfriends." Then, like that Ah Beng lost interest—he just said "Orh" and then walked away, his friends all following behind.

When we discussed it later, Sher actually said, "You know, that Ah Beng was not bad-looking for an Ah Beng." It's true lah—when I thought about it, he was tall, skinny, had a Cantopop nose and his hair wasn't so stiff and poufed up, like all his friends'.

"Aiyoh, Sher—come on lah," I said. "Ah Beng is still Ah Beng. Once you go with one, you are nothing better than an Ah Lian."

Which is why, even if it's a secret, I don't know if I can ever sleep with a Malay guy. Must always maintain standards.

And this was clearly something Sher never understood, considering the Ah Beng she ended up marrying.

Not that I had a lot of time to sit around thinking about big tongues and Ah Bengs that Sunday morning. Kin Meng this week was on holiday so, feeling super free, he decided to organize a brunch. At first, I was not so interested—his friends are all quite snobby. And they are all Singaporean! If some of them are ang moh, then they at least have some reason to be snobby. But when he told me where they were brunching, I said, OK—set.

By the time I arrived at Relish, the place was already damn happening. I had only been here for dinner once before, on a weeknight some more, but even then I already knew that this one was a potentially good place to meet guys. Bukit Timah neighborhood is where all the expats live, after all—so if you want to meet an ang moh, must sometimes come and just casually hang out where they go and makan, pretend like you always hang out there. No pressure, just smile sweetly, act like you belong, then maybe you can make some friends. And Relish is one of those places—casual restaurant with good pastas and burgers. Both of those things are what ang mohs like to eat, so confirm Relish is a good place to go. The one time I went, Sher and I decided to just go and have girls' night dinner by ourselves—the scene was quite slow; some more it was mostly filled with families or couples. "Maybe lunch or brunch better," she whispered to me, after we spent all night looking at cute guys who, if we met them at Harry's or Clarke Quay maybe would buy us a drink, but with their girlfriends or wives around? Forget it—please, they confirm don't even dare look at us.

Kin Meng and his friends all live in Bukit Timah—all born rich, Anglo-Chinese School boys lah—so they were all regulars at Relish, usually for dinner with their wives. When I got there, they were all at their usual table all the way in the back—good spot for people watching. From that back center table you can see everyone who walks into the restaurant—and then you can quickly decide whether you want to make eye contact and say "Hi" or not. The restaurant is on the second floor of this old colonial townhouse so the windows are quite big, got a lot of light type—very easy to spot anyone you want to talk to. Some more in the center usually there's a display of cakes or some shit so you can use that as an excuse to get a closer look at people at the restaurant—and I guess, the cakes also lah.

I've only known Kin Meng a few years—he's an old friend of Louis's. Once Kin Meng got promoted to managing director of his shipping company then he started having to travel and entertain clients a lot and go to KTV lounges all the time. After going to a KTV lounge, he said, regular clubs at Clarke Quay were boring lah! It's so much easier after all to be able to pay a chio girl to sit with you for a few hours, listen to you talk cock and laugh at all your jokes. No strings attached. So we stopped seeing him so much after that. But he and I always got along quite well so I don't mind keeping in touch, even though he's married (and Singaporean).

Kin Meng stood up when I got to the table so he could give me a hug and a kiss. "Hi babes, how are you?" he said. Wah, this uncle today was damn stylo—wearing loose, tailored white cotton cargo pants, brown Gucci sandals (got logo all) and a tight white V-neck T-shirt. His hair, as usual, was only slightly gelled and combed all the way back like Chow Yun-Fat in The God of Gamblers.

"Eh, where's your wife?" I asked.

"Mah-jongg," he said, rolling his eyes. "I don't know how much she's going to lose today, man. Fuck."

Kin Meng's wife ah, is really mah-jongg queen. She started playing when he got promoted and had to travel a lot—everyone needs a way to pass the time, that's what she said. So even though Kin Meng told her that hallo, there are other ways to pass time—for example, maybe she can be like other bored tai-tais and take a flower-arranging course or volunteer at some bullshit charity? Or maybe she can get pregnant? But his wife doesn't want to lose her figure—or freedom—yet. So even though they talk about having a kid nonstop also in the end, it's all lumpah pah lan. Balls bang your cock until both stop motion—no matter what you do, there's no movement anywhere, the outcome also the same. In the end, nothing happens. Just frustration. So, like that lah. No kids, but got lots of mah-jongg. And from the way Kin Meng talks about it, also got lots of money exiting his bank account.

Kin Meng sat back down at the table, in the center of everything as usual. I said hi to Ramesh and his wife, Heidi, some American-born Chinese that Ramesh met at uni in California and somehow managed to persuade to come back to Singapore with him. George, this guy who's the fucking snobbiest one of them all, was there also. He works for some theater company or some shit—and he even has a power British accent all, calling it "theea-TAH" instead of "tear-TERR." His wife, Susan, was there also—not that it mattered. I think in all the years that I've known her, I've only heard her voice three times. Each time for some stupid cock reason like, asking me if I can pass the chili sauce or something.

I got there so late that everybody had ordered already—Kin Meng even ordered for me, said he remembered that I like eggs Benedict or some shit. I don't really care lah. Unless it's at a hawker center, food is just food. All ang moh food is quite the same to me. No matter what it is, put chili sauce on top, then everything will be shiok.

At least that is my strategy now. The first time I went to an ang moh restaurant I still didn't know this because I was quite young. It was Imo's birthday and we were all in Primary Two. Her mum had this idea to bring us all out for a nice lunch at the Dynasty Hotel on Orchard Road after school—at the time I didn't know anything about such places. Imo had been to places like that before lah—not often but at least once or twice with her parents. But the rest of us were still quite toot. (Come to think of it, I'm not sure whether my parents have still ever been to a Western restaurant in an atas hotel—got cold air-con, use fork and knife to eat type of place.) From the moment we walked in though, I wanted to walk out. The restaurant was so beautiful! Everything smelled like air freshener—and not the cheapo metallic kind that really hits your nose if you get too close to the dangling Christmas tree in taxicabs, but like actual roses or something. In fact, the restaurant had vases of flowers all around so after a while I wondered, eh, maybe it wasn't even air freshener. Until that moment, I hadn't even considered that there are some flowers that actually can smell like perfume.

I remember it being really hot that day, so hot that my school pinafore and white blouse had that thick, sour smell from morning sweat drying then mixing with early afternoon sweat. Even my ponytail was greasy. So greasy that I could taste it when I chewed on the tip of it—something I only did when I was nervous. But that day I was damn fucking nervous.

The waiters all wore ties; the waitresses had nice black dresses and deep red lipstick. Everyone had very clean fingernails and everything was quite quiet. We could hear some violins or classical shit playing in the background. When I touched the edges of the white tablecloth before we sat down, the corners made me think of the sharp origami cranes Cikgu Hamidah had just taught us to make in art class. Sher, Fann and I didn't really know what to do so we just followed everything Imo did and let her mum handle everything.

"You girls like sausages, right?" Auntie said. "Like hot dogs but without the bun?" We all just nodded. Since Auntie was paying, whatever she wants, of course we will just follow along.

Auntie had invited one of her girlfriends to come, so once she ordered the sausage plate—no soft drinks because, as she noted, one lousy Sinalco was four dollars each!—for all of us, the two of them just sat in a corner and started yapping. The rest of us were just left alone. Usually, the four of us always had a lot to talk about. There were the St. Michael's boys on the bus, of course—all of us at the time were wondering whether Simon, the Eurasian boy in Primary Four, would ever notice us—and our stupid teachers, especially Mrs. Ting, who always made us do extra sit-ups in PE because she probably knew we stuck out our tongues at her whenever she turned her back. And actually, that year we had just started playing dirty Barbie—the week after exams were over we always were allowed to bring toys and books to share with each other. At that time, no matter how poor you were, you also got at least one Barbie. It's the one toy all parents, even if you are working in a longkang shit job, also know that you must buy for your daughter. So when we could bring toys, we all brought our Barbies to school. Since we were still quite young at first, our Barbie games were still decent. Actually, when I think back to that time I also don't remember what was so fun about it—we just sat around combing our doll's hair and exchanging clothes. For fuck? But in Primary Two, Jill Ong's mum bought her a Ken doll. At first we just had the Barbies all fighting for his attention but then one day Veera Yap brought in a magazine she found under her parents' bed. Wah—naked pictures of women all over the place! Some also had men in the photos, rubba-ing here and there. We weren't quite sure what was going on but I remember it making us feel very excited, even though we didn't know why. Set lah! After that our Barbie storylines suddenly became damn happening. For some of them we even called Ken "Simon."

These kinds of topic, though, how to discuss in such a nice restaurant? So the four of us just sat there—Imo looking at me, me looking at Sher, Sher looking at Fann, that kind of stupid thing. All of us were also not sure what to do. That's mainly what I remember about the lunch—I can't even recall what the sausages tasted like, whether Imo's one slice of nine-dollar black forest birthday cake that we all shared was good or not. I just remember feeling scared.

All around us, everyone was so proper. And there I was in my lousy pinafore and my moldy school blouse. I bet the waitress could smell me. If I could definitely smell myself—I forgot about the nice lunch that day and was wearing the one blouse that was starting to get yellow stains at the armpits—then so could she. Die lah.

I had never been around so many ang mohs before—and all were so nicely dressed! Not like those tourists in shorts and slippers that you sometimes see at the botanical gardens. No, these ang mohs were all tall, looked damn smart, wear glasses type. The guys were all good looking—not say cute like Scott Baio but good-looking in a normal way. And not too hairy. Or red-faced and pig-nosed. The women looked so sweet; each handbag next to them had a shiny logo. Everyone was smiling, quietly chitchatting. Sometimes you could hear a bit of soft laughter—the refined kind, not like those noisy Ah Cheks in kopitiams who, I tell you, if one of them tells some joke, then the whole gang of them will start shouting and laughing so loud that even if you're on the tenth floor, you confirm also can hear.

I guess it was then that I realized. I told myself, Jazzy, if you are going to want anything in life, this is what you should want. All this—this world.

Which is why even if I think Kin Meng's friends are all jokers, if they are meeting in Relish then I don't mind coming. This is the life, this is the world. Once my eggs Benedict came I decided to try and at least be nice and make some conversation. Not that they really asked me about my job or that I remembered anything that they said lah. But still, it was nice. For an hour, at least I could somewhat pretend that I already belong.

On the way home, in Kin Meng's new Mercedes SUV, I was still thinking about brunch. The bright airy restaurant, sunlight coming in the large colonial windows, the clean white furniture that was atas country house–style, like the ones you see in those actor's houses in *Vogue*. Kin Meng had the air-con on so high in his car I wish I'd brought a sweater. "Why—cold ah?" he said, leaning to press a button. The leather seat underneath me started to throb.

"Crazy ah," I said, laughing a bit. "Singapore so hot—why the fuck do you need seat warmers?"

"They offered what—so why not?" he just said, pulling down his Dolce & Gabbana aviators from the top of his head and turning to smile at me. "Also, hello—it's called foreplay." I whacked him on the arm.

I was looking out the window, watching the wide sleepy Bukit Timah streets roll by. On each median the grass was perfectly green, each tree was evenly spaced apart, all bushes were nicely shaped. Yah lah, the government street workers really know how to take care of landscaping everywhere—even in my longkang housing estate, lorries of Malay workers come by once every two weeks to prune everything. But somehow in the expat neighborhoods the bushes always seemed more perfectly round, the trees fuller, the grass brighter.

I didn't feel like talking but didn't want Kin Meng to think I was treating him like a taxi uncle. "How's work?" I asked.

"Busy, but boring," he said, sighing. "Clients keep coming in. Night after night I have to go to KTV lounges—after a while, even that can become damn boring. Also, must be careful lah—you see the same girls over and over again. Give them the wrong impression only. Uncle over here is not the 'Let's be texting friends, I buy Gucci for you' type. Please, I already have one of those bossy women at home."

This one, I knew was not entirely true—the last time I saw Kin Meng, we were having a beer at Bar Bar Black Sheep, this outdoor pub in Bukit Timah that was kind of like an ang moh kopitiam. Guys in slippers and shorts were sitting by the roadside on British pub-style benches, having an early Sunday beer with chips. Even though they were by a longkang, this was still atas in a way. No nose digging or foot scratching. The conversation was civilized. I can't remember how Kin Meng and I got on the subject—not hard, actually, considering it's his favorite topic—but he was telling me about the KTV lounges he was going to these days.

"Eh—how? Cute or not?" he had said after we'd been sitting for half a pint and he'd already finished his first cigarette. Kin Meng pulled out his iPhone, swiped the screen with his finger a few times before showing me a photo. The girl was one of the more high quality ones, I could tell—fair skin, but just dark enough to be a bit Korean-ish. For a long time, the Japanese girls used to be the most expensive—if you go to any KTV lounge, if the menu has Japanese girls, then you'd better make sure you have a platinum card.

If not, maybe you can settle for the Japanese-looking girls—white white complexion, eyes big big one. If she has a dimple on one cheek—wah, those are the best. (Those look the most like porny schoolgirls in Japanese blue movies.) But these days, with K-pop girl bands and all, the Korean-Korean look was starting to become damn happening in clubs and KTV lounges. Long light brown hair, wispy fringe falling all over your face, sort of fair skin, big eyes, full lips—those were the girls that were now making guys like Kin Meng steam.

I looked at the girl—she looked like she was about sixteen. Her face was tilted to one side so her fringe was draped over one eye; her dark pink glossy lips formed an O, as if she was sucking a lollipop that wasn't there.

"Steam, right?" he said, taking the phone back from me, looking at it and letting out a big sigh. Then he swiped his finger across the screen again and handed it back to me. "This one also not bad."

A different girl this time—same complexion, with a little darker hair but with her head tilted the same way so hair fell over the side of her face. This one had a demure slight smile; the way her eyes looked up in the camera, I could almost imagine her peeking up at a client, offering herself.

"Akiko," Kin Meng said. "We all know she's not Japanese, of course. The moment she opens her mouth, hello, anybody can tell she's just Chinese. But she told us she chose the name to fit her bedroom personality. Wah—with a girl like that, how not to steam?"

Now, I don't care about Kin Meng in that way lah—and I definitely heck care about his gambling den wife so I don't give a shit who he's fucking. But I didn't know that KTV girls were so daring— sending pictures to clients and all. Wasn't the point of a KTV lounge that it's a one-time business transaction kind of thing?

"Oi, Kin Meng—how come you have all these pictures of KTV girls? Your girlfriends ah?"

"No lah—crazy!" he said, quickly taking his phone back from me. "Just text buddies. These are their WhatsApp profile photos. Now and then, if I'm bored, I'll just send them an SMS. Just flirt flirt only. No harm."

No harm? As if it wasn't enough that we had all these guniangs in clubs and bars to compete with and the China girls coming over to spoil our market. Now we have to think about KTV girls trying to climb their way out of their lousy lives by stealing decent guys like Kin Meng?

"But these girls are so dirty! Don't you know how many guys they entertain each night?" I asked. "Why don't you just do the usual thing and get a regular girlfriend?"

Kin Meng laughed so hard he snorted. "Aiyoh, Jazzy. These KTV girls are pros!"

I must have looked confused—after all, yeah, who wouldn't know these KTV girls are working girls? What do you think? They are rubba-ing you because they genuinely like your backside, is it?

Kin Meng took out another cigarette and lit it, putting both elbows on the table and leaning forward to get closer, looking serious for a moment.

"You see, it's very simple," he said. "Girlfriends? Please. They're too much work! Especially Singaporean girls—whatever you give them, they just keep expecting more. And if it lasts longer than a few months, forget about it—either they want you to leave your wife, they get jealous if you go to a KTV lounge or go out with other girls when your wife lets you out of the house, or you end up paying big bucks. The presents they expect will only get bigger the longer you are fucking them."

He stopped to take a long drag from his ciggie before shaking his head and continuing. "Even the Malaysian girls these days are getting to be more like Singaporeans. It's all too much. But these KTV girls—so sweet, so friendly. When you text them just to say hi and chitchat a bit, they confirm will text you right back. And they know the boundaries. I tell you, if they bump into you on Orchard Road on a Sunday when you're out with your wife, they won't even look you in the eye. They'll walk right by you like you're any other guy on the street. Like I said—they are pros."

Until then, I hadn't even considered KTV girls seriously when we were watching out for all the women getting in our way. But clearly I had been wrong.

"But aren't you afraid they'll get too attached to you and start expecting things?" I asked. "I mean, even KTV girls still have that *Pretty Woman* dream of meeting a rich guy and getting married and all, right?"

Kin Meng laughed again. "Of course lah—girls everywhere, all the same one. But you have to just manage their expectations." The way he was talking, I could see how he'd risen so far up in his company.

"You see, the girls only get attached if you form a professional relationship with them—if you just text them now and then, it's no problem. But if you go and keep requesting the same girl each time, for example, you're just asking for trouble. After a while, they start to feel like you're a 'couple' or some shit like that—then if you go sometime and decide you want a different girl, my god, sometimes they'll give you a pouty face and all. Kani nah—if you let it get to that point, it is all habis already."

"But don't you go and . . . you know?" I asked, pushing my fist in the air a few times to illustrate a bit, just in case he didn't understand me. "That level of girl—they're all looking for rich guys. Even if you just pok them one time and start texting them after, wouldn't they still think you want something more, no?"

"That's why you must be smart," Kin Meng said, shaking his head as if I'm so toot. "I never fuck those girls. The most I'll do is get a Japanese bath. They just strip me, bathe me and, aiyah, you know lah. Like that, I can still come home and answer questions honestly. A blow job, some people still consider is sex but jerking you off—confirm is not sex! When wifey actually bothers to come home from her mah-jongg game and ask me whether I did anything bad, I can honestly say 'No.'"

In Kin Meng's car, I thought about reminding him about this conversation and all his photos and KTV text buddies. But he was in such a good mood, I thought maybe better not. But I did want to ask him something though.

"Kin Meng—at these KTV lounges, do they allow girls to come inside?" I had been thinking that I'd never been to one. But so many guys I know—and probably guys that I want to know in the future—go to KTV lounges all the time. Maybe if I see it once, I can at least understand the system a bit.

"My god, no lah," he said. "Other girls are competition for their business! Unless . . . it's a work situation. You know how it is—nowadays there are women managers and everything. Sometimes we cannot help it. Must let them in otherwise they might scream sexual discrimination or some shit like that. KTV entertaining is business, after all. The lounge managers don't like it, but they know they have to let them in sometimes."

This was my chance. "Bring me," I said.

Kin Meng turned to look at me. "You serious? Why?"

"I just want to see. Why not, right?"

He was quiet for a bit. I was just thinking he was going to just say no.

"You can behave or not?" he asked.

Wah, guniang here was damn surprised. Of course I nodded.

"You'll dress exactly as I tell you and do everything I say?" he said. "If so, I could actually use a non-KTV girl in the group for some clients I need to bring out tomorrow night. See how."

Set lah!

After that I quickly switched the subject so he couldn't change his mind. But when Kin Meng dropped me off at my block, he kissed me on the cheek and said, "I'll text you tomorrow, babes."

Walking through the gray concrete void deck underneath my apartment block, past the wrinkled uncles playing Chinese checkers, past the aunties burning joss paper offerings in the giant red communal barrels by the dustbins, I began to wonder what the scene would be like at a KTV lounge. If going to Lunar and seeing those shameless China girls was already so terrible, leaving us all feeling so bad, then wouldn't a KTV lounge be worse?

But Jazzy, I thought, you cannot be so scared. Must "yong gan de zhou." Bravely walk.

Thinking about our mums—maybe not Imo's but definitely mine, Sher's and Fann's—they just did the same thing their mums did. They all had the same boring tunnel-visioned approach to finding a suitable man and figuring out the husband landscape. So in the end, nothing happened for them! They never went anywhere. They just ended up having the same lousy lives that their mums had. And now Sher was doing the exact same thing. I can tell you her Ah Huat is never going to bring her to brunch at Relish. Ever.

Just thinking about Relish made me happy again—so white, so clean, so perfect. Then the lift doors in my building opened and some small sweaty fat fuck ran out, almost knocking me over. His mum just casually walked behind him, not even bothering to apologize. When she noticed that I was staring at her, she just stared back and said, "Got problem is it?" and walked away.

Getting into the tiny five-person lift, I could feel the air, hot and sticky, seeping into my hair. As the lift went up, floor by floor, I felt like I was swallowing warm clouds of urine and cigarettes. Bloody hell. And as usual, when I got to the flat, before I could even open the door, just from the turn of my door key, it all started back up again.

"Ah Huay?" my mum shouted from all the way back in the kitchen. "Finally come home already ah?"

Bloody hell. Kin Meng, as always, was late.

Not that I was that anxious to get to the KTV lounge or to see the fucker's face. But I had already told Albert I had to rush off to an appointment and now fifteen minutes later, guniang was still standing on the curb outside of Front Page waiting for Kin Meng. If Albert comes out for a smoke or something, he will think I was lying! Since it was Monday, it was a fairly quiet night at Mohamed Sultan—on weekends, forget about trying to walk a straight line along the neighborhood's narrow pavements outside the rows of little prewar townhouses. The bars in those old shophouses are always jammed, which means the pavement is confirmed also jammed. Tonight though, there was almost no one around. So if Albert looked out, he'd definitely see me still standing there. What's worse, my toes were damn painful from the office pumps I wore just for Kin Meng. In this heat, I'm not used to closed-toed shoes lah—but as Kin Meng instructed, if I want to be less slutty for KTV mamasan approval then confirm cannot wear strappy heels. So, no choice.

But the main problem was that I was damn grumpy. That weird conversation with Albert on Friday—aiyoh, I couldn't stop thinking about it today. Was Albert really thinking it's time for me to go? Why else would he be bringing up circulation as a good move for me in the company? Everyone knows that the girls in circulation are basically complete fucking idiots or are leftover girls from other parts of the company who are just shoved there to be forgotten about. And what was up with all that lecherous rubba-ing? Did I somehow give him the impression that I wanted something? Of course he was right—I know that I'm not getting any younger. Of course I understand that it's high time to grow up already. But it's not like I'm just sitting around waiting for my wrinkles to appear, not doing anything. Why else would I be trying so hard to hook an ang moh now?

Even though guniang here was upset I still had to touch up lipstick and pretend to be happy once five o'clock came because I had already promised Albert I would help him to entertain his guests, who in the end were quite interesting lah. The main guy was the foreign editor of some Ozzie or Kiwi newspaper. I know I should remember these things, but to be honest, Ozzie and Kiwi are all the same to me—seriously, is there any difference? The guys usually look the same and sound the same. Unless it's an ang moh I think I might pok, once they tell me they are Ozzie or Kiwi I don't really care which one is which. All I know is that unless the ang moh is very rich, if it's a Kiwi guy, I definitely don't want. If we get serious and get married, then how? Who wants to move there one day and live in a country filled with sheep and grass? Fate worse than death, man.

Whether he's Ozzie or Kiwi, Leonard the foreign editor guy was bloody charming—longish white hair combed back, high nose, nice wire-rim glasses. Very cultured-looking. If he wasn't so old I might consider. Albert also brought along his foreign editor, a Eurasian guy he went to uni with a long time ago. Even though Sean is half ang moh, he grew up here so he talks like a Singaporean—not like me or Fann, but more like Imo, when she's at work and must impress people, that kind of thing.

Sean usually just ignores me—when he needs to see Albert he

never even says "Hi" before knocking on his door. And in the cafeteria he only talks to other editors or people higher than him. Sometimes, Eurasians are just like that—just because of that little bit of white blood from how many donkey's years ago, they think they are better than most Singaporeans. But who can blame them? They are part ang moh after all. (Some more the ones who are guys usually know they are very good-looking—aiyah, this is from years of sarong party girls throwing themselves at them. Even if they are not fully ang moh, for those SPGs with lower standards, half or quarter ang moh guys sometimes also can.) So I guess, at the end of the day, they do deserve that special treatment anyway.

But that night Sean was quite nice to me—probably because even though he and Albert kept trying to ask Leonard questions, Leonard only wanted to ask me questions. Before Albert's bottle of Chivas appeared, Leonard already started interrogating. "So, Jazeline, what is it like to be a modern Singaporean woman?"

Hah? What kind of nonsense question is that? When I first heard it, I felt quite blur. This kind of question, nobody has ever asked me before. Usually Albert's guests mostly just want to flirt a bit with me, maybe touch my knee or elbow now and then, but the serious questions? Those they will only ask Albert. Why should they ask me? Everyone knows that guys are the ones who actually know these things.

"Well . . ." I started to say, trying to smile and think at the same time. How to answer? Ask me where to eat the best chicken rice, which Hotel 81 is the cleanest for one hour or where to buy the best Vietnamese girls, these kinds of questions I confirm know what to say. But what it's like to be Singaporean woman? Aiyoh. We're all in a bar situation, you know—it's not an O-level exam! I could see Sean turning his face to one side so Leonard and Albert couldn't see it. I bet he was rolling his eyes. Kani nah.

The truth is, even if I felt like I could speak honestly, I didn't know how to explain everything—or anything, really. How to tell him about a society where girls grow up watching their fathers have mistresses and second families on the side? Or one in which you find out one day that it is your mother who is the concubine and that you are the second family? A society that makes you say, when you are twelve or fourteen or seventeen, "No matter what, when I grow up, I am never going to be the woman that tolerates that!" But then you actually grow up and you look around, and the men who are all around you, the boys you grew up with, no matter how sweet or kind or promising they were, that somehow they have turned into the men that all our fathers were and still are. And you suddenly know what you have to accept—that yes, no matter what you hoped for before, well, fuck, lumpar, kani nah etc., this cock road is just how my life is going to turn out also. Unless, unless . . . you can find your own way out to a different life.

"Well, if you ask me," Albert suddenly said, when it looked like I was about to open my mouth and say something, "I think life in Singapore is great for women of Jazzy's age now."

I could see him gesturing to the waiter on the side to bring his bottle over even more fasterly before he continued. "They get to have good jobs like hers, the freedom to dress however they want—look at how sexy she is today! And the independence to date whomever they want! They are in the real positions of power in Singapore today, Leonard. We men are nothing but peons!"

Leonard didn't say anything—though he did look at me a bit funny. I almost felt as if he was still half-waiting for me to jump in and say something. And kani nah, guniang here actually half-considered it! The one time Jazzy miraculously thinks of something that might be even halfway smart to say and Albert cuts me off.

Bloody hell. I looked at Albert, who was now cheerfully chitchatting about some other cock topic and thought, I really don't want to go to circulation. So I just smiled and quickly looked away, pretending that I needed to take some tissue paper out of my handbag, and hoped that Leonard wouldn't still be looking when I actually did manage to find the stupid packet of tissues. At that moment, Albert started laughing—even winking at me and everything. So of course Sean and I quickly laughed along with him. Luckily, at that moment the bottle arrived so Albert could just start pouring. After that, Leonard asked me a few more questions—but those were more easy. Like, Did you grow up in Singapore? What do young people do for fun? That kind of no-point question. I think, in the end, Albert was a bit relieved when I said I had to leave.

"Eh, woman! Daydreaming about me ah?"

Finally. I looked at my phone. Fucker was thirty minutes late. I made sure Kin Meng could see my third finger before opening the car door.

"Hey, don't be like that—not nice, you know," he said, leaning over a bit so he could pinch my cheek. "Be a good girl tonight, OK?"

Once we started driving, Kin Meng explained some things. "So I have these clients who are in town from a bunch of places. They're here to . . . aiyah, you don't need to worry your pretty little head about these things. You won't understand anyway. They are all quite fun guys—my assistant thinks one of them is gay. And you know lah, those types of guys can feel a little weird in KTV lounges sometimes, so it's good to have a girl from the office or someone normal to just chitchat with them while all that other shit is happening, take their minds and eyes off the action a bit. So when we get there—the guy's name is Keith. You just make sure you sit next to him and help me keep him entertained and distracted, OK?"

This one is confirm can for me lah. Jazzy here is happening, OK—so of course I've had some gay friends in the past. Usually we just went clubbing together lah. But even if there's no dancing involved, they usually can be quite fun. "Can," I told Kin Meng. "As long as you are buying drinks."

"Of course I'm buying lah! Please—don't be stupid. Hallo, we are going to the best KTV lounge in Singapore. You save up for six months also cannot afford tonight's bill, I can tell you right now."

It's true—I had heard that KTV places were damn fucking expensive. Sometimes one night you can end up spending tens of thousands of dollars—and that is not even counting what you might have to pay your individual hostesses for extras and bed rental. That's why most of the guys who go are either on expense accounts or they have a super-rich lecherous friend who's happy to pay for everything so he doesn't feel like the only dirty old man around. Kin Meng at least is one of the decent guys—I can tell that he only goes to KTV lounges out of duty. Business is business—if you have to go to a KTV lounge for it, then you really have no choice. But many guys out there—I tell you—they are just sitting around waiting for clients to come in from out of town so they can finally have some fun. When clients finally fly in, wah—they get excited like hell. Finally! They have an excuse to go to KTV! Company will pay some more. Being a guy in Singapore—sometimes it really is a good life, man.

"Jazzy, when we go in, don't talk to the guys—except for Keith," Kin Meng said as his car slowed down near a bright car park near Tiong Bahru. "Keith is OK because he's gay. Mamasan will know that tonight, he is a losing proposition. Since she confirm cannot make money on him, it's OK for you to hog his attention. But the rest of the guys? Hands off, otherwise mamasan will stare and stare and then later come and whack your face. If that happens, guniang—

even I cannot save you. The mamasan at Temple of Heaven is damn fucking power."

As Kin Meng turned into the car park, his SUV was suddenly filled with bright neon lights. I had passed by this place many times before—usually in a taxi going to Tiong Bahru for supper after clubbing, so I'm definitely quite mabuk at those times. And when you are busy trying not to throw up you don't really notice a lot of things around you lah—so I never really looked twice at Temple of Heaven even though the flashing signboard outside was so large it almost covered the entire front of the three-story building. The sign was shaped like a pagoda—like the actual Temple of Heaven in Beijing, I guess—and outlined in Chinese New Year red and lucky yellow neon lights. And right in the middle were the two Chinese words for Temple of Heaven: Tian Tan. And underneath that, in words that were almost as huge: MARTELL.

Even before Kin Meng stopped his SUV, two tall slender women wearing tight red cheongsams (and at least five-inch high heels) ran up to open his door. "Hi, hi—ni hao!" they both said, smiling and ushering him in. One of them came to my side to open my door too, but when she saw I wasn't a guy, her smile disappeared. Kani nah. I wanted to slap her face one time.

Kin Meng was already halfway up the steps by the time I got out of the car. Wah, these steps were crazy—covered in thick red carpet, with a shiny gold railing on each side and big lights shining down on you from the ceiling. Taking each step up made me feel damn high-class—I felt like I was in one of those Hollywood movies where Marilyn Monroe is walking up the steps to an old glamorous hotel in Italy or some shit and all these guys in white suits are all around, treating her like a queen. I never thought that just walking up steps could make you feel beautiful.

"Miss? Miss?"

I turned around to see an Ah Beng in a black tuxedo chasing me up the stairs.

"Miss? Stop! Stop, please!! What are you doing here ah?" he asked.

Luckily Kin Meng bothered to wait for me at the top of the steps.

"Boy—she's with me," he said. The Ah Beng bowed and ran back down again.

Aiyoh. This one—North Korea is it? Want to enter KTV lounge also get interrogated until like that.

"Jazzy—stick close to me ah?" Kin Meng said. "Oh, and remember—don't try to get friendly, even chitchat, with any of the girls. That kind of lesbian shit—not allowed. They confirm will throw you out."

The mamasan appeared as soon as Kin Meng stepped through the round doorway—kind of like the ones I saw in the Qing Dynasty Village years ago when I went there on primary school excursion. It was quite a toot amusement park lah—no wonder so quickly close down—but I remember thinking those old doorways and Chinese buildings looked quite authentic.

"Huanyin, huanyin! Long time never come!" mamasan said, leaning forward so Kin Meng could kiss her on the cheek. When he mentioned a power mamasan I had expected some old, powdery, sharp-chinned dragon lady with fierce eyes and one of those Chinese fans that you know she's just waiting to use to whack you on the head. But this woman looked young and she was quite pretty—a bit like Gong Li. Not the Gong Li now lah but back when she was still a young hot actress and Zhang Yimou still wanted to fuck her. The fierce eyes were definitely there though.

"We booked the usual room, Mr. Tay—your colleagues are already here," mamasan said, turning to walk up a wide grand marble staircase in the middle of the room. If it weren't for the gaudy gold lights and cheongsams all around, this place could perhaps pass as an old French palace, man. The ceilings were so high; everything looked so drama.

At the top of the stairs, mamasan led us down a long, wide hall, opening the door to a room that looked like a dark red nest. The walls were lined on three sides with plump cushioned seating and on the fourth wall, there was a big flat TV screen. Leslie Cheung, wearing silver sequined hotpants, no shirt and a tight white jacket with feathers sewn all the way down each sleeve, was dancing around onstage. Seeing this almost made me cry. So classic—1980s Cantopop is really the best.

Everything in the room was red—the walls were covered in shiny red wallpaper; the cushions were all covered in slippery red silk. Maybe the dim lighting wasn't red (I couldn't be sure) but it really looked that way since everything else was red.

Once my eyes adjusted I could see three ang mohs and one Chinese guy, who seemed to be busy mixing whiskey sodas. "Hey, thanks for hurrying so much to come and see us ah?" the Chinese guy shouted. "Boss, we were waiting for you until our balls were turning blue, man."

"Sorry, sorry—I had to pick this one up," Kin Meng said, pointing over at me. "Jazzy—meet the guys: Sam works with me in the Singapore office; Nigel and George came in from London; and Keith over here just flew in from Hong Kong."

After shaking everybody's hand, I felt Kin Meng nudge me in the back to go and sit next to Keith.

Keith was quite a good-looking guy in that slightly nerdy British way—tall, clean-cut and skinny; he even had a thin boyish face. (And since Kin Meng was entertaining him in Singapore's number one KTV lounge that means Keith must have money—or at least must be quite important.) Aiyoh, so wasted. If only he liked girls! And this one is confirm true lah—I could tell from how he didn't even look for one second at my tetek or backside that I'm not his type for pok-ing.

"Hi," Keith said, leaning close to me to whisper. "This is a little awkward, isn't it?"

I didn't know what to say so I just covered my mouth and giggled. Keith laughed too.

After Kin Meng settled in next to me, the mamasan got serious.

"Tonight, do you want butterfly or by the hour?" she asked.

Kin Meng looked at his watch—it was 9 P.M. "Not much time left in the early shift," he said. "We'll do the hourly girls. Butterfly—wasting time only."

Butterfly? Kin Meng could see from my face that Jazzy here catch no ball so he came closer and whispered, "Butterfly girls fly from one room to another. Those girls split one hour among four rooms, so you only get each one for fifteen minutes. It's cheaper, yes, but not so worth it right now. The late shift is starting soon—the girls, the drinks, everything gets much more expensive then. Better get our fun in quickly."

"Mr. Tay, the girls—the usual kind?" mamasan asked.

Kin Meng looked around at the guys—he seemed to be mentally calculating something.

"Tonight we have a range of tastes—just bring a variety so people can pick," he said. "You know what kind I like, but also throw in one with big breasts, a tall one with very nice legs . . . eh, Sam, these days, what are you in the mood for?"

"Hmm—you got new China girls?" Sam asked.

Mamasan nodded.

"OK, then China lah," Sam said. "Madam!" he shouted after the mamasan as she started to leave the room. "Very young ones, OK?"

Mamasan disappeared, returning a few minutes later with ten girls, all of them looking cheerful and smiling, all of them wearing sexy shiny dresses. Mamasan was good lah—the group had a few girls fitting each of Kin Meng's descriptions. Plus, the young China girls Sam ordered were wearing dark red lipstick and tight mini cheongsams with big slits down each side.

"Aiseh!" Sam said quite loudly, jumping up so he could inspect them closely, as if he'd never seen women in his life before.

Nigel got the big-boobs one, George picked one with such long legs she looked like runway model and Kin Meng chose a Korean-ish girl with the same look as the girls he had in his phone. (But later when she had to introduce herself to him I realized she wasn't one of his previous girls.)

Sam was taking quite long to pick from the three China girls. "How?" he said, turning to look at Kin Meng as if he was begging him. "Boss—cannot take it lah. All of them also make me steam! How—can I have two?"

"Don't even think about it—as if you can handle more than one!" Kin Meng said. "Hurry up—you're holding everyone up."

So Sam just did an eeny-meeny-miney-moe and ended up with the shortest smallest one—so small in fact that she looked like she was about fourteen. The leftover girls quietly left.

Once the girls sat down next to their guys, they started mixing drinks for themselves.

"Come, come," Big Boobs said. "Let's bottoms up!"

Everyone clinked their glasses and drank. Even though I never say no to free whiskey—I'd already had a few at Front Page so I only drank half. When I put my glass down, I saw that Keith also only drank half.

The girls immediately noticed Keith's glass and started pestering him. "Wah, how can be like that? Must bottoms up!" They kept cho-cho-ing him until he agreed to bottoms-up the whole thing. None of them bothered to say anything to me. Once Keith put his glass down, Big Boobs and China Girl made another round of drinks for everyone. Everyone except me, that is. Wah lao, guniang here was invisible.

Sam started frenching China girl the moment she finished making drinks. I could hear her giggling and saying, "Aiyoh! You're so naughty!"

"Come! Another bottoms up!" Big Boobs announced.

Everyone clinked their glasses again. (Only Keith clinked his glass with mine. Kani nah.) While China Girl started making another round, Sam got up to walk toward the door. Before closing it again, he looked back, nodded at Kin Meng and said, "Boss, I go toilet ah?"

As soon as we heard the door close, Kin Meng said to China Girl, "*Xiao jie*—sorry, but my friend's not feeling well."

The girl actually looked angry for a second, then quickly went back to smiling. "No problem," she said, smoothing down her cheongsam and getting up to leave. Now that her business in this room was over, her English suddenly sounded much more Singaporean than broken Chinese-y. "I hope he feels better," she said, not even looking back at Kin Meng.

As soon as she left, mamasan reappeared with three more young China girls—none of them were the ones from before. First, she came over to talk to Kin Meng though. Mamasan's face was blank, but even I could tell she was irritated.

"Madam—he just had a quick taste only, nothing serious yet," Kin Meng said. "But if there's a problem, just charge me for her also. No trouble, OK?"

Mamasan nodded and went over to wait by her girls. Sam re-appeared so quickly I could tell he didn't go to the loo. This time, he quickly picked one—the one with the biggest eyes and fairest skin.

"What happened?" Kin Meng asked when Sam sat back down.

"Bad breath," Sam said, picking up his glass and downing his drink, taking a long time to swirl the last sip around his mouth before swallowing. New China Girl grabbed the whiskey bottle to refill his glass even before he could set it back down.

Kin Meng just nodded and put his arm around his Korean girl again. When he saw me staring at him, he whispered, "It's always easier to have someone else get rid of your girl. More polite."

Everything had happened so quickly once we got to Temple of Heaven that I was still trying to absorb what I had seen. I had heard what happens in KTV lounges of course, but to see it happen in front of me . . . young girls getting picked or rejected like chickens in a wet market? I am very open-minded, but even I think maybe this is not quite right. Even though I didn't have that much to drink that evening—usually I only start to get high after six or seven whiskeys and maybe feel sick after ten or so—I started to feel something in my chest and coming up the back of my throat. Jazzy, I told myself, you'd better buck up! You promised to help Kin Meng out—and you asked to tag along anyway. Don't be a spoilsport!

New China Girl had switched off the Leslie Cheung concert video and was starting to sing some Elva Hsiao song. That singer is a good choice lah—although a lot of guys still think Sammi Cheng is damn pretty and has the better songs, hallo, she's forty already! Who wants to hit their own handgun while thinking about someone their auntie's age? So even though Sammi's songs are all very nice to hear and sing, in a KTV room, if you're one of these lounge girls, maybe it's better to choose a younger singer. Elva is not say that young but at least she's not antique.

Big Boobs was trying to instigate a few more rounds of bottoms up—if the two bottles of Chivas quickly disappeared then she could try to persuade get Kin Meng to buy Veuve, after all. (Which is not more expensive than Chivas, but people always drink champagne much faster. So in the end, Kin Meng's bill confirm will be bigger.) George and Long Legs had disappeared god knows where and Sam was rubba-ing New China Girl all over—her backside, under her skirt, up her thighs—as she sang. Kin Meng wasn't doing any of that shit—I guess he meant it when he was telling me that one time that he only does naked Japanese baths with these girls; no hanky panky. But he had his arm around Korean Girl, her head on his chest, her right hand stroking his knee.

"I guess I'm supposed to understand why this has to be a part of doing business when I'm in Singapore," Keith suddenly said, putting away his phone. He had been glued to it, texting, since the singing started. He was smiling at me though, so I guess he wasn't upset about the situation. "Are you OK, Jazzy?"

Am I OK? Usually, when I'm out like this, there's one person who asks me that question—Sher. I suddenly wished she was there. Unlike me, she would have the balls to say something polite (but with attitude) to the guys and tell them she has to leave so that we could escape. But then again, why would I wish this kind of dirty scene on someone I care about?

"Yeah, I'm fine," I said, smiling back at Keith. "I guess . . . it's just more shocking than I thought it would be. I've never been inside a KTV lounge before!"

"I can imagine," Keith said, laughing. "You seem like a nice girl, Jazzy."

That's when the shouting started.

"Aiyoh, aiyoh, aiyoh!" Sam said. He was standing up now, jumping up and down and pointing at the far darkest corner of the room. I couldn't really see what he was pointing at so I stood up also. I could sort of make out a small love seat and some movement.

But it turns out I didn't need to squint so hard because Sam took out his iPhone and turned on the flashlight, shining it at the corner. Long Legs was seated, her minidress bunched up at her hips, her legs spread wide open, dangling off the sides of the chair. And I guess she wasn't wearing panties because George was kneeling in front of her with his face in her you know where!

"My god, George! Why on earth are you doing that?" Sam shouted.

George had stopped and turned around now, looking a little embarrassed. Long Legs quickly closed her legs and sat properly, taking a tissue out of her handbag to wipe George's mouth, helping him off his knees and onto the love seat. Sam's light was still on them so we could see everything.

"KTV girls are the last kinds of girls you should do that with—aiyoh, they are so dirty!" Sam continued. Kin Meng stared hard at him—no matter what they thought of what we all had just seen George do, he was still their business client after all. He should never be insulted—especially not in front of girls. Sam was really throwing away Kin Meng's face.

Sam tried to make it seem like it was a joke and started to laugh. Kin Meng quickly laughed along too. And once that happened the KTV girls also joined in, giggling along. Sam decided to try and say something funny to defuse the situation more. "Hey, George," he said, "I don't know how your women treat you in the UK, but you come here to buy these girls so you don't have to do that kind of shit. You don't have to win these girls over by pretending you like that kind of gross shit!" He started laughing again. But Kin Meng didn't laugh along this time.

"Well, as a matter of fact, I happen to like it . . ." George said.

I could see Kin Meng's shoulders tensing up. He was probably worried that the clients would get upset.

"Sam," he whispered, "quiet lah. You know these ang moh guys— sometimes they just like this kind of weird shit. If he wants to do that, then just let him do it."

Sam turned off his iPhone light. Kin Meng waved over to George and said, "Come, George, why don't you take . . . um sorry, I forget her name, somewhere more private?"

Kin Meng picked up the receiver of the plastic red phone in the center of the tinted glass coffee table in front of us. "Yah, hello, we want to dapao one—yes, just one. For now. . . . What? Oh, yes, of course five-star room. . . . Hmm, I don't know—one? Maybe two hours? . . ." Kin Meng put the phone down so he could look over at George, who had Long Legs on his lap now and was violently frenching her.

Kin Meng quietly laughed and shook his head then picked the phone back up. "Just book it for the whole night. Thanks."

In just a minute, mamasan appeared again. She smiled at Long Legs, bowed slightly at Kin Meng and then whisked George and the girl away.

New China Girl had stopped singing while all the excitement was happening, so all we heard now was the melody of what must be one of Elva's sad songs. (Not that I knew the song—I only guessed this because Elva's face was on the TV, looking like she was going to cry.)

"Come, bottoms up! Bottoms up!" Big Boobs said, holding up her glass. This time I also joined in, throwing my head back as I drank and really cleaning out my glass. The ragged feeling of the whiskey burning down my throat warmed my face and nipped the feeling that my eyes were about to tear up. Even then, when I did tear up a bit, I just told Keith, who had noticed, "Whiskey sometimes does that to me—too strong, too strong!" I even fanned my mouth with my hand to make him believe.

The thing is, I always knew shit like that happens in these places. Growing up in Singapore with KTV bars in so many neighborhoods—how not to know? But to see it happening in front of me—girls getting packed up to go just like a box of noodles at a hawker center—is a bit too much lah. How can these girls possibly be paid enough for a job like this to be worth it? And these guys—I don't know about George or Nigel but Kin Meng is married, Sam's wife is seven months pregnant with their first kid. Even if you marry someone who seems like a good guy, in this kind of working environment, is it confirmed that this kind of thing will happen anyway?

"Do you want to get out of here?" Keith asked.

My god, yes. I grabbed my handbag. Keith whispered to Kin Meng, who nodded and tilted his head to look at me, waving. Keith took my hand and led me toward the door. Just before we closed it, I saw Big Boobs climb onto Nigel, straddling him and lifting her long hair up at the neck so he could run his hands all the way up her back as she gave him a lap dance. I guess now that the boring gay guy and square female colleague are not there anymore, the fun could really begin.

I was still a bit dazed as we slowly walked down the stairs, which seemed as grand and beautiful as it did earlier—maybe even a little bit more, since Keith was still holding my hand and guiding me down the stairs. I tried to block out everything I saw that night—if I did, I could at least pretend in my head for a few minutes that he was my date and he was leading us down the stairs to our Rolls-Royce outside.

"Why were you here, Jazzy?" he asked.

"Well, Kin Meng thought you might need some normal company... you know," I said.

Keith's face got serious a bit. "Oh goodness—I never need the company in that kind of setting that badly," he said. "He really shouldn't have brought you there. I'm very very sorry, Jazzy."

At the foot of the stairs, we heard music. Some kind of Mandopop in the background, layered with waves and waves of cheering and laughing. Eh? Were people watching a football match in there?

I followed the sound to a heavy bronze door on the other side of the lobby. A stocky Ah Beng in a tuxedo opened the door for us even before Keith and I got to it. Once we stepped through, the cheering and laughing got louder all around us. The room was quite big—not as big as Lunar or any of those clubs but larger than your usual bar. And all around us were cushioned circular banquettes filled with men in suits—a floor of padded pods all facing a stage. Onstage, a row of nine girls in strapless mini sequined dresses lined the background while one stood in the front, her shiny gold heels just a few centimeters away from the tip of the stage, where a row of men were seated on bar stools, leaning forward.

"More! More! More! More!" The guys were shouting all together. A short Ah Beng, also in a tux, was walking up and down the stage with a mic in one hand, using his other hand to wave and rile the crowd up even more.

"Hallo, hallo, gentlemen! Are there any more people who want to hang flowers on this beautiful lady? Look at how chio she is! Her hair like silk, face like fairy, legs long long," the Ah Beng said. "Hallo, little girl—come, show them a bit!" The crowd cheered louder. The girl tucked her hair behind one ear, winked at the crowd and bent over to pull up her minidress very very slowly. The guys started shouting even more, but she stopped just before getting close to her panties. (As if she was wearing any.) A few started booing but a young guy in the front row jumped up and said, "OK—I buy her the five-thousand-dollar garland!"

Once there were really no other bids, a fresh-faced girl got onstage holding a garland of red plastic flowers. The minidressed girl bent her head so the garland could be placed around her neck, then she waved at the crowd, blew a few kisses to the guy in the front row and joined the rest of the girls in the back row.

"Don't worry," Keith said. I guess he noticed the worried look on my face. "He's not buying her services—well, not really. She does have to come and sit with him for a drink—and if she is open to more, she can negotiate. But the five thousand dollars doesn't buy him a night or anything like that."

"Then—why is he paying so much?" I asked. I tell you ah—guys sometimes are damn fucking crazy. Pay that much—at least must get some product out of it! What's the point of throwing away thousands of dollars on a few plastic flowers. If you go to a wet market, you can buy the same thing for fifty cents!

Keith shrugged. "Competition? Winning? Showing other guys that you are the one who can spend the most? Isn't that what guys care about in Singapore?"

The room was very quiet now. The Ah Beng onstage was in the middle of introducing a new girl, one who looked exactly like all the others except that her minidress was powder blue. (Each girl was wearing a different color—it made me think of *Teletubbies*.)

"One hundred dollars!"

"Two hundred dollars!"

"Five hundred dollars!"

"Eight hundred eighty-eight dollars!"

A bidding war was going on between two banquettes of balding Chinese guys in the middle of the room.

Keith elbowed me softly and leaned over. "Shall we?"

"Are you crazy? How would I have that kind of money?"

"Kin Meng's company does," he said, grinning. "Don't worry— I'm going to sign that contract they want tomorrow. Well? Go on."

So I stepped into the center of the main aisle, waved my hands until Ah Beng looked over, probably wondering what in fuck's sake I was trying to do. Before he could say anything, I shouted, "Ten thousand dollars!"

It wasn't that I had a cock day at work.

No—I guess what was more disturbing was that it wasn't as ob-vious as that. I mean, things were still a bit weird with Albert after our talk in his office yesterday and that whole crazy business about asking me to think about the circulation department and all. I kept wondering what he might be planning, but thank god he didn't bring it up again. So, who knows?

I was distracted all day, however, because I couldn't stop going over all the things I saw at Temple of Heaven last night. China Girl, New China Girl, George going down on Long Legs right in front of us. I thought about texting Fann and Imo about it, but I didn't even know where to begin. (At least Kin Meng was nice and texted me in the morning asking if I had a good time. Of course I said yes. Though I was mainly just glad that he didn't seem angry about my ten-thousand-dollar garland. I guess the deal Keith signed must have been fucking huge. I wish I had thought of exchanging phone numbers with Keith when he dropped me off. Even if he's gay, if he's in that kind of money range—who knows? I'm sure he has straight ang moh friends who also make that kind of cash! Aiyoh, Jazzy here sometimes really doesn't think straight.)

Just thinking about that KTV room, that night, that club, made me feel damn dirty. Of course I'm not so naive as to believe that girls like that don't exist everywhere in the world. But to see respectable men—husbands!—like Sam or Kin Meng in that environment, just going along with all of it. Aiyoh—how can? But what was making my heart the most pain right now was the thought that Sher—our sweet Sher—now had one of these exact types of lousy Singaporean husbands. My god! What did she do to herself?

I still remember the night when I first realized that things were really going to shit for Sher—and, I guess in a way, all of us as a group. The four of us—and Ah Huat—were all squeezed around a small table at Chin Chin Eating House. We had just finished eating our pork chops and chicken rice; we still had beer on the table, so the Chin Chin uncle still hadn't come over to ask us to fuck off yet. Just before that, Ah Huat had invited us to come see his tuition school over at Peace Center. Walao, I tell you, this locale is a damn funny place for tuition school, man—with all those sleazy KTV lounges surrounding it, which parents in the world would want to send their kids there for physics and chemistry tuition? But Ah Huat had told us his school was actually quite successful—and since I didn't believe him, we agreed to go and look-see look-see.

It turned out that I was wrong. Ah Huat, in the end, was quite an entertaining teacher, jumping around the front of the class, madly scribbling all these crazy equations on the board, explaining science and all this super complex maths in his Ah Beng lingo, swearing and telling dirty jokes all the way. His students all called him "Ah Lim," and his classroom was very small but somehow he managed to pack in forty to fifty students each hour. He just rotated his subjects all day—one hour teaching chemistry, one hour teaching maths, then physics next, etc. He was quite funny lah—even if I don't know pythar gorass theorem is what cock, when Ah Huat explained it with his smelly Ah Beng attitude, I also listened. I guess if you can make people laugh they confirm will pay more attention. And I could tell so did the students—they were all leaning forward at their desks, listening carefully to every single thing he was saying. Even I could see that Ah Huat was actually teaching them something. For a former teacher from some lousy government school, he really had made something of himself lah.

So, no choice—I had to admit that I was wrong, and Ah Huat almost dropped his chalk when I did. "You know," he said, staring at me with his squinty Ah Beng eyes and stroking his chin as if he had a Confucius beard, "you should come and work for me. The school is growing so quickly I can't handle all the admin and managerial work. I really need some sort of assistant or business manager . . ." I tell you—if I was drinking anything at the time I would have laughed so hard I'd spit it out right in Ah Huat's face. So typical of these kinds of people—you say one nice thing to them and suddenly they think that they are equals with you. Please—my god! As if I'll ever work for a smelly Ah Beng!

I didn't want to be rude, though—he had been nice enough to show us around his tuition school and all. So I just laughed and said, "Aiyah, come, come, I'll buy everyone dinner." So we all walked over to Chin Chin for pork chops. Everything was going OK—it wasn't say, very fun but it also was not terrible. We all didn't know Ah Huat that well—because hello, do we look like the sort of girls who would actually be seen with him? But Sher had known him since they were teenagers because their mothers were mah-jongg friends for donkey's years. At some point in our early twenties, of course both aunties had started hinting to the two of them that maybe they should go see a movie or something. But when Sher mentioned it to us—aiyoh—the three of us laughed so hard that she looked bloody embarrassed for even mentioning it.

That night at Chin Chin though, we knew that Sher had started hanging out with him a bit—we had not been so successful with ang moh guys for a few months, I told her I guess it's OK to just hang out with him lah. Better to keep busy otherwise we might lose practice. Also, if you have someone to buy you dinner now and then, what's the harm? As long as I don't see Ah Huat's fuck face so much around the four of us—in public—I also don't really care.

Halfway through the dinner, Fann poked my elbow—her eyes rolling from side to side, asking me to look over at Sher. Aiyoh, Sher was picking out nice pieces of chicken from the big platter to put on Ah Huat's plate! I remember thinking, this girl—my god—she's really getting out of control. "Kani nah—tomorrow ah," I whispered to Fann, "we'd better talk to Sher. Acting so romantic? We must stop this!" I think Sher noticed us whispering because after that she didn't feed him anymore.

When we finished eating, Ah Huat pulled out his box of Marlboro Reds and lit one up. Imo was telling us about how her dad was saying that day that the new HDB flats were quite nice-looking, asking whether she had a serious boyfriend or not. Apparently the new flats were so nice that Uncle was saying that people should fasterly get married just so they can buy one. So he was advising her, "Imo, if you even have a not-so-serious boyfriend, maybe you can at least consider whether can get more serious lah—the new flats are so beautiful. They're a very good investment! Just go to the registry of marriage, quickly buy a flat first, then deal with everything else later." Wah, when we heard Uncle's advice, Fann and I started laughing and laughing. Please! Yah lah, if you want to buy a government-subsidized flat then sure, you have to get married and preferably do it by a certain age. And it's true lah—the whole country had been talking about how nice the new ones are. Some are located downtown and all—and look even more atas than some private condominiums! In fact, the other day Fann almost got slapped for saying to Imo that Waikiki Towers looks more like an HDB flat than the new HDB flats. Even so, is Uncle blind? Surely he should know by now that his daughter and all of us are never going to be like those loser Singaporeans who get married just so they can buy a flat. *Cheh!*

Ah Huat also laughed a little bit, then he sucked hard on his cigarette and nodded his head over at Sher. "Eh, how?" he said, smelly puffs of smoke coming out of his chubby hairy nostrils as he talked. "Want to register for flat or not?"

Fann, Imo and I started laughing and laughing. We laughed for so long that we actually had to stop and take a sip of water—that type of laughing. Until we suddenly realized that Sher and Ah Huat were not laughing! Then all of a sudden, everything felt quite scary. Ah Huat was looking at Sher. We were staring at Sher. Sher was looking down at the chicken bones next to her orange plastic plate.

"Well, it seems like a good deal—those flats are quite nice," she finally said. "OK."

Ah Huat was suddenly so happy he actually pumped his fist into the air as if he won some cock competition. He raised his beer glass to try and cheers with all of us but we were so stunned we didn't move. Sher couldn't even look at us.

Imo was the first one to say something. "Sher, are you sure . . ."

Sher just cut her off and said, "It's a good time, Imo. OK?"

"Sher," I said, reaching over for her hand. I suddenly felt like throwing up.

Sher grasped my hand in hers first though. "Jazzy," she said, looking very seriously at me. "Please—just don't. Not now."

I couldn't believe it. I tried to look at Sher one more time but this time she not only could not look up at me but she also actually turned her head and looked away.

Oh, for fuck's sake. I took fifty dollars out of my wallet and threw it on the table. "Come," I said to Fann and Imo, "let's go."

Thinking back to that day, I wish I had said something—anything—that could have made that cock marriage proposal disappear. Instead I'd gotten angry like a baby and stormed off. I should have reasoned with Sher, taken her out for drinks after. If I had, would we have lost her forever to a loser Singaporean who's probably going to behave just like Kin Meng or Sam at those KTV clubs before too long?

I mean—forget Kin Meng and Sam. Even the Singaporean guys who don't have the money—or expense accounts—for KTV lounges are also doing funny business outside of their marriages. A few years ago, the girls and I really liked Hard Rock Cafe—we had just started hanging out with this group of English ruggers that we had met there, so we were feeling a little hopeful. One Saturday at Hard Rock when we girls had just climbed onto the dinner tables and were still sweating from swinging our long hair and going crazy to "Sweet Child of Mine," some guy near our feet suddenly said, "Eh, Jazzy and Sher ah?" At first we didn't recognize him. Some Singaporean guy at Hard Rock—who cares? But then Sher said, "Eh, I think it's Aileen's husband."

My first thought was, "Cannot be." Aileen just got married—how come her husband is already going clubbing without her? But it confirm was him! Well, we liked Aileen, so we got down from the tabletops to say hello. Her husband bought us a pitcher of Long Island Iced Tea and we talk-talked with him for a while, passing around the pitcher with two long straws so everyone could sip it. When the pitcher was empty, he bought another one. That was when I noticed he was suddenly standing right next to me, rubba-ing more and more as each song came on. I asked, "Eh, what you think you doing?"

"Aiyah, Jazzy, don't be so serious lah. Let's just get high and have a good time. Come, later I send you home." Aileen's husband kept rubba-ing—even using his left hand to hold on to the back of my neck so I felt like I was in one of those thick dog collars. At first I thought, OK, be nice lah, Jazzy. People just bought us all drinks— better to just swallow it, smile and say nothing.

But then I thought—kani nah, Aileen is our friend!

So I elbowed him and pushed him away. "You think we who? One of those China girls who can actually pretend they like sucking your small cock?"

That was when he got angry. He just wiped his mouth and spat on the floor. "You all ah," he said, pointing slowly at each one of us, "are nothing but a bunch of lousy sarong party girls. You think all these ang mohs will treat you any better than we will? Lan jiao, lah!" And then he walked away. I just couldn't believe it—even the not good-looking, not rich Singaporean guys are like that. So you tell me—what kind of hope do we girls have?

My head felt like it was going to explode thinking about last night at the KTV lounge, about Sher, about Aileen. So after I knocked off from work, I took the MRT down to Orchard Road and walked over to Paragon. Walking along its gleaming corridors and peeking into its perfumed cocoons filled with handbags and shoes always made me feel better. Prada, Loewe—even Coach. No matter what happened, these were the friends who could always instantly cheer me up.

I know this kind of thinking is quite materialistic lah. (Although, at the same time I also think—what the hell is wrong with that? Doesn't PM Lee always say it's good to have goals?) But since teenage times, I guess I've always been like this. And I guess walking these expensive corridors now always reminds me of the first guy who actually made me think that this was the life I could have someday.

There is only one Singaporean guy I ever considered worth marrying. Maybe.

This was a long time ago when I was still young. I knew about Gavin from the first week at JC—we were both in the same year in the commerce faculty, so even though we weren't in the same class I always saw him in econs and maths lectures. He was damn hard to get to know at first, because we were nowhere near being in the same circles. Even though he only managed to get into lousy Changi Junior College, his family was fucking rich. So each day, from the moment he parked his older brother's BMW in the teachers' car park to the time he left, he always had a big group following him around. Mostly guys, but since he was the richest guy in school, of course there were always a few girls—all the pretty ones, even a few Eurasians. The fucker knew this, of course—you could always see him walking around the school corridors with major attitude, like he's George Clooney at that atas French film festival or some shit.

So even though I thought he was cute—tall tall skinny skinny one, with small backside and sweet cheeky smile, and his school uniform shirt collar was always turned up a bit, like Cantopop singers in those paparazzi shots of them on vacation and all—I thought, this kind of guy, I confirm have no chance with him. If he has Eurasian girls wanting to date him, why on earth would he consider me? For me to dream about being his girlfriend—waste time only lah. I might as well try to date George Clooney. Same same.

But one day Gavin was late for econs lecture and I guess his gang forgot to save a seat for him—and usually I sit with Sher, but that day she was sick so there was a big empty seat next to me. Ten minutes after Mrs. Ho started talking about diminishing returns or some shit I heard someone sneaking into Sher's usual chair. When I looked to my left and saw it was Gavin, I was so shocked my mouth dropped open and I even stopped writing notes. Fucker saw that and just laughed quietly, shaking his head. *Babi!*

I thought, OK lah, if he wants to be like that, guniang will be a bit stuck-up with him. I just turned back to my notes and didn't look at him again during the whole lecture. At the end, when he winked at me and just got up quickly to leave, I wasn't surprised. Probably had some hot date at recess or something. Cheh!

I saw him around school the next few days, of course—fucker would wink at me here and there but never bothered to come over and say hello. But then a few days later, I happened to be leaving school late—so late that the bus stop outside was empty. Gavin was sitting on the railing at the bus stop, just casually smoking, looking a bit action. Damn funny—I whole life never see him at bus stop before. He had a BMW after all—and even if he didn't have his car that day, his mum could always send her driver to come and fetch him. What's he doing at a bus stop? The mighty Gavin taking public transportation? As if!

When I got to the bus stop though, Gavin threw his ciggie into the longkang and hopped off the railing.

"Why are you so late?" he asked.

I was so stunned I had to look around me for a moment to make sure he wasn't actually talking to someone behind me.

"Come," he said. "I send you home."

I usually try to be a bit proud—but then again, I also never say no to free car ride. (At that time, buses got no air-con, you know—if you have to take long bus trip in the middle of the afternoon . . . very hardship!) So I just nodded and follow him to his BMW.

"You live near town, right?" he said after he started the engine—

this engine was damn power, man. It sounded like one of those Formula One cars! (Not that I'd actually ever been close enough to a sports car to hear something like this. But hello, even if Jazzy here is not rich, she has some imagination.)

"Yah," I said, suddenly wondering how he knew where I live. I had never even said "Hello" to him before—how the hell did he know all these things?

"OK, I bring you to King's Hotel for lunch first," he said. "The chicken rice there, quite good."

Go to a hotel to eat chicken rice? I whole life never hear something so stupid before. Chicken rice is hawker food, hello—the hawker center across from my block alone has so many good kinds, and all just the two-dollar three-dollar type! If you are toot enough to go to a hotel for chicken rice, you must know you're going to cough up at least ten dollars for a plate! And GST on top of that! But I assumed he was paying, so I just kept quiet. In fact, being quiet was not so hard at that point. Gavin's air-con was as power as his engine—everything was so cold and shiok I was getting a bit sleepy. I actually wished he wasn't there so I could just close my eyes and take a nap. But babi was not only sitting next to me—he kept looking at me, like he wanted to see if I was OK or not. So I just looked out the window and counted the angsana trees flashing by.

"I'm Gavin," he said.

"You think I don't know, is it?"

I heard him laugh, so I turned around to look at him.

"What?" I asked.

"Nothing, nothing," he said. I could see that he was still smiling. "Just wondering why you are being so attitude with me. It's not like I did something to you before. Excuse me, uncle over here is even fetching you home and all."

OK lah. He had a point. I guess I was on edge because I wasn't really sure what was going on. Is he treating me like a charity case? Or did he want to ask me for favor? (My god, if he wants to copy my econs homework, he's even more stupid than I think.) This kind of situation—rich handsome guy; poor not bad-looking girl—usually never ends well in those films in the cinema. Often the guy's friends dare him to ask her out or something—and in the end they always end up making fun of the girl and how poor she is. Jazzy may not have money lah, but she's not a goondu!

I didn't know what to say so I just turned around and carried on looking out the window.

Gavin had turned onto the ECP by then and revved up his engine so we went a bit faster. I wished he would slow down. I had only been on this part of the ECP a few times before because guniang usually only took buses at that time. (And buses never go on the ECP, which is why all the bus rides from Changi all take so long. Sometimes, it feels like we have to get through one thousand traffic lights and even more bus stops before I get home, man.) It had already rained that day so the sky was damn blue and I could see a few people walking near the beach, the rows of skinny, short holiday chalets, the tall palm trees all around, the seaside hawker center that I heard had very shiok satay. I bet every day when Gavin drives to school he never even looks out his window at all this. When the fucker wants to go to a beach I bet he just flies to Bali or some shit.

"How you know I live in Tiong Bahru?" I asked.

"I asked around," he said. "And I've been noticing you. You're quite popular, you know. There are a lot of guys in school who are just waiting for a chance to take you out."

Popular? Fucker must be pulling my leg. I know I'm a bit cute lah—some more I make sure to keep my school uniform skirt damn short. Some girls in school—even Eurasians!—have even quietly taken me aside before to ask me to show them my technique for rolling up my skirt at the waistband so the skirt rides up but also flares out nicely in that way that suggests that maybe guys can see a bit of backside if they look hard enough but hello, of course we girls know better than to actually give the whole show away for free.

No, usually when strange guys start talking to me, it's usually because they want to get closer to Sher. Back then, I had better legs lah (hence the emphasis on skirt-rolling) but Sher was already damn pretty. Even so, she wasn't that busy on the dating scene because the truth is, she just couldn't be bothered. Of all of us, she was the most focused on studies—so when she was in school, she actually cared about going to classes type. (And when she was there, she actually listened.) I could always see guys—really good-looking ones, too—trying to get close enough to her to say hello. But usually only the really nerdy smart ones were the only ones who succeeded because Sher was mostly interested in asking them about homework and other cock shit like that. I had heard that some guys in school had started calling her "Ice Princess" because she never talked to people she didn't know. I guess they thought they could get to her through me because I was a bit more friendly. (Or desperate? Babi.)

I wanted to say something to Gavin—like "Don't talk cock lah!"—but decided to act cool. So I just nodded and kept looking out the window.

"You know," I said. "Usually when guys ask a girl out, they do it nicely, sometimes bringing flowers all. They don't kidnap them at a bus stop and force them to go and eat chicken rice."

"Kidnap?" he said, laughing again, shaking his head. "You are really something, Jazeline."

After that, we were stuck together like superglue. We went to lectures together, studied together at McDonald's after school, on weekends we'd go to shows at Lido, holding hands for the world to see that we were a couple. The one year we were together was quite fantasy lah. If it was Bollywood movie we confirm would be running around a tree.

Even though I thought at first that Gavin was damn attitude, he actually turned out to be a very good boyfriend. Always pick me up in his BMW; always send me home. Some more each month on the fourteenth—the anniversary of our first bus stop date—he always gave me a present. Something branded some more—not a flashy or expensive present, usually something small like a Gucci keychain or the cheapest Tiffany pen. But on my birthday he gave me a Louis Vuitton wallet—the one with the logos all over so everyone could see it was LV!

Things were going so well after a few months that I actually allowed myself to start imagining what it would be like to be Mrs. Gavin Lim. To live in big house, have two maids, maybe even a Malay driver. Win lottery! This kind of life, I confirm don't mind. I wasn't sure how rich Gavin was exactly—and honestly, I didn't really care. I got the sense that he was definitely rich enough for more than one maid. But I did hope that he could give me enough to buy a nice house for my mum and dad also, and make sure they also had a maid to take care of them. I know back then we were still pretty young but it was a little bit different than it is now. When you're in school, some of the relationships you have, you'll stick with them until early twenties and when it's a decent enough age, you get married. Those kinds of school relationships were much simpler than now lah—now, aiyoh, it's all about hooking up and getting free drinks. Somewhere along the way between JC and real life, everything always changes when it comes to dating. If you're one of the lucky ones, you'll snag that good guy before he sees the opportunities out there and any of that crap can change him.

Then a few months before our A-level preliminary exams, Gavin took me to dinner at Nadaman at the Shang. Nice Japanese dinner at Nadaman? Must be something important. Could it be? Just in case, I made sure my mascara was waterproof that night. So when I make those few tears of joy at least we can still take a nice photo afterward.

The dinner was damn shiok—foie gras chawanmushi, super expensive sashimi and all—but guniang here was not even halfway through eating when Gavin dropped his fucking bomb.

"I think we should take a break," he said, reaching across the table to take my hand.

I just laughed. Things were going so well—why was he saying such cock words? "Crazy, ah?" I said, laughing even more.

"Jazz, I'm serious," he said. "The A-levels are so important. My mum says I need to really focus. She wants me to come straight home after school every day and take extra tuition classes before the preliminary exams. I can't afford to bollocks this up."

His mum! Of course she is behind this. I always try not to be rude to my elders but Auntie Lim is a fucking chee bye, man. From the first time I met her until now, she was always damn stuck-up around me, always pulling a dark face if Gavin invites me to family parties. I know she thinks her precious son can do better.

"Did your mum ask you to break up with me?" I asked.

"Break up? No! This is not that, Jazz. She just thought maybe it's good to take a break. Just at least until the A's are over."

"Why do we need a break? We can see each other less often. Do you think I don't know how important the A's are? I also need to study! You're not the only one who is trying to have a future, Gav!"

"I know, I know. Jazz, please don't be upset."

He was trying to bend across the table to kiss me now but I just leaned back and folded my arms.

"Jazz," he said, sighing. "You know I love you. My mother . . . you know what she's like. I need to at least pass my A's. The future chairman of Lim Yee Sheng Exports cannot retake his A's! Do you know how embarrassing that would be? My parents won't be able to show their faces at Chinese New Year!"

I refused to say anything and just looked away. I was still waiting for him to tell me this is a joke. Or that he's going to tell his mum to go fly a kite.

"My mother said if I don't at least show I'm serious about it and break up with you—for now—she's going to take away my car. And cut my allowance. Do you know how hard that would be? I would have to take a bus to school! I won't even have enough money to take a taxi to school! Do you understand?"

At that point, I finally did. I guess I had thought Gavin was different.

I folded my napkin, put it on the table and picked up my handbag.

"Jazz, please, don't go. Don't be so petty. I know you love me. Think about my future. Please?"

I just got up and walked away.

Gavin shouted behind me, "It's just temporary!"

But of course it wasn't.

And ever since then, even though now and then of course there will be some rich Singaporean guys who want to chase me, I never say yes. Date these spineless babies who at the end of the day will always kowtow to their snobby mums? No thank you. Please—waste time only.

Even though I hated Gavin, he still popped into my head now and then. Last I heard, he was in the States—California or some shit—studying business after he finished with his army training. Not married yet, but I can confirm I'll never hear from him again. His mother would probably vomit blood and die if she ever heard the name "Jazeline" ever again, I'm sure. And boys like Gavin will always keep that in mind once they get close to marrying age.

Even so, kani nah—eight years later and I still think about him whenever I see a Gucci handbag. Damn pathetic, right?

I guess, since he was the first person who gave me branded gifts, I can't help but think of him whenever I go to Paragon. There's Bottega lah, Chanel lah, Gucci lah; the air-con is cold cold and all, the toilets so nice they have a sofa, pink carpet and must pay twenty cents to even enter type. All these things somehow make me think of Gavin. I guess I imagined that one day I would be able to come to Paragon and actually buy something for myself, not just look-see look-see.

Even though this mall makes me think of him and that cock time before Jazzy here smartened up, I still come. Just seeing all the logo handbags and big fashion show catwalk posters, the expensive lipsticks and thousand-dollar high heels—even if it's through the window—can always cheer me up. And this evening I really needed cheering up.

"Jazzy?" I heard someone say. "Is that you?"

I didn't recognize the voice but when I turned to look, I recognized the face—Sharon! God, I hadn't seen her since secondary school. Her face was a bit fatter—and so were her hips. Must have had a kid already. But she still looked the same otherwise.

"Sharon! Eh, woman, you still look damn happening!" I said, giving her a hug.

"Talk rubbish!" she said. "You are the happening one—look at you!" (We both knew she was the only one not talking rubbish.)

We caught up a bit—she was always damn smart so she went

to Raffles JC and then National University of Singapore after our secondary school days, even studied law and all. But then she fell in love with some ang moh barrister and had a kid right away, so she quit her job at Allen & Gledhill to be at home. I was a bit shy about telling her what I do exactly so I just said, "Oh, I work at the *New Times*."

"Oh wow!" she said. "Everybody subscribes to the *New Times*! Good for you, Jazzy."

I always liked Sharon, even though we didn't keep in touch after she went to Raffles—no point lah. Why on earth would she want to mix with some Changi Junior College friend when she has her clever Raffles classmates to talk to? But bumping into her made me a bit nostalgic for our old school days. So I suggested that we go across the street and grab dinner to catch up more.

"You know that old beef ball noodles at Scotts Picnic that we used to go to after school?" I said. "It's over at Ion now! Still damn shiok."

I was never that close to Sharon—even in secondary school, Sher was my best friend—but she and I did always take the same bus home. So sometimes if we didn't have lunch waiting for us at home, we would stop at Scotts for noodles. Sharon always tried to encourage me to study harder, aim higher and all that crap. I was thankful for that, yes, but I also knew that at the end of the day, my brain and her brain is not same same lah. She's the type to be a future CEO, lawyer or maybe even minister of parliament! Me? I'd be lucky if she thought I had enough brains to be her future assistant. Beef ball noodles, though—that's what we always had in common.

Sharon laughed and said, "I can't believe that place is still around!"

When we got to the air-conditioned food court at Ion, the line for the stall was as long. And it turned out the noodles were as shiok as they used to be. And it was quite fun to chitchat and tell her about all the things that had happened recently—not last night, of course. But I filled her in on Sher getting married, Imo working at her power fashion job and Fann . . . I didn't have much to say about Fann lah, but she understood.

"Eh, how's the life of a married lady with a Chanel baby?" I asked. She had just taken out her phone and shown me many screens of her and her husband Alistair holidaying here and there—Greece lah, Paris lah. Even New York! And also photos of her daughter, who looked more British than Chinese. Aiyoh, when you have one of those types of Chanel babies—the really obvious ang moh ones—this one is really win.

"I guess I can't complain . . ." Sharon said. And then she didn't say anything more for a while.

After her noodles were gone, she took out a packet of tissue from her Givenchy tote—from this season some more! I just saw one in a window at Paragon.

Sharon took a tissue out, daintily dabbed the sides of her mouth—and started crying!

Guniang here was so stunned I didn't know what to do.

"Oh Jazzy, I'm so sorry—I'm never like this," Sharon said. (Usually when people say something like that, it's when they start to slow down or stop crying. But she really had no shame—she was still crying!) I reached over and patted her shoulder.

"Don't cry, don't cry," I said. "Just tell me what's wrong."

Sharon kept crying for a few minutes—softly, thank god. But it was still so obvious that people around us were beginning to look over at us. A small boy even walked by our table very slowly so he could see what was going on. (I just told him, "Stare what stare? Got problem is it?" Fucker ran away.)

"I'm sorry, I'm sorry," she said when she finally stopped. "It's just . . . I think my husband is having an affair."

I looked at her again from head to toe—hair a bit messy, fat face, chubby hips, baggy dress, auntie-style Ferragamo flats and from the look of her skin I don't think she'd had a facial in at least six months. OK lah, I can see it. Which ang moh wants to come home to this shit?

"No! I'm sure he's not!" I said. "You are so happening!"

Even if these were all lies, at least I made her smile.

"You're sweet, Jazzy," Sharon said. "But I'm pretty certain. He's started going out on weekends until the wee hours of the morning, coming home pissed—so pissed I sometimes have to wake up and help him up the steps to our bedroom. And he smells of perfume sometimes, even when he says he's just been working late at the office or entertaining clients. I know the women he works with— they don't wear perfume!"

I was trying to figure out how to tell her what I think she needs to know, but she kept going.

"And he was never like that, Jazzy! He's never been that type of guy! But these few months—oh, I just don't know what to do . . ." Sharon said, starting to cry again.

"Well . . ." I said. "Have you . . . have you thought about going shopping?"

"I beg your pardon?" Sharon said, putting her tissue down. She was still breathing damn hard but had stopped crying.

"Shopping—you know, to get a makeover," I said. "You're still very pretty, you know—but maybe you just need a bit of a touch-up? Sharon—maybe it's not my place to say this, but guys . . . guys, even after they are married, still care about looks. How their wives dress, whether they still wear lipstick and eye shadow, dye their hair, go for facials—you know, all the things you used to do before you got married. I mean, I know you recently had your daughter, but, I don't know—maybe if you tried a bit?"

Sharon stopped her heavy breathing.

She was really looking at me now so I guess she was listening. So I decided to carry on. "You've probably put on a bit of weight since the baby so maybe that's a factor also?" I said. "It's unfair lah—but guys are just like that. Want to keep their attention then maybe you need to just look nicer a bit, maybe suggest romantic holiday to Bali or something to try and win him back or . . ."

"You're right, Jazzy," she said. Her voice got a bit sharp. (My mother and her wet market lectures suddenly popped into my head.) "You're right that it's not your place to say any of this. Please—look at who you are and who I am. Are you married? No. When was the last time you had a boyfriend who wasn't a smelly Ah Beng? I don't even know. And let's not even get into success, smarts and all that jazz. Who are you to assume you can give me such shallow, self-loathing, misogynistic, pitiful advice like that?"

Wah. Some of those words I don't even understand. But from the way she was staring at me, I knew they must mean damn bitchy things. When she paused, I thought Sharon was finished but she kept going on.

"I'm sorry," she said. Wah—finally, I thought. She's going to apologize for being a bloody chee bye to me. All I was doing was trying to help her!

"I guess I shouldn't have said anything at all—I'm sorry I did," she said. Then she just picked up her handbag and left.

Kani nah. I was so shocked I had to sit there for a while. When I got up to walk over to the bus stop, it suddenly occurred to me another piece of advice I should have given Sharon.

"Givenchy? Please. It's been yonks since even anyone's mother wanted to carry that brand."

World War III had started by the time I got home.

All I did was not look at my phone between the MRT station and my bedroom and that was enough time for Fann and Imo to send seventy text messages. My god. What do they think? Texting is like air is it—free? (OK, actually it is free—I think—but you get the point.)

At first I was fucking annoyed. But after I read all the texts, I realized the situation was quite bad. Most of them went something like this: "I CAN'T BELIEVE Fann is such a fucking CHEE BYE!!!!" and so on. And some came from Fann too, trying to explain but then also calling Imo a fucking baby, etc. Apparently Louis kissed Fann goodnight or some fuck, when he dropped her off on Saturday night. And Imo finally heard about it because Fann was feeling bad about it and decided to tell her. All Imo's texts were about how Fann should have slapped him or something. Although, from what I sort of remembered of last night, I think Fann was quite gone. Imo was too—which is why she should be understanding a bit! It's not like Louis is hers, after all. The fucker can kiss whoever he wants. If Mary doesn't care, why should she? Waste time only.

"GIRLS," I texted. "Just shut the fuck up. Both of you are in the wrong. Both of you apologize. Louis is just Louis. Don't forget our goal."

My god, this day was never-ending. I was damn tired. Even though it was early, I needed to turn on the air-con and lie down a bit. Even though I was tired, I knew there was no danger of falling asleep. My bed since secondary school days was damn uncomfortable—lumpy

lumpy one. Plus, it's so small—my parents, I think, didn't want to buy me a full or queen bed because they think I'll bring guys home or some shit. (It's true lah—I only did it once or twice and my god, it was really uncomfortable. My bed was so narrow—our hands and knees where to put, we also don't know. Might as well be doing it in public toilet.)

Actually, I don't know why my parents refuse to change my room. All the cupboards, shelves and desk and chair have all been around from not just secondary school, you know—some date back to primary school! I mean, they're still in good condition, so I actually can understand a bit when they tell me no need to change, buy new furniture—waste money only. But hello, the desk even still has some of the Little Twin Stars stickers I stuck on it in primary school, man. People here are twenty-six years old already, you know—how can I still have cartoon stickers on my bedroom furniture? Apart from that, I admit that the rest of the shit in the room is my own fault. My photos from primary school, my sparkly gold piggy bank with the fat lipstick mouth, that hundred-meters medal I got on Primary 4 Sports Day. And even until recently I still had that poster of Christian Slater from *Gleaming the Cube* up on the wall. But that movie is damn power! Some more he was so cute in it! Cuter than now when he has that balding spot on one side all—aiyoh! Guniang had to go all over Far East Plaza to all those cheapo poster shops to find one you know. So of course I didn't want to take down. (Until recently when the Scotch tape was so yellow and old that the poster just fell off. Then, OK lah, I thought, this is a sign.)

There's one thing my mum always nags me to throw away—this big thing of dried flowers that yes, I know, is not fresh anymore. But it's also quite crumbling and crackly, so much so that each time you try to pick up and move it, confirm will have petals falling off in pieces. But I think it still looks quite nice. Back when I first got them I made sure to preserve them carefully after just a few days, hanging them upside down to dry in the original plastic wrapping so the overall look is still quite can. (Even got red ribbon around it and all!) But every time my mum comes in to clean my room and I'm around, she confirm will shout "Aiyoh, AH HUAY! These ants are all coming into your room because of these flowers! Die so long ago already still want to keep . . ."

It's not like they're really pretty, I know. But this guy gave them to me a long time ago. At the time I was still only going out with Chinese-Singaporean guys—and maybe sometimes local Indian guys. Indian guys, after all, are quite like ang mohs in some ways— more gentlemanly. Not spoilt big babies like all these Chinese guys who, no matter how old they are, their mothers still pick out all the meat from crab shells for them at the dinner table. But with Indian guys, you must try to find the ones that have a China doll fetish— those will actually bother to take you out to nice dinner, treat you like a princess. It's quite sad lah—those kinds are the ones who I think look down a bit on Indian girls and don't want to date them. I also don't know why because Indian girls, come to think of it, actually seem quite nice. One time I made friends with this one girl Sheela from the office—it's not like we were close enough to say, go clubbing, but we were actually friendly enough to grab lunch together a few times. Once we even went for after-work drinks together, just the two of us. But even so, there are some Indian guys out there who, no matter what, just don't want to date their own kind of girls, even nice guniangs like Sheela. Such a waste, you know. I think maybe they think Chinese girls are more high-class. Singapore sometimes is just like that one.

But then one day this guy from the States came to help my boss with some project. At that time I had just started working for Albert at the *New Times*. I was still quite new—and happening! Because I was the very young chio new girl in the office, my god, all these people kept asking me out. Even so, I wasn't interested. What for? Guniang here just started work, OK—must at least try and act professional a bit.

Until this guy Nathan showed up in the office—wah, tall tall, white white, cute cute one. His smile was so big and friendly. He told me he came from some place called Savannah so that's why when he talked he sounded a bit different from those people on *Friends*. I also don't know where this Savannah is lah but hey, he's ang moh—like that is can already. Plus, he was very sweet—when taking me to see a movie, he'd always buy tickets in advance. When he took me out to drink coffee, it was always at nice air-con cafe and all. Not some sweaty kopitiam! No Ah Cheks sitting around scratching their balls and chain-smoking! So, yah lah. Is can.

But in the end, Nathan was only here for one month—to help my boss redesign the newspaper front page or some shit. And when he left, he left. I guess we could email and keep in touch lah, but in the end, for what fuck? Not say the States is very near, you know. Also, not say I know where this Savannah is. So, that was that.

Before he left, he took me out for one last nice dinner, showing up at my doorstep with that bouquet of flowers in hand. (Even my mum was damn stunned. Until cannot even open her mouth to say hello kind of stunned.) After he left, guniang actually cried. Not in front of him, of course. No matter what, I always know that in front of ang moh guys must act high-class a bit. Well, life is just like that. And my mum knows that if she dares to touch those flowers I'll heck care respect and hantam her one time.

Which is why this Imo-Fann-Louis thing really made me angry.

Waste time on Louis for what? Guys like that will only give you flowers once in a long time and only then if they have something to say sorry about. All that sweet crap is only for their wives. If you expect anything else, you are just a fucking goondu. No point.

No—we guniangs must focus!

CHAPTER 10

Guniang here had already deleted Roy's mobile number when the fucker texted me.

"U out tonight?"

Since I'd deleted his number, I of course had absolutely no idea who this was. (Plus, I'd actually gotten the first text on the KTV lounge night, so my mind was quite occupied.) When I saw the message the next morning, I had to think hard about who it might be. Maybe it was some lech anyhow texting, just shooting out random arrows to see whether some chio girl would respond? In any case, I didn't answer, of course. Then I got another text. "Late night out last night? :)" My god—this was now getting too personal. So I ignored this too. Babi, if it happened one more time, I was going to call Sing-Tel to block this number and see whether I could get the fucker's number canceled or some shit.

But then later in the afternoon the asshole texted again. "Hey, it's Roy. Would love to see you. Let me know when I can take you out."

Ahh. Well, I guess this was not bad—I was playing hard to get without even knowing it! This was the first time I could see my tootness actually producing a result. I made a mental note: next time more toot equals more better. Even though I saw the text when I was sitting at my desk, shaking my leg, waiting for Albert to come back from some long liquor lunch, I purposely waited until after I'd finished dinner with Sharon before texting back: "Tomorrow night. Maybe." Right away, the fucker damn steam!

He texted back immediately, "Let me take you out for drinks. Que Pasa, 8 pm?"

So I guess we were going on a date.

Before Roy texted me, I had actually been thinking that this guy—maybe it's better to write him off. It's not as if he's super handsome, and hallo, I still couldn't forget his hairy nose. But even more important—I don't exactly know what he does! All I know is that he works on an oil refinery—and we all know how uncouth those guys can be. And seriously, what kind of future is that? It's not like he's some guy who works in bank or is a lawyer or some shit at that level.

I know how this must make me sound. And honestly, when we were all growing up and were still naive young girls with stars (and not yet Gucci logos) in our eyes, I would see women who are so obviously going after guys just for status and really look down on them. What kind of woman is so pathetic to chase after a husband just for the kind of handbag, car or condo they can buy them? What about love? Shouldn't that be the most important thing? The only thing?

But that was before Gavin. I mean, the thing is, you can go around being as trusting and sweet as you want and believe in the goodness of the world and people and all that. But if you are a not rich, not that smart (school-smart anyway) girl whose best asset—let's face it—is a nice sweet face and not bad body, then being naive is only going to land you in some cock situation in the end.

I still remember career day in school—in my school this was quite a joke lah. Career? Please. Talk what kind of cock? Many of the girls there are probably going to be married and pregnant before they reach twenty-three and the guys—aiyoh, don't even get me started. Unless squatting by a longkang and smoking a cigarette is an actual skill that you can put on your CV, then please, these guys—all no hope lah.

When I think about it really hard though, of course it would be nice to have a career, one that I like even. I mean, marrying an ang moh guy is nice and all but it would be nice, at the end of the day, to have something to call my own. From seeing all the marriages around me, even if you marry a good catch, no matter how trustworthy or solid the guy is, you still never know all the things, all the girls, that can happen along the way to make his heart turn—whether at the end, no matter how good a wife, a mother, you've tried to be, you will somehow end up being the one left all by yourself.

The problem is that I don't know what I would actually be good at. Imo has always been into fashion so working at Club 21 was always her dream; Fann loves dogs and her dad always told her that it's most stable to be your own boss—unless you're really fucking toot, you will never want to fire yourself—so she knew early on that she wanted to start a pet business. And Sher—Sher is a bit more like me, but much less aimless when it comes to her career. Even though she (like me) felt that she doesn't have any obvious talent that can be turned into a career, she just started working in a cafe after we left school and somehow eventually turned that into a job where she now is an assistant manager at a restaurant! Not one of those atas restaurants lah—but one of those neighborhood British-y family restaurants that families go on weekends type. It's not, say, a very sexy or name-brand (or even good) restaurant but still, it's stable—and it's a job that makes her happy.

Guniang here? Even though I thought for many years about it, I wasn't sure what I would be good at—I mean, really good at. Yes, I'm very sociable and I like talking to people. Guys especially always say that I make them feel very fun, funny, smart and comfortable—that I'm sweet and very easy to hang out with, especially for drinks or dinner, that kind of thing. I tell you, when we had career day and had to list out our best talents and I wrote these down—kani nah, the main thing I could think of that this would be suitable for is being one of those KTV lounge girls or some bar hostess! Aiyoh. How—like that?

Thinking about it all made me realize that I'm very organized though, which is what led me to being an executive assistant, I guess. And now that I'm doing this job I realize that I'm actually very good at not just organizing people's lives and days but also organizing events. Albert already trusts me now with putting together department promotion or birthday parties and holiday lunches and shit like that. So—who knows? Maybe one day.

But this kind of thing—think about it too much right now is wasting time only lah. What's the point of chasing unlikely dreams like that? The main thing we must focus on now is finding an ang moh husband! Hallo, guniang here is twenty-six already, you know—no time to play anymore. Which is why even though Roy was still a bit of a question mark, I figured, I might as well go on one date and see how. Also, free drinks is free drinks lah. Guniang here never says no to that.

Even though I was only few minutes late getting to Que Pasa (walking up cobblestoned Emerald Hill, along the uneven historic tiled sidewalks to get to this bar is always damn harrowing), Roy was already there. The fucker was so eager he even reserved a table in the back room. So prepared? Desperate is it?

Maybe this was true lah, because when he saw me walk in, he quickly jumped up, hugged me and tried to kiss me on lips and all. (Luckily that one I already anticipated—I fasterly turned my face so he only kena my cheek instead.)

"How are you doing?" he asked, grinning really broadly.

"Fine," I replied, purposely just smiling a very little bit while sitting down.

"I . . . I realize I don't even know what you like to drink," he said. "Although I seem to recall you were open to a lot of things . . . would you like a red? Or white?"

"Bubbly," I said.

Fucker looked like he didn't want to argue so he quickly ordered a bottle of cava.

"Have you eaten? Do you want anything?"

I was starting to get a little suspicious—why was he being so nice to me? I just shook my head and he waved the waitress away.

This kind of date, I actually have never been on many times before. Usually when I meet the kind of ang moh I go on dates with, usually we have already talk-talked a bit over beers and playing darts at some pub so we at least know each other a bit already. Since I usually at least try not to ruin prospects right away by opening the kitchen too early, usually on a first date like this, I still haven't hooked up with the guy lah—so, everything is still mystery mystery a bit. (Make them steam!)

The ang mohs I quickly hook up all the way with, I often never keep in touch with them. Usually what's happened is some mistake at the end of the night, when I've had too much to drink and the guy somehow ends up looking quite cute or hot in the dark or some shit. The next day, it's just better to forget them and hope they forget me so it's not so awkward overall. (Aiyah—to them, Asian girls all look the same. So as long as I don't give them my phone number—and usually they are so mabuk they sure don't remember my name— then confirm everything is OK lah. Even if I see them at club again, they usually don't remember me.)

But here, like that how? Roy had already sampled everything.

Some more he has this guniang's phone number. And he confirm remembers me—and everything that happened. I don't even know what to talk to him about, since this oil refinery guy is not an ang moh I would actually arrow in a club with dating in mind.

"What do you do?" I asked him.

"I'm here with Chevron," he said. "I'm one of the people brought in to oversee managing the distribution of oil. It's . . . oh, never mind, I shan't bore you with the details. And believe me, they are boring!"

He laughed a little bit so I smiled again. Just following along lah. Besides, I was starting to like him a bit more. A manager must be quite a big deal right? At least he wasn't one of those foremen on the rigs. Maybe he even had an office and all. In fact, he looked like he just came from work and he was wearing a white collared shirt—no tie—and nice tailored pants. If he has to dress like this for work then maybe he's not so unimportant? Maybe later I should ask him for a business card so I can confirm what exactly it is that he does.

"What about you?" he asked. "I realized . . ." he added, pausing. Was the fucker actually blushing? Kani nah. Maybe he was actually a nice guy after all. I tried to squint a bit, to see whether he was pretending or not.

"Well, I realized that we didn't quite have a chance to talk that night," he said, really blushing now. His skin was so fair I could actually see it turn red. "And I'm really really sorry for that. I really never do get that pissed. I've only just moved to Singapore, the boys at work were taking me out on the town to see the nightlife, the company was buying drinks, it had gotten very late and I saw you and . . . well, anyway. I just thought you looked really sexy in those jeans—and beautiful of course! I'd never danced so closely with such a beautiful Asian girl. I really want you to know that I never do that sort of thing right when I meet a girl. And you . . . you really do seem like a nice girl. I'm sorry."

Aiyoh—he was sounding damn sincere. If he's acting, he confirm can win a prize, man. If he's not acting, then he's really damn fucking blind. Nice girl? Walao. Who is he talking about? But if he thinks so, then this could work in my favor.

I decided maybe it might help if I started acting the part. So I looked down and tried to act as if I was embarrassed a bit. When I looked back up, the fucker looked happy and all. OK lah. This one— is maybe can. In fact, when I looked closer at him, he looked like maybe he had even waxed his nose. So at least he seemed to have some awareness of lousy things that need to be changed.

"OK," I said. "I work at the *New Times*. It's all right. Not bad hours, decent pay. I like my boss."

"Wow, a real media person!" he said, looking quite impressed. "I'll drink to that!"

So we toasted and then talk-talked some more. And when the bottle was empty, he ordered some more and some cheese and meats for us to share.

"You know," he said, "until I moved here, I led quite a sheltered life in the UK. Until I joined Chevron, I didn't travel much. BP never sent me anywhere. But here, Asia is just eye-opening." I just smiled. This, he had actually told me earlier tonight when I first sat down. Repeating already? Maybe he was getting sloshed.

"And Asian women . . ." he said. "Can I tell you a secret?"

Of course I nodded.

"I'd never been with an Asian girl until that night," he said. "I mean, of course I've been with women—not that many, but not too few, mind you! But you Asians—whoo . . . just, wow! Your skin, your eyes, your hair—my god!"

Aiyoh, this kind of obvious thing also must say. But I don't quite understand why he telling me all this. He's trying to make me feel special is it? Say my skill very good is it? Kani nah. Maybe I should fasterly go home.

"It's getting late," I said.

"Yes, yes, of course," he said. "I'm sorry—may I send you home?"

This one—is very nice offer. Usually it's the Singaporean guys who care so much about sending you home—like they think that if you somehow don't make it home safe, your mum is going to come to their doorstep and hantam them or something. But I didn't really want Roy to see where I live. (Even though his condo is not, say, super nice, it is at least condo—not a lousy government flat.)

"No worries," I said, reaching across the table to squeeze his hand.

When the waitress brought the bill over, Roy pulled out his wallet—the leather had that telltale crisscross woven pattern and all. Bottega Veneta. Fucking expensive. Good, good. He confirm has some potential.

So, when Roy found a taxi for me, I decided I should probably give him a signal before I go. I pulled him close to my body—walao, I could feel that the fucker was getting a bit steam—and looked up at his face, smiling. This time when he kissed me, he wasn't too slobbery and messy. Actually, it was quite nice and sweet and I kissed him back a little fiercely. Good—give him something shiok to think about tonight.

Right when his breathing was starting to get damn heavy I quickly cut it off.

"Goodnight," I said, waving and jumping into the taxi. Fucker just stood there waving and waving until my taxi was at least one traffic light away.

I guess this guy . . . is maybe can consider. At least I should go out with him one more time and see how. Oil refining business is not the dream goal for Jazzy lah, but if he's a manager and all, maybe he's quite power. Besides, he at least has the money to buy Bottega! Got hope.

Taxi uncle was quiet the whole time after I told him where to bring me. These taxi uncles sometimes are like that. They hate expats so much that if they see Singaporean girls with ang mohs they sometimes act damn snobby, even give us mean looks and all. Like, hello—even if I wasn't a sarong party girl, do you actually think I'm going to throw my life away on a taxi uncle? Uncle, please—you never had chance to begin with lah. So stop acting like these ang mohs are actually stealing your women.

"Uncle, drop me here can?" I said, when we got to the bus stop near my block. Easier lah. Also, I didn't mind having some time to walk and think about the evening before I had to deal with my mum and her "Ah Huay ah!" nonsense again.

But then, bloody hell. The moment I got out of taxi, I heard "Oi— Jazzy!"

Kani nah. It was Seng, that smelly Ah Beng, sitting on the plastic orange seat of the bus stop.

"My god, tolong—what you want now?" I said, trying to walk faster so maybe he wouldn't follow.

But of course the fucker even more fasterly got up and started following me. "Eh—don't walk so fast lah," he said. "Why so snobby tonight? I so nice all, walk you home so you don't kena rape and all."

When I didn't say anything, Seng just lit a cigarette. "You tonight go where?" he asked.

"Your business, is it?" I asked.

"True, true—I know lah, uncle here got the wrong color skin," he said, laughing. "Guniang, just for you I can consider that Michael Jackson surgery. How? If my skin turns white, then you want me or not?"

Fucker was even making kissing noises and all. Kani nah. This Ah Beng was really too much.

"My god—you!" I said, whacking him on the arm. Fucker was so stunned he almost dropped his cigarette. "Talk cock lah!" I added. Seng just laughed.

I guess he decided to stop talking, because we managed to walk quietly for a bit—so quietly that I could actually hear the night crickets. I remember sometimes when we were young, Seng and I used to sit at the bus stop and smoke until early early in the morning. Both of us had nowhere to go, we had no money to do anything fun. And both of us didn't want to go home. We talked a lot lah, but sometimes, back then, no need to talk could also be quite shiok. Just to sit there, smoke smoke smoke, dream about the future, listen to crickets . . . Where did those simple days go?

But more important, how come Seng is this old already and he's still sitting at the bus stop until late at night, doing this kind of kampong shit?

We didn't say anything else until we reached my block. "OK, goodnight," I said, waving at him.

Seng just nodded, stopping so he could squat by the longkang near the lift and finish his ciggie. Like I said before—I really don't know when he became so Ah Beng. Whatever lah. It's his life.

He was still squatting and smoking and staring at me when the lift came and I got inside. As the doors slowly closed, the fucker was still looking.

CHAPTER 11

"We need to talk."

Louis whole life has never said words like that to me. So, when I got his text the next morning at work, I knew it must be about Imo and Fann. I fasterly canceled after-work drinks with the girls that night. I know they were going to complain—Fann kept saying that she had something to tell us but didn't want to text it to us. Some more—it was Thursday night! Almost Friday already—time to start revving up for chionging! But to get a text like that from Louis, I knew I really had no choice.

Jazzy here was feeling chio that day—still a bit high from the date with Roy last night, probably. The guy even texted me half an hour after I got in the taxi, making sure I got home safe, saying he hoped to see me again soon. Wah—I guess my calculated standoff-ishness worked! So today—this guniang was feeling damn good.

I put on a new sleeveless workdress, quite short and tight (but not like Orchard Towers tight), plus, I threw on a skinny belt to make my waist look smaller. (Imo's fashion discount sometimes is quite power.) Although, dressing up for work today made me angry with Sharon all over again. Just thinking about how our dinner ended the other night still made my blood boil. So ungrateful! Guniang here was just trying to help her, and she just shot me right down. That woman—I tell you—is really too much. But I was still feeling so good about Roy that I decided—aiyah, heck care Sharon! And heck care Kin Meng and his stupid KTV lounge and all his sleazy colleagues and those disgusting girls! Today Jazzy here must dress lively lively sexy sexy—energy a bit. This is how it's supposed to be done! I even blasted Rick Astley while I was putting on my clothes, until my mother hammered on the door, screaming and all. "Ah Huay ah! You want people in Johor Bahru to hear your ang moh song is it?"

But hallo, this one is good strategy lah—I looked so good and was so wide awake that when I got to work even Albert was happy, telling me I was looking damn chio. Boss good mood; everyone good mood. I was just happy that things were back to normal with Albert after our weird chitchat the other day. Things had gotten a little strange for a bit—yes, of course because of the chat about circulation and all, which made me try to look a bit more hardworking than usual. (If Albert wanted anything done, I would quickly jump up and say, "Yes, boss!" A few times I even gave him a fake salute. He thought it was being damn toot at first but now he just laughs.)

But also, I guess I was getting a bit distracted by our SPG mission—I mean, for years we'd already been on this quest, though not in any focused way at all. Now that we had spelled things out a little bit and were being more analytical about it, I was really kicking myself for not thinking of this earlier! Although, the way things were going with Roy—it was a good beginning. Who knows how long I would need to be on this mission? I had to keep stopping myself from thinking too much of this though—better don't jinx things! (And besides, Albert had already caught me once or twice this week when I was deep in thought and come over to tap me on the head, saying, "Excuse me, I pay you to sit here and daydream, is it?")

After work that day, Louis was already almost done with his first martini by the time I got to Mezza9—not usually a bar I'd hang out in on a Thursday night. (It's one of those atas hotel bars that boring middle managers and tourists go for happy hours. But the drinks are really cheap during those happy hours and you do get some ang mohs there, so we don't mind going sometimes.) But whatever Louis says always goes—he's buying all the drinks, after all.

"Hello, hello," he said after we finished the double air kiss. "I didn't ask them to unlock my bottles since the happy hour martinis are quite shiok. What you want to drink? Crème brûlée martini? Lychee?"

"Er . . . just a champagne," I said. "Those martinis—all too strong for me." Louis wiggled his index finger at a waitress, who ran over and wrote down his order for a bottle of Veuve.

"Whole bottle?" I said when she left. "Crazy, is it? I'm the only one drinking! How to finish?"

"Aiyah," he said, shrugging. "I'll have a bit. Cannot finish then cannot finish—just give it to the waitress. Who cares? Anyway, Andrew is joining us in a bit. If we have a bottle of anything already open, he'll just drink. The cheapskate doesn't care—as long as he doesn't have to pay."

Louis seemed to be in a good mood—he was even looking over the catalog of cigars on the menu and wondering out loud if we should ask for a table in the smoking room instead. (I was hoping not—this smoking "room" was more like cancer closet. It had a short banquette and two small bar tables but every time I'd been in there, each seat was full and everyone was chain-smoking. If you look through the glass wall from the outside, sometimes all you can see is clouds and clouds puffing around people's heads. Like those old Chinese paintings of the mountains and scenery like that— except the clouds there were probably more healthy.)

"Eh, Louis, I think Andrew doesn't smoke, right?" I said.

"Good point, good point," he said, closing the menu.

Louis picked up his glass again and finished his martini in one long sip. As soon as that happened, a waiter appeared to clear it; our waitress was right behind him with the Veuve.

"So?" I said, as she poured out two glasses. "What's so urgent?"

Louis leaned back in his chair and shook his head. "You heard about what happened with Fann last weekend, right?"

My god—I had known that this meeting was probably about that bullshit crap but part of me had really been hoping that it had blown over.

"Yah," I quickly said. "But don't worry about it! Clubbing is clubbing—all kinds of things can happen. Everyone knows that. Don't worry! Come, come—let's cheers." I smiled and held up my glass. Louis frowned a bit but then grabbed his flute to tap it to mine anyway.

"The thing is," he said after taking a sip and putting his glass down again and running his hands through his hair to flip up his floppy fringe, "I don't want any trouble. I don't want any of that childish secondary school pettiness in our crowd. If I want that kind of shit, I can go home for it. Please, I don't need that outside. I know everything is cool with Fann—it was nothing, after all. She, of all people, should know that. Look at her! But Imo is the one I'm worried about. She was so upset about it! She was texting me angry messages and all; calling me to cry. This kind of thing, Jazzy—it's damn uncool."

"Aiyoh," I said, suddenly feeling very bad. "I didn't know about any of this." I guess I should have known that Imo was more affected by this than she wanted to show—she's quite proud, always thinking about face and appearances. (Whereas Fann, Sher and I always have been a bit more heck care about that. If people want to think something of us—go ahead! Who cares?) I guess because of all that weird shit with her dad having a secret second family—excuse me, with her family being the secret second family—she wants people to think that she has this perfect perfect life, where everything is pretty, everyone is happy. And I also know that even if she doesn't want to admit it, she probably wants to be Louis's girlfriend. Like, the solo girlfriend; no other girls—besides his wife, of course.

But even if we cannot blame Imo for getting upset, this is all too much. Hasn't she listened to anything I've tried to teach her over the years about how to handle men?

"Look," Louis said, "you know I like her. And I want her to be happy. Hell, I like making her happy! I love seeing her smile—you know that. She's a very sweet girl. But she needs to understand her place, OK? I don't want things to get even more awkward. If things get to that level, then what's the point? No fun lah. And I really shouldn't need to be sitting here having to tell you all this.

"Jazzy," he added, "if you want what's best for her—for all of you—please, control your friend."

Louis didn't seem angry or upset as he was saying all this. In fact, his face was very calm—as if he was simply holding a business meeting.

"Come," he said, throwing back the rest of his champagne and grabbing the bottle. "Enough serious talk—boring lah! Andrew just texted that he's parking the car so he'll be here soon. Jazzy, bottoms up! I'll pour another round."

By the time Andrew showed up a few minutes later the Imo topic was long forgotten—by Louis anyway. He had already moved on to planning our chionging this weekend and what new clubs he was hearing about that we might like. I guess now it was just up to me to settle the Imo situation. My god—I hope this wasn't going to be too hard. If Sher was here, she would be the one who would know exactly how to handle it. Bloody hell—why was everything now my responsibility?

"Hallo! Welcome back, old married guy!" Louis said, standing up and loudly whacking Andrew on the back. Andrew just smiled and gave him the third finger.

"Fucker—don't be a chee bye!" Andrew said, lowering his voice. "Please—not so loud. There might be chio girls around—don't spoil the market!" Both of them were laughing damn loud now. So I also laughed.

I didn't know Andrew very well—in fact, tonight was the first time I saw him before 1 A.M. Usually when I see him, he's already fucking mabuk from chugging Kilkennys from happy hour until clubbing hour and then coming out to find Louis wherever he is at midnight. So, even though guniang here has known him a few years already, I never knew what he's like when he's not trying to rubba me, smack my backside while dancing or stop himself from throwing up. But, from what Louis was now saying, I guess he just got married.

"Eh, thank you! You get married never invite me, is it?" I said, whacking him on the arm.

"Aiyoh—Jazzy, I don't invite you is for your own good lah," Andrew said. "Saving you from the red bomb! You should thank me."

It's true lah—weddings these days are all bloody terok. Hotel banquet halls now charge so much, if you get stuck with a wedding invitation—my god, you must give the couple a really big red packet. And these days you can't just anyhow guess. For Sher's wedding, Fann even showed me some website to check to see what the proper market rate for red packets are based on what hotel the banquet is in. If you get invited to a wedding at the Raffles—my god, the red packet can eat up one week's paycheck just like that. And if you somehow give wrongly, you'll get scolded for years. (Or the couple's family and friends will just gossip about you behind your back. I don't know which fate is worse.) And at the end of the day, you confirm will see a few hundred dollars go out just for one boring evening of eating lousy shark's fin soup and cock dishes like Buddha jumping over the moon or some shit. No thank you. The big red bomb is always better to avoid.

"So? How was the honeymoon?" I asked. "Where did you go?"

"This guy—I tell you—just spoiling the market for the rest of us," Louis said. "He cannot go on his honeymoon in normal places you know—must go holiday in bloody romantic, expensive places. Milan lah, Paris lah—London also. Kani nah. Andrew—since Mary heard about your multi-city honeymoon she's been pestering me to take her back to Europe for shopping. Thank you!"

Aiyoh—Andrew was really spoiling his new bride. The funniest thing is—he married a China girl! These girls—the ones that you directly pluck from China, that is, not the ones who hook you here in Singapore—usually don't expect shit! They're just grateful to be brought to Singapore and out of their own longkang of a country. It's usually only after some time in Singapore that they learn the ways and start insisting on the branded handbags and all that crap.

Even so, when Andrew first met his wife we were all damn worried. I don't know what her Chinese name is lah, but many of those toot Chinese girls like to pick some name that they think sounds cute or has some special meaning in English so when this girl came to Singapore, she asked everyone to call her "Moony."

Andrew is quite handsome, you know—fair skin, very tall forehead (which means he's very smart; look at Lee Kuan Yew—very big forehead!) and actually, he's quite smart also. Even though he's only thirty-something, he's already chairman of his dad's furniture import-export company. And their business is all over Asia—Brunei lah, Hong Kong lah, Philippines also got. So, the business is bloody happening. And since the business runs so well on its own, Andrew is damn free to sit down and shake his leg all the time. Even if he hardly goes into office also every month got a big check coming in for him and his mum. His bank account has at least $50 million since he inherited everything when his dad died ten years ago. Even if he sells off the company and doesn't work for the rest of his life, Sher once calculated that the interest from his bank account would be more than enough for him and his mum for the rest of their lives. He could even buy her a Prada handbag every month some more. I tell you—Andrew is the super jackpot.

"Brother—I think maybe you were right lah," Andrew said to Louis. "Maybe Europe as our first big trip together was too much. That girl really knows how to shop! I tried to bring her to all those places I know she'd never been before—Eiffel Tower, the gardens in Versailles, all those damn happening churches in Milan, Big Ben. But all she wanted to do was go shopping. We spent an entire day at Chanel in Paris! The sales manager there served us champagne all day, even catered in a big lunch from this super atas bistro nearby because Moony was taking so long there. I think she bought everything in the Chanel spring collection—some pieces of clothing, we even have two or three, different color versions and all. By the time we got to London I gave up. I had my bank make her her own credit card and just sent her out. I got to spend a lot of time watching football with the blokes in pubs though. Eh, Louis, I should have texted you to fly out for a few days of boys' time with me."

Louis was laughing like mad now. "Serves you right!" he said, pointing both index fingers at Andrew, who just used his hands to make the "fuck you" sign.

I didn't find anything funny though. I couldn't even imagine how much money this China girl had spent in each shop, in each city, on the whole trip. Kani nah. Probably her shopping bill on their whole holiday was the equivalent of what I make in five years! I know Andrew is in a different world lah—being so super rich and all. But Moony was nobody! Before she met him at some bar in Shanghai, she was just a receptionist at some kampong textile company! Who is she to come in and start blowing his inheritance like that the moment she becomes Mrs. Yap?

What is funny though is that when Andrew first started seeing Moony, we were quite surprised because he had never shown an interest in Mainland girls before. His girlfriends before were all Singaporean, all damn chio, all damn funny and fun to go chionging with. But when we met Moony and she was so (fake) demure and quiet, I actually asked him, "Um, this girl—a bit different from your usual type, right?"

I still remember his answer. "Jazzy, when it comes to dating, yes, it's fun to date the happening, damn daring, outgoing girls," Andrew said. "But when it comes to choosing a wife, I want someone who is quiet, who, when I have my friends come over for drinks or to watch a football match, she will just quietly let me be. She won't talk too much or challenge me—she'll let me do the talking. My dad always said that's the recipe for a happy household!"

Now though, it looked as if Andrew was wondering whether he ended up marrying one of those daring girls anyway. I almost laughed.

"I had no choice but to let her shop lah," Andrew said, shrugging. "Shopping was the only time Moony was happy on the honeymoon!

She didn't even like all the restaurants our concierge arranged. In Italy, she insisted on eating only Chinese food after the first few days. She said the Italian food there was terrible. She actually called over the manager of this super atas restaurant in Milan and complained that their way of cooking pasta was not right—too hard. He was very nice and tried to politely explain that the noodles are meant to be nicely al dente, but she kept telling him that if the restaurant charges so much for a plate of pasta they should at least know how to cook it properly. And that if he wants to really learn how it's done, he should check out these Italian restaurants in Shanghai—she even listed some of them for him! I was damn embarrassed. But what to do? Married already!"

As cock as I think his situation is, I can't blame Andrew for being so blind. I knew the kind of girl Moony was from the first time I met her. When he first brought her back from China—at that time on some temporary visa and he was just trying to see if she liked Singapore (not bad) and if his mum liked her (no). Andrew told everyone she was not like most China girls, that Moony, though very pretty and sophisticated-looking, was actually very humble, came from a simple background and wasn't interested in any branded goods or going to nice restaurants. In fact, when he wanted to buy her a Marc Jacobs wallet because her old Flying Horse or some shit brand plastic wallet finally pecah she begged him not to, saying that all she needs is a cheap cheap one from the Chinese Friendship store.

"She even looked at it in the Marc Jacobs window longingly but refused to go in and touch it, you know!" he told us. I remember thinking at the time that this lumpar story makes me want to laugh and vomit at the same time. (Of course when Andrew secretly went and bought the wallet—together with a nice new Marc Jacobs handbag—Moony didn't say no.)

When Andrew finally brought Moony out to meet us, she was

very shy and polite with everybody—even covering her mouth and bending her head down when she laughed. But this was only when she was around the guys and atas girls. Around people like me, Sher, Fann and Imo, she confirm was very heck care about what we think—she never talked to us, never smiled. This kind of attitude is very hard for us Singaporean girls to swallow, you know. Especially coming from a Chinese girl from China. Hallo, doesn't she remember that our ancestors thought China was such a longkang that they risked their lives to jump on boats and sail to Singapore?

"Louis," I remember saying at the time after meeting Moony. "You better tell Andrew to watch out. This girl Moony—I have a bad feeling about her."

Louis just laughed and said. "Oi, don't be jealous, Jazzy—not pretty lah. Andrew's not even your type anyway. Why you bother to care so much?"

Crazy! As if I ever would like Andrew. But see lah, now that Andrew finally married that girl and her true colors came out— who was the one who was right from the beginning? (I thought about whispering something about it to Louis but Andrew looked so stressed I thought, maybe I'd better not.)

I guess the interesting thing to watch is how she plays her strategy from now. Now that she's married—and probably will get her permanent resident card soon—she has two options. If she wants an even bigger fish than Andrew after that (because let's face it, that's how these girls all think—look at Wendi Deng and Rupert Murdoch! Ultimate success story, that one), that's also possible. But if Moony wants to seal her place with Andrew, then she'd better fasterly pop out a baby boy. I know that even though they're now married, Andrew's mum still probably hates her—so this Moony had better have a boy soon. Until then, his mum still has the power.

"Aiyah," Andrew said, gesturing to the waitress to bring another bottle of Veuve out. "Money is just money lah. Doesn't matter in the end."

Louis held up his glass and said, "I'll cheers to that." So we all clinked glasses.

"More importantly," Andrew said, "who is that girl over there? Tight jeans, red blouse, long straight hair, fair skin. Louis, look!"

I wasn't sure where to look but tried to follow Louis's eyes. "Ah," he finally said, after looking around at the banquettes around us and then at the bar. "At the corner of the bar, is it?"

Andrew nodded. "But I can't really tell," he said, "got gap or not?"

That's right. Louis had told me once that Andrew only goes out with girls with a gap between their thighs when they stand up. If there's no gap and the tops of the thighs actually touch each other, the girl is too fat.

Louis had the best view of the girl so he squinted hard, looking looking.

"Got, got!" he said, winking at Andrew. "Go lah, brother—what are you waiting for?"

Andrew waited for the waitress, who just came back, to pour him a full glass, then he smoothed down his hair with his right hand like those guys in Cantopop music videos, grabbed his glass and got up. Louis and I didn't say anything as we watched him casually walk over to the bar and start talking to the girl. I guess he said something funny because she laughed right away, then let him buy her a drink.

"Good for him lah," Louis said, picking up the cigar menu again and flipping through. "After that nightmare honeymoon he deserves a bit of fun."

CHAPTER 12

How to control my friend?

I guess if I think about it, I know I should be angry with Louis. Kani nah—I don't care how much money he has. How can he tell me I have to control one of my best friends? Treating me like one of his servants, is it? But on the other hand, Louis is so good to us, he never cares how much we drink, what we want to drink, always never thinks twice about ordering whatever we want to make us happy at clubs. This—this is really true friendship lah. I should try to listen to him.

I remember one time when my mum saw Louis sending me home in one of his more expensive cars—wah, the old lady got damn excited. Finally—a Chinese boy sending her daughter home! In a nice car some more!

The next morning, before my eyes could even fully open, my mum was by my bed with a small bowl of bird's nest soup. "Ah Huay, come—I got this from the market this morning," she said, cho-cho-ing me to sit up so she could spoon some of it into my mouth. "It's still quite warm—better eat it quickly."

At that moment, I was still so blur that I had forgotten that Louis had sent me home. (It wasn't just me lah—he sent Imo home too. Thank goodness, he's never tried anything funny with me. Awkward!) So I was quite suspicious of my mum and her morning bird's nest soup. (Bird's nest is fucking expensive, you know!) What did she want from me? But since she rarely starts my day without some lecture of some sort, I figured I'd better just enjoy this rare occasion. Long long time then come once—better don't argue. Just sit up and savor!

The soup was actually quite good—not too sweet, not too clumpy. After a few spoonfuls I began to look at my mum a little, wondering why she's just sitting by my bed staring at me eat. Hallo, guniang here how old already? As if my mum is not tired of seeing me stuff food in my mouth after twenty-six years?

"Ma—what?" I asked about halfway through.

"Who's that boy?" she immediately asked, even sitting up straighter. "He seemed nice."

Nice? I don't know how she could tell. I know we don't live on a high floor but could she really have been looking out the window at the exact time in the early early morning when Louis popped out of the car to give me a double kiss and hug goodnight? From the looks of it—and the big smile on her face—I guess so.

"Aiyoh, please!" I said. "This one is married lah! You want me to go and steal other people's husbands, is it?"

My mother's smile vanished. I actually started to feel a bit bad. I know she and I don't wish the same things for my life—but at the end of the day, I do love her.

"Then what are you doing going out with him until odd hours of the night, having him send you home and all?" she asked. "Ah Huay—you are a nice girl, you know. You cannot forget that!"

"Ma—please, don't try and lecture me on things you don't understand," I said, putting the bowl aside now. Guniang here suddenly had no more appetite to eat. "Louis is just a friend—a good friend who likes us girls to come out and hang out with him and his friends, drink drink, dance dance, talk talk, that's all. Good clean fun. And he always buys us drinks some more—so, everyone wins lah!"

"You mean he buys you all drinks? All the time?" my mum said, shaking her head. I nodded.

"What does he do? His family printing money, is it?"

Actually, I wasn't quite sure what Louis or his family did. I just knew that they were massively rich. I think his family is one of the original banking families of Singapore—or something like that. Anyway I just told my mum I had no idea.

"But why does he buy you all drinks? Doesn't he want to save money and bring his wife on a nice holiday?" my mum asked, shaking her head again. I could tell that she was not only confused but also getting quite disgusted with this Louis character.

"Aiyoh—Ma, please don't try and understand all these modern, young people things that you cannot understand," I said. "Louis works hard during the week—on weekends, he just likes to go out to clubs and have a good time with his friends. And when he does, he wants everyone to have a good time and drink and have fun. If you want to have an entourage come out with you wherever you go, I guess that's the price you just pay. It's just like that one. And it's not like money matters that much to him or his family anyway. You compare the fortune god's bank account with Louis's—I can't tell you whose is bigger!"

My mum was damn quiet now—maybe she finally understood lah. Good—the next time Louis is so generous to send me home again I don't want to get another lecture or interrogation.

I watched while my mum quickly got up to pick up the bowl of half-eaten bird's nest off my nightstand. Just before she headed to the door, she paused, however. I saw her thinking for a minute before opening her mouth again.

"Ah Huay, I know you think your ma is old and useless," she said softly. "But I do know some things—and I also know that some things never change. Nothing is for free—and if you think that it is, you're just looking for problems."

She looked at me; I looked at her. Neither of us had anything to say so she just turned around and went back to the kitchen.

Aiyoh—I tell you. Some people no matter how old already will still never learn, I guess. I couldn't think of any other way to explain this whole thing to her more clearly. Waste my saliva only. But who knows—maybe one day she'll see that she really doesn't understand how the world works these days for us modern young women.

Just when I was thinking about all that (while sitting at my office desk, headset on, shuffling papers around, trying to look busy because there was still thirty minutes to kill before lunchtime), the phone rang. Sher's number popped up.

Back from her honeymoon so soon? Cannot be.

Should I answer? My first thought was, Of course not lah!

The last time I talked to Sher—like, really talked to Sher—it was about a week after the proposal. After that cock proposal, I ignored her for a few days, which to us is sort of the equivalent of many months. Since primary school, Sher and I talked at least a few times a day. If we don't talk for one day, it's because we're either on holiday with our parents or really sick, that kind of thing. But then, the more I thought about Ah Huat's proposal, I wondered if maybe I'm approaching this the wrong way—instead of ignoring Sher because I'm so shocked (and feel like vomiting blood), I should be proactive! Maybe try and sit her down and explain why she's throwing her life away if she goes through with this. Sher and I have been so close for so long—surely she will listen to me!

Things went well at first when we met for drinks that time. I'd asked her to meet me at this new tapas bar on Club Street. When we were growing up, Club Street was a bit shady lah—not like Orchard

Towers shady but even so, nice girls really didn't go there. Not even to eat. It's funny because it's so near Chinatown—and that area actually does have some good hawker stalls—but even so, we never dared to spend much time in that area at night because long long time ago it used to be a red-light district filled with Chinese prostitutes. This was during the British times lah—I guess Raffles or one of his coolies decided that all the Chinese guys coming over to work in Singapore need some entertainment so, like that lah. All of a sudden there was a little red-light district around Club Street just for those Chinese guys.

These days though, that whole area is damn happening! Aiyah, Singapore is like that one. The country is so small, the government has to somehow keep coming up with new cool neighborhoods for people to hang out in. If you keep having new bars and restaurants and clubs open up in new little happening hubs then Singaporeans won't get so bored and start thinking maybe it's cooler to live in New York or London or some shit like that, after all. If we have all this here, no need to move anywhere! Singapore really is home sweet home in some ways.

I asked Sher to meet me on a Friday night. Saturday night is also very happening, of course. But Friday night has a different energy lah. No matter what you do in Singapore—or anywhere, too, I guess—let's face it. Most people hate their jobs. Who enjoys going to an office early in the morning and sitting in front of a computer for hours and hours, doing bullshit work for god knows who? But work is no choice lah. Must get paid, after all. So, just slog. That's why by the time Friday rolls around, people have usually been waiting for it for so long, they have so much pent-up energy, you can sometimes see guys just looking like they're about to explode when they walk into a bar and see all the chio girls in front of them. Good formula for success lah, this one.

The bar I picked was a new one so it was packed by the time we got there at 10 P.M.—so packed that it took us forever to reach the bar to order a drink. (On the way some guy even sloshed his beer all over the front of my dress. Ang moh guy—normally I would be quite happy but when I saw his face and how toot it looked and how drunk he was already, I just blinked at him and carried on. Tonight—I had a mission!)

Sher had somehow managed to score a small table by the time I got us vodka Ribenas from the bar. She always had a knack for stuff like that—really pretty girls really do have a leg up in life sometimes. (Especially pretty girls who don't think or act like they're pretty.)

I set the glasses down on top of the already soggy napkins at their bases and slid into the narrow cushioned booth next to Sher. The bar was so loud we had to really huddle together so we could talk without shouting. I always liked feeling Sher so close—somehow it always reminded me of when we were kids, how freely we would just put our arms around each other or fall asleep on each other's shoulders on the school bus. I mean, I know that we still care a lot about each other—despite this toot Ah Huat business—but somehow, it's sad, but when you get older you just automatically get less affectionate with your girlfriends. I remember one time I was hanging out with Sher after school watching the guys at rugby practice. It wasn't too hot a day so the scratchy concrete step wasn't burning my backside like it usually does. At the time Sher had a small crush on one of the ruggers so we used to just go and sit there, sometimes pretending to do homework or read—ha! As if—while watching them practice. It was such a comfortable day, everything was fairly quiet off the field, and I guess I was feeling a little happy, which made me feel sleepy. So I just put my head on Sher's shoulder; I felt her put her right arm around me and squeeze my shoulder as I started drifting off. I was just about to really fall asleep when I heard some Ah Bengs shuffling by—you can usually hear them from a distance, all their lan jiao talk here and kani nah there.

As they got closer though, they started shouting at us! "Eh, eh, eh!" one of them said, pointing pointing and all. I could hear some of the others laughing. Then another said, "Wah—lesbo is it?" And then more laughter! Kani nah. I mean, who cares what Ah Bengs think? But anyway, I sat up straight and Sher took her arm away. "Just heck care them lah," Sher whispered. I nodded. (But still, I turned around and gave them my finger.)

"Come, come—cheers," I said, picking up my glass and clinking it with Sher's. She smiled at me, relieved, I think, that I seemed to be in a good mood and wasn't starting our evening by hantaming her for agreeing to marry Ah Huat. We sipped our drinks slowly, both not feeling eager to have to get up and get another round in that scrum again.

Side by side, we looked out at the crush of people for a few minutes, not saying a word. "So . . ." we both started to say at the same time, before laughing, also at the same time.

"You go first lah," Sher said, turning to look at me.

I took a long look at her and wondered where I could possibly start. There was too much to say. "Why?" I simply asked.

Sher didn't look surprised. From the way she took a small breath and immediately started speaking, I could tell she had rehearsed what was coming out. "Jazz, I know you don't understand, but try to see things from my eyes—"

I cut her off. "You're right—I don't understand!" I said. I could see her slumping down a little and looking at me, a bit worried. I could tell this was what she'd been expecting since she walked into the bar. "Sher, all I've ever done is see things from your eyes. We have the same eyes! Don't you think I've always just wanted the best life ahead for the two of us? Have you thought—really thought—of what your life with Ah Huat is going to be like? What being an Ah Beng's wife is like? This kind of life—where got future? You're going to find yourself living in some lousy government housing building in some dark flat where you're chained to the kitchen making soup for your Ah Beng babies and no one is going to care about you. What about all our plans and dreams of living overseas one day, having beautiful Chanel babies? We are so close! Why give up now?"

Sher sighed and looked away from me, staring at the guys hovering by the bar. I could feel Sher slipping away. And I felt a dull pain forming in my chest. The thought of not having her in my life, answering my texts, holding my hair back—all of that, it was just too much. We had been through so, so much. Could she really be choosing Ah Huat over me? Over us? Over our future lives together?

"Sher," I said, really looking at her now, trying to get her to stop staring at the fuckers in front of us and just look back at me. I was almost begging now, from the tone of my voice. "You are so pretty— you still have so much potential! Please, tolong, don't throw it all away."

Sher looked hard at me, sighed, then took a large sip before slowly setting the glass down and looking out again at the crowd. She was quiet for what seemed like a long time—though it probably was only actually a minute or two. I looked out at the crowd, too, trying to figure out what she was seeing. I was so busy scanning her field of vision I almost didn't hear her voice.

"I'm tired," Sher said, so quietly.

"Tired?" I asked, a bit disbelieving. "Of what?"

"Of this, Jazzy—this! All this," Sher suddenly said quite loudly, waving her hand at the scrum all around us. "Aren't you? We've been doing this for how many donkey's years already—since we were sixteen! That's ten long years, almost half our lives! You still not tired?"

I looked at the people around us. The setting didn't seem any different from any of the bars and clubs we always went to on weekends. Singaporean girls, some Singaporean guys, lots of ang mohs— what was Sher's problem? What did she expect? What did she want beyond all this? Life in Singapore is just like that, after all—if you want to meet anyone good, you just have to do the bar scene. I don't care how tired you are, you still must just go out there and chong. Otherwise—do what? Stay at home and look at your mum; your mum look at you, is it?

"Of course I am tired sometimes," I said. "Of course I wish I was married already. But things that are worth it never come easily, hallo. We have to keep trying, Sher. Please? I mean, I get that OK, maybe ang mohs in the end may not be for you—but an Ah Beng? Come on, there are so many better Singaporean-Chinese guys out there than that. You can do so much better. If you told me you want to be Louis's secret mistress, even I would support that more than this. You marrying Ah Huat—it's just so wasted! As your best friend, I can't just stand by and watch you do this to yourself."

Sher turned away from me and was silent again. I tried to imagine what she was thinking at that moment. Usually, Sher and I were *xin lin xiang tong*—hearts and minds perfectly aligned. But now— now, after all the words that I had just heard out of her mouth, I couldn't even imagine what she might be thinking. Something had shifted.

"You know," Sher finally said, "when I told my mum Ah Huat proposed, do you know how happy she was? I've never seen my mum so happy, Jazz. You know our parents—they have so little to get happy about. But my mum, she was really really happy. All these guys we've dated all these years, I never even once thought about bringing them back to meet my mum because—what could they possibly talk about? An ang moh guy in my parents' little flat? They can't even speak the same language! But Ah Huat—he's a good guy and he treats my mum well, always bringing her things to eat and renting her favorite Cantonese shows to bring to her. He's going to be good to her. And I think he's going to be good to me. And our children."

By this point, Sher was just talking a lot because, to be honest, guniang over here was speechless. When I asked Sher to come out tonight, I still didn't think that my mission was such a gone case. But I was starting to understand that I was very wrong.

"Jazz," Sher continued, "when I told my mum, she even turned off the TV and took my hand and dragged me to her bedroom. She knelt down on her floor—not even complaining and you know how her knees have really been hurting recently—and pulled out this small wooden box from under her bed. Once we were sitting on her bed, she opened it and started pulling the few things in there out for me to see. Not much lah—a thin jade bangle, a pair of small pearl earrings, three bright yellow-gold bracelets. One of them was quite fat actually—it was made of these mah-jongg tile–like charms that had "double happiness" all over them. My mum put each of the bracelets on my wrists, one by one, and held up the earrings by my face.

"It was her wedding jewelry, Jazz. She had just been waiting all these years to give it to me. 'All grown up now,' she told me. 'Finally, my mind can rest.'"

I really didn't know what to say. Invoking Auntie in her defense? This one is one damn power move. How could I possibly say anything bad about what Auntie might want? (Especially Sher's mum, who was the sweetest to us of all our mums.)

"Sher, please, at least just think about it a bit before planning anything real . . ." I started to say.

"We've booked the banquet hall," she said, looking a bit sheepish. "Deposit put down already."

I thought for a moment. They had paid the deposit. So I guess like that, everything was over already. Even worse—kani nah, even if I hated the fact that this wedding was happening I still had to deal with the bloody red bomb.

I looked straight ahead, picked up my glass and slowly finished my vodka Ribena. (Heartbreak or not—drinks still better don't waste.) "Sher, I'm going outside for some air, OK?" I said. She looked at me like she knew not to believe me. I quickly picked up my handbag and shoved my way back outside.

Standing outside on the patio outside the bar, looking at narrow, crooked Club Street, lined with concrete prewar shophouses, the road itself filled with a thick, bobbing river of SPGs and ang moh guys, some draped over each another, staggering together.

When I left Sher, I had every intention of going back into the bar after I'd had a moment to myself. (I think.) But at that moment I was just too tired for any more of that bullshit. I remember taking my phone out and typing: "Sher, not feeling well—I make a move first. Talk to you tomorrow."

The next time I would see her was at her wedding.

That day, however, Sher, in fact, was not only on my mind—she was actually in my office, in a way. My office phone just wouldn't stop ringing! Four times already I'd let it ring until the bitter end. And still, Sher would call back.

Finally, after the fourth time—I was really staring at the phone by now—there was silence. I felt relieved at first. Then, a bit sad. I missed Sher. Even after all these months it still felt strange not to hear her voice every day. (Not that I would ever tell her, of course.) No matter how much I tried not to think about her whenever I saw Fann or Imo—or whenever anything big happened, like meeting Roy or that bitch Sharon—Sher was always on my mind, the first person I wanted to share my stories with.

Suddenly, the ringing stopped. Then, a beep. I checked my handphone: "Jazz," a text said, "Just back from Batam. Dropped in to see if you're free for lunch. Brought back some of your favorite squid crackers. Should I just leave them at the front desk?"

I hit DELETE.

CHAPTER 13

The thing about clubbing is, if you don't have some rich (or stupid) guy buying you drinks the whole night, your life is really quite pathetic.

So I knew this problem with Louis and Imo better be solved ASAP. How? My head was starting to hurt. OK lah—no choice. Just call for another girls' meeting after work at Ice Cold Beer and see how to bring it up. This bar was a good choice—mellow mellow type, plus, it was in the middle of a quite touristy area so there would definitely be ang mohs there. So even if Imo and Fann wanted to shout and whack each other in the face, I knew they wouldn't dare to do it in front of potential ang moh boyfriends. Face is face lah. The expat community is so small—if you lose your temper once in public, everyone will talk.

I asked Fann to get there early so we could chitchat before Imo came—besides, this being Friday night it might be nice to be out and about early anyway, check out the scenery and all.

"Fann, listen—I want you to apologize to Imo . . ." I said, holding up my hand to Fann's face before she started trying to interrupt, telling me that kani nah she'd already apologized to Imo how many times already, why is it her fault when Louis was the one who started it and all?

"Look, I don't care how many times you texted or called her—you haven't done it face-to-face," I said, pinching her nose to get her to stop talking. This move always embarrasses her, but since secondary school, it's always been the most effective method.

"Just do it OK?" I continued, now that she was silent. "And you'd better make it sound bloody sincere, like you are practically on your knees, begging for her forgiveness. Don't actually get on your knees, of course. But just make it sound like it, OK? Otherwise, I tell you, this sisterhood may be over already. We've already lost Sher—if we lose Imo, then how? Just you and me going chionging together? Boring lah! If Imo leaves, we are over. So please—just swallow your pride and say you're sorry. The real kind of sorry."

I only let go of her nose after I was done talking. Fann started being damn drama and all, rubbing her nose and breathing hard, staring at me.

"Understood?" I said. Fann nodded, then took her Chanel compact out of her handbag to quickly touch up her nose before anyone else could see.

Now that that was settled, we could focus on more important things—ordering drinks! I waved at the waitress and ordered three vodka green teas. Good choice—the green tea has caffeine. (I think?) Maybe it would help me energy a bit—we had a long night ahead of us. Fann said she had something special planned later on!

Imo showed up just after our conversation ended, walking past Fann's chair, her face like stone. Of course she didn't say "Hi" or acknowledge Fann in any way; she just came over to give me a hug, then sat down next to me.

I looked over at Fann, she looked away, picking up her phone to see if she had gotten any new texts. Bloody hell.

"Fann," I said, "weren't you just telling me something right before Imo came?"

Idiot didn't look up from her phone.

"Oi!" I said. "Fann?"

Finally, Fann put her phone down and looked at Imo. "I'm really sorry, Imo."

I kept staring at Fann.

So she continued. "Look, I don't know what really happened—I was so drunk! You know how sometimes when you are too high you make bloody lousy decisions? That's all it was, Imo—I made a mistake. A really big one. Please, Imo, I don't know how many times I can say sorry. But I know that in your heart, you must treasure our friendship right? We've been friends—no, sisters—for how long already? Please?"

Imo, we all know, is bloody softhearted. She cannot stay angry at anybody for long—especially people she cares about. We've seen this how many times with Louis already! No matter what he does, no matter who he sends home, no matter who he snogs right in front of her on the dance floor, in the end, she always forgives him. (Or, looks the other way, I suppose. I don't get the sense that these things can really be forgiven—but that's just me.) No matter what, Imo just wants everything to be OK. That's her most important thing: appearances.

"OK," Imo quietly said. "But," she added, her voice sounding a bit fierce, "*never* again, OK?"

Fann offered her small finger and Imo hooked it with hers and said, "Set."

"OK, come, come, come, drinks are here!" I said, raising my glass so we could all cheers.

"So," I said, after we all had taken a few sips, "what's the report, girls? Any action since last weekend?" Imo looked embarrassed.

"Aiyoh, my god," I said. "Don't tell me you've been spending this whole time moping about this stupid thing?"

When Imo didn't say anything, I was about to scold her for not being serious. But then I thought, It's OK, she's been through a lot. Some more, I think maybe her mission was becoming a little different than ours. Maybe life is just like that—a mistress's daughter perhaps is always destined to be a mistress also? Maybe it's point-less to fight it. Sad lah, but if she wants to throw herself away, we also cannot say anything. Bang balls only.

If this is the path she's chosen though, I wondered if I should say something.

"Imo, you know Louis cares a lot about you," I said, reaching over to squeeze her hand. Imo smiled, blushing a little. "The thing is, guys like that—I hate to say it, but you must know your place some-times. The only people really allowed to throw tantrums with them are their wives. One dragon lady at home is more than enough. If number two is also a dragon lady, I tell you, she won't be shooting her fire around him for very long."

Imo looked a bit sheepish at this point. As much as she didn't want to openly admit it—or her relationship with Louis, I guess—she understood perfectly clearly what I was talking about. I didn't want to embarrass her anymore so I quickly changed the subject.

"Fann? You leh?" I asked.

Fann smiled and said, "Guniang here had a hot date—don't play play! Remember Melvin the Australian?" she said.

I didn't, but who cares? Australians are confirm OK. So I nodded.

"Sher was right when she told me last month to just ignore his texts—he started calling and texting, even dropping by my pet store, pretending he just 'happened to be in the neighborhood!'" Fann said, smiling.

Aiseh! This one is quite win.

"So yesterday, I finally agreed to let him take me out for dinner," she went on. "Very nice restaurant some more—you know that new happening Spanish place on Keong Saik Road? The guy cooked for that big chef in London or something?"

I tell you, I don't know why she's trying to tell us these kinds of stupid details. Who cares? Food is food. Unless it's super good chicken rice or barbecue stingray then I really don't give a flying shit.

"Hallo—guniang," I said, "please, fast-forward all that Food Network crap and get to the important part."

"OK, OK," she said, blinking her eyes one time at me before carrying on.

"It was nice—a real date! He didn't even bring up the fact that we had hooked up a few times when we were drunk. He was very gentlemanly and sweet. And I realized it was actually nice to talk to him."

Fann looked so happy, I guess I should be happy too. Now I remember who this guy was. And if he's the one I think he was—hallo, her hookup history simply had too many Australians—then he's quite good-looking!

"Well anyway," Fann continued, "Melvin promised us a power night tonight!"

Apparently, the Australian has a friend who just opened a bar near Boat Quay. Since it's not been open for that long, right now it's just his ang moh friends and their friends who know about it. But everyone was supposed to spread the word to come out for a big opening party that night. Ang mohs and their ang moh friends? Set lah! Plus, since Melvin knows the owner—hello, free drinks! So this was what it was. I had been wondering all day what on earth was happening.

"Wear a skirt—and nice panties," Fann had texted to me and Imo earlier in the day. When I texted back, "Why?" Fann didn't respond. The whole day I kept wondering what Fann could possibly have planned—all the possibilities made me laugh. Albert even asked me at some point, "Jazzy—why you smiling so much today? Good sex last night, is it?"

"Aiyoh, boss, no lah," I just said. "If it's not with you, how can the sex be good?"

This actually made Albert stop walking. Then we both laughed until I had to fetch some water since he started coughing. (Can't have him dying on my shift, man—I'll be jinxed for life! No one will ever hire me again as an executive assistant.)

Laughing aside, I was glad things were back to normal with Albert—he hadn't mentioned our conversation again that week and I didn't ask him anything. After the four o'clock meeting, he even stopped by my desk and rubba-ed my neck a bit. Just like old times.

That night, after settling up at Ice Cold Beer, Fann instructed us all to powder our noses, touch up lipstick and wash all the chicken wing grease off our fingers. Good that we were all together, Fann said. Better to walk in all together—more impact; three super chio girls coming in at same time is better than one. I was getting quite excited about tonight lah. Even though my date with Roy went well, guniang must keep options open! I was still not quite sure if the oil refinery thing was for me. Plus, you never know when you're going to find someone better. Must always have an open mind.

So I had worn this short flared black skirt—imitation Gucci from a few years ago! Don't play play, I tell you. (At that time when this Gucci skirt was fashion, I even saw Anne Hathaway wear one in a magazine photo.) And on top I had this stretchy red blouse with a V-neck. Guniang here doesn't have much tetek, so must add push-up bra.

Once we neared the bar, Fann got serious and looked closely at me, from my fluffy blow-dried hair to my red top and small skirt to my skinny black heels.

"Can," she said, nodding and then pointing at Imo. "This one here—never listen. Look at her!"

Imo looked chio as always but she was wearing pants! Baggy baggy harem pants, some more.

"Aiyoh—you think this bar is what? Magic bottle is it?" I said.

"Shut up lah," Imo answered. "I had no time to go home and change after work today. And hello, these pants this season are very fashion, you know!"

Please, I don't care how fashion they are—any pants that make my backside look like I need a giant diaper is confirm not sexy. I'll stick to my few-seasons-old pretend-Gucci skirt, thank you very much.

Fann was patting some powder on her nose to get ready then she said, "Come, let's go." She didn't tell us that much about the bar but from what she did say I gathered that the bar sounded quite mellow, one of those hangout places for low-key ang mohs. I know this is Friday night and we should be out chionging the clubs somewhere—Louis certainly had tried to get us to go out with him but Fann put her foot down. But sometimes I guess a change of scene may not be bad. Plus, the name was promising—Carlyle's. Quite atas sounding, right?

When we got close to the bar though, we could tell right away that it was anything but mellow. The scene was just like Studemeyer's or Attica—there was even a queue outside! And through the glass windows, we could see that the bar was damn packed—people's dancing bodies were pressing against the glass and all. What was happening? It was only 10 P.M. At this point—the night technically hadn't even really started yet!

Luckily, Melvin was standing outside waiting for us. Not bad—score points already. His smile got huge when he saw Fann and he quickly started walking toward us to give her a big hug. She just laughed and gave him her cheek to kiss. Good strategy. (I started thinking maybe last night at the end, I shouldn't have kissed Roy so hot and heavy. Today, the bugger didn't text me!)

"Hi, I'm Melvin," he said, shaking my hand and then Imo's.

"Imogen," Imo said, smiling. "But everyone calls me Imo."

"And I'm Jazeline—but you can call me Jazzy," I said. Fann gave me a long stare. My god—don't tell me guniang thinks I'm flirting with her boy. (Plus, hallo—she is one to talk! Who is the one who cannot be trusted around guys we've already reserved?)

"I'm afraid that it's a little more crowded than usual," Melvin said, pointing at the long line. "*Time Out Singapore* just wrote about this place so I guess the masses have come to check it out. I mean, it's good for my friend Steve but . . . well, anyway, let's check it out. It's a fun place and I promise you'll get good drinks. Steve's said he'll take care of us."

Melvin put his arm around Fann's waist and led her to the door. The bouncer, I guess, knew Melvin because they high-fived each other before the guy unhooked the velvet rope and let us all in. Just before we entered, I looked back at the long line. I could tell many of the girls in line were SPGs and some were now glaring at us. Aiyoh, so petty. If they are not in the in crowd then they're just not in lah. Why should they be jealous? Wasting energy.

Katy Perry was blasting through the whole bar when we got inside. The place itself was quite small but along one long wall there was big bar with a wide wooden counter. On the ceiling, all along the bar, there was a thick railing, almost like those old handrails on public buses, but this one was shiny and gold-plated. Quite interesting, I suppose.

The crowd was damn thick—everyone was moving, dancing a bit to the music and just clogging the whole area. I also didn't know where to go. Melvin was leading Fann somewhere though—toward the back, near the end of the long bar. Fann reached back to hold my hand so I reached back to hold Imo's hand. By the time we got to the end of the bar, guniang here already had beer spilled on me three times. Kani nah. But at least the table that we were given was a bit more quiet. And it was right next to the bar, so we could see all the action. I guess Melvin's friend had already prepped the table—there was a big ice bucket, a tower of glasses, carafes of orange juice and soda. Nice!

After we sat down, Melvin started shouting across the table. But I couldn't hear a thing—it was so fucking loud. Fann whispered in his ear and he went off toward the bar—I guess, to order our drinks.

"Oi, Fann," I said. "You sure we want to stay here? This bar is practically a rugby field—except there are scrums everywhere and guys don't care if you're a guniang or a guy, everyone's just pushing. How is this fun? Should we see if Louis has his usual table at Studemeyer's?"

"We have to stay, Jazz—Melvin will be upset," Fann said. "Just stay for a while lah—he says it will get more fun. And excuse me, how many times have I followed you all over Singapore to this bar or that club, no questions asked, just because you want to maybe see someone there?"

Right then, Melvin came back with a tray of Sex on the Beach shots—the tray was so big there were about thirty-plus shots there!

"I think each one of us gets about eight!" he shouted, setting down the tray and grabbing two shots. "Bottoms up!"

So we followed him—each person grabbed two glasses, clinked them and then whacked both shots, one after the other. The shots were not strong at all—more sweet and fruity than strong. My god, all this sugar—make us fat only. I made a mental note to make sure to vomit extra hard later. But for now, aiyah—just drink lah.

We quickly did a bottoms up a few more times until all the shots gone. A waitress appeared to clear the table, disappeared and then came back holding an unopened bottle of Grey Goose and a bottle of Jack Daniel's. Grey Goose is not bad. And Jack Daniel's is not as expensive as Chivas—but hey, if it's free, we anything also will whack.

Fann was right—it was getting to be more fun already. Imo reached over and started to put some ice in a glass but Melvin stopped her. "Allow me!" he shouted.

Wah, this one is quite not bad! (I quietly gave Fann a thumbs-up sign.)

Melvin mixed four vodka sodas then passed them around. We quickly did one bottoms up so we could quickly get a bit high, since those shots really didn't do anything except make us feel like peeing. I tell you—those Sex on the Beach shots probably were mostly food coloring and fruit juice. None of us were feeling even a bit buzzed. But I could see that Melvin was trying to make up for them—his vodka sodas were damn power! After just the first bottoms up, my eyes couldn't focus for a few seconds.

After that, we slowed down a bit—Melvin mixed another round of vodka sodas for us to sip and passed the glasses back to us. Not really thinking about it, I took a short red cocktail straw and knotted it twice, popping it into my glass. This way, I could differentiate my glass from all of theirs, otherwise bloody hell, all the drinks look the same, and all of us just end up sharing saliva. Seeing the straw made me feel a bit bad. Seng was the one who taught me that strategy years ago when we were teenagers and first started going to clubs—he always made one knot on his straw so I made two. Usually, especially later and later in the night, when it was just the two of us left, we could really tell whose drink was whose. I always pitied all the others around us—just passing germs to each other by accidentally sharing drinks.

That afternoon, Seng had texted a few times, asking me to come out with him and his friends tonight. They were going to some cock club in near Marina. Just seeing the name, I knew that this club confirm is one of those places where no ang mohs go—guniang here had never heard of it before! Plus, none of the ang mohs I know had ever mentioned it before. Jazzy? Go to this kind of club? Waste time only.

"Eh, don't be so proud lah," Seng finally texted. "Why no give me face? Trying to make me beg you to come out with me tonight, is it? Uncle here getting too old to kneel lah."

I didn't bother to respond.

Imo was starting to look a bit bored—her eyes were glued to her phone, which she put on the table so she could keep an eye on it even when we were all chitchatting. But it didn't vibrate even once. Fann was sitting very close to Melvin, who was rubba-ing her arm and kissing her cheek now and then. And her top—bloody good choice—had a low cowl neck, so if you were taller than her (which Melvin definitely was), all you had to do was look down a bit only to see everything. (And Fann of course didn't wear bra. Good girl!) This, Melvin had obviously figured out already because he kept looking down, while Fann just purposely moved around now and then, letting her shirt fall even farther down occasionally before giggling, covering her mouth and pulling it back up. Walao. I was so touched I almost shed a tear—the student was becoming the master.

Melvin—confirm blue balls, man. I could see the look on his face—he looked like he was sweating a bit, clearly getting more and more desperate. Plus Fann told me today she was definitely not going to let him pok her again until she officially became his girlfriend. Good lah—even if Imo is a gone case and I'm not so successful yet, if Fann manages to hook him, then at least we have a 33 percent success rate. We would have something to show.

Who knew that of the three of us, the least chio one is the one who win first? Aiyoh—sometimes life is like that. You just cannot predict. Even though of course I am happy for Fann, I started to feel a bit sad for myself. I don't understand why I can't just find a nice cute cute ang moh guy with a good job (like, not at an oil refinery) who wants me—for more than just one or two fun nights. Yah, I know—I'm not as pretty as Sher, my backside is not as nice as Fann's and my clothes are not as atas as Imo's, but I'm also not bad, I think. I'm such a nice girl—why doesn't anybody just want that?

The music suddenly started to get a bit louder—some Lady Gaga shit or something and people all over the bar were going crazy. Melvin opened the bottle of Jack Daniel's and made four whiskey sodas. I was about to lean over and thank him when he pointed toward the bar, asking me to turn around. "Watch," he said to all of us. "This is the fun part."

Everyone was watching the bartenders now—these three buff Eurasian-looking young guys with short cropped hair who looked just like American sailors during Fleet Week. The guys were doing that *Cocktail* act—throwing bottles around and shaking and mixing. After they finished, they shouted together: "Kamikaze!"

The one in the middle looked around the bar, at all the tables—then pointed at me. "You—come up, lady!" I didn't know what was going on so I was a bit scared. I just started waving my hands "No" and shaking my head but the crowd all around me started clapping and shouting all together, "Why are we waiting? Why are we waiting?" I felt someone pinch my arm damn bloody hard—kani nah! So I turned around.

"Just hurry up and go!" Fann said. "Don't be so embarrassing!"

Since it was her night, her bar, her boyfriend, I felt like I had no choice. When I stood up, the whole bar started cheering damn loudly. Guniang here was feeling a bit dizzy from the drinks so far. And once I got near the bar, these few guys standing in front of the bar grabbed me—aiyoh! I had no idea what was going on so I struggled a bit. But these tall ang moh guys—they were all too strong! They lifted me onto the bar and left me lying down. Of course I immediately tried to get up but the bartenders were holding me down—one holding my ankles, the other pressing down my shoulders. The middle guy just said, "Don't worry—this is just a bit of good clean fun," and winked at me. Good clean fun? Guniang here was feeling so blur and getting damn bloody scared—how can this be good clean fun?

But I didn't want to embarrass Fann or Melvin, so I just smiled back at the bartender. Whatever happens, it couldn't be so bad right? After all, this is a public bar. And even if it gets bad I'm sure Fann and Imo will try and save me. (As long as one isn't too busy snogging her ang moh while the other is too busy staring at her nonvibrating phone, that is.)

So I tried to relax a bit. The bartenders were shaking their shakers once again and threw them up in the air a few times before shouting all together: "Body shot!"

Oh, just a body shot? Why didn't the bartender just say so earlier? If he had, I wouldn't have been so worried. Cheh! A body shot is nothing. Guniang here has done it many times before—one time, it was even Fann who was the one who licked a Lemon Drop out of my navel! Don't play play!

"Who's up?" the middle one said. Immediately, there was a scrum in front of the bar.

"Wait! Wait!" the bartender said. "Men—don't fight. The lady gets to choose."

OK, this was looking promising. Who knew? Maybe I would meet a boyfriend out of this? I smiled, thinking about how we would have to explain this to our grandkids. "So your ah-ma here was spread out on the bar and a kamikaze shot was poured all over her . . ." Aiyah— good, let them know that their grandparents were happening once.

I looked around at the guys in front of the bar, all fighting one another to get close to me. (I have to admit that guniang over here did feel quite shiok about this. All this attention? As if I'm a super-model or some shit.)

Who to pick? There was a range of guys—cute cute ones but also got damn ugly chee bye face ones. Among them, one of them look a bit familiar—ang moh, a bit older, around forty maybe, with a bit of longish shaggy gray hair, not bad-looking lah but from his big eye bags and saggy skin, he didn't look so healthy. I was trying to think of how I knew him—not very possible that I actually did, I was thinking, since the ang mohs I actually bother to talk to at clubs are never that old. So I stared a bit longer, squinting squinting and all. The guy noticed me staring at him and my god, he started pushing his way up to the front saying, "I think the lady has chosen!" Once he got to the front, he turned around to face the crowd behind him and pumped both fists into the air.

Aiyoh, who does he think he is? Champion boxer, is it? But even if I didn't actually choose him, this situation was habis—everybody started cheering right then, so it was all confirmed. Bloody hell.

When the guy turned back around, I realized how I know him—I had seen a phone-full of pictures of him just a few days before. It was Sharon's husband!

I could feel the two bartenders at the ends holding my shoulders and ankles down again. The middle bartender pulled up my red blouse until it reached almost the bottom of my push-up bra. Walao—Sharon's husband's eyes got damn bloody big. I was not very happy but I really didn't want to spoil the moment or embarrass Fann and Melvin so I just smiled at him.

"Hey, lovebirds—stop making eyes at each other," the middle bartender shouted. "There's time for plenty of that—and much more—later!" The crowd started clapping and cheering again.

"Ready?" the bartender asked.

Sharon's husband nodded and bent down a bit. The moment the bartender started pouring his shaker all over my stomach, Sharon's husband was suddenly super action! I could feel his fat tongue all over my stomach, fasterly licking and licking, his head was frantically bobbing up and down, from side to side, trying to catch all the liquid before it rolled off. To get a firmer grip the fucker at some point even grabbed the waistband of my skirt—I could feel him pulling it down a bit so his tongue could get some of the shot that was dripping down there. I tried to move a bit, to try and signal him to stop being so lecherous but all this did was make the two bartenders hold my ankles and arms down even more firmly. There was so much noise, so much movement, that no one seemed to notice any of this.

It was never-ending. How much more liquid could there be in that shaker? How many shots were there?

"And that's the last drop!" the bartender suddenly announced, pouring the last few splashes of it onto my stomach. Thank goodness. Sharon's husband was still licking though.

"Hey there, fella—enough already!" the bartender said. "There's a Hotel 81 near here—just get a room!" The crowd erupted in cheers and laughter again.

Even Sharon's husband knew that it was finally time to stop lah—even though I could tell that the fucker was damn reluctant. He gave my stomach a few final slow licks, then dug his tongue into my navel before kissing it. As he stood back up, he pumped his fists into the air again. Everyone cheered.

Guniang was feeling a bit shocked. Luckily one of the bartenders was nice enough to pull my blouse back down for me—and thankfully, in a decent way, too. I appreciated that he didn't try and touch my tetek or anything.

"I think you . . . what's your name?" he said, helping me sit up on the bar.

"Jazzy," I said.

"Jazzy—what a musical name!" he said. "Jazzy—I think you deserve some kamikazes of your own. Boys, don't you think?"

The crowd started cheering, so he poured me two shots and said, "Carry on!"

After the bad feeling of the body shot, I could still feel Sharon's husband's tongue on my skin—guniang here really did feel like she needed to get fucking high. So I grabbed both shots, raised them to the crowd and drained each one.

My god—these shots were definitely not like the Sex on the Beach shots. Each one was bloody strong! But good—I was immediately high!

The music—which I guess had been turned down a bit during the Jazzy Body Shot time—suddenly blasted back on. This time, it was another Katy Perry song—"Firework" or some shit—and everyone started dancing like mad again. Two skinny Singaporean girls in minidresses and heels started climbing onto the bar, one on each side of me. My goodness me—I was feeling quite blur at this point so I didn't really know what to do lah. But then the girls grabbed my arms and helped me up so I suddenly found myself standing on the bar. I wanted to immediately climb back down but when I glanced over at our table, Imo and Melvin were clapping along to the beats and Fann gave me two thumbs up. So, no choice.

I was feeling slightly like an auntie at this point, looking at these young girls in high heels, wondering how come they're so daring, not afraid of falling off the fucking bar. (Then I caught myself realizing that that's exactly something that my mum would say.) I was damn worried about falling myself, given how tipsy I was feeling. Then I saw the girls each using one hand to hold the gold railing on the ceiling for support, so I followed.

The shots were starting to make me feel good—and being that high above everyone else made me feel like I was floating. I knew the guys below me could probably see my lacy red panties every time I shook my backside and moved my legs but I didn't care. Some of them were cute after all—as Albert sometimes liked to say, "Any publicity is good publicity."

Looking out at the crowd—guys were staring at me, confirm quite interested, and a few ang moh women were giving me dagger eyes. Good! I purposely shook my backside at them a bit more. I felt good—perhaps even like a celebrity. In between songs, the bartender kept giving us shots, too—each one wasn't that strong but they did make me feel more wild. I was really dancing like madwoman now, sometimes use my free hand to push up my boobs and all. The guys—I could tell from their eyes. They were all damn steam.

After a few songs, guniang's feet were hurting so I squatted down. Before I could try and figure out how to climb off, three guys rushed forward to help me get off the bar counter! I'd never felt so special, man. Good to have this feeling, especially after this cock week and last weekend. I guess I should thank Fann and Melvin.

I was adjusting my skirt, getting ready to walk back to the table when a short ang moh guy with a paunch and messy gray beard tapped me on the shoulder. My god—of all the handsome guys at the bar, this one is the one who wants to chase me? Why is my life so unfortunate?

I blinked at him and started to walk away but he said, "Jazzy? I'm Steve—Steve Carlyle, Melvin's friend." Oh—bar owner! Of course I should be nice to him. So I turned around and smiled.

"You were terrific up there! Really lit up the room," Steve said, shaking my hand. "Do you want to be one of my regular bar-top girls? I can't pay you—not like Galaxy or one of those bigger flashier clubs. But I will give you free bottles. And you and your friends never have to queue up; you'll always have a table."

Wah—guniang here has been going clubbing for so long but I'd never been asked to be podium girl before! I'd always thought this kind of podium-girl arrangement is a bit LC. It's true that podium girls at bars and clubs are just regular girls, not pros, who are just good at dancing and look quite cute but still—hallo, how much different is this arrangement, at the end of the day, from KTV hostesses entertaining guys by throwing around their body? And those girls get paid more! With LV handbags on the side if they are really smart about their strategies! Although I'd always thought that—that was based on having never actually tried it. In the end, after dancing up on the bar with those girls at Carlyle's, the whole thing actually was quite fun lah. Plus, I didn't want to be rude to Melvin's friend.

"I'll think about it," I said, making sure to smile at him really sweetly before walking away.

"By the way," I quickly added, winking at him, "could we have some Chivas at our table?"

By the time I got back to the table and sat down, I could see the waitress walking over with a bottle of Chivas from the bar.

"Eh—where did Imo go?" I asked, looking at her empty seat. Her phone wasn't on the table either.

Fann just shrugged—that woman was a bit mabuk, I could tell. Her eyes were half-closed; her body swaying a bit. The bottle of Jack was almost empty, surrounded by a few small glasses—I guess they had been doing shots. When the waitress showed up with the bottle of Chivas and opened it, sticking a spout in, Fann suddenly got damn energy, clapping her hands and all.

"Come—another round!" Melvin said, pouring three big shots of Jack, wiping out the bottle. The two of them bottoms-up their glasses but I just sipped mine. Not that they noticed—Melvin had started to stick his hand inside Fann's blouse, pretending to be holding her waist but from the way the fabric was moving I could see it gradually moving upward. I considered taking Fann to the ladies' room to remind her of her grand plan to not let Melvin get any action until she became his girlfriend but the woman was too far gone. Shameless!

"Aiyoh!" Fann said, squealing and swatting Melvin's arm so he immediately moved his hand back down to her waist. "How can you go there? We're in public! You are *so* bad, Melvin. Just for that, you must be punished."

Fann climbed on top of Melvin, sitting on his lap. Holding his head, she started frenching him deeply and moving her hips around, clearly rubba-ing his cock. These two—my god, it was like I was not even there. Just when he started to rubba her backside with his hands, she whacked him.

"No!" she said, taking the bottle of Chivas and sticking it inside her cleavage. "You must be punished," she said, kneeling on his thighs now so the spout was just over his mouth.

When she said, "Drink!" she leaned forward, using her hands to cup her boobs up and steady the bottle. Then she started pouring Chivas into his mouth.

Kani nah. That was my hard-earned Chivas! You think I let that gross guy do a body shot on me, dance until my feet hurt, show my panties to the whole bar—all that so that I can sit here and watch Fann use her pushed-up boobs to pour my Chivas down her boyfriend's throat?

But guniang here knows when she has become an extra. It was time to get lost.

Fann and Melvin of course didn't even notice when I finished my whiskey, grabbed my handbag and got up.

Once I got outside the bar, it hit me how drunk I was. It hadn't rained that day so the air was still bloody humid. I could feel my blouse and skirt glued to my sticky skin. Damn gross.

"Jazzy! Right? It is Jazzy?" I heard one of the ang mohs sitting outside the bar say.

I turned around to look but it was so dark and I was a bit dizzy so I wasn't sure who was talking to me at first. Then, aiyoh, my god—it was Sharon's husband!

"I'm Alistair," he said, taking my left hand and kissing it.

I wanted to throw up—of all the guys in the bar, I would pick him to be the second-last guy I wanted kissing my hand. (Steve the paunchy bar owner would be the first.)

"Nice to meet you, but I'm not feeling well," I said, taking my hand back and walking away. "I'm going to make a move first."

"Wait!" he said, walking quickly to catch up with me. "May I send you home?"

Aiyoh—this guy really has balls, man. I stopped and quickly turned around, quite pissed off. I was about to say something like, "I'm your wife's friend, you know! Don't you give a shit about Sharon and your baby at home?"

But then I thought about it—is Sharon really my friend? Was she ever really my friend? That stuck-up bitch Sharon? Who called me shallow and all that crap when guniang here was just trying to help her? Whose husband is here steaming over me so much that if I tap his cock one time I bet he confirm will instantly come all over his pants? Besides, from Sharon's Givenchy bag and the photos of her vacations, I was guessing that he was quite loaded.

"Hmm . . ." I said, scrunching my face up a bit and lightly touching his shoulder with my finger and making a little circle, like I was thinking hard about it.

"Please?" he said. His eyes were really begging me. I bet I could get this fucker to do anything I wanted. I should text his wife a photo, man. Who has the power now, Sharon?

"Well," I said, smiling a bit shyly, "your tongue did feel nice . . ."

CHAPTER 14

Even I—Jazeline Lim Boon Huay—know (sometimes) when I have been too much.

I am always right, it's true. But sometimes even I have to admit that perhaps I'm just a little bit wrong. Waking up the next morning, I definitely knew that this was one of those times.

As much as I hated Sharon for being such a bitch to me—should I really have done what I did?

I know I was sloshed (which is actually a good excuse) and yes, Sharon had really pissed me off (also a very good reason) and I was feeling a bit gross and awful about the whole Carlyle's scene (I guess maybe I am a bit to blame for not saying no at any point when I sort of could have?). Also, I was feeling a little sad that Roy hadn't texted so I guess guniang here was looking for some comfort—somewhere. (OK, this one even I will admit is quite a cock excuse.) But when I woke up the morning after, all I could think about was the sound of Sharon crying at the food court a few days ago.

Her husband, Alistair, surprisingly, was quite a gentleman once we were alone; he was even a bit sweet. He didn't make a big fuss when he said goodbye to his friends to send me home. I don't even think they knew he was leaving because of a girl. And in fact, he seemed a little shy once we got inside the taxi, keeping quite quiet, sitting all the way over on his side of the seat. I wondered if maybe he was feeling awkward about asking me right away whether I actually wanted to be sent home or wouldn't mind going to hotel for a bit. So he was just asking me stupid questions like "Where do you work?" That kind of shit. (I also pretended to ask him some questions back, even though I already knew where he worked and what he does. He didn't mention Sharon at all. And of course he wore no wedding ring. Typical.)

But when the taxi was almost in my neighborhood, he moved a bit closer. "It's not that late, actually . . ." he said. "Just after midnight?"

"Yeah—so?" I said, pretending to yawn a little. Guniang was a bit mabuk, yes, but not so drunk that I didn't know how to make him sweat a bit.

Alistair looked a bit worried. "I guess if you're tired . . ." he started to say, then quickly added, "but if you're not too tired . . ."

"If not, then?" I said, purposely acting a little blur.

"Then . . . would you like to get a drink?" he asked, getting closer so he could put his arm around me now. I could see taxi uncle staring at us in his rearview mirror, shaking his head and then blinking his eyes.

"Like, at another bar?" I asked, leaning a bit closer to him and tracing one of my fingers on his thigh. I could hear him breathing heavily now. Pathetic fucker.

"Jesus Christ," he said very softly.

I could see from his face that he was thinking quite hard. Was he feeling bad? Interesting—if so, this was definitely the first time I'd come across this kind of thing. Could it be that guys like these sometimes could actually have a conscience? Just the thought of that made me suddenly feel a little tender toward Alistair.

Besides, before Sharon got fat and obsessed with her baby, even though she wasn't Miss Chinatown material, she was not terrible-looking. If this guy actually married her, perhaps he did actually love her.

The taxi uncle was slowing down a bit now, reaching my block. When I felt Alistair pull away from me, I thought, OK, this guy—he's really not bad. Good for Sharon. Maybe she's wrong after all about why her hubby goes out so late so much. Maybe he's just sowing wild oats by drinking and flirting with guniangs at the bar, never following through and going all the way.

But then Alistair leaned forward and said to taxi uncle: "Actually—Fauntleroy Hotel, please? Sorry, we're not stopping here."

I guess at that moment, I could still stop it. I could say, "Sorry, I'm tired. Maybe another day." And I honestly hadn't thought much about whether I would go through with it at this point. Part of me wanted to find out whether Alistair was really the guy that Sharon thought he had turned into—and, if I was wrong, then I'd figure out a way to tell her. (Without incriminating myself of course.) But to be honest, guniang was feeling a bit sad after watching Fann and Melvin snog all night. Roy still hadn't texted me; and even though I had felt quite happening to be dancing on the bartop at Carlyle's with all these guys looking at me, in the end, none of the cute guys ended up coming to talk to me or buy me drink. Like that—how can? At least here—here was a guy, married or not, who could provide some comfort and entertainment for a few hours.

Also, I know we girls are supposed to think hooking up is bad, but I think this kind of experience, always somehow ends up being useful—it's like research. Cock sometimes small, cock sometimes big; sometimes the method is more action action, sometimes it's more slow and romantic. And sometimes I even learn a new technique, different ways of teasing that can get ang mohs even more steam. Kind of like that old government "Productivity" song they taught us in primary school. "Good, better, best—never let it rest. Till your good is better, and your better best!"

On top of all that, I guess I was a bit itchy. Go home alone to my sad bedroom and lousy single bed? Boring lah! Plus, the Fauntleroy Hotel is quite atas. Definitely not Hotel 81! This is one of the big downtown hotels, by the Singapore River and all. I had been there before—but only for high-class wedding dinners. I never knew anyone who had the kind of throwaway money to just anyhow stay there. So in the end, I just didn't stop Alistair.

Alistair was holding my hand, stroking it gently, by the time we got to the Fauntleroy. He helped me out of the taxi—not bad, quite the gentleman—but once we were outside, he made sure to walk a little bit ahead of me as we entered.

"Welcome back, Mr. Davis," the doorman said, bowing as he opened the heavy gold door for us.

Alistair waved at him slightly then quickly walked through.

"It's not that I do this often," he said, looking a bit embarrassed as we crossed the very quiet marble lobby. "My firm does a lot of business with the Fauntleroy—they let us have a room whenever we want it so I end up having a lot of meetings here."

OK—whatever he says. Hallo, he's not my husband after all—like I give a shit what he uses the Fauntleroy for.

I decided to wait by the lift lobby while he took care of business at the reception desk. Better lah. No matter how polite those receptionists are—they always gossip. Alistair didn't say anything when he came back to the lift lobby and we were silent all the way up to the top floor, all the way to the room at the end of a long corridor.

When he opened the door—wah! It was a suite! I had never been to a suite for hookup before! But guniang made sure to act cool. I pretended to look around and seem bored.

"Is this OK?" he said, looking a bit worried as he closed the door. "I can get something else . . . or we can go somewhere else, if you prefer? I just thought it might be a little more private—and quiet —to have a drink in a room."

I walked over to the big glass window—a serious one! Extending all the way from the floor to the ceiling type. From there I could look out at the small tourist boats on the river, the bright lights of the tall casinos, the ocean. I felt so tall, so big, like a god looking out at all of Singapore or some shit.

"No, this is fine," I said, turning away from the window and smiling at him.

Now that we were in the room, standing around, feeling a bit awkward, he seemed even more shy. What happened to the mabuk guy frantically licking my stomach at Carlyle's? Maybe he really doesn't do this that much? Cannot be. But who knows? (And who cares?)

"I guess . . . we should have that drink I promised you," he said, looking carefully at the fridge—at the bottles, not the price list! It was the first time I'd seen anyone go to a hotel minibar and not look at the prices at all.

"I noticed you drinking Chivas at Carlyle's—is that all right?"

I just nodded. So he opened a medium-sized bottle of Chivas and poured two glasses on the rocks, bringing one over to me by the window.

"Cheers," he said, clinking his glass with mine. We both took a few long sips, standing side by side, looking out at the lights. I could feel him slowly rubba-ing my back, stroking my hair—it was actually feeling bloody good. I bet he gives a good massage, I thought. He bent down to kiss me, very slowly but very sweetly. A warm warm soft soft one. I could feel his cock pressing my thigh—not only was it bloody hard already, but it was also damn bloody big. Wah, that Sharon—lucky girl!

I moved my hand over to rub his cock but he stopped me.

"Not yet," he said. "Can you take your clothes off for me?"

I started to pull my blouse off but he stopped me again. "No—sweetly, slowly," he said, walking over to sit on the couch. He put his glass down on the gold-rimmed coffee table so he could hold his hands up, using his thumbs and index fingers to make a rectangle, as if he was taking a photo of me standing in front of the window. Then he smiled and put his hands back down again.

I was beginning to think this was turning out a bit strange. These types of hookups usually are never like this. (Not that I do this that often lah—you must believe me, this is really true.) But these types of things—usually are just fast fast hard hard type; no storybook kind of set up. Married guys, especially, usually have to go home quickly after all, so the moment they're inside the room, pants come off already. But this one, it was as if he was shooting blue movie in his head. I wasn't sure what to do with this—and if I should be offended. The way he was bossing me around, it made me feel a bit like a pro! I'd never experienced anything like this before. But I had already gone this far—I didn't want to offend him or make things not nice. So I thought—why not? It's quite simple to just go along with this—at least for a bit.

So if Alistair wanted a show, then I decided I would give him a show. Guniang was already inside the room—might as well go all the way. Besides, it could be fun? First, I took another sip of whiskey, then licked the entire rim of the glass before putting it down on the floor. Then I leaned back against the glass window and spread my legs a bit. Slowly, slowly, I peeled up my skintight red blouse. I could hear him sighing loudly as he slowly saw my black lace push-up bra appear. Then, I unhooked the back of my skirt and unzipped it—but this one, I couldn't control how slowly this went though. The skirt was flared, so the whole thing just fell off in one second. Alistair had already see my red lacy panties before but still, he couldn't stop staring. Good.

Next, the bra was unhooked. I covered my breasts with one hand and used the other one to throw the bra at Alistair. He was staring so hard at me, waiting for me to take my hand away from my chest, that he couldn't even react in time to catch it.

"More," he said. "Please?"

When I moved my hand away, he sighed damn loud. I know my boobs and butt are not say as nice as Fann's lah. But I been told before that my body was like a little Japanese girl's body—everything is small and tight. This kind of body is actually quite popular with ang mohs—I think they have some fantasy of being our uncles and protecting us or some shit. And I guess if your wife is now a fatty, maybe you really miss this kind of look. Poor Alistair.

I refused to take my panties off though.

"Kitchen closed," I said. "Now—you." I started to unbuckle the straps on my heels. After all that, my feet were really hurting.

"Don't," he said, standing up and walking over. Were we going to fuck by the window? Not bad—I had never done it facing all of Singapore before. Instead, he suddenly picked me up and carried me like a baby to the bedroom, throwing me on the bed. Damn strong! Guniang here was starting to get quite horny and tried to unbuckle his belt.

"Not yet," Alistair said, pushing me back on the bed and pulling down my panties, spreading my legs apart, stroking my feet and high heels. "I think I should finish cleaning you up first." And then he started licking me all over, from my toes to my legs to, OK, you know where. All the way up and back down again, then he kept licking me there. Guniang here don't want to say too much lah so I'll just say I didn't have to fake anything. In fact, all I could see for a while right after that was large white dots. This—confirm—had never happened to me before.

By the time Alistair took off his clothes, guniang here was so high that I didn't even care that his body was not great—not fat, mind you, and you can tell he does work out, but his skin all over was super pasty, like those oily white Hainanese chickens you see hanging on a hook in the hawker stall, and his chest was filled with curly gray hair.

By that point, I couldn't think. All I could do was stare at him while he fumbled to open a condom wrapper.

"Oi," I said, giving him a bloody dirty look. "Hurry up!"

Alistair laughed. But he did hurry up. By the time we left the room two hours later, the pack of three rubbers he said—as if—he bought for a friend at 7-Eleven earlier that night was all habis.

Thinking about it the morning after, I started to feel a little hot all over again. And then I felt terrible. Jazzy, what's wrong with you? Even if you're feeling lonely and sad for yourself and horny—there are so many guys in the world. Why would you go with your school-mate's husband? In fact, after Alistair sent me home—for real—it was all I could think about. The guy was even nice enough to ask if I was hungry and wanted to order anything off room service right after, but all I could think about was whether Sharon was going to give him hell for creeping home at five in the morning. So, I just hurried us both out of there.

I had no answer for why I did what I did. But now that I'd done it, I couldn't stop thinking about how good Alistair felt. I needed to snap out of this. But how?

"Ah Huay!"

Perfect timing. For once, I was happy to hear my mum's voice. "Yes? What?" I said, getting up and opening my bedroom door before she could even put her hand on the knob. When it swung open, she just stared at me a bit shocked. This eagerness to see my mum had never happened before.

My mum paused for a second and said, "I know you're always very busy—don't know doing what in this messy room of yours," she said, looking around and sighing. (It's true lah—I hadn't swept the floor in a week now. Dust and *Her World* magazines were all over the floor.) "But I need your help in the kitchen."

Once again, she looked shocked when I just nodded and followed her out. From the slight smile on her face though, I could see she was happy.

My mum had the table all set up in the kitchen already—one giant tub of bean sprouts. "This whole thing of tau gay—can you peel for me?" she asked, pointing over at the bean sprouts. When I just walked over and sat down, drawing my plastic stool closer to the small round kitchen table, I could see her raising her eyebrows. (I bet the old lady was wondering who was this person and what happened to her real daughter.) My mum paused, as if she was thinking of saying something, but then she turned around and went to the sink to drain a tub of green beans she was soaking,

Bringing the tub over to the kitchen table, she pulled up a stool and sat down next to me, starting to snap the beans one by one. The kitchen was dark—this one, cannot help it lah. When our first flat was old enough that we were finally eligible to buy another HDB flat, there were a few blocks of apartments in this neighborhood that suddenly opened up. This neighborhood is damn central—few minutes to Orchard Road, the financial district, Marina Bay and everything. So everyone wants to live here. So the moment the government announced these new buildings, everybody wanted one! My mum spent days and days nagging my pa to quickly go and apply for one, since they had just become eligible for a new flat. But of course he was so lazy—and so hates to be nagged—that he purposely ignored her for a while. By the time he got off his backside to file the application, all the high floors had been snapped up already. That's how we ended up with a third-floor flat that's not only quite small but one with a kitchen that's super dark because it's blocked by other buildings from the sun and also faces this wall of gigantic rubbish bins. On really hot days in Singapore, the smell—aiyoh, you don't want to imagine.

But at least we live in Tiong Bahru. The location really is A-plus-plus.

As always, it was so dark in the kitchen even though it was not even 11 A.M., so we had to really squint a bit to see what we were peeling. It was fine lah—after all these years of helping my mum, I'm used to it already lah.

Side by side we worked, not saying a word. It was somewhat comforting to hear the rhythmic snapping of the green beans from my side and to feel my fingers breaking off the crisp, tough roots of the bean sprouts in my basket and tossing them onto the old Chinese newspaper my mum had laid out for rubbish. I was so focused on this that Alistair and the debauchery of last night quickly vanished. This was simple; this felt good. I know I always look down on shit like this lah, saying that I'm going to have a maid in the future to do this kind of crap job for me—but my mum is right about things (sometimes). Of course it's nice to have a maid—or two, like future Jazzy will have—but simple hard work like this also can be satisfying. Later on, when I eat my mum's stir-fry I confirm will feel a bit more shiok. Guniang here earned it after all, my hands here peeling all my mum's bean sprouts until sore!

"Ah Huay," my mum suddenly said, interrupting my blank thoughts. "You OK or not? Not feeling well, is it? Is something wrong? Want me to boil some barley water for you?"

My god. And she wonders why I don't like helping her. Guni-ang here decides to finally be nice to her mum without complaining about having to spend a morning peeling bean sprouts for her also end up getting interrogated like this.

"Yah?" I said. "Don't worry. All OK."

My mum looked at me, still snapping her green beans, her mouth opening slightly. "Ah Huay ah," she said very quietly. "Your ah pa and I are getting very worried about you, you know. You always go out so late, we don't know who you are with, you come home drunk, we also don't know what you're up to when you're out . . . Decent girls don't act like that, you know. If you carry on like that, one day something bad is going to happen to you." She looked so sad that I was actually feeling a bit bad. I thought about trying to explain to her how everything I was doing was my only chance at actually finding a good husband—that this is what all the girls were doing these days anyway. Besides, most nights, it actually was fun!

"You ah," my mum said, sighing very loudly, "always sailing too close to the wind."

"Ma—just don't worry," I said, smiling at her. "Everything's OK. OK?"

She didn't say anything; just grabbed another handful of green beans. We didn't say another word until the two tubs were empty.

A few hours later, my phone rang—like, actually rang.

Normally, I don't really like talking on the phone these days, unless it's for work lah, so most people know not to actually call me. But guniang here was so stunned to hear the phone ring that I just picked up the call.

"Oi!" was all I heard. Ah, Fann.

"Yes?" I said. "Finished your sex fest with Melvin yet?"

Fann snorted. "Talk rubbish lah!" she said. "I stuck to my plan of course. Just snogging and rubba-ing. I refused to follow him home. The guy had super blue balls, man! He's already been texting me all morning asking when he'll see me again."

Bloody hell. In the end Fann managed to win while I ended up opening my whole kitchen?

"Anyway," Fann said, "I'm downstairs. My mum sent me to your neighborhood seamstress to pick up a dress. Are you home?"

"Yah, yah," I said. "Come up—my mum's just putting lunch on the table."

A few minutes later, after Fann had said hello to my mum and given her the oranges she quickly bought before coming up, we found ourselves sitting down in the kitchen. The small table was already filled with dishes. Some of them, I know, my mum had planned to save for dinner that night. But once she heard that we were having a guest, my mum decided to just bring everything out, so we had my dad's favorite salted mustard greens soup lah, some braised duck and fatty roast pork, stir-fried noodles with green beans and bean sprouts, some leftover fried tofu from yesterday.

"Wah—aunty! Such a happening lunch!" Fann said.

My mother smiled a little and gestured to us to quickly eat. "You girls eat first," she said. "I'll wait for your pa to come home then eat with him." Fann started to protest and ask her to sit and eat with us but my mum just waved her away, walking out to the living room to turn the TV on. Aiyah, our parents' generation is just like that—they think the youngsters feel more comfortable if they're not around. Which is actually true lah.

The moment my mum left the kitchen, Fann grabbed her chopsticks and started piling all sorts of food on her rice bowl. Watching her, I realized how hungry I was so I did the same. We didn't really pause again until our rice bowls were half-empty.

"Jazzy," Fann said after a long sip of chrysanthemum tea in between bites. "So . . . what did you think?"

"Of? The club? The cute bartenders? The shots?" I said, reaching for more roast pork.

Fann slapped my hand. "Aiyoh—don't be like that lah!" she said. "You know what I'm asking!"

I wasn't sure what to say—but I knew I shouldn't pause too long or Fann would think I didn't like Melvin. It's true that Melvin probably wouldn't be the type of ang moh I'd like to end up with. There was something too—quick—about him. Yes, I know it's ironic considering I was the one who spent the night with an ang moh—something I wasn't about to tell Fann with my mum sitting in the next room. But at the same time, I had been very clearheaded about Alistair. I wasn't expecting anything more from him than a few hours of fun, though it was a few hours I was regretting more and more each time I thought about Sharon. With Melvin though, if Fann saw him as a real prospect, we needed to judge him by different standards! To have him pawing at her breasts like that in a public bar? Aiyoh—is that really what a guy who is serious about a girl does?

"Well," I said, "he seems nice."

Fann wrinkled her nose. "Oi, woman—if you have something to say, just directly say it lah," she said.

"OK then," I said. "Is he serious?"

Fann smiled at this question. Now I was really curious.

"Well, I have one thing to say," Fann said, picking up her chop-sticks again and reaching over to pick up the nicest-looking, fattiest piece of roast pork on the table. Bloody hell—I'd had my eye on that since we sat down but thought I should save it for my mum.

"Brunch," she said, once she'd examined the pork closely, decided it would definitely do and put it in her bowl. "He's invited me to Sunday brunch—at the Australian Club. With his close friends. And their wives or girlfriends."

Jazzy here almost started tearing up after hearing this. Brunch? A daylight activity? With friends and their wives? In an ang moh club, no less! This was some serious shit going on right here.

I reached over and squeezed Fann's hand. She looked at me and I looked right back at her—and we both started squealing.

CHAPTER 15

Saturday night started out damn cock.

First, Imo suggested going to Studemeyer's. "The deejay tonight is quite good!" she texted. So, OK, we all agreed to go. But then, when Fann and I showed up at the VIP table Louis booked, Imo stood us up! Turns out she left Carlyle's early last night because she wasn't feeling well. Then, it turns out she was actually quite sick, so all we got once we were already at Studemeyer's was a text from her saying, "Sorry, sorry!" (And a bunch of lines about how much exactly she was hugging the toilet bowl, which we looked at one time and fasterly deleted. Who needs that kind of shit floating around our heads on a happening Saturday night out?)

But at least Louis booked a table at Studemeyer's and even though he hadn't come out yet, he let us pull out his bottles from his liquor locker and all. So Andrew and Kelvin—who were so happy their wives let them come out to chiong for the night that they arrived at Studemeyer's super early—had been drinking there since 9 P.M. By the time Fann and I got there, Louis's bottle of Chivas was gone and they were asking the manager to bring out his Grey Goose and whatever the hell unfinished bottles Louis had in his locker.

"Come, come, cheers!" Andrew said, making vodka sodas for us four and passing them around.

"Eh, ladies," Kelvin said after we bottoms-up and Andrew started making another round. "Tonight—be prepared. There's an extra special show!"

When Kelvin said that, guniang here panicked a bit. I remember the last time we were out with Louis and his gang and they were talking about a special show coming on—my god, I could still taste the sourness of defeat from that night at Lunar, that Chinese club.

I looked at Fann, who was looking at her phone. I considered gesturing to her that perhaps we should leave. (Although I guess the more effective way of communicating that to her would have been to text her, even though she was sitting just one seat over.) The truth is, I was not feeling much like being in a club that night at all. Guniang here didn't need any drinks to feel high—I was already feeling quite buzzed from a date with Roy. Yes—Roy!

My mum always says that good deeds bring good karma and guniang here has always thought that's a bit bullshit lah. This kind of zen-zen-type stuff—please, it's not very modern thinking! You think this one is what—ancient Japan, is it? (I know I should respect it and all but I always think it's a bit wasting time only.) But this morning, after peeling all those bean sprouts and being a good girl for my mum, even clearing all the dishes after lunch, I got back to my room to find my phone beeping.

"I know it's a bit late to be asking but are you free for coffee this afternoon?" Roy said.

After the awfulness of last night, guniang here was so happy to hear from Roy that I almost wanted to run back outside and hug my mum, I tell you. Maybe things were looking up a bit after all.

Of course, I waited half an hour before texting back—good, make him worry. Then I said, "OK."

Roy had warned me to wear really comfortable walking shoes—a bit strange but I thought, OK, maybe he wants to go walking along Orchard Road to go shopping or something? It's true—sometimes, when you're doing heavy-duty shopping, especially on Sunday when all the families and kids are out, better be prepared to fasterly maneuver through all that crap. So I made sure to put on my nice sneakers—these were about five years old but guniang here uses them so little they're still shiny shiny and all. I tell you—they look so new that if you put them on display in the store right now, people wouldn't think twice about trying them on.

Roy had taken my coffee order by text so he had two medium-sized styrofoam cups in his car when he showed up downstairs. His car wasn't too big or flashy—no Mercedes SUV here—but it wasn't terrible. It was one of those MINI Coopers that were in fashion these days. Forest green, with one fat white stripe running down the side of it—not bad. Masculine and not that boring lucky red like so many Singaporeans were choosing when buying that kind of cute car.

The fact that he even had a car—and I deduced it was his because most companies wouldn't buy a MINI as their company car, let's face it—was promising. Cars are so expensive in Singapore—the island is so small, the government wants to discourage people from buying too many and clogging the roadways and all. So, first of all, they're all imported and taxes on them are crazy. On top of that, even before you buy the car you have to bid on a certificate of entitlement to buy a car—each year the government only issues so few. So, my god, once those COEs are issued, everyone bids like crazy to get one. All in, you should know that if you want to buy a decent car, you know you'd better have at least a hundred thousand dollars in your bank account or you can forget about it.

So the fact that Roy has one—it's not bad. Either he's making enough to buy one himself or he's valuable enough to his company that they factored a Singapore car allowance into his contract. Or maybe he came from a super rich family? From the looks of it, it was a brand-new MINI too. When guniang here saw the car—wah, I was immediately damn happy. This was promising!

Roy reached over to give me a hello kiss on the lips the moment I slid into his car. I turned my face slightly so he got my cheek instead, but made sure to give him a sweet little smile.

"Afternoon," he said, smiling and turning his music down a little. I had thought he might be listening to pop or club music—I guess I'll always associate him with that since that's what was playing when we first met. But he was actually listening to the Beach Boys. Interesting. I wondered if he'd lived in the States before—or if maybe he might get posted there in the future? A lot of these oil guys I know often get stationed in Houston or some shit. I don't really know how I would like living there lah—but it seems pretty fun from all the movies I've seen. I was trying to think whether that's where all the cowboy movies are? Can consider.

We chitchatted a bit as he drove—nothing serious lah. Just how was your morning (I didn't tell him about the bean sprout peeling—too LC), what have you been up to, that kind of thing. I was hoping he'd say something about why he hadn't texted me since our date a few nights ago (and wondered about asking or commenting on it, but I didn't want to seem needy). Besides, I guess it had really only been just over a day, really.

At that moment, I was just feeling happy to be sitting in this cute little car, with Roy, slowly driving past the tall boring buildings in my housing estate, turning onto a road near downtown that would lead us to leafy Bukit Timah, where the rich or expats with kids live. The trees, each one perfectly spaced apart and elegantly shaped, along the wide road medians were getting greener and fuller. As we neared the botanical gardens, Roy slowed down, turning into the car park. Ah, this kind of walk. To be honest, guniang here is not really a nature nature type of girl. (Please, not many Singaporeans truly are. If they say they are, I can tell you—confirm it's all lies and posing. With all these great malls and cinemas around—who wants to spend time in a dirty garden?) But I had decided that Roy had potential—and he did seem sweet. So I guess, why not?

Roy handed me my coffee—"milk, two sugars, right?"—as we got out of the car. "It was such a nice day," he said as we entered the tall iron gates to the gardens. "I thought perhaps it might be nice to get out."

Once we got inside the park, I let Roy take the lead. Seemed like he'd been here before and probably knew his way around. Of course I'd been to the botanical gardens before—only once though, on a primary school excursion and even then I found it damn boring. Except for the couples doing photo shoots in their wedding outfits, seriously—what else was there to see in this place? But if Roy likes it then I'll keep an open mind lah.

"I like coming here to clear my head," Roy said, leading me down a narrow path toward the heart of the gardens. "Singapore's so different from where I grew up—not quite the countryside but definitely not the city," he added. I tried to think about whether I'd asked where he grew up in the UK. And decided not to risk asking him again, in case we'd already had this discussion that night when I was drunk.

I was starting to feel strange. Not with Roy, but just the general feeling that something very odd was happening. It wasn't that I hadn't been around gardens before—it's true, I hadn't done this that often but hello, once you've seen one bush or one orchid jungle, do you really need to see more? Is each one really that different? I mean, of course if I had bothered to go on one of those school trips to Malaysia to go camping or some shit I might know a bit more about wilderness lah. But please—ask me to spend money on these kinds of toot things? Might as well ask me to buy ticket to see an opera or some useless crap like that. It's not as if I'm printing money.

But I quickly realized what it was that made me feel like something was off—the silence! Roy wasn't talking; neither was I. And while there were people around us—joggers, couples, the occasional family—everyone was fairly quiet, just slowly strolling, looking at flowers. I even heard birds. My god, I couldn't remember the last time I heard birds just chirping at each other in Singapore—actually, maybe like in the 1990s, when for a few years it was quite happening among old uncles at the kopitiams to buy parakeets or other small songbirds and put them in pretty little round bamboo cages and bring them to the coffee shop early in the morning to show off. Back then, I tell you, this trend became so popular that kopitiams all over Singapore actually started creating sections of their terraces where there were hooks on the ceilings for these Ah Cheks to hang their birdcages.

Don't ask me why this was fashion. Please—these are really old uncles we're talking about. Who cares? But if I have to guess, I think it's maybe something quite symbolic, that if their real birds cannot perform anymore then they might as well buy birds to rear and compete so they can at least feel better about one thing in their pathetic lives. You know how guys are lah—no more good bird to fight also still want to fight.

I guess that's why when it was so quiet that I could hear birds in the air—immediately, I felt like something was wrong. After all, we definitely weren't in a 1990s kopitiam!

"Shall we sit?" Roy suddenly said, bursting my kopitiam uncle-bird memories. We had come upon a bench in the shade. I looked around—Roy wasn't bad. He had managed to pick the only bench all around us that was nicely painted and not speckled with birdshit. (Although if my mum was here, she would say, "Bird shit—very lucky!" Not that she would actually dare go near a bench that was filled with bird shit, of course.)

Roy quickened his step a little before getting to the bench, taking out a packet of tissue from his pocket, pulling a sheet out and wiping down the bench before looking over at me. Tilting his head a little, he waved his hand with a big flourish, like those emcees onstage before introducing a singer or some shit.

"My lady?" he said, smiling and bowing a bit. OK lah—this move, even I have to admit, is quite can. It's stupid lah. My god. So stupid. But I couldn't help but smile.

We sat quietly for a bit, just sipping our coffees—lattes from Starbucks, mind you. (The thought of Seng buying me kopi at the kopitiam popped into my head all of a sudden. I was trying to imagine him asking me out on a coffee date like this in the park. My god, the guy would confirm show up with those old coolie-style clear plastic bags filled with kopi and then tied together with fluorescent pink plastic string into a loop so you can hook the hot bag of kopi on your finger and bring back a whole bunch, one for each of your Ah Beng friends. That's just what happens when you buy takeaway kopi from a kopitiam. I wondered if Seng had ever even been inside a Starbucks and actually laughed out loud.)

"What's so funny?" Roy asked.

"Nothing, nothing," I said, feeling a bit embarrassed. When he still looked a bit curious, I figured I should say something. "Just happy to be here."

Roy smiled. "Good, I'm really glad, Jazzy," he said, taking a long sip. "You know, I asked you out here today so we could maybe get to know each other in a slightly more relaxed setting. I was starting to think maybe we'd started out on a bit of an intense footing, with, you know . . ." He looked over at me, slightly embarrassed.

"I mean, don't get me wrong," he continued, "it was lovely how things began. You were so lovely. But it's just not how I usually go about things. I'm really not like that back in England. I just . . . wanted to slow things down a little. See where things go."

Interesting. In all my years of dating—especially with ang mohs—I had never heard such a speech before. Usually when guys reach the promised land, they like to stay there. No need to go anywhere else type. But here Roy was saying he wanted to get to know me outside of clubs and the bedroom? I wasn't quite sure how to respond to this piece of information. But then I remembered that he did just move to Singapore not too long ago. The scene probably hadn't corrupted him—yet.

So I just smiled and said, "I'm glad." From the slightly relieved smile on his face, I could tell it was the right response.

"You know," Roy said, leaning back, draping his arm around my shoulder and looking out at the trees, the pond, the swans in front of us, "in some ways, I feel I was destined to come to Singapore. When I was ten, one of my dad's friends who had come here on a business trip gave me this Singapore five-dollar bill and it had this drawing of the bulbul on it—do you know what that is? No? It's a small tropical bird that you find in various parts of the world. It's nothing very special to look at but it's a songbird . . . Anyway, I was just getting really into bird-watching at the time and had just been reading about the bulbul—the idea of it being on a five-dollar bill, wow. I couldn't get over it! I guess Singapore has been on my mind ever since . . ."

Bulbul? Bird-watching? This guniang was definitely in new territory here. If it had been any of my friends telling cock stories like this I would have just laughed and whacked them on the head and said, "You talking what cock? Don't pretend to be deep lah!" But I remembered Roy's car. And how tenderly he wiped down the bench for me, for us. And I decided to just be quiet a bit. Let him talk. See how. And actually, by the time we finished our coffees and walked back to the car, I was feeling like maybe—just maybe—even if the oil refinery career is not quite part of the big plan, even if he has that bloody hairy nose, maybe Roy has real potential.

Just thinking about our walk while at Studemeyer's with Fann and the guys was still making me smile. That's how happy I was, I guess. I took out my phone and thought about texting Roy, wondering what he was up to tonight. But I thought, I just saw him earlier today. Just let it rest for a bit. See how. I put my phone back in my clutch.

At that moment, Kelvin pointed to the small oblong podium in the middle of the dance floor that was, as usual, jammed with four or five people trying to action for everyone to see. When Studemeyer's first opened and they were still trying to be a bit atas, they actually selected podium people—sexy sexy girls and guys who actually know how to dance, dress well and also look quite steam lah. At that time, those podium people were quite inspiration—you see them dancing like in those music videos (sometimes even making the exact moves—this was especially effective with Janet Jackson songs), it just makes you want to dance harder and look sexier. Everybody feels good. But as I mentioned before, their standards really dropped after the Ah Bengs started coming. Now, they just anyhow let people go on the podium and dance. Good clubs—how can they let such things happen? No wonder all the serious clubbers don't really like coming here anymore.

The podium tonight was a perfect example of this—my god, the variety of losers on it were A-plus-plus, man. There was one classic Ah Beng with the gelled hair and lumpar face, two Ah Lians, both wearing sequin cheena dresses like those KTV bar girls, one fat ang moh guy who confirm is a tourist—must be American, some more, judging from his T-shirt and baggy berms. I tell you—sometimes being ang moh is quite the good life. When they go to a club, they're not Singaporeans so they don't need to watch the dress code. Whatever you wear also any club will let you in.

And then—wah, this one I actually had never seen on the podium before—there was one vainpot auntie up there, a bit chubby chubby but still damn bloody vain. Auntie looked quite old—maybe thirty-something?—but even so, somehow she was the most energy, the most action of all the podium dancers. She was wearing tight jeans— but not those fashion fashion dark blue one. Hers were light blue; the denim looked like those cheapo, buy from the "fashion" stalls at the wet market kind. And yeah, her jeans were damn tight on her—but I can tell you it's not because the jeans were designed to be tight. Even though the dance floor was quite dark, I could see from here that her legs were blown up like two sausage rolls. But lagi best was her top—she wore this loose, a bit see-through white tank top with such big arm holes that you could see her lacy bra. And this auntie's bra— don't play play! Fluorescent orange! Plus, she danced until so powerful that her bra straps kept slipping, so every few minutes auntie had to stop dancing, catch her breath and pull up her bra. She would stop, rest for a few seconds and then—action again!

I tell you, the four of us watched her for a few songs—and we laughed until we almost fell over the railing, man!

"Ladies," Kelvin said, raising his glass to cheers with us again. "Please—promise me that when you are that old I won't see your saggy backsides up on that podium!"

Aiyoh, socks-crotch tonight was really quite daring—having the balls to arrow us like that.

"Eh, Kelvin," I said, clinking my glass with his. "Thanks for the advice—I see you are listening to your own advice as well? You and auntie over there are both the same age but I don't see you joining her up there on the podium."

Kelvin stopped smiling—his face had this bang balls look. He gave me the third finger but Andrew, Fann and I just laughed and laughed.

Just when I started to be in OK mood, settling into the clubbing scene and not really thinking about texting Roy anymore or wondering what he's doing tonight, I saw someone waving at me from the dance floor. Kani nah—it's Seng! Why does he have to be so bloody GPS—know how to find me and all? I didn't want to be rude, so I just waved back then looked away. But ten minutes later, the fucker showed up on our level and was standing next to me in our booth!

"Excuse me?" Kelvin said to Seng and the even bigger Ah Beng friend he had dragged up with him to the VIP section. "Sorry, but this is a private table that we have reserved."

"It's OK," Seng said, giving Kelvin a big fuck-off face. "That one," he added, pointing at me, "my friend."

Kelvin laughed, then looked at me. "Jazz? Real or not?"

Seng look at me; I look at him. I felt quite bad, especially after thinking about what my mum told me the other day, about how he bought her and Pa breakfast last week and all.

"Yeah, yeah, no problems—he's my old friend," I said, feeling damn bloody embarrassed. "But this one—is from a very long time ago!"

Kelvin just shook his head and gave me a dagger look before going over to whisper to Andrew. Fann looked at me and mouthed the words: "Why is he here?" I had nothing to say.

"Jazzy—this one, my friend Richard; Richard—Jazzy, my neighbor," Seng said. His friend was one of those really smelly-face Ah Bengs—the kind of face that always looks like he just ate something wrong. Richard just looked at me, tilted his chin up and nodded. When Ah Bengs say hallo—is like that one. They never shake hands.

"What are you doing here?" I asked Seng.

"I sometimes come here," he said. "Studemeyer's is damn happening!"

Aiyoh, my god. Of course Seng is the exact sort of guy who would think this club is still happening.

"Don't angry lah, Jazzy," Seng said. "Long long time never see you in club already. Let's just dance a bit."

I was trying to think about what to do when the deejay started playing Black Eyed Peas and everyone around us started dancing like crazy and singing, "I gotta feeling . . . that tonight's gonna be a good night!" and all. I didn't want to kill the mood so I decided to dance along, but each time I looked over at Seng and Richard, my blood would really boil. The Ah Bengs were just happily dancing along, ignoring the dirty looks that Fann, Kelvin and Andrew were giving them. Why on earth was Seng here? Isn't it bad enough that he harasses me in my own neighborhood, he comes to my house when I'm not there, but now he has to talk to me in clubs when I'm with my atas friends? And he even dares to bring his mega Ah Beng friend along when bothering me! Please. He really doesn't understand his place in life.

Halfway through the song, Andrew slowly danced closer to me, moving between me and Seng, who gave him a dirty look. Andrew leaned close to my ear and said, "This bugger—is he really your friend?"

I nodded but made sure to roll my eyes.

"He keeps giving me dirty looks—bodyguard, is it? Or boy toy?" Andrew said, purposely putting his arm around me now. I've never been Andrew's type so he's never done anything like this to me before—and I knew that this move tonight wasn't about that, really. And I knew his strategy worked—I could see Seng glaring at him even more.

"Aiyoh, Jazzy," Andrew said, getting closer and really whispering in my ear now. "We've been partying together for so long, why are you giving us no face by bringing an Ah Beng cock blocker? Want to make us jealous, is it?"

Andrew was rubbing his nose on my ear now and kept looking over at Seng to make sure he was seeing everything. This was getting out of hand. I don't know what Andrew was playing at but guniang tonight had no mood to flirt with anybody. Not even with Chairman Andrew with his millions of dollars, thank you very much. After last night with Alistair and then today's sweet walk with Roy, all I wanted tonight was some good clean fun—no hooking up, no drama. My god, that Alistair guy was still texting me! Guniang here just wanted to forget that it ever happened.

I sweetly smiled and moved away from Andrew. "No lah," I said, smiling even more. "This guy is my teenage friend—from a long time ago. I also don't know what longkang he came from tonight. Trust me—this kind of guy, I definitely didn't invite him."

I looked over at Fann, who had stopped dancing awhile ago and was sitting on the banquette, texting and looking grumpy. I looked over at Seng, who was staring at me and Andrew, probably trying to figure out if he should interfere and try to whack Andrew's face or something. Like that—how?

My phone was in my pocket vibrating—actually, it had vibrated a few times that night but I didn't care about answering since it was probably Alistair. But at this moment, I needed an excuse to take a break from all this manhood crap so I sat down next to Fann and checked my texts.

There were two texts from Alistair. I didn't bother to look at them.

Then, from Louis: "Jazz—Inferno is damn happening tonight. You girls come here lah. I'm not going to Studemeyer's." After that he sent a few more saying, "Hello? Hello?" then "Coming or not?"

"Fann," I said, "let's go."

"Thank god," she said, quickly picking up her handbag and getting up. "Bloody boring here, man."

"Andrew," I said, giving him a hug. "We make a move first."

As Fann and I ran out, I gave a quick wave to Kelvin, Seng and Richard. They all looked a bit blur. I could see them wondering if we were going to the toilet or leaving for good. Whatever, lah.

Once we were outside, Fann said, "Eh, I think I'll go home first."

"Home your head lah—it's only eleven P.M.!" I said. "You think I don't know where you going—to see Melvin, right?"

At least Fann had the decency to look a bit embarrassed.

"Aiyoh—it's Saturday night!" I said. "Come on, woman—this is not nice."

"Jazzy," she said. "Weren't you the one who told us that we must be focused on our mission? I am being focused! Melvin is a good catch. Things are going well," she said, smiling as if she was remembering something about him, and then giggling a little.

Watching her made me feel bad. It's true. I shouldn't lose sight of the mission. If Fann has a chance to be happy, then I really shouldn't be so selfish. I guess this is how it is lah—when people have wings already, they know how to fly. You cannot hold them back.

"Aiyah, OK fine—just go and give your backside to him lah!" I said, smacking her pantat one time and smiling.

Fann pointed her third finger at me. "You? What are you going to do?"

"Don't worry—I'll join Louis at Inferno," I said. "The night is still young—maybe I'll meet my ang moh billionaire tonight!"

CHAPTER 16

There was a unicorn at the door when I got to Inferno.

Of course, not a real unicorn lah. But some tall, buff guy dressed like a unicorn; the horn at the top of his mask was even long and sharp—sharp enough to seriously hurt someone, probably. Wah, I thought, if there's a fight here tonight, this guy no need to carry parang also can win. Nowadays in Singapore, you cannot be too careful. Just last month, some guy was walking by the McDonald's near the cinema on Orchard Road minding his own business when some Ah Beng gang thought he was acting too ya ya or some shit and whacked him with a parang! That guy was slashed with that machete I don't know how many times, go hospital all; blood all over the place. There were even kids all around watching this happening—the Ah Bengs just didn't care.

Ah Bengs these days—really getting to be too much. That's why I don't really understand Seng. Picking up all these Ah Beng habits is a slippery slope, you know—one day you are growing a long fingernail to dig your ears and saying "jee-lo" instead of "zero" and the next day you may find yourself holding parang and whacking innocent people on the street just because you think they're staring at you. All I know is, guniang here better just stay out of it all.

Inferno is safe though—this kind of club, confirm will have no Ah Bengs. Since it opened last month, it's not only one of the hottest clubs in Singapore, but actually, in the world! Just yesterday, the *New Times* wrote a big story that the *Perth Tribune* called Inferno the "Best New Bar in Southeast Asia," all. If a newspaper in Perth is actually saying that then this club is confirm happening!

Once the unicorn ushered me into the club, a tall and pretty Eurasian girl in a sexy black dress—short, yes, but with a classy classy cut—welcomed me and led me to a reception room. "And you are with?" she said in a British accent, pulling out an iPad wrapped in zebra skin. I was quite impressed—I whole life never see this kind of iPad cover before. I wanted to ask her whether I could touch it or not but thought, Jazzy, please, wake up your head. You cannot be so LC!

"Louis," I said. "Louis . . ." Babi, I was blanking on this—what was his surname again ah?

But luckily I guess either Louis spends enough here or is considered rich enough that they definitely radar him. So, I didn't need to say his surname at all.

"Ah, yes," she said, smiling more broadly now. "This way, please."

I followed her to a small door hidden in a dark corner of the room, which was damn quiet until she pressed a button next to the door and half the wall slid open. Wah! All of a sudden there was house music and lights flashing flashing all over the place.

Not bad, I thought—now, tonight is confirm on!

The room overall was quite dark, even with the laser lights shooting all across it, except for a fluorescent pink glass walkway that cut diagonally across everything. The walkway was a little raised and on each side there were people dancing or drinking at big cushioned booths.

The hostess led me to the back of the room, where there was a grand glass staircase where each step was a glowing white light. At the top of the stairs was a thick neon pink velvet rope. The bouncer let us through immediately and Louis's VIP table was in a corner—it was a dark spot but it had a terrific sweeping view of the whole room.

"Jazzy! Finally!" he said, getting up when he saw me. From the way he was wobbling a little, I could tell he was already a bit mabuk.

After I double-air-kissed him, he introduced me to the two ang moh guys with him. "Francis, Benedict—colleagues from Hong Kong," he said. "And this is Jazzy, one of my closest friends."

Wah, "closest"? I had known him for how many years and had never heard him call me that before. How mabuk was he? Or maybe he meant it? Guniang actually felt a bit touched.

"Come, come—Jazzy, you are definitely not high enough," he said, grabbing this atas-looking tall glass bottle that said "Diva" in cursive on the side. In the center of the bottle there was some kind of long tube filled with shiny red and pink stones. Louis poured everyone one shot and poured me two.

"This vodka—don't play play! There are Swarovski crystals inside," he said, pushing the two shots in my hands. "You'd better catch up—bottoms up!"

After the first two shots, Louis just kept pouring, ordering more bottles of Diva whenever we ran out. Even though I was high, I wasn't so high that I felt sick—I guess because we were dancing like crazy in between shots. At one point the boys even cleared away some of the bottles off the leopard-skin ("Real one," Louis whispered to me. "The owner says he even shot some of these buggers in Africa himself so he had enough for his VIP section.") table so that Francis and I could climb on top and dance for ten minutes.

I felt the stresses of Seng and Andrew facing off—and my god, being even remotely associated with Seng's super Ah Beng friend Richard in a club—all of that, I felt it fading. After all that action, and my night with Alistair, which was still making me cringe whenever I thought about it (and every time I felt my phone vibrate), I felt like I earned one night where I could just have some simple fun.

Drinks, dancing—checking out a new club, the richest hottest club in Singapore—this was just the right medicine. I wished Fann and Imo—and yes, Sher—were here but this was fun anyway. I looked over at Louis, feeling grateful that we were friends—one of his closest friends, in fact! In life, it's true lah—you are nothing without good friends. I raised my glass and caught Louis's eye. He smiled and winked at me.

All of us didn't talk much as all this dancing was happening—the music was too loud. This was a pity because on my way here, I had been thinking about work and Albert's hints about the circulation department and all, and I was thinking of asking Louis for some career advice, maybe tell him that I was thinking of switching jobs, maybe trying something I was actually interested in like event planning or something. Besides the loud music though, Louis was probably too mabuk to have any conversations like that. Although, as mabuk as he was, the other two guys were even more gone and mostly just closed their eyes and danced like possessed mediums in those dusty Chinese temples. Suddenly, the music got more quiet and all the laser lights focused at one spot near the center of the room, where there was a shiny white dentist's chair with silver handles.

"And the lucky lady this hour is . . . Sylvia Pereira!" a bloody stiff British man's voice announced. I guess his mic had some special sound effect because his voice had some action action echo and all.

The crowd went mad, cheering even louder than the pounding music. A light-skinned Eurasian girl with long wavy brown hair, a leather bustier and red hot pants ran up to the chair. Two unicorns appeared to strap her wrists and ankles to the chair and recline her seat. Then one of them tied a fluorescent pink paper bib around her neck. The crowd cheered even louder.

"Ready?" the booming voice said. Two more unicorns appeared, each one holding a bottle of Diva. The girl closed her eyes, tilted her head back and opened her mouth wide. "Set? Go!"

The two unicorns were suddenly damn action—each one held the bottle up high, in a drama drama way. Then at the exact same time they started pouring Diva down the girl's throat! Even from this far away, we could see the two steady streams of vodka slicing through the air in long sparkling ribbons before landing perfectly in the eager girl's mouth. This went on for almost a minute! I was impressed—this girl was damn power. How could she drink for so long without vomiting?

"And . . ." the British voice came back. "Over!"

The two unicorns put their bottles down in sync, bowed and then marched away. The first two unicorns stepped forward to unstrap the girl, who seemed a bit wet around her face and chest.

"Let's give a round of applause to . . . Sylvia!" the voice said. People were clapping; the lights were all brightly focused on her now. Sylvia gave a big smile, raising her hands to do that Princess Kate wave to everyone, then she started to sit up and her face changed a bit. Her smile was now habis—she had to sit back down and was bending over the side of the chair a bit. The four unicorns rushed to surround her, making a circle. The lights quickly started flashing and moving around the room again so we suddenly couldn't see Sylvia or the chair anymore. The music got louder, much louder than it had ever been before.

"How— Jazzy, should we put your name in for the dentist's chair?" Louis said, putting his arm around me.

"Tolong—no," I said, giving him the third finger.

"Why not? Free double shots, you know!" Louis added, circling his arm tighter around my neck and pulling me closer so he can whisper, "You know how expensive Diva is or not? Each bottle is $2,888!"

My god. I tried to count in my head how many bottles we had already opened that night. Confirm three—and who knows how many they had had before I got there?

Louis didn't seem to care though—so why should I care?

"No wonder so shiok," I said, shrugging. "Come, another bottoms up!" This time I poured two shots for everyone and made them all drink quickly.

Around this time, I started to think maybe it's time to call it a night. Tonight is confirm no new prospects—even though Inferno was filled with rich guys (or guys who looked really rich) I was there as Louis's guest so I couldn't leave him to go wander around the dance floor chatting up other guys. That really would be giving him no face. And his friends Francis and Ben were both quite cute—but if they were Louis's colleagues then I definitely didn't want to pok them. Too close to home. Since they don't live here, whatever we did, confirm, would be a one-night stand. The worst would be the after—if they gossiped about it with Louis and Louis gossiped with Kelvin and Andrew. Better don't mix business with pleasure.

"Eh, Louis, I think I'd better go home before I start feeling super mabuk," I said.

Louis nodded. "Yeah," he said. "Me also. We've been drinking since six!"

The guys were not ready to balik kampong yet though so Louis just signed the bill and told the waitress to bring out more Divas if the guys needed them and put them on his tab.

"Come," he said, after we said goodbye to the guys and were walking out the door. "I send you home."

I was more mabuk than I first thought, so I was glad Louis was sending me home. Plus, he even had a company driver waiting outside in a silver Mercedes, so we didn't need to finagle with the taxi queue, which I could see was already damn long. This life Louis had . . . damn difficult, eh?

When we reached my block and the car stopped, I leaned over to air-kiss Louis but he said, "Not yet. You're so mabuk, I'd better walk you up."

This was true. I couldn't remember how many shots I'd had but I was feeling damn tired, even though it was only 2 A.M. Maybe safer to let him send me up.

When we got in the lift, I started to feel damn embarrassed though. Usually the lift smells a little like smoke and urine, but tonight the scent was even more thick—someone must have come home from clubbing and couldn't wait to reach home. Aiyoh. I'm sure Louis, with his big Nassim Hill mansion, had never breathed in this kind of air in a very long time. I should have thought about this before letting him walk me up. No matter how mabuk I was, the embarrassment of this was just too much. I would have gladly preferred to fall on my face in a puddle of urine from being too drunk to stagger home than let Louis see my daily living environment like this.

Louis didn't seem to mind though—in fact, he was humming one of the house music tunes from Inferno, half-closing his eyes. I had never felt more relieved as when the lift door opened. The air had also never smelled more sweet. I could feel my armpits getting wet. As we walked down the narrow corridor, carefully stepping past my neighbors' giant pots of money plants, with leaves growing all over half the walkway, I realized why I was feeling a bit nervous. All the years that Louis has sometimes sent me home, he had always dropped me off downstairs. I guess now, for the first time, he's really seeing how I live. Aiyoh—like that, how? Would he still think I'm atas enough to come out clubbing with him?

At the end of the corridor, I quickly opened my gate, hoping he was mabuk enough that he didn't notice the brown rusted spots all over it. Before I opened the door, I leaned in again to air-kiss him.

"Can I come in?" he whispered, smiling, still with his eyes half-closed.

Guniang here was stunned. This. Now, this really had never happened before. I tried to think of how to be polite about it. My mind was cotton balls.

"It's very late, you know . . ." I whispered back.

"I know—just for a bit."

"My flat is very quiet—my parents would be unhappy if I had a friend . . ."

"I'll be very very quiet—I promise," he said, squeezing my hand.

We didn't say anything for a moment—me, because I really couldn't think of what to say. This was wrong. On so many levels. Forget Mary—she really was never a factor in anything. But Imo, sweet Imo. Not to mention Roy. Or the fact that I thought of Louis as a brother. And the fact that I didn't want to. And I was drunk. And I just wanted to crawl into bed and sleep. And . . .

Louis sighed. His eyes had a slightly narrow look to them. He seemed impatient—something I had seen only a few times before because Louis was generally so good-natured. But the times that I had—just tiny tiny flashes of impatience—I had thought, My god, I never want that directed at me.

"Jazzy," Louis finally whispered, "didn't you have a good time tonight?"

Suddenly, I saw his point. I had no choice.

I tried to reason with myself. Well . . . I had always liked Louis a lot as a friend. And I guess I did think he was cute, even if I never found him attractive in that way, because of Imo. And, after all our years of partying together and all those free drinks, I guess I owed him as much as Imo ever did. What did I think—that this was all free?

I had no valid reason to say no.

My first reaction was to sigh but I stopped myself. I felt a little nauseous and took a deep breath and swallowed hard. OK, Jazzy, I thought, let's just get this over and done with.

I put my finger to my lips to remind Louis to be quiet, then very very slowly opened the door so the creaking could barely be heard and then very very slowly closed it after we were inside. Then I took his hand and brought him to my bedroom.

Once we were inside and the door was shuffled shut, Louis quickly took off his shoes so I also took mine off. It was damn dark but the room was so small, if he even moved a bit, he would feel the bed bumping his knee. I sat on the bed and he sat very close to me—we had no choice. The bed was so narrow, after all.

Louis gently pushed me back on the bed so I was lying down, looking up at him. Then he got up, removed his Rolex Oyster and put it in his pants pocket, took something plasticky out of his wallet, then took off his pants and briefs, carefully setting them on the floor, right by the foot of the bed. Then he climbed on top of me and started kissing.

At the time, I was just kind of analyzing everything as it was happening—his kisses, quite interesting, actually. Considering how much money he has, I always thought that his kisses would surely be quite forceful. But in real life, it was actually soft and bloody wet. I wondered if that was what kissing a girl's chee bye was like. Nice and warm and wet, but at the end of the day, the chee bye doesn't give you much energy—doesn't kiss you back.

I also suddenly realized how not mabuk he was. Even in the dark, he seemed to know where everything was. While he was kissing me, his left hand could still fasterly find the buttons of my tight shirt and undo them, then unhook my front-hook bra and rub my tetek. After a few seconds of this, he sat back up and fiddled with the plastic thing in his right hand. Ah—rubber.

I heard him slip it on, felt him roll my panties off me, then quickly slip inside. I was a bit wet, but actually even if I wasn't that wet, it would also have been OK. Louis was damn small! He lay down on top of me again and started pumping away, fast and stabbing. I thought of the sleek Inferno waitresses breaking up ice in our bucket with their long silver picks.

Louis kept his promise—he was very quiet. So quiet that after less than a minute of this, he came without me even noticing. Guni-ang at first thought he was only taking a break—but when he pulled out and rolled over to lie by my side, I realized he had finished.

We lay side by side, squeezed together like sardines on my bed. I could hear him breathing damn heavily. I guess he had a good time?

"Sorry," he finally whispered. "It's been a long time. You know lah—Imo was avoiding me and then she was too sick to come out tonight."

Imo! My god, thinking about her again, lying in bed with my bra open, my panties gone, the guy she loves lying next to me, panting and now, rolling off a soggy condom—this, this really killed me. Die lah. This one is really really die.

"No worries," Louis whispered again. "I brought two rubbers. Rest a bit, then we can go again."

What? One more time? Kani nah!

I could feel his head moving around a bit, like he was looking around the room or something. I guess maybe his eyes were now adjusted to the dark; he could see a bit more. I wondered if he could see my lousy desk and all my secondary school crap, how small the room was and how the paint around the window was peeling.

"What time is it?" he whispered.

I started to move so I could try and find my phone.

"No, no, don't worry," he said. "I know it must be late."

His head was still moving around a bit—I guess he could probably see some things in the darkness. He was silent for a moment.

"Maybe," he whispered, "maybe I'd better make a move first."

"OK," I whispered back. Before I could sit up he was already standing. I quickly buttoned half my blouse and slipped on a pair of shorts so I could walk him to the door.

Ten minutes later, after closing the gate and going to the toilet for a very long time to rinse everything off down there, I lay flat on my bed, still wearing my unhooked bra under my half-buttoned shirt, staring at the ceiling, looking around the room, trying to figure out how much of this room someone could actually see in the dark, but also wondering how on earth I could possibly explain any of this to Imo and Fann. My phone suddenly buzzed.

"Wow," Louis's text said. "I always wondered what it would be like to try you. Thank you."

At first I thought I should be polite and text back but then I thought, no, it's so late in the night, I have the right to not respond. I have a good excuse. I hoped he didn't think I was rude though. I hoped that he thought I was so tired from his fantastic sex that I fell asleep.

A few minutes later, my phone buzzed again.

"I know you're a smart girl and I don't need to tell you," the text said. "But this is our little secret."

CHAPTER 17

Sometimes, when I feel like everything is going to shit, I like to watch the old uncles play Ping-Pong.

From young, I was always like that. If I had exam stress or I thought my boyfriend was losing interest, I would go and buy a plastic bag of ice kopi, slowly walk to Tiong Bahru community center, sit on one of those old stone benches, shake leg a bit and watch the gray-haired uncles in their baggy white shorts and T-shirts running around the Ping-Pong table, whacking balls.

These uncles, no matter how old they are they also try damn hard. Win or lose, they also happy. Happy just to be alive, I guess. Happy they still have energy to run around killing each other at some cock pointless game.

Even if these uncles are all damn bloody toot—I still find them to be very inspiration.

I hadn't been to see the Ping-Pong uncles in a long time—I guess that's a good sign. That means life recently hadn't been too stressful. But on Sunday in the early afternoon, the moment my mum started up with her nagging, I quickly left the house—too early to meet the girls for high tea, so I went to community center to shake leg for a bit.

When I got there, the Ping-Pong uncles at first stared at me a bit. Usually I show up in shorts and T-shirt, but today because I was going to the Shang for tea I was dressed up. Not like sexy nice, but heels and knee-length skirt, carry fake branded handbag type of nice. Walao, one uncle stared at me until a Ping-Pong ball almost whacked his face, man. But I just glared at him one time and uncle fasterly looked away. Pathetic.

Since I was wearing a skirt today, I couldn't fully prop my leg up and think, but just sitting there made me feel quite shiok. The whole morning had felt damn weird at home. At first, I wondered if my mum or pa heard anything last night, so maybe they were acting funny around me. So I purposely spent time with my mum this morning, helping her cook porridge for my dad and all. Usually these are her primo lecture times lah—when she can corner me anywhere for more than ten minutes she confirm will start trying to tell me either some life story or her life lessons. (Either way, I also lose. Even when I've listened until my ears damn pain the woman will still keep talking.) But when my mum didn't mention anything at all and even seemed a bit cheerful (perhaps thinking I'm turning over a new leaf after my obedient bean-sprout-peeling session in the kitchen with her yesterday), then I know she confirm didn't hear Louis in my room last night.

When I thought about it more, I realized why I was feeling so strange. Every time I was in my room, sitting on my bed or even just looking at my bed, all I could think about is Louis there, Louis on top, Louis . . . aiyoh, I didn't even want to think about that. But how not to think? I wanted to change sheets but also cannot—my mum confirm would scold me for making her wash the sheets when she just changed them a few days ago. (Plus, I figured it was better not to do anything to make her suspicious. Guniang here never paid any attention to housework, much less when my sheets are changed. If I suddenly asked her to change them out of schedule, she confirm would think that something had happened.)

It's not that I don't like Louis—of course I like him a lot. But he's been my good friend for how long? And now he wants to try this kind of thing with me? Obviously I shouldn't mind—he's not bad-looking for a Singaporean guy, after all. And obviously he's fucking loaded. But something is just not quite right with what happened last night.

Normally, when this kind of thing happens, the first thing to do is call a meeting with the girls and discuss discuss, see how to solve problem. But I can't even do that! Imo confirm will don't friend me anymore—and Fann will probably copy her. (Even though she was the first one to be two-faced one, snogging Louis and all. Kani nah.) And Sher, well, she's out of the picture. But of the three of them, she would probably be the only one to understand what happened to me, who might even be able to convince the other girls to forgive me. But no point thinking about her—she made the decision to fuck off out of our lives with her Ah Beng husband and leave us behind.

Even if I wanted to tell them, obviously I couldn't because I can't betray Louis. So in the end, I'm just left like this. Can only suffer alone. And Alistair—aiyoh, Alistair. I don't even know what to do about that one. He really couldn't take a hint—after my nonre-sponse, he was texting me a bit less now, so I guess he wasn't really a stalker. But he was still texting, asking when I'm free, when he can buy me coffee. As if all he wants is to do is watch me drink coffee. What does he think I am—born yesterday, is it?

Roy—got potential. Of all the guys I've met recently, he is really the only decent one. Yes, we started out by hooking up. But meeting people is sometimes like that—you cannot judge everything on how you first meet. Since then though, he has seemed nothing but nice, quite genuine, not lecherous, never pressurizing me to go home with him. Good guy lah, even if he hadn't texted me since our date at the botanical gardens. I wondered what he did last night.

Sometimes I just really don't understand. Why do I have such bad luck? Look at Fann—so fast can find ang moh boyfriend already, and one who treats her really nicely, inviting her to brunch to meet his friends and all. And Imo, even though Louis has his flaws, at least he is faithful to her—at least emotionally. Even though he's quite the *flower prince*, obviously he really cares about Imo and genuinely wants her to be happy—otherwise why would he insist that I keep last night a secret from her?

But me? What do I have?

Watching the uncles made me feel a bit more calm at least. Today they were damn happening, with four games going at once—one table even had four uncles playing doubles, fierce fierce type, pushing each other aside to hit the ball and all. I watched the balls go back and forth, back and forth, sometimes one side wins, sometimes the other side wins. In the end, who cares? If only life were really that simple.

What was I going to do?

Aiyoh, Jazzy. Better stop moping here otherwise confirm will start crying. Crying will only spoil my eye makeup and make my cheeks puffy—what's the point? Hallo, guniang, time to buck up! Well, time to meet the girls anyway. And who knows? Maybe today I will meet my Prince Charming at the Shang!

When Jazzy gets married, it's going to happen at the Shang.

This one, I long time ago decided already. There are many atas hotels in Singapore of course—first, there's the Raffles. And now here, we had even gotten those American-branded hotels like Four Seasons and Saint Something or Other—don't play play! But the Shangri-La was the first really atas modern hotel in Singapore. Classy classy, with a big white lobby, high ceilings, gigantic crystal

chandeliers; plus, the gardens all around it were just like the botanical gardens, all lush and green. Bloody relaxing.

The first time I saw the Shang was when I was in primary school—at
that time my mum's brother was driving a taxi for a while so sometimes
on Sunday he would come and bring us out for a joyride. We never went
far—hallo, do you know how expensive petrol is?—but he always tried
to bring us to places that we didn't normally see. So one Sunday we
were driving along Nassim Hill, looking at all the bloody three-story,
four-story mansions when we passed by the Shang.

"Kuku," I said, tapping on my uncle's wooden-bead seat cushion.
"What's that?"

"Oh—that one is high-class hotel, one of the most high-class! Ah
Huay ah—when you grow up ah, if you ever can go and eat inside
the Shangri-La Hotel ah—you confirm succeed already."

"Aiyoh—please don't go and put these kinds of funny ideas in
her head, make her think too big!" my mum said, turning around
to look at me. "These kinds of places, Ah Huay—they are not meant
for everybody, you know."

I remember fasterly kneeling on the seat, at first staring staring
out the side window, then as my uncle passed the hotel, desperately
trying to look out the back of the taxi window to get another look
at the Shang, but by that time we were too far away already. But
my kuku saw me looking disappointed, I guess, because he made a
U-turn so he could take us back.

As we got closer to the gate, kuku slowed down a bit—then he
turned into the Shang!

"Aiyoh," my mum said, sighing. Guniang over here was so happy
I wanted to roll down the window so I could poke my head out! (But
then I decided I'd better not—see, even when I was eight, guniang
here already knew how to act a bit cool.)

The driveway, I remember, was very wide—like those big roads leading to old English castles I'd seen on the TV. And since kuku was driving slowly, as we approached the big white hotel, the building very very slowly got grander and grander each second. Through the large glass walls in front, I could see the sparkling white lobby inside with its bright chandeliers. A tall Indian man wearing black pants, a red Indian-style long tunic and a black and gold hat with a tall black feather sprouting out of it started waving at my kuku as we got closer to the entrance. So my kuku slowed down. I guess the guy wanted us to stop.

Once kuku pulled on his handbrake, the doorman opened my door, smiled at me and bowed. Wah! Guniang had never felt so special before.

That lasted all of one second—that's when I heard my kuku frantically rolling down his squeaky window. "Oh, I'm so sorry, I'm so sorry!" he said to the doorman, bowing his head a few times as he talked. I remember thinking, What the hell is he doing? It's not like we are those Japanese tourists or sumo wrestlers who spend half their lives bowing to shit.

"We are at the wrong place; not dropping here," my uncle said. "Sorry, sorry. Very sorry to waste your time."

I could see the guard's face suddenly change for a second, especially as his eyes quickly moved down and he noticed what we were wearing. I don't remember exactly what I had on but it was probably just shorts, T-shirt and flip-flops. (Later on when I got older, I understood the guard's look—it pretty much said, "Bloody hell.") But it was just for a bit, then he went back to smiling.

"Of course," he said in a British accent, softly closing the taxi door.

Nobody said anything as kuku quickly drove away from the Shang, but I could see my mum in the front seat crouching down, not looking out the window, just looking down.

To this day my mum has never set foot at the Shang. But I—I of course am a different story. It's not like I come here very often but sometimes I do have to follow Albert when he comes here for business lunches. And there was that one time that Gavin took me here for dinner—of course, it was the dinner where he broke up with me lah. But still, I'd once had a boyfriend who was atas enough to take me to dinner at the Shang! Now, once in a long while, if there's a special occasion, the girls will book table for drinks or high tea.

And today, one of our secondary school friends Keira had just come back from England with a new baby, so she called us all to come out and see her at the Shang for tea.

I don't really know Keira that well—last time she was a lot closer to Sher and Imo, not me and Fann. (I always had the feeling that it's because she thinks Sher and Imo are more chio, so she prefers to associate with them more. This one is not confirmed lah—just my dirty feeling.) But old friends are old friends—since she hadn't been home in a long time, we were all happy to come out and see her. Must remember to call her Keira though. Our whole life we knew her as Xiu Ying—or Ah Ying usually. But when she met her boyfriend—now husband—at some SPG bar and started hanging with his friends from London then suddenly her name became Keira. "Keira Knightley is so happening what," she explained.

I remember telling her, "If you're going to pick a celebrity's name, why choose the one with flat-flat tetek? Why not choose some big-boobs actress so the name at least has some good karma?" My god, this comment made her angry. But it's true! If you want to give yourself some new ang moh name, must at least be a bit smart lah. Keira? It's just a damn cock name.

Anyway, now we're all good friends—especially since Keira had successfully married an ang moh and moved to the UK. So who knows? Maybe she has some kind of on-the-ground connections to help us find boyfriends.

Fann, Imo and Keira were all there already by the time I got to the Shang. Three of them were sitting close together, bending their necks, oohing and aahing. Ah—baby.

"Hi hi!" I said, remembering to smile and then waving at all of them.

"Jazzy! Thanks for coming!" Keira said, waving back at me. The other two didn't even look up; they were both just in a daze, staring at the fat whitish baby in Keira's lap, pinching its legs.

"Jazz, say hi to Charles," Keira said, propping the baby up on her lap and holding his chubby hand up to wave at me.

"Hi!" I said, waving back. I tell you—I know the goal is to have a Chanel baby. But babies are actually damn fucking boring. What to do or say to them? I also never know. But still, I felt I had to find something to say.

"Eh, Keira, your boy has so much black hair!" I said, saying the first thing that came to my mind. "Very Asian, no?"

Silence. Keira stopped smiling.

"Choi!" Imo quickly said, violently flapping her hands as if to wave away the bad luck I'd just introduced with that notion. "Don't listen to her, Keira. If you ask anybody, confirm they will tell you they can't even tell he's half Singaporean."

Imo. Aiyoh—seeing made thoughts of Louis in my bedroom last night pop right back into my head. I felt like I couldn't look her in the face. But bloody hell, if I act weird, she might suspect something. Die die must act normal.

So I just giggled. "Yes, yes, Keira," I said. "Just joking!"

The girls had ordered the all-you-can-drink champagne high tea so we already had glasses sitting on the table.

"Come, come—cheers first!" I said, trying to make Keira smile again. It worked of course. Some things never change. If there's alcohol, Keira's always happy. You can take the sarong party girl out of Singapore . . .

After we toasted each other, Fann said, "Imo—tell Jazzy about the present!"

My god, what present? Don't tell me we were supposed to bring Keira present? Kani nah—she is the one coming back from far away. She's supposed to be bringing us all presents!

Imo just looked down a little and blushed. I leaned forward. OK, this must be something interesting.

"Aiyah," she said, smiling a bit more. "It's nothing lah. Louis just sent me a bouquet of flowers this morning. Sunday delivery, you know—more expensive!"

"Some more it's a dozen roses, you know," Fann said, jumping in. "Red ones!"

"Stop it lah!" Imo said, laughing. "I'm sure it's only because he wanted to cheer me up because I was sick."

Fann just snorted. "Please—use your brain!" Fann said. "The guy has never given you flowers before but suddenly—on a Sunday, his day at home with Mary—he sends you a dozen roses? Maybe he's finally getting serious."

Imo was really blushing now. I wanted to vomit.

"My god," I said. "Girls—please! If you want to jinx things then please, go ahead and keep talking about it."

After that, they immediately shut up the topic. Partly because at that time someone else joined us—Sher! My god. As if my day couldn't get any worse.

The only available chair was the one next to me. Of course.

"Hi dear!" Keira said, almost squealing. "I've missed you so much!"

"Me too! Me too!" Sher said, looking only briefly at Keira and then looking over at me.

"Jazz," she said quietly. Her eyes were a bit sad all of a sudden. "How are you?"

Good god. After ignoring all her texts and not even bothering to listen to her voice messages or read her emails since she came back from her Ah Beng honeymoon, I really didn't want to talk to her. But this was Keira's party; I must show her face.

"OK lah," I just said, forcing out a smile before looking back at the girls across the table. "Same same."

After we got another champagne glass, we all did a cheers together, then it was down to the gossip. Since Keira was the only one who had managed to achieve the SPG dream—so far—wah, that guniang was suddenly acting like an expert. When Fann filled her in about Melvin, she just nodded and smiled, telling her she's doing well—on the right track! Keira even gave her a thumbs-up sign when Fann mentioned the brunch invitation. I didn't want to say much—definitely not about Alistair, confirm not about Louis and especially not the fact that Roy, my only real prospect, works on oil refinery—so I just said, "Well I met this sweet British guy—but it's still early! I don't want to jinx it by saying too much."

Keira and the other two just nodded; Sher looked like she wanted to ask me more but decided to keep quiet.

I had to admit that Sher looked good—she looked a bit darker so she probably went to some beach resort on Batam for her honeymoon. I couldn't even bother to ask her which one. But Keira of course asked, so I had to hear the long story about how they stayed at one of those family resorts so it was a bit noisy but still quite nice, the food was not bad—Ah Huat complained a bit that the dishes were not as good as those at Singapore hawker centers and damn expensive but they did taste nice. Blah blah blah. For most of the conversation, I actually stoned out a bit, not because what they said wasn't interesting—I don't mind hearing about Keira and her life in England, even if I don't know where the fuck Hackney is. (Hallo—if you're going to England to live, if you're not living in London then you at least must live somewhere that people have actually heard of before, like Liverpool or Manchester or Aston Villa. Come back to Singapore and tell people you live in Hackney? Might as well say you're living in Ang Mo Kio—if people have never heard of this bumfuck place before, then it is confirm quite LC.) But Fann and Melvin—boring lah. I already heard that long story over lunch yesterday. And I definitely don't want to hear anything about Sher and her cock life.

The more I looked at Imo, how happy she seemed that day, how she has no idea what I did, the more I felt sick.

"Jazzy, are you feeling OK?" Sher asked.

Of course she's the only one who noticed. But now that she said that, everyone suddenly looked at me, a bit concerned. Escape plan!

"I might be coming down with something," I said. "Maybe I'd better make a move first."

I took out my wallet and left eighty dollars on the table, looked around at the girls and pretended to cough. "Sorry, Keira," I said. "But I'd better not make your baby sick anyway. You take care ah?"

Keira just nodded, so I fasterly got up and left. I looked back once as I was leaving—the three girls on one side, back to oohing and aahing over the baby. Sher was the only one looking at me as I walked away. I bet she was wondering whether she should chase after me to make sure I could get home OK or just talk a bit.

I just pretended I didn't see her and quickly turned around.

Once I left the restaurant I started to feel a bit better. But still not OK. Every time I closed my eyes or felt distracted, I could see Louis's face on top of me, feel Louis in me, hear Louis talking to me. And the more it happened, the more I thought that I really was a damn shit friend to Imo. At least I know that's what Sher would say. And I know that yes, I'm not friends with Sher anymore. But still, of all the people I know who truly understand any situation, she is the best. So, yes, I really was a damn shit friend.

It's not that I wanted to fuck Louis, you know. The exact opposite! But hallo, even if Sher was the one in that situation, I think she confirm would have said yes to him. You know how Louis is. No one is allowed to say no. No one. I mean, you can. But the consequences—confirm is not fun. And I felt I couldn't just think of myself in that moment, I had to think about the good of the group. You know, harmony, free drinks and all that shit.

There was suddenly some music in the lobby—soft, so it didn't seem to be coming from within the lobby. I followed it outside and saw white ribbons and big bows all over the gazebo in the center of the garden. On one side there were these old Chinese guys in tuxedos, sitting up straight and playing violins or some shit. On the other side was a few rows of chairs. People were still talking talking among themselves so I guess the bride and groom weren't coming down so soon yet.

Quickly, I snuck over toward the side of the courtyard where I knew there were a few benches and picked one that confirm had a good view of the gazebo. The Shang's garden is damn atas—I mean, most hotels that charge these kinds of prices surely have atas gardens but this one was damn super atas. Each bush, each tree—their gardeners spend every day trimming them until all perfectly round or oval type. Sometimes they might even make special shapes and all—one time for Chinese New Year, there was even one with a giant dragon shape. Don't anyhow play!

Guniang was quietly sitting there, looking at the guests, trying to see who was wearing what, carrying what handbag, when all of a sudden someone was talking to me.

"Jazzy?"

Kani nah. Of course it was Sher. I didn't say anything.

"Come on, don't be like that," she said, sitting down next to me. Of course she would have figured out that I might come here. The first few times we came to the Shang, we always came to this garden. If there was a wedding happening, we would come and sit for a bit and stare, imagining. The thought of that made me feel a twinge. At least for me, now, I still have a chance to imagine. For Sher, her SPG life and dreams were over.

"Jazzy, I think we need to talk," Sher said, leaning out now, like she was trying to block my view. Babi.

"Talk? About what?" I said. "Please, everything is OK. We have nothing to say."

Sher opened her mouth, as if she wanted to say something more. But then she closed it again. I didn't want to look at her, but from the side of my eyes I could see her smoothing down her skirt over her knees—walao, guniang married for such a short time only already started wearing these long auntie skirts, covering knees and all. If I didn't already feel like throwing up, then now I confirm would start to feel it.

I was considering getting up to leave, even though the wedding hadn't even started yet. But then a waiter came up to us, holding a tray.

"Ladies," he said, bowing a bit and smiling. "Would you like a glass of champagne?"

Aiyoh, maybe he thinks we're here for the wedding! OK, maybe Sher's auntie-length skirt at least had some use. Sher just smiled at him and took two glasses off the tray, handing me one.

"Cheers!" I said to the waiter as he bowed and walked away.

I looked at Sher and Sher looked at me. Then we both clinked our glasses and laughed.

After we stopped laughing—and after a few sips—Sher leaned back and crossed her legs.

"Jazz," she said. I could feel her watching me so I tried to keep smiling, even though I didn't really want to anymore. I don't know what she was about to say. But hallo, today the gardens were so nice, there was an atas wedding about to happen, the two of us had just laughed together for the first time in god knows how long, why did she have to ruin it?

"Remember Eugene?" she said.

Yah, Eugene. Once I thought of him I couldn't help but smile a bit bigger. Who didn't like Eugene? That guy—my god, that guy—he really was one of the best. We all knew him when we were quite young. I think, twelve or thirteen? He was a few years older—I think fifteen or something at the time. And even though we—and all the girls in the neighborhood—were all damn steam for him, we were all so young, we all confirm had no chance with him. You know how it is when you're that age lah—even a year or two age difference feels like five or ten years sometimes.

But we all lived in the same area, hung out in the same community center, went to the same kopitiam, and on Saturday, Sunday we would see each other with our mothers in the same wet market, that type of thing. So Eugene knew who we were. (He knew that we existed, anyway.) We actually even became friends. Sometimes if Sher and me were alone in the kopitiam he might ask us to join him and his friends, maybe even buy us a plate of chicken rice if we were feeling hungry.

The funny thing about Eugene was that he was the biggest tough guy Ah Beng around. Not the hard-core kind though—just slightly enough of an Ah Beng that he was still cool. He was big on skateboarding then—but since he was quite Ah Beng, he was part of Ah Beng skateboarding group, not the cool ang moh skateboarding teenagers we sometimes saw near Holland Village. And when he was with his gang, he would always be damn act tough—throwing third finger and kani nah around all the time and shouting "Oi, brudder!" to his fellow Ah Bengs a lot. But when he was alone with me and Sher, buying us ice Milo or kaya toast at the kopitiam, he was totally different—sweet sweet one. He always asked us how was school, which boys were trying to chase us, tell us toot jokes to make us smile, sometimes bringing us small boxes of those cute Japanese chocolate cookies shaped like pandas and shit like that. We all knew—even though he's a smelly Ah Beng, whoever ended up marrying Eugene is confirm win lottery one. This guy maybe to the outside world is a tough asshole but at home, no matter what, he will always treat you like a princess.

At that time, Sher and I hoped one of us would end up being the lucky one. We were so young—not SPGs yet. But then after Eugene went to the army, we never saw him again. I don't know why.

"Yeah," I said. "That Eugene really was number one."

Sher smiled, but just a little bit. "Well," she said. "I don't expect you to understand, but Jazzy, Ah Huat is really my Eugene."

Wah, guniang here—stunned. I guess I never really thought about it. In fact, I hadn't thought about Eugene in many donkey's years. And when I thought about it now, I guess I could understand. Back when we first became SPGs, Sher and I would discuss Ah Bengs and we always said yes, Ah Bengs are Ah Bengs but a guy like Eugene, is actually a sexy Ah Beng. He has the best of the Ah Beng qualities—that swagger that makes him act tough to the rest of the world but at home, with people he really cares about? He's just a big cuddly teddy bear. And the sexiest thing though is that you know that whoever he cares about, he cares about fiercely—he'll do anything to defend and protect them. When you think about it, that really is damn bloody sexy.

Although I still wasn't fully convinced, I lifted my glass and smiled at Sher. I'd have to think about this a bit more but for now, sitting in the Shang, a glass of champagne in my hand, I really missed my old friend. I really missed our moments like this.

"Cheers," Sher said—my god, her eyes were watering a bit and all. I figured I'd better fasterly change the subject before this turned into a Taiwanese soap opera.

"So," I said, sounding a bit serious—which I was. "I don't want you to worry. But something happened."

Sher's face got damn serious. Obviously, Sher was now worrying like crazy. Since I almost never begin any conversations like that.

"Are you sick?" she said, grabbing my knee.

"Aiyoh, my god—no!" I said. "Hallo, auntie, sometimes there are worse things than cancer and shit, OK! No, no, no. Just . . . there was this weird situation with this guy, and I couldn't say no, I really couldn't, and now I just feel damn . . ." I didn't even know how to finish my sentence. But I looked over at Sher and I could see that she understood perfectly.

Sher looked concerned. She sighed and took a long sip, then waved her index finger over at the nice waiter and made the "two" sign. The guy jumped up and brought his tray over, lowering it so we could pick up fresh glasses.

"Are you OK?" Sher asked, looking worried. "Do you like this guy?"

"No! I mean, it's not that I don't like him . . . I just don't, I mean . . ." Aiyoh, this one I really didn't know how to explain. If I say too much, Sher knows me and the group so well, she confirm will guess it's

Louis. And if I know Sher, she will insist on me doing the right thing and telling Imo about it. And if Imo knows then Louis will know. And the whole world will just go to shit. No more clubbing in atas clubs, no more VIP lounges and free drinks.

"I mean," I said, "it's just awkward and weird and nothing can happen between us but I keep thinking about it and . . ." I realized I was probably explaining it terribly. The way I was talking about it, I could see Sher possibly guessing that I'm a bit embarrassed and maybe lovesick. My god, that confirm is not the case!

Sher smiled. "Jazzy, don't tell me you don't remember the last-penis theory!" she said.

Wah, this one is confirm misunderstanding. Last-penis theory is for when you really like the guy and you cannot forget him, pining pining for him, that kind of thing. We had read it in some ang moh magazine years ago lah and at first we laughed like crazy over it but then, it turned out, there's probably some truth to it. The theory is that the one thing that can help you forget the guy is if you pok someone else—the new penis in your life, even if you're not a serious relationship, as long as it's a fun fun one, confirm can help push the last penis you had out of your mind.

I started to say something to correct Sher like, no, really, I'm not in love or anything. But then I thought—actually, maybe she has a point. It doesn't matter how I feel about Louis. If I can't stop imagining him in my bed, then maybe . . .

"True, true," I said, winking at Sher. Come, I said, looking at my phone to see what time it was. "Bottoms up!"

Sher didn't walk all the way out with me because she was going to rejoin Keira and the girls. Before she left though, she gave me a hug—one I didn't want at first but feeling her arms fiercely wrapped around me, my chest started to hurt. I hugged her back.

When Sher started to let go, she asked, "Are you still happy at work?"

I paused, wondering what to say. That flicker of silence was enough for Sher to understand.

"Ah," she said. "Listen—Ah Huat really could use a business manager at his place, someone to help him keep things running so he can focus on the classes."

I pulled away from Sher, trying to stop myself from making a face. It had been such a nice moment—why did she have to spoil it with such nonsense? Yes, I was coming around to accepting that maybe it wasn't complete craziness that she had married this Ah Beng—but I sure as hell was never going to lower myself to work for him even so. Jazzy here has a good job with an atas boss! To leave that and work for an Ah Beng? Her husband can go and dream!

"OK, OK," Sher quickly said. "Forget I mentioned it, OK? But, if you ever . . ."

"I'm fine—don't worry," I said, giving her hand a quick squeeze. "Now go—the girls will be waiting for you."

As I watched her walk back to the restaurant, away from me, I thought about our chat; the feeling of Sher sitting next to me again, two girls laughing.

CHAPTER 18

Something very strange happened on Thursday.

The week had passed by quite peacefully at work—nothing more mentioned about circulation from Albert, who seemed to be in a good mood overall. On Thursday morning though, Sean, the foreign editor, came by to tell me he was having a drinks party at his house. Don't know what cock reason he had for throwing the party lah but he'd never invited me before. So even though I don't like him, I felt I had to go.

At first, I thought Albert my boss was going to this party—which is mostly the reason I thought I should go. If the boss is going, then I should be there. But when I asked Albert in the afternoon, "Eh, boss—what time are you going to Sean's party tonight?" he just looked at me blur.

"Sean invited you to his party?" he said, frowning.

Aiyoh—am I not supposed to go? Is this one of those atas parties that only editors attend?

"Boss, if you think I shouldn't go, then of course I won't go," I quickly said. That weird conversation with Albert had only happened last week, after all. Guniang here was still trying to stay on Albert's good side and keep him in happy mood. I confirm don't want him to think I'm starting to think too highly of myself or anything.

"No, no, no," he said—not frowning anymore but still not smiling. He looked like he was thinking hard. "I'm not going. But if he invited you, of course you should go ahead. Only if you want to, of course." And then he didn't say anything more about it for the rest of the day.

Sean's party only started at nine so guniang had time to go home, eat dinner with my mum, bathe and all. He said the party was not formal so I just picked one of my sleeveless casual black dresses—not so short that it will zaogeng and let everyone see my panties, but something above the knee—and nice heels. On the way there, I even had time to stop by a Wine Exchange to buy a nice bottle of red—French, of course. First time at the foreign editor's party—better have manners a bit.

Guniang was feeling good that evening. Alistair was texting less, perhaps starting to get the hint that hallo, he was probably never going to see me again. But the main thing was—Roy finally texted! I hadn't heard from him since our garden walk, which was making me start to wonder.

When I saw his name pop up on my phone after dinner, I at first want to press DELETE without even reading. But OK lah, guniang at least wanted to see what his cock explanation was. It turns out that right after our date he had a big team of clients from the States fly in for a week, and he's been so busy working and entertaining them that he'd had no time for fun. I knew it had to be something serious keeping him from contacting me!

"In fact," he texted, "are you free for dinner tomorrow? There's a goodbye dinner and we're allowed to bring a date if we want."

Wah—dinner to meet not just his friends, but his colleagues? Set lah! This one—confirm is very promising! I wondered what Fann would say. Dinner is better than brunch!

Guniang acted tough a bit, waiting one hour before texting back: "OK."

So, by the time my taxi reached Sean's house—a really nice one near Bukit Timah Hill and all—guniang was in a bloody good mood.

"Jazeline—ah, you're here!" Sean said when he came out to open the tall iron gate. Things felt a little funny right away—Sean was wearing shorts! Nice shorts lah—one of those knee-length tailored berms, maybe even a branded pair, and his button-down work shirt was still on, though it was untucked and his sleeves were rolled up. I guess when he said the party was not formal, he really meant it. I suddenly felt quite shy.

"I suppose I'm overdressed!" I said, laughing a bit. My god—my laugh was so high, surely Sean could hear that I was nervous.

"No, not at all," he said, leaning down to give me an air kiss. "You look just perfect."

After thanking me for the wine, he said, "Well come in, come in—everyone's inside already." So I followed him down the short driveway, squeezing a bit past the big silver Lexus parked right in the middle, kicked off my heels and stepped into his house. It was quite an atas place—a very big corner townhouse surrounded by a large bushy garden on all three sides. Damn quiet, since it's so near Bukit Timah Hill and all those parks that old people like to do qigong in. I guess some people like that kind of thing—for me, once I get married, I'll prefer to live in a house in Holland Village. You still get the good schools there and some parks and playgrounds lah—but at least nearby you have all those ang moh restaurants, bars and shops so even though you're married, you at least still can be happening. Not dead yet.

"Jazeline, I think you probably know everyone—Serene, Su Fen and Vidya are all on the news desk, Shamini's over in sports and that's Lydia, my wife," Sean said, pointing at the women one by one around the room. The news desk girls were squeezed together on one sofa; the other two were half-lounging on fat glossy beanbags on the floor, loudly cracking peanuts and melon seeds open and throwing the shells into a bowl on the glass coffee table. At least they were getting most of them in. Only one or two women bothered to wave "Hallo" at me.

I knew who they were—everyone except Lydia, that is. I had seen them all in the newsroom before—not Shamini so much because sports is on a different floor. But the other girls, I often see them purposely waving their backsides all over the newsroom when they walk so everyone can steam over them. Yah lah—that's the kind of girls they were. Their work is so-so—from what I hear; guniang here doesn't read the newspaper, so how am I supposed to know?—but even so, somehow they always get assigned to cover the front-page stories.

I was quite surprised to see what Sean's wife looked like though. He never brings her to office functions and his desk at work is very empty and clean, so I'd never seen her or her photo before. Because he was Eurasian I always thought his wife confirm was Eurasian—that's how they are. The Eurasian boys will sometimes date Chinese or Indian girls for fun, maybe even keep them as "serious" girl-friends for a few years. But when it comes to marrying, they confirm will prefer to marry other Eurasians one.

"We are such a small, unique race," one of them explained to me a long time ago. This was after we hooked up, when he was explaining why we can be fuck buddies but he can never bring me home. "We really owe it to our ancestors, to Singapore history and identity, to try and preserve the purity of it. Otherwise the Eurasians will just gradually disappear!"

When he explained it like that, I guess I had to understand. Tradition, of course, is very important. So we were quite happy fuck buddies for four and a half months until he started getting serious with a Eurasian girl from church that he ended up marrying.

Lydia, though, was not Eurasian. Not only was she Chinese-Singaporean, but she was not a good-looking Chinese! Aiyoh. I really hope they don't have kids, man—otherwise not only is Sean going to have non-pure Eurasian kids, but he's also going to have backside-face kids. Lydia was one of those slightly chubby face, wear glasses, small flat nose Chinese ladies. No matter how good her personality was, it confirm must not be enough for someone like Sean to marry a face like that. I guessed that she must be very clever, have a lot of money, or come from name-brand family.

"What would you like to drink?" Sean asked. "I've sent the maid off to sleep so I'm afraid I'll have to be the one making your drink."

"Well," I said, quickly looking at what was on the coffee table. I couldn't quite see what they had been drinking but it was obvious that they had been doing it for a while—not only were there peanut shells and half-cracked melon seeds all over the table but there were also a dozen shot glasses and a few larger ones filled with clear drinks. "I guess I'll just have what everyone's drinking?"

"Good!" he said. "Another gin and tonic, then."

Looking at how mabuk some of the girls looked—the two girls on the edges of the sofa were so tipsy they were leaning their heads on the shoulder of Su Fen in the middle—I was starting to wonder when they actually started drinking. Also, I was wondering—where is the rest of the party? I thought this was an official party, with different editors, their friends, maybe even some potential ang mohs to date, that kind of thing. Walao—guniang here even wore nice nice clothes and all! But this just looked like one of those sit around with your old secondary school friends, drink until mabuk and tell cock stories and sex jokes kind of party. Bloody hell! Never mind lah—maybe I could just have a quick drink and say I have to leave. Tomorrow we must work, after all.

"Here you go," Sean said, handing me a big cold glass. "Come, Jazeline—sit next to me."

So I followed behind him as he walked to the other side of the sofa and sat on a wide armchair, patting his hand on the arm of his chair. Aiyoh—there?

Sean must have seen me pause and think a bit because he said, "Well don't just stand there—come on?" he said, patting the arm again. So, no choice.

Of course it was uncomfortable because it was quite high and I'm not that tall, so even though my backside was resting on the arm, it was almost as if I was half-standing.

"Good girl," Sean said, tapping my backside a bit. Walao! Guni-ang here was so shocked I almost spilled my drink! Some more, after Sean finished tapping my backside he kept his hand there. And his wife was just one meter away, sitting on the beanbag! At least she wasn't looking over at us, though. Thank god. But my goodness—this one was really too much. I squirmed my backside to give Sean a hint but he didn't move his hand.

There was nothing more I could do so I just sipped my drink. But the first sip I took—kani nah, I almost spat it out. So bloody strong! Su Fen must have noticed my face, because she started laughing.

"Sean dear, did you make a really strong G and T for—what's your name again?" she said, nudging Mabuk One and Mabuk Two next to her and pointing at me. "Look at her face! Priceless."

Sean also laughed. "Jazeline—you have to catch up, my dear," he said. "We've been drinking since after work. Now go on—drink it all!"

Su Fen started clapping and the Mabuk Twins started staring

so aiyah, OK lah—bottoms up. Plus, if I finish my drink quickly, maybe that would give me an opening to make an excuse and leave faster.

The drink was so strong, this was not easy—my throat was burning, my eyes were wet, so wet I had to close them for a bit. But I did it. When I opened my eyes, I could see Su Fen had gotten up and was making another drink.

"Um—no more, no more! I can't stay long," I said.

"Rubbish! You just got here," Sean said. "Now settle in," he added, tapping my backside again!

I made sure to slowly sip my second drink, which was as strong as the first and had no lime so—babi, the alcohol tasted even stronger.

Sean was telling some story now—something from his time as a hotshot foreign correspondent in Manila or some shit. Only Su Fen was asking him any questions—the other girls were just half-listening but mostly giggling here and there. I guess they were super high. His wife seemed a bit mabuk too—judging from how rosy her fat cheeks were—but she didn't say one word. She just sat there, only smiling a very tiny bit but still looking quite serious. If I had to guess, I would say that she's a lawyer or some banking exec. She just had that perfect "don't blow smoke up my arse" look.

At this point, all the girls started laughing, even the Mabuks. Sean's story probably reached the punch line or something. So I laughed along also. After we all finished, there was just silence. Maybe now was a good time. I bottoms-up the last third of my glass and started to say I have to go but Sean—my god, he really noticed everything—said, "Lydia—Jazeline's done. Make her another one, OK?" And before I could say anything, his wife just got up and did it.

"Well . . ." Su Fen said. "Is it time?"

Shamini and the Mabuks, who I guess had gotten their second wind after all that pretend laughing, said, "Ooh, yes!" So Su Fen got up again and disappeared into what's probably the dining room door, and came back with a big white cardboard box. The Mabuks quickly cleared the coffee table, brushing all the shells and seeds onto the floor so Su Fen could set the box down and take off the lid.

The girls all got off the sofa and the beanbags so they could crowd around the table and start pulling things out of the box. I couldn't see anything at first because they were all crowding around, but one by one they started holding things up, looking at them and then setting them aside on the coffee table. I wasn't quite sure what they were at first but the more I saw, I understood.

Sex toys!

Shamini pulled out a set of what looked like handcuffs ringed with small red feathers, Serene waved around a long black stick that suddenly started making a buzzing sound when she pressed a button, Vidya started opening small vials of lotions, dabbing some on her wrists and smelling them. There were several masks, some sort of board game and a set of large dice with words instead of numbers printed on each side.

I looked around the room to see where Sean's wife was in all this. What could she possibly be thinking?

Lydia was standing by the bottles of alcohol—she had already finished making my drink but she wasn't bringing it over. Instead, she was just standing there, leaning against the table of alcohol, slowly sipping a shot of something, just casually staring at everything with a bored, patient face. Obviously, she'd seen this before.

But surely, she could stop it?

The girls were squealing louder now, taking more and more things out of the box.

"What shall we start with this time, Sean? The dice?" Vidya said, taking off her cardigan, pulling the rubber band out of her ponytail and shaking her head a few times so her long wavy hair fell to her shoulders.

"Yah! Yah! The dice is always a good icebreaker," Su Fen said. "Especially for newcomers!"

Newcomers? Lumpar lah!

I looked back at Lydia, who downed the rest of her shot and firmly put down the glass, grabbed my drink and walked back over. Good—it was high time the woman came over here to set her husband and everyone else straight.

Lydia walked over and handed me the glass, not even looking at me. Then she sat back down on her beanbag and cleared her throat loudly.

"Just pick one lah," she said. "Tomorrow is a working day—let's not go too late this time."

Walao! Guniang here was feeling a bit paralyzed, I have to admit. This kind of thing, I could never have imagined. KTV girls, yes. Prostitutes, yah, I can imagine. But this? Professional girls from my own office? With the foreign editor and his backside-face lawyer-banker wife? My god.

Just then, Sean said, "OK, come, come, come—wifey said, 'Let's go!'" And he patted my backside again, harder this time.

Guniang jumped up right away. "Sean, I'm sorry—but I really think I have to go," I said.

I couldn't even look at any of the other girls or Lydia as I ran out of the door. As I was putting on my heels, Sean was suddenly standing next to me. He looked a bit confused.

"Jazeline—are you OK?"

"Yah—I just . . . I just need to go home," I said.

"I'm sorry—I thought . . ." he said. "Well, this is just a bit of fun we have around the office sometimes . . . it's a rather select group, actually. And it's nothing very serious—just lighthearted games, really. I don't just invite everyone over. And I had assumed that, well, you seem to go out clubbing a lot and have a lot of fun, and well, I had just heard some things and . . ."

"And? And you thought I would be interested in being part of your sex-toy *New Times* harem?"

Guniang here was getting a bit angry now. Which is not bad, I thought—better than losing it inside there around all of them. I thought I had been damn patient all night already. But after everything that happened over the past week, guniang here honestly was losing patience with everything.

At this point, I could see Sean's eyes change a bit. He straightened up and said, "Should I call you a taxi?"

"No, no need," I said. "The main road is nearby. I can just walk. Thank you though. And thank you for the drinks. Please also say thank you to Lydia for me."

Before he could talk again, I quickly started walking to the gate.

"Jazeline?"

"Yah?" I said, turning around just as I opened it.

"I hear congratulations are in order, by the way," he said. I could see him smiling. "When are you moving to circulation?"

CHAPTER 19

Whole day long I was sitting at my desk, thinking about how to bring up the box of sex toys.

Not to Sean of course, but to Albert. I had managed to avoid Sean all day—which wasn't hard because I'm sure he also wanted to avoid me. I did see Su Fen once or twice though and each time she not only didn't quickly look down or avoid me—bloody hell, that girl is really not shy! Instead, she just stared at me, blinked once and then walked away.

Every time I tried to talk to Albert though, he just either rushed right past me and said he had a meeting to go to (even though I know it's lies—hallo, I am the one who keeps his schedule after all) or really must go to the loo. After about the fifth time he did that, I figured out that he must be avoiding me too.

But like that, how? This was the first time guniang really needed his advice, man. Plus, what was this about circulation?

I decided to use my lunch break to kaypoh a bit.

Once Albert had safely disappeared to his business lunch in the financial district, I headed straight over to the next building—the decrepit old one where no one in the newsroom, except Albert, ever went. To the right of the lobby, which looked like it was still firmly in the 1970s, was a big sign: CIRCULATION.

A Malay receptionist greeted me the moment I pushed open the door. "Good afternoon, miss!" she said in a cheery singsong voice. "How can I help you?"

"Oh, I'm here from the news side," I said, flashing my *New Times* pass. She smiled and nodded. "I just wanted to look-see a bit," I added. "Can?"

"Of course, of course," she said, waving me in. "Just go right in."

Past the reception area, there was a large cavernous room filled with neat rows of desks, all in a grid. Even though it was lunchtime, the room was filled with women, some eating sandwiches at their desks, others gathered together, chitchatting over cups of tea. At first I thought I didn't know anyone here but a youngish woman caught my eye in the far corner—wasn't that Michelle? Albert's assistant before me? And that woman she was chatting with—that was Pauline, the one before Michelle! I had met Michelle when I first arrived but knew Pauline from a photo Albert had once shown me. In another corner of the room, I spied a woman I sometimes saw having coffee with Albert in the cafeteria. Could she be another former assistant? I had thought all along that these women left for jobs elsewhere—perhaps they became executive assistants to men higher up than Albert, or for CEOs along Shenton Way. But no, here they all were, in some apparent dumping ground for the assistants Albert had outgrown. As much as I'm sure Albert was going to paint this as a good career move, this was essentially a cemetery for aging women that the *New Times*—or rather, Albert—didn't want anymore!

I was so shocked I didn't even see that Michelle had spotted me. She was waving vigorously by the time I noticed.

I knew what I should do, but I simply couldn't. No, this was not a place for Jazzy—not today and definitely not in the near future. I quickly turned around and walked out, back across the parking lot and into my shiny, clean building. My heart didn't stop racing until I was safely back in my plump swivel chair. "Jazzy," I told myself.

"You need to use your brain to think! This cannot happen to you. It simply cannot."

Albert returned from lunch just slightly mabuk, though still ignoring me. He didn't say a word to me for most of the afternoon. Toward the end of the day though, just as I was starting to put files away and clean my kopi cup, Albert popped his head out of his office and said, "Jazz, can you come in for a minute?"

Finally! "Yes, boss!" I said, and quickly went in.

"Come, sit, sit," he said, opening his drawer and taking out his specs.

Was he doing this to get a better view today? Oh, that's right. Guniang was wearing a skirt today. I started to walk over to his sofa, wondering if I should offer to mix him a drink first, when Albert said, "Not today, Jazz—I'm late for drinks already, so I don't have much time. Just come sit on the chair over here."

OK—guniang today was actually wearing nice panties and all, since I had that dinner tonight with Roy and his company. If Albert didn't care about peeping, it's his own pasal. I just walked over and sat on one of the black metal chairs in front of his desk.

Albert was quiet and looked like he was thinking hard about something. I didn't want to interrupt him but I had decided last night when I got home—if he doesn't know what is happening with Sean, he should know. This kind of shameful thing can be very bad for the *New Times*, you know. I may not read the newspaper but I always look at the headlines, so I know that the *New Times* really likes to splash stories about politicians and CEOs having scandalous affairs all over the front page. If word about Sean's sex-box parties gets out—die lah! The *New Times* will have no more face already. Besides, if Albert sees me as a valuable person who can give him information about his underlings in the newsroom, maybe I won't be moved to circulation after all?

No, Jazzy must be brave. Even if I might get in trouble for being the one to tell on Sean's parties, better to just do it.

"Albert, I really need to tell you something," I said, starting to launch into the story I had been trying to tell him all day. But Albert cut me off!

"I know," he said, looking a bit serious and sad. "No need to say. Actually, I really don't want to hear the details, but I know."

Know? Know what? And how can he know? Babi . . . did that bitch Su Fen tell him something? What did she say?

"No, Albert, I really need to tell you . . ."

"I know, you went to Sean's party," Albert said; his face looking a bit red, patches of it appearing all over his forehead even. Everyone knew whenever that happened, Albert was truly embarrassed. He cleared his throat. "Look—I know what happens there. And I hear the party was a big success, everyone had a good time, et cetera, et cetera. Sean already told a few of us about it after the morning meeting. Wah, that Su Fen—is she really as talented as he says? Wait, don't tell me. I want to find out myself."

What? What did Sean say? What should I say? And then I realized: what can I say that Albert would believe over Sean's word?

"Hey, Albert, you know what kind of girl I am—I didn't . . . I mean, I did go but I didn't . . . I can't . . ." I said. Damn bloody irritating. The story I had been thinking about telling him since I got home last night and practiced during all those hours when guniang couldn't fall asleep suddenly wasn't coming out.

"It's OK, Jazz," he said, looking sad again. "These things happen. Sean is a very handsome guy—and you know, once they move me upstairs he will probably be the one sitting in this chair. So it's good that you played your cards right. But I never doubted you—Jazzy. You have a good head on your shoulders. You're going to be all right."

I couldn't believe I was hearing any of this. I was still trying to think of how to explain and how to make him believe when Albert continued.

"Anyway, I didn't call you in to talk to you about any of this," he said. "Remember our conversation last week? I'm glad we had it because it's so coincidental, I was talking to the head of circulation and he has a very good opening so I thought about you. We had some nice chitchats and it's all settled . . ."

Circulation? What nonsense is he talking?

"Albert, thanks for the offer but I'm very happy working for you—really," I said. "I don't want to move. I really really love working for you."

"Come on, Jazzy—there's no future for you here," he said. "Don't make this difficult, OK? It's a very good job—it even pays a bit more. Win-win! Don't say I never take care of you."

"But, Albert, I—"

"Please. Jazzy, don't make this difficult—be a pro, OK?" he said. "You've been working for me for how long? We've always had a good relationship. You've been great. But it's time."

My mouth was still open but no words were coming out. I could see in Albert's eyes that he was starting to feel a bit bad. Of course he should—I'm the best assistant he's ever had!

"Jazz, eh—what time is it now? Aiyoh, I'm really late. Better make a move," he said, taking off his specs, quickly folding them and putting them back in his drawer.

"Come, come—it's time to knock off! Don't you young people have some big fun to get to on a Friday night?" he said, getting up and gesturing for me to quickly follow him. His face was starting to look impatient.

Quietly, I followed behind him.

"The new girl is coming on Monday, so pack up your desk this weekend," he said. "But come here Monday morning and show her the ropes then report to Gerald Ho over in circulation by eleven. Don't be late. Oh, and since I have that meeting at the printing plant I won't be in until noon, so make sure she's all settled in and knows how to order my lunch before you go."

Albert didn't look back at me as he said any of this. And he didn't turn around once the whole time I watched him walk all the way across the long newsroom and out the door.

The only time I had to think was the thirty-minute taxi drive that evening from the office to Manhattan.

Usually it only takes fifteen or twenty minutes to get to that steak house near Raffles City, but thank god for Friday night clubbers and lovebirds. There were traffic jams everywhere, so at least I could delay things a bit and have more time to think. Taxi uncle was happy of course—he was the kind that, when he sees a chio girl in a short skirt enter his taxi, wah, uncle purposely drives super slowly so he can talk cock a bit more and maybe see if he can get a phone number or not. (As if.) But the moment he started his rubbish chitchat I just said, "Uncle—I've had a bloody hard day already. Please! Don't make it worse." Uncle just stared at me a bit through his rearview mirror and then shut up his mouth for the rest of the drive.

Everything happened so quickly in Albert's office that I didn't have time to fully react until he was long gone. First of all, I still hadn't told him the real story yet about what happened at Sean's. He had been walking around all day thinking that I participated in Sean's sick games? After I thought about it a bit more, I guess I could imagine what Sean said about me. (Fucking chee bye—probably just trying to save his own face so he doesn't have to explain to his work buddies why some peon from the office would rather run out into the darkness and walk to the main road in high heels than stay and suck his Eurasian cock.)

But second of all—and this one was more important—why am I moving to circulation and what can I do to stop it? When I thought about my career trajectory, if there was any job that I thought Albert would be kindhearted enough to help me get—in fact, he even suggested it himself a few times—it was as an events planner for the company or somewhere else. The guy has so many contacts—if anyone can help me make that leap, it's him. And it seemed at some point that he was open to helping me down the road—what happened? And circulation? I mean, yah, he still goes over there to say hello and flirt with his old assistants a bit every week but it's where he shoves people when he no longer has much use for them. How could I possibly be in that category? Jazzy has worked too damn hard for him all these years to end up like those other losers before me. I am not Michelle!

Perhaps I should try and explain the evening at Sean's to Albert a bit more? I know that on weekends, I'm really not allowed to contact him unless it's an emergency like the *New Times* building is burning down or his boss wants to give him company box seats for a soccer match. (And even then, I can make this emergency call only for some games—Singapore versus Kelantan, can; Singapore versus Terengganu? If I dare to call him over that one, I confirm will get a scolding for at least two weeks.) But this issue with Sean's party and circulation—even if it's not an emergency for him, it's an emergency for me! Or maybe I can send him an email or a text to try and explain a bit and beg for my job back?

Aiyoh, this one. How come I have people in my life to advise me on all sorts of things—shopping lah, flirting lah, where to put your tongue on a guy's cock lah. But when I have a career problem, everybody in my life is all bloody goondu about this kind of thing?

I was still thinking about this, with no solution yet, when the taxi uncle pulled up to the Imperial Hotel.

"Well," I thought, as I paid taxi uncle, giving him a twenty-cents tip because he was so nice to keep quiet. (At least uncle couldn't say that guniang here was not appreciative.) "At least there's Roy."

Before heading to the second floor where Manhattan was, even though I was a bit late, I made sure to stop in the loo to powder my nose first. After rinsing my face with some water and blotching it off with a tissue, I looked hard into the mirror. Pretty eyes, not bad nose, clear skin, nice smile. I even blew-dry my hair this morning so it was a bit puffy, got volume and all. And I wore sweet dangly pearl earrings—must look a bit classy for a work dinner after all—to go with my black, slightly clingy silk dress, which was a little longer than the one last night but showed just a bit of cleavage. I even made sure to wear red lacy push-up bra so Roy confirm could get a few small peeps here and there at dinner.

Tonight, I'm going to show him why he needs me! Especially with some new tricks I learned from Alistair last week, I confirm can make Roy more satisfied than any girl has ever even tried.

"Jazzy," I mouthed into the mirror, pointing at my own face, "you are damn happening! Roy would be lucky to have you."

After that, guniang was energy a bit already. No need iPhone music—in my head, I could already hear that Madonna song "Express Yourself."

"Don't go for second best, baby, put your love to the test!"

Guniang was mouthing the lyrics as I put on new lipstick, touched up my mascara and eye shadow, pinched my cheeks a bit to make them rosy, fluffed up my hair and blew a kiss into the mirror and all.

(Of course it's at that last moment that some old auntie walked into the loo and stared at me like I was mad.)

Roy was waiting outside Manhattan when I got off the escalator. Wah—he even had a big smile come on when he saw me. I tell you, after my bloody lousy day and the crazy night last night, seeing his smile made me happier than I'd felt in a long time.

"There you are!" he said, walking forward to hug me—tight. He pulled back a bit, kissed me very softly on the cheek and said, "You're a sight for sore eyes. I've missed you. Sorry that work has been so crazy. I've been dying for it all to be over so I could see you again."

Aiseh. Guniang here was damn happy!

But must act cool a bit lah. "I'm glad," I just said, smiling sweetly.

"Now, before we go in, I have to explain something," Roy said. "This guy is a really big client so I have to be very nice to him. But he's a little . . . unusual, Jazzy. It's hard to explain but he may be a little surprising and I just have to beg you to be a little patient—OK? It's just one dinner—we've just got to get through it."

I was just so happy to be there I just nodded along. It was a work dinner—how bad could it be?

"Great—I'm starving," Roy said, "and everyone's already inside. Shall we?" He stuck out his arm, so I took it, feeling like a lady and all. (Not lady like Camilla—but Lady Diana, of course.)

I had never been to Manhattan before but I had always heard good things about it—Singapore's number one steak house! So of course I had booked Albert dinner reservations there. But this restaurant is so expensive—all the steaks are flown in from New Zealand or New York, that kind of thing, so the starting price for one piece is ninety-six dollars, man. Kani nah! So of course even though Albert did occasionally take me along on his business lunches or dinners, he had never taken me here, not even when his dining companion's company was paying. So when Roy texted that this was where the dinner is—guniang thought, no matter what happens tonight, confirm is a win already.

Lightly holding Roy's arm, guniang here was almost floating as we walked through the restaurant. The burgundy carpeting was so thick that I could feel my heels sink in a bit each time I took a step—in fact, it was so deep and thick, I could feel the soft carpet tickling my toes with each step. The tables were all covered with nicely ironed tablecloths, the waiters all wore tuxedos and had hair combed back neatly, like those old butlers in British shows. And every time one of them was near us, he would stop walking, bow a bit and stick his hands out, as if he were ushering us to a church pew. There was even some kind of violin classical shit playing softly in the background.

This place—it was exactly as I had always imagined in my fantasies of actually being taken here for a meal.

Roy led me all the way to the back of the restaurant, where there was a wide black wooden door—like one of those heavy castle doors you sometimes see in films. The waiter standing outside like a statue quickly jumped forward to open the door for us as we got close. The moment it opened, I could hear people laughing quite loudly inside. Good—I actually had been quite scared that this was going to be some atas party where I don't even know what to say to people. At least it sounded like this could be fun.

Considering how big the door was, the room was actually quite small. Or maybe it was that the table inside was quite big. Either way, there was one long table that filled almost the whole room and all around it were eight men—mostly ang mohs but there were also two toot Chinese faces in there. There was just one woman there—a long-haired young girl, pretty in a flat-faced kind of way,

Asian, though one of those slightly darker-skinned Asians—who was sitting close to the oldest man in the room, a guy with scruffy white hair wearing a flannel collared shirt.

"Finally!" the flannel-shirt guy said, getting up. "We were wondering where you went—I don't want to know but I'm glad you brought us some fresh meat! Now bring that bitty thing over here so we can have a good look!"

I was having a bit of trouble understanding everything the guy was saying—he was talking so loudly and with such a heavy American twang—a bit like those ones you see in those old Clint Eastwood movies or the ones set a long time ago on some kind of plantation. These kinds of accents, you don't normally hear in Singapore so much. Usually the Americans I meet all speak like Keanu Reeves—a little bland, like newscasters on CNN; no accent, really. But I figured that this guy must be a big shot if he is the oldest in the room, and also the loudest. So guniang here knew that she'd better try and follow along!

Roy quickly brought me all the way to the back of the room, since the guy was at the far end of the table, sitting like a king, having dinner with his advisors or something.

"This is Bill Tucker," Roy said, waving at the guy. "Or Tucker—everyone calls him that."

"Hi," I said, smiling and offering my hand for him to shake. "I'm Jazzy."

"My, my," Tucker said, shaking my hand—his grip was so firm my crushed hand immediately started paining a bit. He was looking at me up and down now—even stopped damn long at my boobs. (No shame!) I started wondering if it was such a good idea to wear my red bra—he was so tall, he confirm can look down my dress.

"Aren't you a catch?" Tucker said, shaking his head. "Now why are we so formal? Come over here!"

Before I could figure out what he meant, he yanked my hand toward him so I practically fell into his big chest. Luckily guniang was at least fast enough to turn my face as this was happening so my lipstick didn't end up smearing all over his blue checked shirt. But this wasn't the end—Tucker wrapped me in his strong arms, tight tight type, then cupped his hands over my backside and gave it a big squeeze.

"Aiyoh!" I shouted, then quickly feeling a bit embarrassed— guniang here was damn worried I was a bit too loud. This was Roy's office function, after all. I didn't want to make him feel ashamed about me.

So I quickly said, "Oops, sorry," and giggled a little bit. "I didn't mean to be so loud."

"Oh don't worry, honey—I like loud," Tucker said, laughing so hard that he finally released me—but not before he slapped my backside one time, really hard! The guys at the table quickly laughed along with him, too. I could hear that Roy behind me was joining in. One of the Chinese guys at the other end of the table was laughing a bit less than the rest. I tried to read his face—he looked a bit worried, and maybe sorry for me. I guess in my pearl earrings and nice makeup he must think I'm a nice lady or some shit. When he noticed me noticing him though, he quickly looked away and laughed even harder.

"Now enough of all this—let's sit down so we can finally eat some meat," Tucker said. "Now, y'all over there move so Jazzy over here can sit next to Vanida. You know girls, they like to do everything together—chitchat together, go to the bathroom together, fuck a man together . . ."

Even before the laughter from that disappeared, the two ang mohs sitting next to the girl quickly moved to the other side of the room, where a waiter was now adding chairs so they could sit down.

Tucker started talking again the moment Roy and I sat down. "Now this pretty thing is Vanida," he said.

I stuck out my hand to shake Vanida's. She looked a little surprised to be offered a handshake but adjusted her gauzy silk wrap over her tight bustier dress a bit so she could shake my hand. I was about to introduce myself when Tucker continued talking: "I knew I'd like this one the moment they told me her name—I figured any girl whose parents have the right mind to give their daughter a name that's like 'vagina' have got their priorities straight!" He slapped the leg of his jeans and laughed loudly again. Roy and the boys followed along, laughing even louder.

Now, I know that in some social circles I can be considered a bit kampong lah—I've never been to the States or London before, I'm not rich, and sometimes, even though my English is very good, I still don't quite understand the different language social customs or slangs of different countries. But in my whole life, not even in the sleaziest of clubs and certainly not on any work events that Albert had dragged me to, I had never met anyone like Tucker. I had met Americans before, of course—but none of them were ever like this. Usually, no matter where they came from or how little money they had, they were at least classy a bit. But this guy—my god! But he's an important client of Roy's? No choice, even if I was a bit uncomfortable, I figured I'd better just endure the dinner for Roy. I wanted so desperately to make him see me as good partner material, after all. This was my chance.

So, I just smiled.

I guess they must have ordered already because a round of big steaks started arriving—all American steaks. Even though American steaks are much more expensive than Ozzie or Kiwi steaks, apparently Tucker only eats American beef. And he wants everyone to eat American beef, so we all got one—with mashed potato and grilled asparagus some more. At least this was the one bright spot— the food itself was going to be something like what I had envisioned when I used to dream about eating at Manhattan one day.

"Who are these people?" I whispered to Roy as the table got a bit quiet while everyone was cutting their meat and passing around plates of asparagus.

"Boys in my office," he whispered back. "And Tucker—his firm is one of our really big clients. He's semiretired now but still comes through a few times a year on his way to or from Bangkok."

"And his girlfriend?" I asked.

"Girlfriend? Please," Roy said, laughing a bit and rolling his eyes. "I'm learning more and more about the ways of white men in Asia this week. Apparently it's a new girl for Tucker every time. But he likes this one a little more than the previous ones, I think. He was telling us the other night that he kept her for most of the month he was in Bangkok this time and even paid extra to bring her along with him on his Singapore leg."

I guess I must have looked concerned or something because Roy pinched my cheek and smiled.

"Look, I know it's a bit strange," he said. "But I really did want to see you and I promise you, after this dinner is over, I am all yours. I'll make it up to you."

OK lah—now this evening was actually going somewhere. Guni- ang smiled back.

The whole table around us suddenly got super noisy—everyone was laughing at something that Tucker just said, so Roy and I turned back to them and tried to follow along. I guess one of the Chinese guys had made some comment about not really knowing how to tell whether a woman has come or something. The things that were being discussed at this dinner—just shameful! Americans, I tell you.

"Of course you don't," Tucker said to the Chinese guy. "Small limp dicks, tiny tongues. I can tell you right now, my friend—you have definitely never made any woman come."

The whole table started laughing again—even the two Chinese guys. And even Roy!

"Now, just ask Vanida over here," Tucker continued, putting his arm around Vanida, who was so skinny and small to begin with but looked even skinnier and smaller when she was mashed into his armpit. "Ask her how many times I make her come every night. What is it—three times at least? Four times? You should hear her when she's really going!"

I didn't know what to do. I looked at Vanida, still squeezed under Tucker's arm. She was smiling a very small smile, her eyes looking downward, but she nodded anyway. Everyone started laughing even louder now.

"Roy," I whispered, squeezing his thigh under the table so he would stop laughing and listen to me for a minute. "This is not right."

Roy just looked at me a little apologetically, whispered the words "Not now" and kept laughing along.

I waited for Tucker to release Vanida before taking out one of my business cards. Looking at what it said made me sad again: "*New Times,* assistant to the editor." Would I have the same phone number on Monday? I didn't even know. But at least this was a way to get ahold of me somehow. I must remember to tell the new girl to forward all messages to me in case Vanida calls. I wasn't sure what I'd do if she did but surely there must be some way I can help her.

I thought back to all the women I had come across just in the last two weeks—the girls at the KTV lounges, having to flash bits of their ass, legs, more for lousy garlands from drunk business-men, the China girls at Lunar having to put on that show night after night, the modern SPGs on the bar counter at Carlyle's in their heels and little skirts, kicking up their feet for guys to enjoy. And then, Jazzy. The Jazzy who would never become an event planner now in all probability. The Jazzy who was getting shipped off to cir-culation on Monday like yesterday's fish. The Jazzy who was pushed to invite Louis in. The Jazzy that Sean thought he could add to his sex-toy harem. The Jazzy everyone liked having fun with and no one wanted to keep. Who would protect Jazzy now?

"Vanida," I said as quietly as I could while Tucker was telling his next story—I couldn't really hear but I'm sure it was about sex and his amazing cock. I saw Roy look at me whispering to Vanida, frown very nervously and then look away.

"This is my business card," I said. "If you ever need help, you can always call me. OK?"

I wasn't sure if she understood what I was trying to tell her but she took my card and looked at it for a long time.

"What's this?" Tucker asked, grabbing the card and looking at it closely. "Oh, *New Times*, eh? Exchanging business cards—how cute. You want to keep in touch to swap blowjob tips or go shopping? Or are you one of those bleeding-heart feminists in the media who ac-tually thinks she can help whores like her?"

No one was laughing now. Vanida actually pulled away from me and moved closer to Tucker, her small fingers holding on to his elbow.

"I have to say," Tucker said, chuckling a bit. "Singaporean women like you really crack me up. What do they call you—'sarong party girls'? You think you're so great that you won't date one of those losers sitting over there," he added, pointing at the two Chinese guys at the far end.

"You think only white guys deserve you. But please—you and Vanida, the two of you are the exact same kind of girl. All you're both after is more money, more power in your little world. And you'll do anything to get it. And I'm the sleazy one?" Then he laughed a bit louder, tossed out a loud "Control your woman, Roy!" before giving Vanida a big loud kiss and going back to cutting his steak.

Guniang here was tongue-tied. But then I looked at Roy—wasn't he going to say something to defend me? Roy just gave me an embarrassed look and turned to the guy next to him, asking him to pass the asparagus.

I looked at the plate in front of me. I had only eaten a few bites of steak—it really was damn shiok lah, buttery and fatty fatty. And I hadn't even tried the truffled mashed potatoes yet. But I slowly folded my stiff napkin and put it by my plate.

"Mr. Tucker?" I said, leaning past Vanida, who quickly shrank back the moment she saw me moving toward her, as if I was going to try and talk to her again or some shit.

"Thank you very much for this delicious dinner," I said. "But I really have to go."

The whole room was quiet for only half of my long walk to the door.

"Let the bitch go," I heard Tucker loudly saying to Roy just before the door closed behind me. "We'll find you ten better ones tonight—the kind that knows the only acceptable time to open their mouths is when your cock comes out." The last thing I heard was everyone starting to laugh again.

I couldn't even look at any of the waiters around me as I walked, all by myself, through the big restaurant. Did any of them see how that guy had grabbed me? All the things he had said? If they did, I'm sure they'd have a lot to gossip about. Kani nah! Now I really could never come back to Manhattan.

Outside, I stopped by the escalator and decided to wait a bit. Maybe Roy was stunned in there and didn't have time to react? And then maybe after I left he realized he was wrong and told Tucker off? If he did, I'm sure he wouldn't stay. So, OK. I decided, let's wait a bit.

Guniang waited five minutes. Ten minutes. Then, OK. I guess, it's just like that.

As I got on the escalator down, I didn't know how to feel. There was a jabbing pain in my chest; my heart. And I felt like crying— but Jazzy cannot cry! Maybe I just really needed a hug. Maybe I needed someone who could cheer me up a bit, make me smile. So I took my phone out and texted Alistair: "Free tonight? Fauntleroy? ;)"

He replied right away. "Wish I could, my dear. But the wife has booked us on a sudden weekend trip to Bali. Not sure why. Leaving first thing tomorrow. Text you when I'm back Monday?"

Bali . . . I guess Sharon was taking my advice after all and was trying to mend things by booking a romantic holiday. Good for her. Good to see her trying—trying to win her man back from the fucking slut who borrowed him.

"OK," I texted back. Even though I knew right then that I didn't plan to see him again.

CHAPTER 20

Saturday night. Again.

I was feeling bloody bored.

Whole day long I was damn quiet. I wanted to tell someone, to talk to someone, but I also didn't know what to say. All these things—everything that happened, where to begin? After that awful night at Manhattan, Roy had texted several times to apologize, saying that he had to be polite to Tucker, there was no way he could have said anything to contradict or embarrass him and hey, would I please just let him take me to a nice dinner—a real dinner—so he could explain? I didn't even bother to respond. This kind of no-balls loser—worse than dating an Ah Beng, I tell you!

That Saturday at home I was so quiet that even my mum started to worry—she wondered why I didn't go to the kopitiam to drink kopi and shake leg, why I didn't go shopping with the girls, why I just sat in my room, not talking, not singing, not complaining at her when she burst into my room with her "Ah Huay!" nonsense.

"People here are tired lah," I said for the sixth time in the afternoon, pulling the blanket over my face again when she pushed it off to try to get me to sip her energizing lotus root soup.

I could hear her standing there for quite a while, probably trying to think of something she could do or say, then very quietly leaving the room. She didn't even slam the door as usual.

To prevent her from making even more soup—or worse, taking me to her Chinese doctor for acupuncture or some shit—I figured

I'd better get out of the house on Saturday night. If guniang actually stayed at home on Saturday night—aiyoh, to my mum this confirm means that I am very sick, maybe even dying.

"Tonight, Barracuda, usual time," Louis texted us all at 7 P.M.

At first, I thought, should I not go? I knew from Imo that Louis had been quite sweet with her this week. After sending her flowers that Sunday he even took her out for drinks one night after work to see if she was feeling better. (Fann and I asked her to pretend that she was still sick a bit, to see whether he might send more flowers or—even more best—buy her something that comes in a little blue box. But Imo, I tell you—she was so happy she forgot how to play game. This toot girl—my god, she really is his lapdog now. And Louis knows it.)

But those were the only updates I got about Louis until his group text. I just hope things weren't going to be awkward with him. I mean, yeah, what happened was a bit weird. But I'd already forgotten the whole thing. Or tried to. What's the point in thinking about it? In the end, we've all been such good friends for so long—what's the point of making things weird over one small thing like that. Better to just pretend it never happened.

Anyway, it's good that Louis sent the first text—if he is organizing, that means he confirm is coming. If he's coming, then we not only have a good table but also free drinks all night.

Even though we all know Louis's "usual time" means he wants us to come at 11 P.M. but he actually arrives at midnight or one—so that when he walks in like a superstar we've all already been sitting there for a long time waiting for him—we all decided to meet at eleven. Because Melvin was at a stag night with his friends anyway so he wouldn't be free tonight until much later, Fann agreed to come out. And Imo—aiyah, anytime Louis is showing up anywhere, she confirm will want to be there on time.

And me—if I don't go to Barracuda at eleven, where the fuck else do I have to go?

When I got there at eleven though, I regretted being so on time. I should have known that even though the three of us decided to not be late, everyone would be late. Never mind lah—I figured I'd start whacking Louis's bottles first and all would be good. After last Saturday, if anybody deserves to drink his booze, it's me, after all. So when the waiter asked, "Which bottle would you like us to bring out?" I just said, "The most expensive one. No, two. Yah, bring them both."

Guniang here is not usually the one mixing drinks for myself or other people, so when the bottles came, I didn't know what amount to put in. I sometimes see Kelvin being damn toot, carefully measuring measuring to see whether the glass has two-fingers-high worth of liquor before adding the mixers. But aiyoh, guniang here was lazy lah. (Plus, I didn't want to look toot.) So when the waiter brought out two bottles of Glenfiddich I just poured a little in a shot glass and did a bottoms up. Wah—it felt like fire. Shiok! I did two of these fast then decided to sip the third with some ice.

I was happily sitting there at Louis's table, listening to that Coldplay song that everyone loves—I don't care who you are or what car you drive or who you are. Ah Bengs, ang mohs, atas bitches all jump up whenever they hear the song start and sing each line out loud loud type. Kani nah. All these fucking happy people. I decided to just close my eyes and listen to the song. OK lah, maybe life is not so bad after all.

"Miss? Miss?"

I opened my eyes. Aiyoh. Of course it was an Ah Beng—his eyes all big big, hopeful hopeful type.

"Fuck off," I said, closing my eyes again.

"Hi," another voice said this time. "Here alone?"

This time I started talking even before my eyes opened. "I said—fuck off!"

When I opened my eyes I realized it was actually quite a good-looking ang moh trying to talk to me! Aiyoh! By the time I tried to say, "Wait, wait!" it was too late already. The guy was shaking his head as he walked away.

At first I thought, Aiyoh, like that—so wasted. But then I realized, even if I talked to the guy, maybe go home with him, maybe don't go home with him tonight but we have a date later, and then another date, and another date—in the end, is anything is actually going to happen? In the life of Jazeline Lim, let's face it—probably not.

The moment I thought that, I tried to mentally slap myself. Aiyoh, Jazzy—come on! Cannot be so negative. Somehow or other, must try to stay positive! Just then, Imo and Fann arrived, so this guniang's mood improved a bit. And Kelvin and Andrew were right behind them. Andrew had even invited Kin Meng out and all. Wah—tonight, really is a big night if the gang is all there! So I decided to just heck care everything. Focus on tonight! Especially since I was wearing something especially nice—tonight I was in one of my new fake Herve Leger bandage dresses, which looks like I have tight red stretchy bandages wrapped all around my boobs, waist and backside. The waist looks smaller, boobs look bigger, backside—aiyah, backside just the right size for making guys steam. Not bad!

"Did you cut your hair or something?" Kin Meng asked when he air-kissed me. "You look damn steam! My god, if I didn't know you only like ang mohs I might try and get lucky with you tonight."

"And if you weren't married, I might think you're not a lecherous old man for saying that!" I said, pinching his cheeks and slapping his backside.

Kin Meng look a bit shocked. I guess I'd never called him a lech before. (But hallo, truth is truth.) When he recovered a minute later, he gave me the third finger. I just blew a kiss at him.

Fann had gotten the rest of Louis's bottles from out of his locker and made a round of vodka sodas. "Come," she said, passing one to each one of us. "Bottoms up!"

After two rounds of this Louis finally showed up with three girls behind him. "Gang, this is Akiko, Emi and Naomi," he said. "Ladies, this is the gang."

Until this point, Andrew was in a corner, flirting a bit with Fann while Imo was dancing with Kelvin and Kin Meng but trying to keep her distance, especially from Kelvin, who kept coming up from behind and grinding his socks crotch into her backside. But the moment the Japanese girls showed up, all three guys immediately moved over to talk to them instead. I tell you, Japanese girls—the decent, nice ones, like not the ones you find in KTV lounges or one of those sleazy bars looking for a loaded husband type—are like ganja for guys like Kin Meng and all.

I still remember for Kelvin's stag party a few years ago, Louis flew everyone to Tokyo for a last havoc weekend before the red bomb. They didn't really want to talk much about it when they came back—which made us all think, aiyoh, really serious things must have happened there. Every time we tried and bugged them to tell us about it Louis always stopped everyone from talking by saying, "Fellas—what happens in Roppongi stays in Roppongi."

But since Kin Meng tells me everything because he's just a big gossip, I knew what happened lah. Basically, every kind of Japanese girl they saw, they just tried to whack—but they were very strategy about it. Louis went and did all this research to find out where the decent young chio Japanese girls like to hang out, then they went and pretended that they were just being tourists, want to get to know local girls, buy them lots of drinks—and then aiyah, you know lah. I think they were quite successful—Louis and Kin Meng know how to speak a bit of Japanese, since they often have to go to Tokyo for work and all. So they could automatically talk talk flirt flirt until the groups of chio nice girls were a bit more comfortable with all of them.

For the guys in the group who were less successful—they never said who exactly these were but I suspect Kelvin was one of those of course—Louis also had a backup plan. He had a list of KTV-like bars—but with high-quality local girls. So, worst comes to worst, everyone in the stag party also had someone to party with each night.

I tell you, when I heard this, I wondered why I was so unlucky not to be born a guy! My life where got so easy—having hot people to sleep with me just handed to me on a plate?

Since the guys had disappeared, Imo and Fann both came back to the booth and sat next to me. Imo grabbed the Glenfiddich and poured three full shots, picking one up then pointing at the two of us to fasterly pick ours up.

After we bottoms-up, I was starting to feel quite happy. But Imo's face was damn sour. She had poured a second round of shots for us but instead of downing it she was just sipping—sipping and staring, sipping and staring. But no matter how hard she stared, Louis never looked over at her. I could hear Fann giggling now and then next to me.

"Eh—guniang, you possessed by love magic, is it? Whole life texting Melvin!" I said. "Can you pretend a bit that you actually like hanging out with us?"

Now Fann was also sour-faced, but at least she put away her phone.

I regretted scolding her lah. I know I should be happy for her.

And I'm sure she thinks that I'm just jealous or some shit. In fact, I think Imo was also thinking that I'm jealous of Louis and her lumpar bouquet of flowers. Which only made me feel like telling her, "Hallo—he was only sending you flowers because he was feeling guilty for forcing your best friend to fuck him." But then, when I think about it more, doesn't the fact that he feels guilty mean that he's maybe getting serious with Imo?

I guess they were right perhaps. Maybe I am just not being a very good friend to them.

"Eh, guniangs," I said, grabbing the Glenfiddich and topping up all our glasses before holding mine up. "I think we should do a cheers."

Imo and Fann looked a bit confused. I guess they were still a bit unhappy, wondering what kind of cock thing I'm going to say to make them snap out of it. Even so, they followed me, picking up their glasses and all.

"I'm really happy for you two," I said. "I know these few weeks without Sher—it's been a bit weird lah. But you two are doing so well. Look at Fann—so fast and you're so close to having your mission accomplished! And Imo, aiyah, we just want you to be happy. I'm damn proud, you know. Come . . . cheers! Cheers!"

"It's true," Imo said, smiling for the first time since the Japanese girls appeared. "Bottoms up!"

So we quickly bottoms-up and then hugged each other tightly. "Come," Fann said. "Now let's just heck care all the boys and have fun with each other. Let's dance!"

And actually, after that it was damn fun. We laugh laugh, dance dance, even sing sing a bit. In fact, we were having so much fun, heck caring the boys and the Japanese girls, that at some point they noticed what a happening time we were having. So they came over to join us!

In between all that we bottoms-upped now and then of course. It was good to be able to forget everything for a while, all the cock things that happened so recently. At one point Fann had had so many shots she had to go to the loo and vomit. But it was good. After that happened, she was not only all OK—she was feeling even better than before! "Why are you girls so lazy, sitting down and all?" she said, poking me and Imo in the back when she came back. "Come— bottoms up!" Good times lah—in fact, it was almost like secondary school days. Carefree and all.

My feet were hurting by the time Louis started looking like he was getting ready to make a move. Most of the night, even though he came over to say hi hi a bit with Imo now and then, he was mostly talking and rubba-ing a bit with one of the Japanese girls. (I forget which one—you know how it is lah; Japanese names all sound alike.) And we could kind of tell it was getting to be that time of the night where he has to make a move already. It was now four-something—if Louis leaves now, he can still squeeze in a quick stop and make it home at a decent hour so Mary doesn't spend all day tomorrow throwing tantrums and making him take her shopping at Paragon. That's when I noticed Imo getting a bit sour again, staring at Louis wrapping his arms around the Japanese girl, dancing and rubba-ing.

"Imo," I said. "You OK or not?"

She just blinked and nodded, but her eyes were a bit angry. Actually, not just angry. I've known her for how many years already. I know that when she looks like this, very soon, waterfalls will happen. After the bouquet and the drinks date, I guess maybe she thought tonight would be different.

At this moment though, we noticed Louis breaking away from the Japanese guniang. Imo quickly turned her face away and very fasterly wiped her eyes, then turned back to look straight ahead, as if nothing happened.

"Imo," Louis said, smiling and pinching her cheeks when he came over. "You ready to leave or want to stay some more? I send you home?"

I tell you—Imo's face transformed! One minute she was trying to purposely put on a stone face, the next minute she was practically jumping up into Louis's arms.

"Great," Louis said, pointing at her to grab her handbag. "Come— I'm sending Akiko home also. We'll all go together."

Aiyoh. Aiyoh-yoh. I looked at Imo, whose face was a bit less smiley now. But she just nodded and followed. Before she left, I grabbed her hand and squeezed it, feeling her squeeze it back. I was about to suggest that she and I leave together instead, and maybe grab supper on the way home. But before I could, Imo used her hand to make the telephone sign near her ear and mouthed, "I'll call you."

Fann had gone to the loo again, I guess. (And I guess it was another productive round because she came back looking less mabuk and much more energy than before.)

"Eh," she said. "Where did Imo go?"

"Louis," I said.

Fann smiled and gave me two thumbs up but I just shook my head.

"See how lah," I said. "Louis is sending her and that Japanese girl back also. Aiyoh."

Fann rolled her eyes and pointed her third finger toward the club exit.

"Um, Jazzy," she said. "I make a move first . . . OK with you?"

I looked at my phone. Aiyoh, it was almost 5 A.M. already.

"Of course, of course," I said, waving her to hurry off.

"Thank you," she said. "You're going to be OK right? If I wasn't meeting Melvin . . ."

"Aiyoh, please!" I told her, whacking her arm one time. "Guniang here is how old already? You go and get laid lah—do it for the two of us!"

Fann stuck her third finger at me then grabbed her purse and hugged me goodbye.

I was thinking that maybe I would share a taxi with Kin Meng—he's usually quite good about making sure I get home OK. But tonight, I forgot—with Japanese girls around, confirm is a different case. Just when I was going to ask him about sharing taxi I saw him put his arm around one of the girls and wave goodbye to me and Kelvin. Andrew also did the same with the other girl.

Kelvin and I looked at each other. Kani nah. This wasn't happening.

Now, how?

I had never spent any time alone with Kelvin before and now he was kind of in the position to at least be a gentleman and send me back—unless I opened my mouth to say I was going to leave first. But guniang didn't feel like going home yet. The thought of it, being alone in that room, that bed, tonight, was too sobering.

Luckily, Kelvin spoke first.

"Jazzy—boring now, right?" he said. Which was very true. Barracuda is one of those gigantic clubs where it's only fun if you go with a big group. Plus, since it was almost five, the club was starting to wind down a bit, so you could see big empty spots here and there on the damn bloody huge dance floor—something like the dance floors in those loser nightclubs where everyone's too shy to dance so they just hang around and be wallflowers.

"You ready to go home now or not?" he asked.

When I shook my head, he continued. "Good—me too," he said. "Come, I'll bring you somewhere."

I guess I must have looked nauseous or something, because he quickly added, "Aiyoh, please—don't think that your backside is so great. People here are not trying to make a move on you—I just want to bring you somewhere more fun."

Set! I just laughed, gave him the thumbs-up sign and grabbed my handbag.

The club Kelvin had in mind was actually not far—good lah, no need to queue up for taxi. When he saw me hobbling a bit because my feet were hurting he was actually nice enough to offer me his arm to help me steady steady all. I have to admit that I was a little shocked—I whole life long had never seen this side of Kelvin before. It actually made me feel a bit bad about being so mean about talking about his socks crotch over the years. (But just for a moment.) Then I realized—hallo, if he weren't so toot as to stuff his crotch with socks then we wouldn't have anything to make fun of him about. It's his own bloody fault.

After a few minutes, Kelvin turned into the Dynasty Hotel lobby, which was a bit quiet—of course, it was five-something in the morning after all! I was about to ask him whether there was really a bar or not—the lobby was so deserted. But as we walked through the lobby all the way to the back, I could hear people chitchatting and some muffled clubby music. When we got to the far end of the lobby, there was a small partition and behind that, big double glass doors under the sign SOS. Walao—what kind of toot bar is this?

The moment Kelvin opened the heavy glass door—voom! The music suddenly got damn bloody loud, filling the lobby momentarily. And inside, I could see a big crowd jammed around a bar, and an even bigger crowd cramming a small parquet dance floor. There were a few dark banquettes scattered around—I couldn't really see much but I could see moving shapes in all of them.

I wasn't sure whether I wanted to enter or not but Kelvin had already started walking in, so I fasterly followed. He squeezed his way through to the bar and cleared enough room so I could stand next to him.

"What do you want?" he said, quickly tilting his head up slightly in that attitude Ah Beng way.

I was so confused by the surroundings I didn't know what to say. "Whatever you're having," I said.

"Two Jamesons on the rocks," Kelvin said to the bartender, holding up two fingers and watching him closely as he poured, I guess to make sure that he was getting his money's worth. Since Louis wasn't here, Kelvin was paying for our drinks after all.

"Come—cheers," he said, when the drinks arrived. "Just cheers—no bottoms up. If you want to bottoms-up, you can take out your wallet and buy the next round."

Bloody hell. But, I have to say, fair is fair. I clinked his glass and took a sip.

Kelvin turned around and stood on the raised step underneath the bar so he could get a better look at the dance floor, so I did the same.

"What the hell is this place?" I asked.

"My god, why are you so kampong—you've really never been here before?"

When I nodded, Kelvin shook his head.

"SOS—or, as we call it, 'SBS.' For *si beh sian*—super boring! This is where people come to find the last-chance hookup for the night," he said.

"Now is the damn happening time here lah," he added. "At this time the atas clubs are all doing last call, so if you still haven't found someone to pok yet, then go to SOS. This bar only closes at seven A.M.!

If by seven A.M. you still haven't found a hookup yet, then even you yourself have no choice but to admit you are a loser. Just fuck off and eat breakfast then go home. But most people confirm can find someone here. It's just a matter of adjusting expectations."

Even though Kelvin was talking to me, he wasn't looking at me—he was very carefully staring at each corner of the room, squinting. I could see him making mental calculations in his head—does that girl look chio enough to lose his spot at the bar near the bartender? Or maybe there's someone with more potential who just hasn't shown up yet?

"Eh, Kelvin," I said. "Now what time already—you don't want to go home? Worst-case scenario you can always go home and pok your wife, no? Come here for what?"

"Talk cock lah," he said, laughing a little even though his face didn't look like he was laughing at all. "The bitch is moving out next week. She's been having a bloody affair with her meditation therapist! Fucking lanjiao fucker. She's moving in with that fucking California-educated hippie and all, while trying to take all my money."

I didn't know what to say. So I just joined Kelvin in scanning the room. Together, we leaned back against the bar, quietly, side by side, and just did a look see.

If you just walked in and didn't know anything, you would think that SOS was damn happening. Everywhere people were cheering, bottoms-upping, dancing like crazy, hugging, air-kissing, real kissing, rubba-ing. Every single person was being damn action, as if they were having a number one time. But if you looked closely, you could see that actually, this one is all for show. Even though the mouth is smiling, the eyes are quite sad. The ones who were hooking up didn't look tender or passionate. It was a manic desperation; the fear of being alone, of going home alone. And the only ones who didn't have this kind of look on their faces were the small young Thai girls who, even though it was five-something in the morning, still had perfect hair and makeup and they certainly didn't look mabuk. Calmly, they perched on bar stools or banquets, preening and scanning the crowd, occasionally getting up to circle the dance floor.

"Kelvin," I said, "I think I'd better make a move first."

He didn't look at me—just nodded and kept slowly sipping his Jameson, still scanning the room.

Now I really didn't know what else to say. So I just bottoms-up my drink and fasterly left.

When I got to the front of the hotel, I wondered what to do. Even though it was damn late, I still didn't feel like going home. (Plus, the Dynasty Hotel taxi queue was jammed with SOS people—who looked even more desperate and drunk now that we were outside and the sky was very gradually lightening.)

So, I decided to walk along Orchard Road a little. At this time, the street was especially bright, with the streetlights still beaming down, and although it was almost six, it was actually a bit noisy since post-clubbing people were stumbling about. Slowly, I walked, passing the Crabtree & Evelyn where Imo likes to buy her atas shower gels, past the Ferragamo shop where Imo, Sher and I went to buy Fann a wallet for her birthday last year after saving up money for a few weeks. I was about to head to the bus stop when I noticed a familiar face coming toward me. Kani nah!

I stood very still, hoping that if I didn't move, maybe I wouldn't be noticed.

"Oi, Jazzy—following me around is it?" Seng said when he got closer. I could tell that the fucker had noticed me from far away but was trying to act cool, not even looking at me.

"You go and dream lah," I said, blinking at him.

Seng looked at me up and down, pulled out his pack of menthols and lit one up.

"So late still haven't gone home?" he said, staring at me coolly.

I didn't say anything. I watched as he ran his fingers through his long fringe and swept it back. Fucker was still trying to act cool and all. He took a long drag of his ciggie, still looking at me as he slowly scratched his cheek with his long pinkie fingernail.

"How come one of your atas friends isn't driving you home in his Rolls-Royce?" he said, blinking and looking away for a bit, then looking back. It didn't occur to me until now that I hadn't seen or heard from him since that night when I ditched him at Studemeyer's. I suddenly felt bad. No matter how annoying Seng had been to show up, his heart was always in a good place. Plus, we'd been friends for so long—far longer than I've been with any of these fuckers I've been clubbing with every night.

Also, if I had been nice and stayed there instead of running off to meet Louis, maybe that evening would have turned out a lot different. Maybe a lot of things in my life would have been different if I had just seen things clearer.

I started to feel damn tired. And I guess the fucker probably thought I owed him an apology or some shit. But just when I was thinking of saying something—not apologizing, mind you, but just acknowledging that maybe he expects me to apologize—Seng said, "Aiyoh, aiyoh!" and ran over to the dustbin near the bus stop.

Next to the tall plastic dustbin there was a guy curled up on the floor.

"Oi," Seng said, using the tip of his pointy leather shoe to poke the guy's stomach. "Oi! *Oi!*"

When the guy didn't wake up, I heard him softly say, "Kani nah."

"Who's that?" I asked.

"My friend lah," he said, taking a last long puff of his ciggie and throwing it on the floor near the guy's shoe. "We all thought the fucker went home already when he suddenly just got up and fucked off out of McDonald's thirty minutes ago."

Seng shook his head and exhaled slowly. I could see the smoke coming out of his nostrils as he pursed his lips, thinking, thinking.

"This lanjiao always gets this drunk," he said, shaking his head and looking a bit worried.

Then Seng sighed, bent down and went through the guy's pockets, taking out his iPhone and wallet. He stopped, opened the wallet and thought for a bit, then took out twenty dollars, folding the notes up nicely and carefully tucking them inside the front of his friend's pants.

When I looked confused, Seng winked. "Taxi money," he said, carefully putting the phone and wallet in his pockets. "Robbers won't dare to put their hands into his underwear, even to try and steal money—haha!"

Even I had to laugh at this. As toot as this whole scene was, this actually made sense. I watched Seng dust his hands on his jeans, sigh again and clear his throat, then slowly bend down and carefully pick his friend up. They were both about the same size so Seng was having a hard time of it.

"Eh, you need any help?" I said, stepping closer.

Seng looked at me sternly. "No need, no need," he said. "He's really too heavy. I don't want you hurting yourself."

Silently, I stood there and watched as, inch by inch, Seng staggered over to a long bench under the bus stop canopy and gently laid his friend down. Buses were few and far between at that time, so the place was empty, quiet. And, this being a bus stop in Orchard

Road, the benches were fairly clean. From the guy's heaving chest, I could see he was all right. He even smacked his lips and turned on his side, his arms cradling his chest.

"Shouldn't we send him home or something?" I said.

"No need lah—you see how bloody heavy he is?" Seng said. Which was true. His friend was not say, damn fucking fat but he also confirm was not skinny. Seng had really been staggering.

"Plus, he lives all the way up north, near the Malaysian causeway—do you know how expensive the taxi ride there and back will be?" Seng added, reaching into his pocket to pull out his ciggies, plucking one out and lighting it. "I'll just drop off his stuff tomorrow. I want to make sure you get home soon and safe, Ah Huay. Now what time already? Your mum is really going to worry if you're out much later."

I stood there for a moment, looking down at the guy, still curled up. A ring of cigarette butts and crumpled tissue paper made a halo around his bench. Fucker was even smiling a bit.

"Come," Seng said, holding out his free hand. "Let me send you home."

I had to think for a moment. Was this it?

"Actually," I said, "I'm waiting for someone."

I could see Seng's upper lip curl. He rolled his eyes and said, "Your choice." Then he threw up his hands and walked away.

Alone—really alone, it felt—I wondered what to do next. Next to the bus stop, there was a hive of bright lights and noise—McDonald's. I tell you, at this time of night, McDonald's is the most happening place in town. Post-clubbing hours are a big moneymaking time for them. Even though guniang here didn't want to go and eat with the Ah Bengs inside, smelling the place reminded me that tonight I didn't have supper. If I eat something here now, it's also not bad—chances are, nobody I know (or care about) will spot me here. And by the time I finish, I'm sure the taxi queue would be gone.

I was standing outside looking in, considering, when I noticed the face looking back at me in the glass. After such a long night out, my hair had deflated; long strings of it were whipped haphazardly around my face. My lipstick was mostly gone, chewed off; the mascara was still in place, though I looked a little like a raccoon from the smudges under my eyes. I missed Sher, who always carried around makeup remover towelettes in her handbag and would drag me to the loo when she thought I needed a touch-up. Where was Sher tonight? Sher always knew the right thing to do. Always. She may have married an Ah Beng, but, I realized, at least this was an Ah Beng who was there sleeping by her side at this very moment— maybe even spooning.

Sher had popped by the office one day this week to take me out to lunch. It was a quick one, but sweet. She told me all the toot stories of her Ah Beng honeymoon and I realized I hadn't laughed that much in months—yes, even if some of it was laughing at her precious Ah Huat. Sher was good-natured about it all. I got the sense that she knew what he was and what he wasn't and she was just A-OK with it. I guess there really was nothing left for me to say on the subject at the end of the day. Sher had even hugged me super tightly as she left, asking me once again if I would consider helping Ah Huat at work. "As if!" I had said. Sher just smiled and shrugged as she left.

The lights inside McDonald's were so bright I couldn't see my skin clearly, but from how papery it felt, I knew it was sallow. I suddenly heard my mum's voice in my head: "A young girl's face is her jewel, Ah Huay—take good care of it. Get lots of rest, eat healthily, don't go out so late. The fire in your body increases the later you are up—if you're up too late, the fire will burn you up. Listen to your, Ma—please."

My mum, perhaps, was right all along.

The sky was a pale pinkish blue now; the sun wasn't too far behind. The gigantic shopping malls that lined Orchard Road were towering black blocks against this rapidly lightening canvas. I could barely make out the Prada store sign just across the street.

Something about this dawn was reassuring, even if all around me was an army of mascara-streaked dolls staggering about, occasionally breaking into scuffles whenever a taxicab trundled by. I saw what I should have known all along. I didn't need Seng, or Kelvin, or Louis and most certainly not Roy—not to send me home or fuck me or even to marry me. I didn't need Sean or Albert. And thank god I didn't need Alistair.

I may not know the future but I do know myself. I am Jazzy— and Jazzy doesn't lose! I realized then that I had actually made my decision sometime before, even though I hadn't wanted to admit it.

Taking my phone out, I started typing. "Sher," I said. "OK lah. You can tell your Ah Huat—yes."

Acknowledgments

This book would not have been possible without these people and I give them immense thanks:

To my extraordinary agent, Jin Auh, who believed in and loved Jazzy from the very beginning. Much appreciation to Mike Hale for his encouragement during the early writing of *SPG*. To Gordon Dahlquist, for reading closely each step of the way—Jazzy's world was all the better for having him know it early on. And to John "Nonny" Searles, for his enormous heart.

I am also grateful to the following:

My parents, Tan Soo Liap and Cynthia Wong, and sister, Daphne Tan—their love buoys me each day. And my incredible and always inspiring family in Singapore.

The wonderful team at William Morrow: my amazing editor Rachel Kahan, Tavia Kowalchuk, Lynn Grady, Kelly Rudolph, Shelby Meizlik and Mumtaz Mustafa. As well as Jessica Friedman at the Wylie Agency.

Friends whose love and nudges kept me going: Simpson Wong, Henry Wu, Julia Glass, Drew Larimore, Judy Blume, Jeanette Lai, Kevin Cheng, Regina Jaslow, Brian Fidelman, S.J. Rozan, Sachin Shenolikar, Robert Sabat, Charles Chris Chiang, Hillary Jordan, Willin Low, Diane Cook, A.J. Ashworth, Albert Forns, Chandrahas Choudhury, Bill Goldstein, Emily Miller, Peter Fortunato, Marie-Atina Goldet, Christy Funsch, Theresa Wong, Jonathan Santlofer, Gretchen Somerfeld, Rachel Cantor, Sari Wilson, Camille

DeAngelis, Tony Eprile, Noa Charuvi Shai, Robinson McClellan, Paula Whyman, Natalie Wainwright, Pam Loring, Greg Morago, Clifford Pugh, Donna Kato, Debra Bass, Joe Amodio, Anne Bratskeir, Lauren Young, Monica Drake, Laura Sullivan, Stephanie Desmon, Laura Smitherman, Rachelle Pestikas, Abe Kwok, Robert Christie, Ryan Page, Bobby Caina Calvan, Susan Bolin-Wright, Susan Segrest, Marcus Brauchli and Paul Steiger. And thanks to TalkingCock .com's Colin Goh for Singlish consultation.

Artist colonies that provided havens for writing: Yaddo, Hawthornden Castle, Djerassi Resident Artists Program, The Studios of Key West, Ragdale Foundation, VCCA Le Moulin à Nef and Art OMI's Ledig House, as well as Elaina Richardson, Candace Wait, Margot Haliday Knight, Jed Dodds, Elena Devers, Erin Stover-Sickmen, Cheryl Fortier, Camille Durin, DW Gibson, Skip Gianocca, Georgina Goodall and Mrs. Drue Heinz. Colony chefs who fed me terribly well: Ruth Shannon, Linda Williams, Dan Tosh, Mike Hazard, Rita Soares-Kern.

To the National Arts Council of Singapore.

And Hamish Robinson.